"[ABRAHAMS'S] PROSE IS ELEGANT BY ANY LITERARY STANDARD."
—*Los Angeles Times*

"Abrahams slowly ratchets up the tension. . . . Once again this author finds menace in dailiness, as he creates a scenario that's firmly grounded in real life, but which becomes increasingly (and fascinatingly) skewed. . . . As usual, the author's ear for the diverse details of everyday life is sharp. . . . All the characters here are deftly drawn."
—*Publishers Weekly*

"Sharply written psychological suspense. With details as exact as fingerprints, author Abrahams will convince readers that they've never encountered a suburban family this recognizable."
—*Kirkus Reviews*

"[A] suspense master . . . Besides the kind of breath-catching suspense Abrahams is known for, this novel is blessed with a delightful supporting character, a preteen girl obsessed with Sherlock Holmes. Sure to please."
—*Booklist*

"Recommended . . . Abrahams is in great form with this psychological thriller."

—*Library Journal* (starred review)

By Peter Abrahams

THE FURY OF RACHEL MONETTE
TONGUES OF FIRE
RED MESSAGE
HARD RAIN
PRESSURE DROP
REVOLUTION #9*
THE FAN*
LIGHTS OUT*
A PERFECT CRIME*
CRYING WOLF*
LAST OF THE DIXIE HEROES*
THE TUTOR*
THEIR WILDEST DREAMS*

* Published by Ballantine Books

THE
TUTOR

PETER ABRAHAMS

BALLANTINE BOOKS • NEW YORK

A Ballantine Book
Published by The Random House Publishing Group
Copyright © 2002 by Pas de Deux
Excerpt from *Their Wildest Dreams* copyright © 2003 by Pas de Deux

The Tutor is a work of fiction. Names, places, and incidents are either a product of the author's imagination or are used fictitiously.

This book contains an excerpt from the forthcoming hardcover edition of *Their Wildest Dreams* by Peter Abrahams. This excerpt has been set for this edition only and may not reflect the final content of the forthcoming edition.

www.ballantinebooks.com

ISBN 0-345-43941-4

Manufactured in the United States of America

First Hardcover Edition: July 2002
First Mass Market Edition: August 2003

OPM 10 9 8 7 6 5 4 3 2 1

For my children, Seth, Ben, Lily, and Rosie

For an Undercover Angel, Tracy, with love

Many thanks to Joe Pedlosky, Captain Bill McManamin of the Falmouth Police Department, and Tom Potts at Advest for answering my endless questions so patiently.

And thanks also to my daughter Rosie, whose responses, while less patient perhaps and no doubt deservedly so, were exactly what I needed every time.

I'm very grateful too for the strong and thoughtful support of Peter Borland.

Art in the blood is liable to take the strangest forms.

—A. Conan Doyle, *The Greek Interpreter*

1

Linda Marx Gardner awoke from a dream and felt her husband's erection against her hip. Not nudging it, not demanding; just there. Earlier in her marriage, or maybe more accurately very early, on predawn mornings like this, the bedroom dim and shadowy, Linda would have taken hold of Scott and started something. Those predawn somethings, their bodies still loose and heavy with sleep, would usually turn out pretty good, sometimes better than that.

Linda got out of bed. In her dream she'd been frantically erasing words from sheets of pink paper, but the words themselves were all forgotten. As she went into the bathroom, Scott made a little sound in his sleep, one of those soft grunts that indicate agreement. She had a funny thought, not like her at all: was he erasing something too?

Then she was in the shower, her appointment book opening up in her mind, time blocks dense with her neat writing. There was going to be an overrun on the Skyway account, most of it from the photography screwup, but not all. Linda tried to figure out where the rest of it came from, letting go of everything but work so completely that she jumped as she caught sight of Scott through the steamy glass, his naked back to her as he stood before the toilet.

She called to him: "Can you wake Brandon?"

Scott said something she didn't catch because of the shower's noise, almost a roar—when they'd renovated instead of moving up from West Mill to Old Mill, they'd used nothing but the best, in this case the 10-Jet Tower from Kohler's Body Spa collection—and when she looked again he wasn't there. The water, hot and pounding, felt so good she could have stayed there all day. Linda turned off the shower at once.

She got out, reaching for a towel with one hand, flushing the toilet with the other. Scott always forgot, or didn't bother, or something. Her watch, on the granite sink top—black granite streaked with midnight blue, the nicest feature in the whole house—told her she was running two or three minutes late, nothing to be all tense about. She took a deep breath.

"Bran? Bran? Bran? Bran?"

Over and over. The word penetrated Brandon's dreams, twisted them out of shape, finally woke him.

"Brandon? You awake, buddy? It's late."

Brandon came awake enough to know he had the covers pulled way up, know that he was totally warm, totally fuzzy, totally unable to get up or maybe even move at all. He got one eye open, not much, just enough to peer at his father through gummy lashes. His father: towel wrapped around his waist, shaving cream on his face, razor dripping in his hand.

"I'm really not—"

"Forget it, Brandon. You're going to school."

"I feel like shit."

"You're going. And watch your language."

Brandon didn't say anything.

"Show a little life. Sit up or something. Don't make me come back here."

"All right, all right," Brandon said, but the only thing moving was that one eyelid, closing back down.

"And this room is really getting out of hand."

Brandon, almost asleep, barely caught that last bit. The inner fuzziness repaired itself quickly, knitting up the little hole poked through by his father and then some.

· · ·

A cut-glass prism dangled in the window of the bed-room across the hall from Brandon, a window that always caught the first light. As Brandon sank back into deep sleep, the sun blinked up through the bare tree limbs out back, sending a ray through the prism. A tiny rainbow instantly printed itself on the calendar hanging on the opposite wall, and not only that, but precisely on a special square, the one with the birthday cake drawn inside, eleven flame-tipped candles burning on top. That rainbow, quivering slightly on her upcoming birthday, was the first thing Ruby saw when she opened her eyes.

She held her breath. This was proof of God's existence. That was her first thought. She'd barely begun to deal with it, and its backpack—that's how some thoughts were, they carried backpacks—that God took a personal interest in her, Aruba Nicole Marx Gardner, before her mind got going with the facts: sun, east window, prism, a rainbow that had to land somewhere, coincidence. That was the way Sherlock Holmes would see it, and she respected Sherlock Holmes more than anyone on earth. Didn't love him—Dr. Watson was the lovable one—but respected him.

Still, coincidence could be tricky. Take that time she'd been eating a baloney sandwich and reading a story about a frog, she must have been four, when she'd suddenly puked all over the place, including on Brandon beside her in the backseat, frog and baloney getting all mixed up in some way. That was how she saw it, and hadn't touched baloney since. But she could hear Sherlock Holmes: "A long car trip and a winding road? One could produce the same result with peanut butter and a penguin." Elementary, my dear Ruby.

The rainbow moved on, sliding off her birthday, off the calendar, ballooning along the wall, warping around the cor-ner of her open closet, vanishing in the shadows within. The spinning earth did that, stuck the rainbow in her closet. There would be lots of backpacks to that thought, but Ruby didn't get to them. Some commotion kicked up down the hall, only the sharp notes getting through her door, like when one earphone conks out.

"Scott? Didn't I ask you to get Brandon up?"

Muffle, muffle.

"Well he isn't, as usual, and it's five after seven. Brandon, get up now."

Muffle.

Then came sounds of movement, and Bran yelled, "Fuck. Don't fuckin' do that," in that deep new voice of his, ragged at the edges, that vibrated the walls, and Ruby knew that Mom had ripped the covers off him, which always worked.

The sounds that followed—Bran getting up, banging around in his room, crossing the hall to the bathroom they shared, turning on the shower—faded as Ruby took *The Complete Sherlock Holmes* off her bedside table and found her place: "The Speckled Band." Just from the title, she knew she was going to like it.

Speckled. A word she'd never spoken. She tried it out loud for the first time. "Speckled. Speckled." Her stuffed animals watched in silence from their perches on bookshelves. A strange word, with a kind of power, if that made sense, and maybe not power completely for the good. *Freckled* was on the good side, *heckled* a bit nasty, *speckled* different in some way she didn't know. The garage door opened under her room and her dad's old Triumph rumbled out, sounds that were far, far away.

I had no keener pleasure than in following Holmes in his professional investigations, and in admiring the rapid deductions, as swift as intuitions, and yet always founded on a logical basis, with which he unravelled the problems which were submitted to him.

Yes, that was it, what was so special about him. As Ruby read, her room went still, began to lose its physical properties, became less solid. The bachelor lodgings at 221-B

Baker Street went the other way. Ruby could almost hear the crackle of the fire Mrs. Hudson had had the good sense to light, could almost—

"Ruby! Ruby! Ruby, for God's sake!"

"What?"

"I called you six times." Mom, probably dressed for work, probably standing at the top of the stairs, that impatient look on her face, when the up-and-down line between her eyebrows appeared. "Are you up?"

"Yeah."

"Don't forget tennis after school, sweetheart." Just from the change of tone, Ruby knew the up-and-down line had smoothed itself out. "See you tonight." Mom's voice trailed away as she went down the stairs.

"Bye, Mom."

Maybe not loud enough, because there was no reply. Then Mom was backing out of the garage, lurching just a bit as usual, tires squeaking on the cement floor. The garage door closed—a long whine ending in a thump—and the sound of the Jeep Grand Cherokee, smoother than the Triumph and much less interesting, faded and faded to nothing. Sherlock Holmes deduced from seven spatters of mud that the terrified young lady in his sitting room had had a rough ride in a dogcart. A car honked on the street—Brandon's ride. The terrified young lady was going mad from fear.

Linda was dictating a memo about the Skyway account into her digital organizer when her cell rang. Deborah, her sister-in-law, married to Scott's brother, Tom—Linda always caught her breath for a moment when Deborah called. She was excited about something. Linda could hear it just in the way she said, "Hi."

"Hi."

"Are you at work yet?"

"Stuck in traffic."

"Me too." Pause, but not a long one. "Did you get Brandon's results?"

"What results?"

"The SAT."

"I thought they weren't coming till next week."

"That's if you wait for the mail," Deborah said. "There's a number to call as of seven this morning. You just need a credit card and patience—it took me twenty minutes to get through."

Linda's dashboard clock read 7:32.

"So you got Sam's results?" she said. Sam, Brandon's first cousin, same age.

"Fifteen forty." The volume of Deborah's voice went way up, almost an explosion, like some spike caused by a change in atmospheric conditions. Linda held the phone away from her ear.

"Is that good?"

"Have you forgotten? It's out of sixteen hundred, Linda. Sam's in the ninety-ninth percentile."

Somehow she had forgotten; now it all came back. "That's great," Linda said, stop-and-go on the exit ramp. The homeless guy who worked this spot stared through her window, rattling his Dunkin' Donuts cup. It all came back, including her own score, and she added, "Wow."

"Thanks," said Deborah. "We kind of expected something good because of his PSAT—they track pretty closely—but still. Some kids do get sixteen hundred, of course, but we probably won't have him retake it. With his tennis and community ser—" She stopped herself. "Anyway, here's the number. Good luck."

Linda tried the number. Busy, and it stayed busy until she was about to enter the parking garage under the building, a cellular dead zone. That was when she got through. Linda pulled over to the side, her foot on the brake, the car in gear. Someone honked. Linda followed the automated menu on the other end, her heart suddenly racing. She needed Brandon's social security number, which she had in her organizer, and a Visa or MasterCard number and expiration date, which she had in her head. It cost thirteen dollars.

There was a pause, a long one, during which she found she'd actually broken into a sweat, and then the digital voice uttered Brandon's numbers: "Verbal—five hundred ten. Math—five hundred eighty."

Linda clicked off and, as soon as she had done so, began to doubt she'd heard right. Five hundred ten? Five hundred eighty? That would be what—1090 on the SAT? Impossible. Brandon was a good student, almost always got A's and B's. Those digital voices were sometimes hard to understand—they tended not to emphasize the syllables a normal human being would. Maybe it had been 610 and 680. That would be 1290, the exact score she'd had years before. She didn't think of herself as smarter than Brandon. It must have been 1290.

Linda tried the number again. Busy. The clock now read eight on the button. She was going to be late. No one up there cared about five minutes or even ten, but Linda had never been late, not in the three years she'd been on the job. She let up on the brake, eased the car back into the long-term check-in lane, hit redial. And connected. As she entered the garage, she went through the social security and credit card routine again, paying another thirteen dollars, waited for the long pause. While what? While some computer matched the social security number with the credit card number and activated a voice program. How long could it take? She stuck her parking card in the slot, jammed it in, really, and went through the raised gate as the digital voice said: "Verbal—"

And lost contact, now in the dead zone.

On the elevator, Linda tried once more. The building was seven stories, her office on six. Linda got through to the SAT number as she passed three, repeated the social security and credit card numbers as she was getting out, paying thirteen dollars yet again, listened to the long pause as she walked down the corridor. She opened the office door and saw to her surprise that everyone was gathered around the conference table for a meeting. They all turned to look at her. The digital voice spoke once more: "Five hundred ten. Five hundred eighty." This time she caught the percentile too: "Seventy-fifth."

Brandon got into Dewey's car.

"Hey."

"How's it goin'?"

"I feel like shit."

"Tell me about it."

Dewey, the first of Brandon's friends to get his license, had a joint going, which sometimes happened on the ride home but never in the morning. He passed it to Brandon. Brandon didn't want to go to school fucked up, didn't want to go to school at all, but shit. He didn't take it any further than that, just hit off the joint, passed it back.

"Could use some gas money," Dewey said.

Brandon handed Dewey three ones.

"Am I driving a lawnmower and I don't know it?"

Brandon handed over two more, noticing that the fuel gauge read full. But so what? Dewey pulled away from the curb, squealing the tires just a bit. He switched on a CD, some rap about "fuck you, good as new, all we do, then it's through" that Brandon hadn't heard before. Not too bad.

"School sucks," Dewey said.

"Yeah."

"I'm thinking about dropping out."

"You mean before senior year?"

"I mean like now."

"But what about baseball?" Dewey had been captain of the freshman team and had started a few games for the varsity last spring.

"I'm not going to be eligible anyway," Dewey said. "I'm flunking two courses."

"Still time to get them up."

Dewey took a big hit off the joint, breathed out slow. "Right," he said.

Fuck you, good as new, all we do, then it's through.

Not too bad? It was great.

"Who's this?"

"You don't know who this is? Unka Death."

At that moment, Brandon remembered he had an English test third period, counting for 20 percent of the term grade. *Macbeth*. Hadn't studied for it, had fallen asleep after the first few lines, some weird shit with witches that was meant to be symbolic or ironic or some other term he'd have to define, probably getting points taken off even though he knew damned well what they meant.

"Got an idea," Dewey said. "Let's go to the city."

"What city?"

"New York, for fuck sake. I know this bar in the Village where they don't card anybody."

Almost two hours away. Brandon had been to New York maybe a dozen times, but always with his family. "I've only got, like, ten bucks on me."

"It's cool. I've got a credit card."

"You do?"

"On my mom's account. For emergencies."

Dewey started to laugh. Then Brandon was laughing too. Emergencies: he got it. They drove right past the school. Buses were pulling in and the student lot was filling up. Brandon saw people he knew. Dewey beeped the horn. Brandon thought, *Aw shit,* as they went by. Dewey passed him the joint.

"All yours," he said, ramping up the volume on Unka Death.

The house was quiet. Ruby loved having it to herself. The terrified lady told Holmes: *You may advise me how to walk amid the dangers which encompass me.* Ruby checked the time, stuck in a bookmark, the one with Dilbert's boss—it had finally hit her that the boss's pointy hair was meant to make you think of the devil, she was so slow sometimes—and got up. Out the window, she saw a cardinal at the feeder, poking its red head inside. It suddenly turned toward her window, then rose and shot off into the town forest behind the house.

Ruby brushed her teeth with the Sonicare toothbrush until the inside of her mouth tingled, then smiled into the mirror. Not a real smile with the eyes joining in; this was just an examination of teeth. Dr. Gottlieb said she was going to need braces. How crooked were her teeth anyway? She studied them from several angles. Some days they looked pretty straight. Today she saw a complete jumble.

Brandon hadn't flushed the toilet, also hadn't aimed very well. Careful where she put her feet, Ruby flushed it for him and got in the shower.

She chose the Aussie extra-gentle shampoo with the kangaroo on the front because she liked the combination of shampoo and kangaroo, Helene Curtis Salon Selectives conditioner because it said *completely drenched*, whatever that meant, and Fa body wash because it smelled like kiwi. Clean, dry, smelling great, she wrapped her hair in a towel and got dressed—khakis from the Gap, a long-sleeved T-shirt with a silver star on the front, black clogs with thick soles to make her taller—and went down to the kitchen. Zippy awoke at once, sprang up from under the table, bounded toward her, tail wagging.

"Down, Zippy."

But of course he wouldn't go down, did just the opposite, raising himself higher, resting his front paws on her shoulders.

"Down."

He poked his muzzle in her face, gave her a big wet lick on the nose.

"Up," she said, just as an experiment. Zippy dropped to all fours at once, snagging her T-shirt as he did. Two of the little arms of the silver star now hung loose.

"Zippy. Bad boy."

He wagged his tail.

His water bowl was empty. Ruby filled it. He ignored

the bowl, but as soon as her back was turned she heard him slurping noisily.

Ruby made her breakfast—scrambled eggs, toast, and orange juice. No milk; she only drank milk when forced. Next to her bedroom, the kitchen was her favorite room in the house, the copper pots on the wall, the fruit bowl, now empty but sometimes full of all kinds of fruit, the wooden spoons, the spice rack, the big fridge humming in the corner—she needed both hands to open the door—the walls a lovely light yellow, perfect for the eating of eggs.

Ruby's seat at the table was in the actual sticking-out part of the breakfast nook, with windows on three sides. She ate her yellow eggs in a pool of yellow sunlight, leafing through *The All-American Girls Book of Braiding*, trying to think of the right name for those star arms, totally content.

Maybe her teeth weren't so great, but her hair, that was another story. Thick, glossy brown, full of all kinds of tints—it had a personality of its own. Ruby chose the Thumbelina Braid because the look reminded her of Dilbert's boss. She made two high pigtails, divided each into three strands, braided the strands, coiled them into buns, stuck them in place with bobby pins.

"How do I look, Zippy?"

He poked his head over the tabletop and snatched her last piece of toast, the one with the butter melted in perfectly.

"Zippy!"

He growled at her. She gave him the cold look. Zippy made himself smaller and slunk away, like the coward he was.

Ruby put on her blue jacket with the yellow trim and walked him out back and into the town forest, taking the shortcut to the pond. The banks of the pond were muddy. She let him off the leash.

"Run, Zippy. Make spatters."

He lifted his leg and peed on a tree.

Were dog spatters different from horse spatters, or was

the important difference the one between a dogcart and a horse cart, which would probably stand higher?

"Run, Zippy."

He didn't want to run. She tossed him a stick, which he gazed at. She tossed another one into the pond. It disappeared without a splash, which was kind of strange.

"Go get it, Zippy."

But he wouldn't. She didn't blame him. The water, a blue so pale it was almost white, looked cold. She took him home. He lifted his leg at least a dozen times.

"Poo, Zippy, poo." He finally did, maybe stepping in it just a little.

Ruby loaded the dishwasher, her own dishes and the ones already in the sink, slung on her backpack and left by the front door, making sure it was locked. The school bus pulled up. She got on.

"Hi, beautiful," said the driver.

"Hi, Mr. V."

There was only one seat left, beside Winston. He was picking his nose.

"Don't eat it, Winston," she said.

But he did.

The bus rolled away. All of a sudden and for no reason, she remembered her book of Bible stories, sent by Gram to make up for the fact that Mom and Dad didn't go to church. Specifically, she remembered the story of Lot's wife, who wasn't supposed to look back. She had the strong feeling that it was very important not to look back right now. But she couldn't stop herself. The urge grew and grew in the muscles of her neck. Ruby looked back.

Nothing happened, of course. She didn't turn into a pillar of salt, and the house wasn't going up in flames. It stayed just the way it always was, not the biggest or fanciest house on the block, but square and solid, white with black shutters, the only color the red brick chimney, maybe a little too . . . what was the word? *Imposing;* too imposing for the rest of the house. She'd overheard her aunt Deborah say that the Thanksgiving before last.

Winston tore a Snickers in two. "Want some?" he said.

Ruby gave him a close look to see if this was some kind of joke. But no, he'd made no connection between the nose picking and his dirty fingernails on the candy bar. He was just sharing.

"Maybe Amanda wants some," Ruby said.

Amanda leaned over, with her goddamn pierced ears— Ruby had to wait another year. "Maybe Amanda wants some what?" Amanda said.

And what was that? She was wearing lipstick?

"Snickers," Ruby said, all of a sudden feeling the power of those devilish horns on her head. "You like Snickers, don't you?"

"Oh, my favorite," said Amanda.

Winston handed her the thing. Ruby watched till she'd popped it in her mouth.

"Mmmm," said Amanda.

2

Linda's meeting ran until nine-thirty. One minute later, she was in her office—a cubicle, really, they all worked in cubicles as part of the new team concept—calling Scott.

"There's been some disturbing news," she said.

"The Skyway account?"

That too. "I got Brandon's SAT results."

"So did I."

"Tom told you about the credit card thing?"

"What a racket," Scott said. He laughed. "And we paid double." Linda didn't inform him they'd paid four times now to hear the news. "I guess they both did pretty well," Scott said. "What's disturbing?"

"I'm not following you," Linda said. Had there been some sort of computerized mix-up, had Scott heard the real score, much higher?

"Brandon and Sam," Scott said. "Tom said Sam did okay, and Brandon's in the seventy-fifth percentile, right? Nothing wrong with that."

Where to begin. Linda found herself squeezing the phone in frustration. She had a thought, a series of thoughts, not nice: Had Scott ever talked about his own SAT results? Had she ever asked? If not, why not?

"First of all," she said, "are you telling me that Tom didn't mention Sam's score?"

"Just said he did all right."

"Sam got fifteen forty. Almost perfect, Scott. He's in the ninety-ninth percentile."

Silence.

"Ten ninety is terrible," Linda said. "The worst thing we can do now is fool ourselves about that."

"I don't get it," Scott said. "Brandon's always been a good student. What's his GPA?"

"It was three four but he slipped to three three—three two nine, actually—last term."

"Three three's not bad—A's and B's, right?"

Linda tried to relax her grip on the phone. "A's and B's at West Mill High aren't A's and B's at Andover."

"What's that supposed to mean?" Sam was at Andover.

"It means that colleges know the difference, and a ten ninety SAT and a three three from West Mill High tells the Ivies to not even look at him. It's probably programmed in their computers."

"There's always Amherst or someplace like that," Scott said.

"Amherst? Are you dreaming? Forget Amherst. You can forget Trinity, for God's sake."

"Forget Trinity?"

"Forget NYU, forget BC, forget BU, even. Don't you get it? The SAT ranks every kid in the nation. Seventy-fifth percentile means there are hundreds of thousands ahead of him, maybe millions. The good schools can fill their classes without going anywhere near Brandon. We screwed up."

"How?"

"In our usual way—by not seeing this coming."

"What could we have done?"

"Made him retake the PSAT for starters."

"The PSAT?"

Come on, Scott. "Don't you remember? He felt sick, supposedly, and left after five minutes."

"I don't see—"

"So we never got a score, and the PSAT tracks the SAT. We've missed a whole year."

"Of what?"

"Preparation," Linda said. "Maybe at boarding school."

"But we discussed that. We didn't want him to go away. And he didn't want to go away. And don't we believe in public education?"

"Don't we believe in Brandon first? And you left out not being able to afford it."

Pause. "So what are we going to do?"

"I don't know. Get him right into an SAT prep course, that's one thing."

"Maybe he just had a bad day."

"I hope to God that's it, but we can't take the chance. We should probably have his IQ tested, just to see what we have the right to expect."

There was a long silence. She could feel his resistance, not thought out, something deep in his character, genetic. Tom's DNA was different. That thought just popped up, nothing she could do.

"We're talking about Brandon's future," Linda said.

"What his life's going to be when he's on his own, when he's our age."

More silence. Then Scott said: "Sam's in the ninety-ninth percentile?"

"Correct. Harvard, Brown, Williams—they're going to be beating down his door."

At that moment, Tom came into Scott's office, raised his eyebrows, pointed to his watch.

"Gotta go," Scott said.

There were lots of things Ruby didn't like about school, but Mad Minute was the worst. "All right," said Ms. Freleng, welcoming them back from recess. "Time for Mad Minute." Like it was a treat, going to the circus or the beach. Ms. Freleng passed out the papers, everybody getting a sheet covered with rows of multiplication problems.

"Wait for it," said Ms. Freleng, taking out her stupid stopwatch. "Three, two, one . . . go!"

Ruby gazed down at the sheet. First question: thirty-seven times ninety-two. Christ on a crutch. *Seven times two is*—she liked that expression, Christ on a crutch, although she really didn't get what it meant—*fourteen, write the four and carry one. Seven times nine is . . . fifty-six?* This was one of the tricky ones. *Sixty-three! Got it. Plus one makes four. Skip a space. Three times two is . . .* There was also shit on a stick. She liked that too. She became aware of her hand moving along the rows of numbers, attacking the problems on its own.

Eight times seven. There's your fifty-six. Write down the six, carry the . . . Crutch was a bit like *cross*, and Christ had died on a cross. Another thing Ruby didn't like was turning the pages of one of the art books in the living room and suddenly coming across a painting of the crucifixion. She'd be willing to bet that *crutch* meant "cross," or had been *cross* at one time, or something like that. And that crown of thorns. She felt prickling all around her head.

Her hand plowed on. *Six times nine makes fifty—*

"Time's up, class. Pencils down."

Six. Write six, carry the five.

"Everybody. Pencils down this instant."

Not six. Four. Fifty-four. Why the hell—

"Everybody includes Ruby."

Ruby laid down her pencil, counted the problems she'd done. Eight.

"Now exchange papers with your neighbor for grading."

Ruby exchanged Mad Minute papers with Amanda, saw that Amanda had answered every single one. Amanda gave her a friendly smile. Her teeth were huge and white, of course, goddamn perfect.

"The answer to number one is—"

And the guy who actually put the crown of thorns on Christ's head—how come he didn't get thorns stuck in his own hand? If those thorns were anything like the briars in the town forest . . . Had he worn gloves? It wasn't the kind of climate for gloves—they were in the desert, right?—but didn't some of those gladiator types wear—Ruby glanced up, saw that Ms. Freleng was eyeing her for some reason.

"Are all of us, each and every, ready for number two?"

Ruby looked down at Amanda's answer to number one, thirty-seven times ninety-two. What had Ms. Freleng just said? Ruby couldn't bring the number back, but Amanda's answer struck her as wrong in some way, certainly wasn't what she remembered getting herself. She marked an *X* beside it and waited for the answer to number two, all ears.

"What's it gonna be, guys?"

There were like fifty beers on tap, literally. This was the coolest place Brandon had ever been in. The long bar, some kind of dull metal, was cool, the music was cool, the people sitting around or shooting pool were cool, the bartender was cool, the bartender's tattoo, a perfect likeness of herself right on the side of her face, was cool.

Brandon pointed to the nearest tap, the one with a picture

of a bear. The bartender poured him a glass. She had muscular bare arms, the coolest arms he'd ever seen on a woman. The beer was dark brown, unlike any beer he knew. He took a sip. It was horrible.

"You like that porter shit?" said Dewey. The bartender was pouring him something that looked more like beer.

"This one's pretty good," Brandon said, taking another sip. The taste didn't get any better.

"Five bucks," said the bartender.

"I'll get this round," said Brandon, handing over his ten-dollar bill.

"Then it's nine fifty altogether." The bartender rang it up, placed two quarters on the dull metal bar.

Brandon copied a gesture he'd seen in a movie, meaning it was all hers.

"Thanks," said the bartender.

Brandon ordered the same on the next round—Dewey took out the emergency credit card and the bartender opened a tab—just to show how into porter he was, but the round after that he switched to what Dewey was having. It wasn't that big an emergency. He kept that joke, if it was a joke, to himself, not sure how it would come across.

Dewey was gazing around the room. He smiled at a big girl with a huge head of blond hair, and the girl smiled back. When Dewey wasn't looking, Brandon tried smiling at her too. He got a smile back, maybe even friendlier.

"Think I'll move down here," said Dewey. "Get a job as one of those bicycle messengers. They make three hundred bucks a day."

"They do?"

"At least." Dewey ordered another round, plus cigars. They smoked and drank. Interesting-looking people went by on the street outside, not the kind of people you saw in West Mill or even Hartford. Take that tow truck driver—he had a red bandanna on his head and an eye patch, just like a pirate.

Brandon got up to go to the bathroom. Hey! The porter

hit him at that moment, and he felt a little unsteady. Nothing noticeable, nothing uncool, and he recovered right away, although maybe not completely because he went into the wrong bathroom. The big blond girl was inside. On the other hand, she was pissing at the urinal, her leather skirt hiked up and—

Brandon backed outside, waited in the hallway by the pay phone. On the street, a woman carrying a bass drum on her head went by, and then the tow truck guy came back the other way, a car hooked up behind. Brandon watched the woman till she was out of sight to make sure that was what she was. He barely noticed the car.

They sat in Tom's office, the office that had been the old man's, Tom behind the desk, Scott on the couch that hadn't been there in the old man's day.

"So Brandon did well too?" Tom said.

"Not bad."

"Glad to hear it. He's such a funny kid."

"Funny?"

"That crooked smile of his. Wouldn't it be something if they ended up at the same college somewhere? Like us."

"Like us?"

"At UConn."

True that they'd both gone to UConn, but Scott's arrival as a freshman coincided with Tom's transfer to Yale for his last two years.

"Think of the tailgate parties. And can't you imagine Mom's reaction, say they were both at Princeton or someplace?"

Scott didn't reply. Maybe Tom thought he was imagining Mom's reaction. "There's kind of a situation," Scott said.

Tom gave him a look, a look that went way back, that Scott couldn't put into words, that said a lot anyway.

"Money?"

"If you want to put it that way. You know Mickey Gudukas?"

"Bald lefty who foot-faults all the time? A real sleaze-ball?"

"He gets good information."

"What kind of information?"

"On the market."

"He's a broker now? I thought he was a claims adjuster or something."

"He was. Then a broker. At Denman, Howe. He's still a broker, just not with them anymore."

"Canned from Denman, Howe? What line do you have to cross for that?"

"He was the one gave me the Stentech tip. You made out all right off that, as I recall."

Tom nodded. "But I checked into it pretty carefully before I bought." The only stock market investment Tom had ever made, outside of indexed mutual funds.

"Sure. The thing is, I ran into him picking up Ruby from tennis a while back and he gave me another tip. Same kind of deal—a biotech with a new product coming out of testing. This one's called Symptomatica."

"How's her game?"

"Whose game?" Tom could be confusing sometimes.

"Ruby's."

"Okay, I guess."

"She likes it?"

"Tennis? Sure." Didn't she? She'd been taking lessons for years. Ruby was pretty quick but kind of small, hard to tell whether she'd develop into a real player. But it was important to demonstrate a long-term commitment to a sport, preferably two sports, even if you weren't athletic scholarship material—parents around the court were talking about that just the other day. Maybe Brandon would move up the ladder this year, not necessarily to Sam's level—Sam was already playing number three at Andover—but at least getting to where some Division III coach might put in a word for him at the admissions department. Ninety-ninth fucking percentile.

"A cute kid," Tom said.

"Who?"

"Ruby."

"Yeah. The thing is, this Symptomatica deal is the reverse of the last one. Their hot product isn't going to work. So the play's to go short."

"Selling short? You're getting involved in shit like that?"

"Never," Scott said, and it was almost true. "But in this case there's no risk. It's like seeing into the future."

Tom glanced at the portrait on the wall, the old man, a year or two after he got sick. To everyone else on the planet, that glance could have meant anything or nothing, but Scott got the message. Seeing the future: was that any way for an insurance man to talk? The foundation of their business was the uncertainty of the future.

"How do you know this product or whatever it is will fail?" Tom said.

"Gudukas met one of their scientists on a cruise. Guy's teaching at MIT now. He cashed out when he realized the thing was doomed. They're still scrambling around to save it but there's no way. They made some huge mistake right off the bat."

"What mistake?"

"Something about junk DNA. Gudukas drew the whole thing out on a napkin for me and I understood it at the time, but it's all very technical and doesn't matter in the end. What matters is the day those test results come in, the stock will tank."

"What's it trading at?"

"Closed at twelve and change yesterday. It's going down to zero, Tom. I was thinking of twenty thousand shares, ten each. We'd clear almost a quarter million."

"What's Gudukas's angle?"

"Full-rate commission, if that's an angle."

Tom rocked back and forth in the chair, just like the old man used to do. Scott grew aware of a strange triangle in the room—portrait, Tom, himself. The truth was neither of them looked much like the old man. They resembled their mother, resembled each other even more, Scott being a little bigger, Tom a little darker, his features a little more prominent. Their voices were almost identical—everyone mentioned that.

"Count me out," Tom said.

"You're walking away from a quarter million, just like that?"

"I'm not stopping you."

Scott took a deep breath. "His brokerage wants some collateral on a deal like this."

"Move your account over there."

"Not enough."

"But what about all that Stentech stock?"

"Paid for the renovations."

"You spent eighty grand on those renovations?"

"We got our money's worth," Scott said. He didn't mention that some of the eighty grand had gone into another stock that hadn't worked out as well. He also said nothing about his house being just as nice as Tom's, maybe nicer. Put it on the same street up in Old Mill, it would be worth . . . a lot more than Tom's, leave it at that.

"You've got a great house," Tom said. "I wasn't saying that." Like he'd been listening inside.

Scott shrugged. "I can't use the retirement account—there's some SEC thing. And putting up the house would require Linda's signature."

"She doesn't know about this?"

"You know how she is."

Tom didn't answer that, just stopped rocking.

"That leaves the business," Scott said.

"The business?"

"My share. As collateral."

Tom was rocking again. H. W. Gardner Insurance: 35 percent Tom, 25 percent him, 40 percent the estate, meaning their mom, now in Arizona.

"I don't even know if it's possible," Tom said. "At a minimum, it would require my signature and Mom's on some sort of document, I don't even know what."

Scott said: "I'll cover any legal fees, goes without saying."

Tom said: "Can't you just walk away from this one?"

They gazed at each other. This had always been hard for Scott—so much like gazing at himself in the mirror, but a strange self, pained and not fully cooperative. It had nothing to do with the thirty-five/twenty-five split. That was fair: Tom had started with the old man right out of college, while Scott had kicked around for ten or twelve years, first in Boston, then in Hartford, climbing the corporate ladder at Prudential, then Travelers, finally Allstate.

"Don't you ever dream of independence, Tom?"

Tom blinked. "Independence?"

"Financial independence. Just being free to . . . I don't know."

"We're doing pretty good here, Scott, both of us. The wives, the kids, everybody."

You are, Scott thought. *You're doing good.* But he didn't say it.

"What about Mom?" Tom said.

"She'll do whatever you say, you know that."

Tom looked away.

"I'll think about it," he said. "That's the best I can do."

Think fast, for once, Scott thought. *The clock is ticking.* He meant that just in the narrow sense of the Symptomatica deal, but right away he knew it was bigger than that: why couldn't Tom hear that goddamn ticking?

3

Kyla Gudukas started the deciding point by serving to Ruby's backhand. Every lesson ended with a round robin, the finalists playing a four no-ad game set, the winner, almost always Kyla, getting a prize like grip tape, Gatorade, or a can of balls from Erich, the pro at the indoor club.

Ruby got her racket back, stepped into the ball, low to high, low to high as Erich repeated over and over until she wanted to scream, and hit a nice backhand crosscourt. Kyla hit it back, one of those deep shots of hers that was mostly a lob, not hit hard, just getting it back. Ruby hit another backhand crosscourt, maybe even better than the one before. Kyla lobbed it back. Ruby tried hitting the next one to Kyla's forehand. Kyla lobbed it back. Ruby went to Kyla's forehand a couple more times. Lob, lob. Then the backhand again. Lob. Three more times. Lob, lob, lob. Thrice—was that a word? A nice one, maybe even a great one. Ruby had a word list where she ranked all—

She hit the next shot into the net. She must have because there it was, *bouncy bouncy,* on her side. Game, set, match. They went to the net, shook hands.

"Nice game."

"Nice game."

Erich came over with a bottle of Gatorade, the blue kind that Ruby liked best. "Here you go, champ," he said, handing it to Kyla, but with his Swiss accent or whatever it sounded just like *chump*, so Ruby started feeling better almost right away. "See everyone here next Monday," Erich said.

"Effreyone will be here," said Ruby, very quietly.

"What was that, Ruby?"

Maybe not quietly enough. She gave him a winning smile. "Thanks for the lesson."

"Oh. You are most welcome."

Velcome, velcome, effreyone's velcome. Ruby zipped her racket into its cover. Four men with knee braces, arm braces, hairy arms, loud voices, came onto the court.

"Get the court good and warm for us, kids?" said one of them.

"Don't burn your feet," Ruby said.

Kyla laughed; she had a funny little laugh that Ruby liked.

They went into the lobby. Ruby drank from the fountain, hardly getting up on her tiptoes at all. Someone had left gum in there.

"Your mom called, Ruby," said the lady at the desk. "She's going to be a little late."

Ruby sat on a bench by the vending machine, checked in her backpack. Had she remembered *The Complete Sherlock Holmes*? No. Did she have any money left over from lunch, just sixty-five cents for M&M's? No. She gazed at the M&M's row through the glass of the vending machine, noticed that the lead pack was half hanging over the edge. Then, without quite being aware of it, she was on her feet, facing the machine. Maybe just a little nudge, completely accidental, like so—

"Ruby?"

She whipped around. Kyla, by the front door.

"My dad says we can give you a ride home."

Ruby heard a thud behind her, but soft.

Mr. Gudukas had a nice car, all soft leather in the back where Ruby and Kyla sat. Alone in front, he glanced at Ruby in the mirror.

"Where do you live, exactly?" he said.

Ruby told him.

"You're Scott Gardner's kid, right?"

"Yeah."

"He and I go way back."

Ruby picked out a red one and a green one, passed the M&M's to Kyla.

"He hit a pretty good ball back when. Played for UConn, wasn't it?"

"Yeah," said Ruby. She had the green one on the right side of her mouth, red on the left, like a ship. They tasted very, very good. *Just shippin' M&M's, baby.*

"This your street?"

"Yeah."

"Nice."

So if he wasn't sure Dad went to UConn, they only went so far back, Dr. Watson.

"Don't let me go past it."

"Next one," Ruby said.

Mr. Gudukas parked on the street. An empty Budweiser can rolled out from under the seat in front of Ruby.

"Very nice," said Mr. Gudukas, looking at the house. He twisted around and smiled at her, but all she really saw was his mustache, so weird. Mustaches were saying something. Whatever it was, Ruby didn't want to hear.

"How long you been living here?" he said.

"Since before I was born," Ruby said, opening the door.

"That conservation land out back?"

"Yeah," said Ruby, getting out. It was cold.

"How many bedrooms?"

"Four," Ruby said. Mom and Dad's, Brandon's, hers, the empty one at the end of the hall and up those little stairs. She didn't like being reminded of that empty one. "Thanks for the drive."

"Anytime, honey," said Mr. Gudukas.

The sky was already that dark blue and purple color that Ruby didn't like, the color of the bottom of the deep cold sea. The house was dark too. She wished she'd turned some lights on in the morning, and had a funny thought as she unlocked the door: *Mrs. Lot comes home.* Could make a good caption for one of those *Far Side* cartoons that were so funny, although what sort of picture would—

Zippy bolted out the moment she opened the door, streaked right by her, made a beeline for the Strombolis' house across the street. His feet on their driveway, or his motion or something, triggered all their outdoor lights, which flashed on like Christmas. Zippy couldn't have been more visible, darting up to their front door—a huge gleaming thing, big enough for a castle, the gleams clear from all the way across the street—darting up to that front door, lifting his leg and peeing all over it. Ruby could see the yellow stain flowing slowly down, the lights were that good. Zippy couldn't have done a worse thing. The Strombolis hated him, hated the whole family because of him. Lights were going on all over their goddamn house.

Ruby had read about people freezing in a crisis, completely paralyzed. She hadn't believed it till now, now that she appeared to be one of them, even incapable of that one simple step into the house, banging the door closed, safety. And now came Zippy, pelting back across the street, all four paws in the air at once, his ears going every which way. As he hit the front lawn, the Strombolis' huge gleaming door started to open. Ruby couldn't budge. Zippy, eyes wide, bowled smack into her, knocking her clear into the front hall. Ruby kicked the door closed as she fell, backpack and tennis racket flying, M&M's clicking across the tile floor.

Ruby lay in darkness, Zippy panting beside her. She was panting too. She thought of telling him what a bad dog he was, but why? He was hopeless and at the same time he could be worse.

"Like the hound of the Baskervilles," she told him. "That would be worse."

But he wasn't listening, was already going after the M&M's; she could hear them skittering away from him. Ruby got up, started switching on lights. Like idea bulbs in a cartoon; and the moment she had that thought it hit her that tennis and math were a lot alike, the Mad Minute and those stupid four no-ad game sets being almost identical. The backpack thought to that was—

The phone rang. It made her jump, even cry out a little, although she might have imagined that part. Were the Strombolis nuts? Did they really believe she'd answer?

The machine picked up. Ruby heard angry Stromboli breathing, then a hang-up. It rang again two seconds later.

"Knock it off, Strombolis," Ruby said.

The machine took the call again. No angry breathing this time. "Anybody home?" said Brandon. Ruby picked up.

"Hey," she said. Or maybe, *Hey!* She was glad to hear his voice.

"Who's home?"

"Me."

"Who else?"

"And Zippy. You know what he—"

"Forget about fuckin' Zippy."

That little explosion took Ruby by surprise. She was silent.

"Ruby?" he said, his voice not so harsh. "You still there?"

"Yeah."

"Tell Mom and Dad I'll be a little late."

"How late?"

"Jesus—"

"They're gonna ask."

"Okay, okay, not too late. I'm over at Dewey's." Ruby heard rap in the background. It sounded like Unka Death, maybe that one about "fuck you all we do." "Working on an essay," Brandon added.

"What's it about?"

"What's that to you?" He hung up without saying goodbye.

She was just interested, that was all. Big-brother shit: nothing to think twice about, but Ruby looked immediately in the obvious place anyway, at the framed color photograph hanging over the hall table. There was the family at the beach in Jamaica a few years before, Brandon not much older than Ruby now. Everyone was smiling except Ruby, who was laughing her head off. Brandon stood behind her, his hand on her shoulder.

Ruby went into the kitchen. Through the sticking-out window she could see a crescent moon just above the dark mass of the forest. The air was clear or her eyesight especially keen tonight, because the two points of the crescent looked sharp. She switched on the lights and the outside went away.

Points—that was what those arms on a star were called! Sometimes she was so slow. Zippy's water bowl was empty again. She filled it.

"How about hot dogs?" she said. Hot dogs sounded good. She took a package from the freezer. Hot dogs tasted better on the grill and Ruby knew how to work it, turning on the gas, then pressing the button that made the spark, but she didn't feel like going out on the deck. Not because of the darkness, nothing like that, don't think that for a moment. Too cold for grilling, nothing more.

Ruby boiled two hot dogs, found they were out of buns, stuck them inside folded slices of bread, sat down at the table with everything she needed: mustard, relish, Sprite, *The Complete Sherlock Holmes*. The sitting room at 221-B Baker Street in early April 1883 materialized, grew more and more solid.

"I am a dangerous man to fall foul of!" said Dr. Roylott, the terrified woman's stepfather. Then he seized Holmes's poker *and bent it into a curve with his huge brown hands*.

The brown was because of all those years in India, the same reason the cheetah and the baboon were running around his crumbling manor—whoa! No cheetahs and baboons in India: Africa, my dear Watson, as Ruby knew from the Discovery Channel. So was this a clue? She'd come back

to that later. What was bothering her—*What? What?* she
thought as she took a big relishy bite of hot dog—had more
to do with . . . the poker. Dr. Roylott bent that poker to show
how dangerous he was. But—Ruby ran her eye back up the
page—there, only a few paragraphs above, Dr. Roylott
stepped forward, *shaking his hunting crop.* No mention in
between of him putting the hunting crop down, or sticking it
in his teeth, or asking Watson to hold it for a sec. So was she
supposed to think that he'd twisted the poker with his huge
brown hands while holding the hunting crop at the same
time? Or—could it be that this was some kind of mistake, a
mistake by the guy clever enough to think up Sherlock
Holmes, the cleverest detective in the world? Or—

"Ruby?"

Ruby looked up. There was Mom, in the kitchen.

"Didn't you hear me come in?" Mom was still in her
coat, that beautiful gray one with the black fur collar, but the
side door to the garage was already closed.

"Hi, Mom."

"What have you done to your hair?"

"Thumbelina," Ruby said. "You like it?"

"It's different," Mom said. Mom's own hair was as black
as that collar and glossy too; Mom had gorgeous hair, no
doubt about that. "Kyla's father drove you home?"

"Yeah."

"You remembered to thank him?"

"Yeah."

"How was your day?"

"Good."

"Got much homework?"

"A little," Ruby said, although that was more an impression than hard fact.

"I've brought some dinner," Mom said, lifting a bag
from the Blue Dragon with a grunt, as though she found it
heavy, and setting it on the butcher block. Ruby smelled oyster sauce, which meant that duck thing that no one ever ate.

Mom's eyes had crescents under them that reminded Ruby of the moon, except they were dark.

"Or have you eaten already?"

"Just a snack," Ruby said, although she was about full.

Mom glanced up at the clock—7:55—got busy with the cartons, plates, forks, spoons.

"Why don't you take your coat off, Mom?"

Her mother looked at her in a funny way. For a second Ruby thought she was going to come over and give her a hug, which would have been nice, not that Ruby didn't get hugs, just that now would have been nice. Instead Mom took a step toward the mudroom, where the coat pegs were. Then she turned, came right over to Ruby—almost shy, Ruby thought, which was crazy—and kissed her on the top of her head.

"You've got the best hair in the world," Mom said.

"Not as nice as yours."

"A thousand times nicer."

Mom went into the mudroom. Ruby knew hair couldn't feel anything, but that kiss lingered in her hair anyway.

Mom came back, coat off. "Brandon's not home?"

She'd have seen that his jacket, the varsity jacket with West Mill Tennis on the back, wasn't there. "He's at Dewey's," Ruby said. The up-and-down line appeared between Mom's eyes. "Working on an essay."

"At Dewey's?"

Ruby nodded.

"Did he say when he'll be home?"

"Not too late."

Ruby heard Mom taking a deep breath. Then the garage door was whining open, the Triumph rumbling in, and Dad came in through the side door.

"Hi, everybody," he said. He went to the butcher block, grabbed a ball of orange chicken right from the carton. "Where's Brandon?"

"At Dewey's, evidently," said Mom. "Working on an essay."

Dad glanced up, a second orange chicken ball in his hand. "Where's Dewey going to college?"

"That's an interesting question," Mom said.

Ruby got ready for an interesting answer, but that wasn't what came next.

"How so?" Dad said.

All of a sudden they were on the edge of fighting about something. Dewey? Were they going to fight about Dewey's college plans? Ruby liked Dewey. He had the funniest bumper sticker she'd ever seen but you had to get real close to read it: Fuck You You Fuckin Fuck. Driving around with that on the back of his car! She almost started laughing right there at the table.

"Just that we should have been taking a little more notice of the college plans of Brandon's peer group," Mom said.

Mom and Dad exchanged a look that Ruby didn't get. "Where's Bran going to college?" she said, reaching for a fortune cookie.

"There's another good question," Mom said.

Mom and Dad were still looking at each other, communicating something. Dad broke off whatever it was first, turned to Ruby and said: "How was your day, sweetheart?"

"Great," said Ruby, removing the crinkly wrapper from the fortune cookie.

"Did you see that girl, what's her name, Mickey Gudukas's daughter?"

"Kyla. We played in the round robin."

"Whip her butt?"

"Nope."

Dad came over, sat down at the table. "How do you like tennis, anyway?" he said.

"How do I like it?"

"Yeah. As a game, if you see what I'm getting at."

He had a strange look on his face, like her opinion mattered to him. He was a great dad. She knew exactly what he was getting at and told him the complete truth. "It's just like math."

"What did that mean?" Scott asked after Ruby went upstairs to do her homework.

"No idea," said Linda. "But she's not doing well at math. I don't think she even knows her times tables."

"Oh, boy," Scott said, a commonplace remark, but it set her thinking, and him too: Linda could see it in his eyes, an inward look combined with a hint of moisture, as though he'd blinked too much. Fifth grade, where Ruby was now, had been Adam's last year of school. Along with everything else, he'd been captain of the math team.

"It's not too early to start worrying about her," Linda said. "Can you imagine how competitive it's going to be when she starts applying to college?"

Scott undid the top button on his pants—did he have to do that every night?—and ate the rest of Ruby's egg roll. Then he got up, went to the liquor cabinet, poured himself a Scotch.

"I hope you're taking this seriously."

"Of course I am. Something to drink?"

"We're going to have to be united on this."

"On what, exactly?"

"Making Brandon look like the best candidate we can. It's not just the academics." Linda started making notes on a Blue Dragon paper napkin. "The academics boil down to three things—GPA, course difficulty, SAT. Then there's community service, of which he has none, and sports. Is he any good at tennis? We might as well face this right now."

"He was better at soccer, if you want my true opinion."

"Then why did you let him drop it?"

"*I* let him drop it?"

"You're the one he talked to."

"You mean that scene in the car after the Old Mill game? He was going to do it no matter what I said. The coach is an asshole—he's right about that."

"Everybody has to learn how to get along with assholes."

Scott gazed into his glass. Was he thinking about what she'd just said? The glass was empty. He got up to pour another.

Soccer was in the past. "Let's get back to tennis," Linda said. "Is he even good enough to play D three?"

"Back when I played college? Yeah. Now, I don't know. It's tougher."

"Who would know?"

"Erich," Scott said. "I'll ask him." Erich coached the West Mill varsity.

"Thank you," Linda said, writing *Erich* on the napkin, under the dragon's tail. Beside that she wrote: *Special talents?* Zip. At least Ruby had her saxophone. She made a mental note to get a progress report from the band teacher. All this would have to go on the computer. Linda started organizing future files in her head.

Then Scott surprised her. He opened his briefcase, took out two cardboard boxes, the size and shape of library card index drawers. Each was marked *SAT Survival Kit.* "Picked these up on the way home," he said, sliding them across the table.

Linda opened the boxes. They were packed tight with SAT flash cards, one box verbal, one box math. Linda opened the math box, plucked a card at random.

A line has x-intercept at $x + 3$ and y-intercept at $y = -\frac{1}{4}$. Find the slope of the line.
A) $-\frac{1}{12}$
B) $\frac{1}{12}$
C) 12
D) -12
E) None of the above

"Oh, Scott," she said, "this is going to be all right, isn't it?"

She leaned down and kissed him, mostly on the side of the face, a little overlap on the ear. He was going to take this seriously; they were going to pull together, get Brandon into somewhere really good.

"Sure," he said. "Stop worrying."

They heard the front door open.

4

"**H**ey," said Brandon, coming into the kitchen.

"Hello, Brandon," said Linda.

"How's it goin'?" said Scott.

"Same old same old," said Brandon, flipping open the carton of duck with oyster sauce, moving on to the orange chicken instead.

"Feeling all right?" said Linda. "You look a little flushed."

"Feel great," said Brandon, opening the fridge, drinking orange juice from the carton.

"A glass, please," said Linda.

"Oops," said Brandon, and gulped some more.

"How's Dewey these days?" said Scott.

"Decent," said Brandon.

"What are his college plans?" said Linda.

Brandon shrugged.

"Did he take the SAT?" said Linda.

"I guess."

"Any idea how he did?"

"Nope."

"You don't discuss this kind of thing with your friends?"

"What kind of thing?"

"The SAT, college," said Scott.

"The future," said Linda.

"They're my friends," Brandon said. "Why would we talk about that?"

"What *do* you talk about?" Linda said.

Brandon knew his mother was a pretty smart woman, but had he ever heard a stupider question than that? "You know," he said. "Stuff."

There was a silence. Brandon dug a fork into the Mongolian beef. It was good. Fucking Blue Dragon, coming through again. He was so hungry, could have just sat down and eaten everything on the table. On the other hand, the smart move was maybe to get up to his room, disappear. He was about to take the first step.

Linda said: "How did the essay go?"

"Essay?" The room was unsteady for a moment. Brandon caught his reflection in the window behind Ruby's seat. He looked totally bombed. Why? He'd had only eight or ten beers the whole day. Must have been those porters to start. Had there been another one later on?

"That you worked on at Dewey's."

"Oh, it's just a rough draft."

"On what subject?" Linda said. Scott had the last chicken ball.

"Macbeth," said Brandon. Quick thinking, and the smart thing to do once he was up in his room would be to study for the *Macbeth* test and arrange for a makeup. He grabbed an egg roll and turned to go.

"I loved *Macbeth*," Linda said.

"You did?"

"I had a great teacher. He knew the whole play by heart."

Brandon thought of Mr. Monson, putting in time till retirement, the Cliffs Notes for *Macbeth* half hidden in the drawer of his desk. "Cool," he said, because it kind of was. But not an impossible feat of memory: in one day, this day, he himself had already learned the lyrics of three or four cuts on the Unka Death CD, without even trying.

"What's the theme?" Linda said.

"Theme?"

"Of your essay."

Mom had been an English major, loved to read books by the pool when they were on vacation, but Christ, why now? "The witches," he said. He had nowhere else to go.

"What about them?" She had that look she got when company came over and some interesting intellectual discussion was about to begin.

"Shouldn't we be getting down to business here?" Scott said.

"Can't you see this is all part of it?" said Linda.

"What's going on?" said Brandon.

"Just tell me what about the witches. I'm interested."

Brandon took a guess. "How they stir up trouble," he said.

"An undercurrent of fate moving the whole story? That sounds very promising, Brandon."

"Thanks." He took one last forkful of Mongolian beef. "I'll just be—"

"Sit down a minute," Scott said.

"Huh?"

"Please," said Linda. "This is important."

They both looked pale. Brandon got scared: that pale look, the empty bedroom. "Is someone sick?"

"Nothing like that," said Linda. "Let's all just sit down."

They sat at the table, Scott at one end, Linda at the other, Brandon between them, facing the bow window.

"We had some alarming—"

"Disturbing," Linda said.

"Disturbing news today," Scott said.

How? How the fuck had that happened? Had the school called and all that shit about Dewey and the essay was just to let him dig in deeper? But the school only started calling when you got to level two, and Brandon was barely halfway to one, for Christ's sake. Unless—was it possible that the parking lot monitor had seen them cruise by and later checked to see if they were in class? That fucking Mr. Kranepool—the biggest asshole in the school. Brandon got ready for a scene.

"We found out your SAT results," Linda said.

"That's it?"

"Ten ninety."

Thank Christ. Brandon let out a big sigh of relief. His mom must have misinterpreted that, had to since she didn't know the real story—he was in the clear!—because she said:

"Now don't be too upset."

"About what?"

"Your SAT score."

"I'm not," Brandon said. Then he remembered hearing somewhere that the scores weren't coming till next week, or maybe next month. "It came early or something?" he said, just to make a little conversation.

"There's a number you can call."

"A number?"

"One of those credit card things," Scott said.

"It cost money?"

"Only thirteen dollars," Scott said.

They glanced at each other, Mom and Dad. They weren't telling the truth about the thirteen bucks? Must be something else.

"You couldn't wait?" Brandon said. They could be pretty weird.

"It's kind of important," Scott said.

"Ten ninety, putting you in the seventy-fifth percentile," Linda said.

Brandon shrugged. "Not bad, huh?" Was that the test where he skipped a whole page of questions by mistake, just a little wrecked from the Friday night keg party in the woods after the Old Mill game, or was he mixing it up with geometry? Months ago, or weeks, anyway, hard to remember.

"First, Brandon, I want you to understand that your father and I both know you're very bright."

"Big brain in there, kid," said Scott.

"The problem is, some very bright kids haven't yet learned the skills that allow them to show how bright they are on these kinds of tests."

Yakety fuckin' yak. Where the hell was this going? And all of a sudden, with that funny way beer had, he needed to piss.

"Do you understand the relationship of the SAT to college acceptance?" Linda said.

"Is that a trick question?" Brandon said.

"Hey," said Scott. "This is serious."

"Colleges make you take it," Brandon said.

"Right," said Linda. "But I meant the numerical relationship. I did a little research today. Guess what the median SAT score for last year's freshman class at Yale was."

"Three thousand."

"It's out of sixteen hundred, Brandon."

"Sixteen oh one."

"Knock it off," said Scott. Those little pink anger patches that hardly ever appeared on his cheeks were just visible now.

"Fourteen thirty," said Linda. She was looking at him with big eyes, like she was trying to hypnotize him or something.

"Who wants to go to Yale?" Brandon said.

Linda got up, went out to the garage. Brandon heard her car door open and close. Scott sat back in his chair, kind of like he was on a break. Linda returned with a stack of thick books. *College, College, College,* it said on every one. She leafed through the top book.

"Twelve thousand and forty-six applicants wanted to go to Yale last year. They accepted eighteen percent."

"Good for them," said Brandon.

"Or take Brown," said Linda. "Providence is nice, remember?" She found the page. "Fourteen thousand nine hundred applied, eighteen percent accepted. Average verbal six ninety, average math six ninety."

"What's so nice about Providence?" Brandon said.

"Federal Hill? The restaurant we went to after that tournament?"

"The food sucked."

"Damn it," Scott said. He grabbed one of the books, whipped through, stabbing schools with his index finger. "Amherst—six ninety-eight verbal, seven hundred math. Haverford—middle fifty percent range, verbal six forty to seven twenty, math six thirty to seven thirty. Dartmouth—seven eleven, seven oh four. BU, BU for Christ's sake—six thirty, six thirty-two." He looked up at Brandon. Mom was watching from the other side. Crosshairs.

"What does it say for UConn?" he said.

"What is that supposed to mean?" said Scott.

"You both went there."

"Things were different then," Linda said.

"How? You guys went to UConn, you're successful."

"You're missing the point," Linda said. "Nowadays it's vital to get into a top college. Do you know what a difference it makes if you've got Princeton or Stanford or somewhere on your resume? I see it all the time. And as you must realize from just this brief survey, even someplace like BU is going to be a stretch for you if things keep up the way they are."

"Okay, okay," Brandon said, standing up. "I'll do better next time."

"Great, Brandon," said Linda.

"What we were hoping you'd say," said Scott.

"Hey, no problem," said Brandon, rolling up a quick moo shu pork to go. Was that all it took? Those were the magic words? *I'll do better?* You never knew.

"We'll sign you up for an SAT prep course tomorrow," Linda said. "Kaplan or Princeton Review? Completely your choice."

"About what?" Brandon, already out of there in his mind and really needing to piss, missed that one.

"Which course to take," Linda said. "I checked the Web sites. They're both twice a week, one night and Saturday mornings, which shouldn't affect tennis, and of course we'll want to fit in community service at some point, sooner the better, but—"

"I'm not taking any fucking SAT course."

The pink patches on Scott's face went red.

"Do you know what would have happened if I'd talked to my old man like that?"

Brandon rolled his eyes; made him a bit dizzy, he wouldn't do it again. "I'm not taking any SAT course."

"But Brandon," Linda said, "haven't you been listening?"

"Forget it." He started walking away.

"Do you think Sam would act this way?" Scott said.

"Sam? What's that asshole got to do with it?"

"That asshole," said Scott, "will probably go to Harvard."

"He'll still be an asshole," Brandon said, walking out of the kitchen, into the front hall, on the way to a good long piss, his room, an end to all this bullshit. He raised his voice to make sure they'd hear. "And no way on that goddamn course. You can't make me and that's that."

The front doorbell rang. Brandon happened to be right there. He opened the door. It was true: they couldn't make him. They could drop him off at Kaplan, Princeton Review, whatever it was, and pick him up, but they couldn't make him listen to one word, make one mark on a sheet of paper, answer a single question. The course wasn't going to happen. End of story.

There in the doorway stood Dewey's mom.

"Are your parents in?" she said. Or something like that; mostly he was just taking in the glare she gave him.

Brandon thought fast, but no good ideas came. He tried the best of what he had: "I think they're eating dinner right now. Is there something I could—"

"Brandon?" Linda called from the kitchen. "Who's at the door?"

"It's, uh, Mrs. Brickham."

"Mrs. Brickham?"

"Dewey's mom."

Then Linda was in the front hall too, everything happening too fast. "Mrs. Brickham? Nice to meet you at last. I'm Brandon's mom." Brandon watched his mom taking in the expression on Mrs. Brickham's face. "Is something wrong?"

"Yes indeed," said Mrs. Brickham, turning that glare right back on him.

Upstairs, Ruby was running into a little problem with "A Scandal in Bohemia." Holmes was a cocaine user, she knew that—in fact she was considering bringing it up during discussion period at the next schoolwide DARE conference—but she'd been taught that cocaine revved you up, and here was Dr. Watson talking about the drowsiness of the drug and how Holmes had to rise out of his drug-created dreams to get on with the business of solving crimes. Was this another mistake, like the hunting crop and poker mess-up? If so, there was something wrong with Sherlock Holmes, like he didn't quite make sense, fit together, and Ruby didn't want that. She got up and started down the hall to the stairs. In the mirror at the top, she saw that her right side Thumbelina had unraveled, leaving just one horn sticking up on the left. Cool.

Ruby went downstairs, taking the last three in one jump—landing with both feet inside a black square—heard talking in the kitchen, ran in. "Is cocaine an upper or a downer?"

The talking stopped and everyone turned to her: Mom, Dad, Brandon, and some fierce gray-haired lady she didn't know.

"Our daughter, Ruby," Mom said. The woman's angry gaze rested on Ruby's single Thumbelina. A scary woman:

on Halloween she'd make a perfect Wicked Witch of the West. Ruby herself always went as Princess Di. She had a huge tiara with a heart-shaped ruby, her favorite gem, of course, and she said, "Trick or treat?" with an English accent.

"How about watching TV for a half hour or so, angel?" Mom said.

"Sure," said Ruby, and left the room. Left it with every intention of going downstairs to the home entertainment center, with the big TV, surround sound, DVD, but out in the hall she heard her Dad say:

"The car got towed?"

"To the pound," said the fierce woman. "Right out from under their drunken noses. That's what led to their undoing."

Led to their undoing—right out of *Sherlock Holmes!* Who could blame Ruby for lingering in the hall?

"How was that?" she heard Dad say.

"The cost was over three hundred dollars," said the woman, "and the pound takes cash only. So Dewey and your son"—that *your son* part sounded very nasty the way she, Dewey's mom, of course, said it—"took the credit card into a bank and tried to get a cash advance. The bank called MasterCard and MasterCard called me. I approved the advance without letting on, and they came driving merrily back in Dewey's car—the car that was Dewey's and is now for sale—with some story about working late on a science project."

"Is this true, Brandon?" said Mom.

No answer.

"Brandon?" said Dad.

A little grunt, more yes than no.

Ruby was transfixed. This sounded like *Ferris Bueller,* one of her favorite movies, but happening for real. Ferris: her own brother! She had a million questions, one of which was: *Are you going to take that bumper sticker off before you sell the car? If you do, I want it.*

". . . reimburse half," Dad was saying.

"I'll accept your money," said Dewey's mom, "but it's not why I came. I wanted to inform you as to the character of your son, in case you didn't know already."

"I understand your feelings, Mrs. Brickham," Mom said, "but I think that's a little harsh."

"If you choose to defend his actions, so be it," said Dewey's mom. A chair scraped on the kitchen floor, then another.

"Here's a check," said Dad. *Yes!* He was a great dad.

Footsteps came toward the hall. Ruby lit out for the entertainment center. She found Zippy gnawing on a pool cue and little puddles of something here and there.

Dewey's mom left, Brandon got up.

"Where do you think you're going?" said Scott.

"Taking a fucking piss," Brandon said, or shouted. In the bathroom off the front hall, with those lacy towels that didn't absorb water, Brandon finally had time to think, but his only thought was, *Jesus Christ. You can't do the simplest goddamn thing.* His parents were assholes, Dewey's mom was an even bigger asshole, the tow truck driver was an asshole, those assholes at the car pound were assholes.

Brandon left the bathroom. They were waiting on the other side of the door.

"I can't even take a piss around here."

"You realize the discussion about the prep course is over," Linda said.

"You're taking it," Scott said.

Brandon felt much too hot. His clothes were uncomfortable. A zit was about to erupt on the tip of his nose. He could feel its push, like a goddamn volcano.

"Do whatever you want," he said, went past them, not really pushing, up to his room, slammed the door, lay on his bed. The message light on his phone was blinking. He hit the button.

Dewey. "This is so fucked, man." Unka Death was in the background. "How does that bicycle messenger job sound?"

Real good. *Fuck you good as new all we do then it's through.*

Linda checked the time, realized the SAT prep offices might still be open for night sessions. She called Kaplan, then Princeton Review, learned there wasn't an opening in any of their central Connecticut courses until the next cycle, two months away.

"I can't believe this," she said.

Scott opened one of the flash card boxes. "Maybe we could do it ourselves."

"Do what?"

"Teach him." Scott checked the card. "What does *lachrymose* mean?"

"Weepy."

He turned the card over, read the definition. "Hey, you're right." He tried another. *"Perfidious."*

"Traitorous."

Scott looked on the back. "Wow. The English major." He took another card. *"Miscreant."*

"Miscreant," Linda said. "That's a tough one. Liar, maybe?"

Scott checked the answer, shook his head. "Villain."

An English major, Linda thought, *but from UConn.* Didn't make any sense at all, she knew that right away, but it was one of those thoughts that coming out of nowhere had the ring of truth.

"It won't work," Linda said, "us teaching him. He won't cooperate. And we're not teachers."

"Then what?"

"We'll have to find someone, a professional, just till we can get him into one of the courses."

Scott opened the yellow pages. "What should I look under?"

"Tutor."

"Lots of them in here," Scott said. " 'One-on-one instruction in your own home, affordable hourly rates.' "

"We need to do some research first. I'll talk to people in the morning," Linda said. "Make some calls."

"Me too," said Scott.

She glanced at him, about to say, *I'll take care of it,* but he wasn't looking. Instead he was cracking open a fortune cookie, reading the message. He passed it to her.

Happiness is all around.

Scott ate the cookie; *crunch crunch* and it was gone.

5

Julian's phone rang. He was watching a huge flock of starlings, thousands of them, flying nervously back and forth between two groves of bare-limbed trees in the distance; at the same time, he was enjoying the first drag from his first cigarette of the day. Smoking was so pleasant, a perfect harmonizing of the physical and mental, even spiritual. But Julian wasn't stupid, understood the health risk, had even at one time encouraged the growth of nicotine-inspired tumors along the spines of white mice in a biology lab, and therefore limited himself to three Dunhill Internationals a day: on awakening, after dinner, and a third whenever he wanted it, usually when he was feeling especially good, but sometimes the exact opposite.

Julian half sucked a smoke ball over his tongue, letting the smoke absorb his moisture, held it, still a ball, at the back of his mouth, breathed in fully, then let the smoke lazily find its curling way out through his nose and mouth. Tantric smoking. Through the blue-tinged plume of his own making, he saw the starlings rise as one from the tree crowns of the westernmost grove, wheel toward the east, all banking at the identical angle, about forty-five degrees. In their uniformity of movement and solid black coloring was something undeniably fascistic. That thought was pleasant too, intimately associated with the smoke in a way hard to define, although Julian had no doubt he could make the connection crystal clear, given time. Already he knew it had something to do with the utter lack of vulgarity in nature.

The phone, still ringing, or ringing again. Julian picked it up. A woman. Paulette, Pauline, Paula, something.

"Settling in yet?" she said.

Ah, yes, the woman from the front desk at the office. He recalled two shallow horizontal lines, not deep—not deep yet—at the base of her neck and a cheap ornament on a chain, gold-plated head of some bland breed of dog; not much else.

Julian glanced around his Spartan quarters. "Yes, thank you." He was nothing if not polite.

"Had a chance to take in much of the town?"

"Unfortunately not," Julian said.

"I'm sure you'll like it," said the woman. "Everyone does. I'm from Indianapolis originally."

Was this the woman he'd glimpsed in the glass of the front door as he'd left, giving him an appraising look from behind, or had it been the other one, her boss, who'd hired him? Julian didn't mention where he was from originally, just watched the starlings on their metronomic flight path. At that moment, the sun shone through a tiny gap in the clouds, making the flock gleam like an armored column. He took another drag, deeper than the first, breathed it noiselessly into the phone.

"Um, the reason I'm calling," said Paulette, Pauline, Paula, "and I know it's late notice, especially on a Saturday, but one of our people called in sick, and I wondered if you could fill in, just for today."

It wasn't in his plans. Not that he had plans: he didn't require them. He'd always been good at keeping himself amused. Breakfast, a long walk, perhaps some reading. On the other hand, there was always the issue of money. His mood, so relaxed, benign, began to shift a little.

"Margie said we'd waive our percentage—you could keep the whole fee."

"What's involved?"

"SAT prep, initial evaluation. You should have all the materials. They'd be in the green plastic—"

"I'm sure I do."

"Then it's a yes?"

It's a yes. The temptation to mimic her was suddenly very strong. Julian mastered it. "Why not? I might as well start somewhere."

"You're a doll, Julian. Eleven till one, but these evaluations sometimes go longer, depending on the client. It's in West Mill, thirty-seven Robin Road."

He wrote the client's name and the directions on a Moroccan-bound memo pad he carried, using a Mont Blanc fountain pen with dark blue ink, almost black, that came from a shop on Regent Street. Then he opened the green plastic folder to see if there was anything unusual in the manual's approach to bringing the hapless up to speed; at least, what passed for up to speed in this society, in these times. Of course there was not.

> *Inez makes 75 percent of her free throws in basketball. What is the probability, to the nearest tenth of a percent, that she will make her first three free throws and miss her fourth?*

The answer, 10.5 percent, popped up in Julian's mind—literally, white figures on a black mental screen—at once, before he'd even had a chance to scan the multiple choices. There it was, D, 10.5 percent. A, B, and C—100 percent, 75 percent, 25 percent—were to catch the idiots, E—17.5 percent—to catch all the other catchables. Julian checked the step-by-step teaching guide to the Inez problem, thought of one or two variants—although none could resemble the actual unconscious method he used—flipped through to the verbal section.

negligent : forsake ::
A) ostentatious : vaunt
B) illustrious : succeed
C) adamant : concede
D) mendacious : deceive
E) tenacious : clutch

Clearly D. Transparently so, as if there were an arrow pointing to the letter. He envisioned the tedium of explaining to—he checked his memo pad for the name—Brandon why A and E were wrong, hoped he wouldn't have to do the same for B, or heaven help him, C as well.

Julian took a last luxuriant drag from his cigarette, then put it out although an inch or more remained unsmoked. Disgusting to smoke it down to the tiniest butt, evidence of the addict, the pig. On the memo pad he wrote:

negligent is to forsake as
mendacious is to deceive

There was a poem somewhere in that little couplet. What came next? He sat bent over the memo pad, thinking, thinking. Nothing came. His mood, so lighthearted to begin the day—he glanced out, the starlings were gone—darkened some more. He rose and went into his tiny bathroom.

The first thing Julian did, without quite knowing why, a whim, really, was to shave off his beard. How full it had grown, like some woodcutter, hippie, or rabbi. He felt a little mental lift from that triple-barreled joke. Julian used an Eagle Brand straight razor from Thiers-lssard, sharpened to a fine edge on a stone he kept in his kit, shearing off the beard in long tessellated swaths of foamy hair that piled up in the sink. His bare face appeared, section by section like jigsaw pieces, a fine face. When there was nothing left of the beard but that strange little tuft under the lower lip, he paused. There was a name for that tuft, some appropriately low name for what really was a gutter affectation, but Julian couldn't bring himself to shave it off. He liked that little thing. And on a face as distinguished as his, how could the effect be gross? It would be more like a diacritic from an ancient tongue, or a single-lettered surname, or one that began with *ff*. He left it on, a tiny badge of . . . something special.

Julian consulted his USGS map. He believed in good maps, always got one first thing on arriving somewhere new. He found the street of the client—Robin Road—measured the distance with dividers: a very long walk, too long given the time, which meant the bicycle. He had no car, had been carless for some time, didn't mind. Flexibility, adaptability—the keys to resilience, and resilience the key to strength.

The clouds recovered the sun as he dressed. Julian was watching them thicken and darken, a pleasing sight—he didn't like things too bright—when he sensed another person. He went to the window, looked down. His landlady stood in the yard, looking up. Middle-aged, overweight, dressed on a Saturday in red-and-black checked flannel jacket, jeans, waterproof boots. She saw him and waved. Also a smile, too big. She had good teeth and knew it, no doubt. Julian waved back, keeping his own smile to himself. She made a little window-opening gesture, up up. Julian released the catch, an old-fashioned brass one, the brass all brown, and raised the window.

"A letter for you, Mr. Sawyer."

A letter. How was that possible? Julian glanced quickly beyond her, saw nothing but what she called the big house on the other side of the long lane, and in the distance the two groves of trees, empty of starlings. Nothing unusual, then. He left his little room, the only habitable space in what she called the carriage house, and went down the worn stairs, *creak creak*. Cold air rose to meet him even before he opened the outer door. Julian noted it, that was all; he was impervious to the elements.

She came toward him, her lipstick the same shade of red as the checks on her jacket. "Settling in all right, Mr. Sawyer?"

He'd already dealt with that question this morning, inane and nosy at the same time. "Nicely, thanks, Mrs. Bender."

"Gail, please," said Mrs. Bender. "And I haven't been a real Mrs. since the Reagan administration."

"Julian," said Julian. He supposed her voice was a good feature too, humorous, even intelligent, but what he wanted was the letter. She reached through the buttons of the red-and-black jacket, pulled it out, handed it to him, the envelope warm from being in there against her body. Julian took it in an unhurried, unconcerned way, but his eyes found the return address at once: A-Plus Tutorial Center, his employer. His unconcern turned genuine; a very interesting sensation, that change, the make-believe becoming real, quite physical.

She was giving him an odd look, head on a slight tilt. "Why, you've shaved your beard."

"How can I deny it?"

She laughed, and through her laughter gave him a complicated look reflective of several emotions, all receptive.

"Thanks for bringing the letter, Gail. We'll have to arrange some less disruptive method in the future."

She lowered her gaze slightly, down to the little tuft left behind, and locked on it. "It's no trouble," she said, missing the point.

In the envelope, Julian found a dozen A-Plus Tutorial business cards and a note from Margie, the boss, written in big round letters: "So glad to have you on board, Julian. You can ink your name on these for now. We'll have printed ones in a week or two." He put them in his pocket, secured the green plastic folder in the spring-loaded carrier over the rear wheel of his bicycle—not his, but a rather new and sturdy mountain bike he'd found draped in spiderwebs in the cellar of the carriage house—rode up the long lane to Trunk Road and turned right.

So pleasant; and the wind was even at his back. Not that it mattered: he was very strong, legs, back, shoulders, without being at all bulky, thick-necked, clumsy. He pedaled through rolling farm country, seeing no one, then into a suburban landscape, perhaps exurban, since the houses were still far apart, and quite suddenly he was rolling down Main Street in Old Mill, ten minutes earlier than he'd expected.

Julian went into a coffee place, had an espresso, studied his map. He discovered a much shorter route to Robin Road in West Mill, a route that involved cutting through the town forest. No paths were marked on the map, but whoever heard of pathless forests? He ordered a brioche, took out the memo pad, tried again to find the poem:

> *negligent is to forsake as*
> *mendacious is to deceive*

What came next? A poem hid in there, he could feel it, a brilliant poem, the kind that would find its way into the language, be quoted, change the way people thought. But whatever came next didn't come. Julian paid his bill, left the brioche half eaten. Not very good anyway, not a real brioche, and his authentic pronunciation of the word had confused the serving girl. No tip.

A few minutes later, he entered the town forest, the wind dying at once, as though someone had cut off the power. The path—of course there was a path, with the odd root sticking up, the odd rock, but easy for him, he sped up if anything—led through silent woods. This was a good place: Julian knew so at once, full of shadows and strange perspectives. The word that followed *deceive* began to take shape deep in his mind, just out of reach. He passed a little clearing, heaped here and there with beer cans, and the word receded inexorably, like a falling tide.

Julian climbed a long rise, glimpsed a tiny oblong of water in the distance. The blue flicker blinked out the moment he started down, the path now winding. Julian stopped pedaling, just coasted, as silent as the forest around him, the only source of wind he himself. Then water flashed again on his right, many oblongs of it now, the trees concealing them until the last moment. He heard a voice, a child's voice.

"Don't do that, Zippy."

Julian paused by a boulder, the granitic type left by departing glaciers, peered over the top. Below lay a pond, almost a perfect circle, another glacial remnant. On a strand of frozen mud about a hundred feet away stood a girl in a blue jacket with yellow trim. A large mutt was shaking itself off, spraying her with water. Almost a Norman Rockwell scene, but it was much too dark in this forest for Norman Rockwell, and except for the blue-and-yellow jacket, there was no color at all.

"Zippy!" The girl—she wore a strange hat of some kind—raised her hands ineffectually. From that single gesture, and from her piping voice, Julian could tell how commonplace she was. Now the girl threw a stick into the water. The dog refused to chase it. They both stood there, child and dog, gazing, or gaping perhaps, at the expanding circles the stick had made. How bored they were, girl and dog both, and how boring. It would take a very dark Norman Rockwell to make art of this little nonscene, an upside-down Rockwell, and the result would not be uplifting. Julian titled the imaginary painting *Lumpen Child* and rode on, silent, through the woods.

Trees, trees, the wonderful sensation of having the planet to himself, except for the little girl and her dog, of being very big, of bringing the wind: this could go on forever. He'd barely had the thought before the forest journey was over. No trees, the real wind, now in his face, and he was at the edge of someone's backyard.

Julian paused. A big, unfenced backyard, with wood-pile, swing set, a dozen or more tennis balls lying around like dirty yellow flowers, patio, bird feeder. The feeder was in the form of a cute little house, white with black trim, someone's idea of cozy comfort. A crow stood on the perch outside the tiny door, not feeding, but watching him. Beyond the patio rose the real house, which seemed to have sprung from the same sort of esthetic: also white with black trim, also cute, also cozy. The only difference was the tall red-brick chimney, too tall, really, almost unstable-looking, as though a giant could topple it with one casual swat. A matching brick walkway led around the side of the house, past a deck, coiled garden hose, trash cans. Julian dis-mounted, prepared a suitable tale—the woods, a little lost, fill in your own blanks—and walked his bike over the bricks toward the front of the house and Robin Road. He heard a toilet flush as he went by.

But no need to go all the way to the street, because halfway across the front lawn Julian caught the number on the mailbox: 37. He'd homed in exactly on target, like the kind of missile yet to be perfected. He leaned his bike against a lightpost beside the front walkway, removed the green plastic A-Plus Tutorial folder from the carrier, approached the front door.

Black, solid, with solid brass fittings. Julian took out one of his new business cards, put a solid businesslike expression on his face. As he rang the bell he noticed the welcome mat. It actually said *welcome*, the word entwined with daisies. Daisies! His mood, not the best since the failure— not failure, how could that word apply?—to find the word that came after *deceive*, lifted. He heard footsteps coming from the other side of the door, felt his solid businesslike expression altering slightly, striking an added note or two of amiability. From the tiny house in the backyard came the cawing of the crow.

6

Linda opened the door. A tall man stood on the threshold. "Yes?" she said.

The man had a friendly smile. "Julian Sawyer," he said. "From A-Plus Tutorial. I'm here for Brandon's SAT prep."

"You are?" said Linda. "We were expecting someone named Sally."

"Sick today, I'm afraid." He gave her a business card with a mortarboard logo on the front. The shape of his hand caught her eye—a Michelangelo study come to life. "Margie has sent me in her stead."

Not a good start, Linda thought. The reason she'd chosen A-Plus in the first place was this Margie woman's recommendation of Sally's skills with reluctant boys, uncooperative boys, the insanely hostile. Sally was a junior at Trinity, a lacrosse star with five brothers. This man was—what? Too old to be a student, even a graduate student. When she thought of tutors, Linda thought of college kids or schoolmarms, not this. He wasn't right for the part—not that he didn't look intelligent, far from it—certainly wouldn't be right in Brandon's eyes; Brandon, at that moment sulking in his bedroom, headphones clamped on tight.

"I appreciate your coming at the last minute and everything," Linda said. She glanced past him, looking for his car, spotted only a mountain bike leaning against the lightpost. "The problem is that Brandon's not what you'd call enthusiastic about this idea."

"The sacrilege of it."

"Sacrilege?"

"Schooling, on a Saturday."

"Exactly. And Margie thought that since Sally—"

Scott came up from behind her with a handful of Ruby's blue-and-yellow feathered arrows. "Where's her bow?" he said. Then he noticed the substitute tutor, whose name Linda realized she had failed to catch. The first lesson was critical: how to postpone it until Sally was available without being rude to him?

"This gentleman's from the tutoring place," Linda said.

"I thought—"

"She's sick." Linda noticed with surprise that the two men were about the same height, Scott slightly taller if anything, which meant that the other man wasn't even six feet. "The problem is—"

A cry—Ruby's cry—and Zippy shot out from the side walkway, his leash flying free.

"Not again," said Scott. He dropped one of the arrows. Bending to pick it up, he lost control of them all.

At the same moment Ruby appeared, also on the run, her hair in that ridiculous devil do, her jacket missing. Zippy tore across the street, Ruby following, calling, "Zippy, Zippy!" Oh, God. Ruby wasn't going to . . . and she didn't. Didn't stop, didn't look left or right. The burst of fright Linda felt in her chest couldn't have been more powerful if a car had indeed been coming.

"Ruby!"

Then Linda was running too. Zippy bounded onto the Strombolis' lawn, headed straight to their rosebushes, the glory of Robin Road every summer, now hooded in plastic. Without a pause, like a madman with a plan, Zippy started attacking the plastic.

"Zippy!" Ruby dove for his leash, caught it, tried to drag him away, but couldn't. Zippy yanked the plastic free.

"Zippy!" Linda called, from halfway across the street.

Zippy seized the rosebush at the base of its stem, started tugging at it in fury, growling and jerking his head from side to side. The Strombolis' front door opened and Mr. Stromboli came out in a purple robe and slippers, a golf club in his hand. He ran too, surprisingly fast for such a fat man, raising the club high. Ruby, now on her feet, saw him coming, screamed in terror, got tangled in the leash, fell. Zippy strained at the rosebush, blind to everything else. Linda shouted something at Mr. Stromboli, she didn't know what.

Then suddenly the substitute tutor was on the Strombolis' lawn, not running, just there. Ten or fifteen feet from Zippy, he said: "Heel."

Zippy stopped what he was doing at once. His head came up, swiveled. He saw the substitute tutor, trotted over and stood beside him, tail wagging. Everyone else—Linda, Ruby, Mr. Stromboli—froze. It was strangely quiet, like after a jackhammer stops. The substitute tutor helped Ruby to her feet, handed her the leash, then knelt at the rosebush, digging around a little with his hands—Linda could actually hear his fingers in the dirt—repositioning the roots. He replaced the tattered plastic, walked over to Mr. Stromboli, said something Linda didn't catch. Mr. Stromboli replied, the substitute tutor nodded, they shook hands. Mr. Stromboli walked back to his house. Mrs. Stromboli was on her way out, also in a robe, although not carrying a golf club. He spun her around and they both went inside.

The tutor turned to Linda: "No harm done," he said.

She didn't know what to say. For one thing, she still couldn't come up with his name.

Brandon, headphones back on, Unka Death in his ears, sat at the dining-room table, watching the tutor guy grade his evaluation test. *Call me Julian,* he'd said, and added some joke about another guy with a weird name, Ishmael or something, a joke Brandon didn't get. Julian: a gay name for sure, but he didn't seem gay, not literally, not whatever the other term was either, when it's just a metaphor or something. He hadn't said much after that, sitting quietly in Dad's chair at the end of the table while Brandon took the test. For a while he'd gazed at some words on a memo pad, pen in hand although he never wrote anything. Later he'd got up and examined the collage on the wall behind the sideboard, mostly tennis pictures of the kids, none recent: Ruby, Brandon, Adam. After that he'd taken a look at the bottles in the wine rack. That's where he'd been—standing behind Brandon—when he'd said, "Time's up," startling him a little and taking the test booklet away.

Unka Death was something else. And his video was fucking incredible. That girl in the gold shorts and the white old lady wig? He thought about her every night.

> *Fuck you good as new all we do then it's through*
> *The job you got, the brains you spew*
> *Ya horn-hoppin momma just about—*

Brandon became aware of the tutor looking at him, lips moving, smoothing the test booklet under his hand. He lowered the headphones, Unka Death rapping on tinnily around his neck.

". . . projecting the results to a full-length test," Julian was saying, "you did a little better in math this time and about the same on the verbal."

Hey! The tutor guy had one of those soul patches under his lower lip, which was kind of cool.

"Interested in your exact scores?" he said. He also had a great speaking voice, like an actor.

"I guess."

The tutor guy checked his paperwork. "Six hundred math, five hundred verbal, eleven hundred total score."

Six hundred. Didn't sound so bad. What was his name? Julian, but not gay. Brandon waited for him to say, "Not bad," or "Good job," or something like that.

Julian said nothing. He opened his green folder, turned pages, stopped. Brandon read: *questionnaire* upside-down. "What colleges are you interested in?"

"I don't know."

Julian made a check mark in a box.

"GPA?"

"About three two."

"Favorite subject?"

Brandon shrugged.

"Least despised, then."

Brandon thought. School was all so fucking boring. He was half asleep just behind his eyes most of the time. "Maybe history."

Julian wrote it down.

"Best book read in the past year?"

"Helter Skelter." The only book he'd read in the past year—he'd come across it in Dewey's garage.

"Helter Skelter?"

"It's about the Manson family killings."

Julian looked like he was about to smile but didn't. "What did you like about it?"

"Kind of interesting," Brandon said.

Julian watched him, as though maybe waiting for more. Brandon couldn't think of anything else.

"And finally," Julian said, returning to the questionnaire, "any career plans?"

Brandon shook his head.

"I'll just write 'interested in serial killing.' "

So deadpan, Brandon didn't get it right away. Then he did, and started laughing. Now Julian smiled.

"A little surprise for Sally when she comes for your lesson next week."

Brandon laughed again. He switched off his MP3. Julian wrote something on the sheet.

"You're really writing that?" Brandon said.

"Should I?" Julian said.

Brandon shrugged. Julian slid the folder across the table. In the box beside career plans Brandon read: *Indefinite.*

"No need to frighten Sally," Julian said. "But I will leave her a note to spend extra time on analogies."

Brandon hated them.

"Not your favorite?" said Julian.

"They—" He shook his head.

"Suck?"

"Yeah." The exact word he had in mind, although it sounded weird coming out of Julian's mouth, almost like Brandon was hearing it for the first time.

Julian opened the test booklet. " 'Revenge is to blood-shed,'" he said. "You circled C—'as sadness is to death.'"

"Wrong?"

Julian came around the table, sat down, placed the booklet in front of him.

A) knife : wound
B) rain : corn
C) sadness : death
D) electricity : light
E) mercy : healing

Brandon gazed at the question, his brain now too tired to think, to even absorb the individual meanings of everyday words. Maybe he really was stupid. And who was the ass-hole who dreamed up that little system of colons? He felt Julian's gaze.

"Any thoughts?" said Julian.

Brandon shook his head.

"Why don't you try cause and effect?"

"Cause and effect?"

"As a method. For example, revenge leads to bloodshed. Similarly, does knife lead to wound?"

"Yeah."

"What about a bread knife?"

While Brandon was thinking about that, Julian said: "Rain to corn?"

"Kind of," Brandon said.

"Tip number one," Julian said. "Eliminate all kind ofs. Electricity to light?"

"Sure," Brandon said, but he wasn't feeling sure.

Julian reached into his pocket, pulled out a wooden match. Not a box of them, just one. He ignited it with his thumbnail, real easy, not even looking at it, his eyes on Brandon. What was he getting at? That you could have light without electricity? Ah.

"Mercy to healing?" Julian said.

"I guess that's the one," said Brandon. "I had it the other way around."

"The other way around?" Julian was looking at him closely. There was something about his eyes, like the chip driving them was the very latest.

Brandon nodded.

"Death causing sadness?" Julian said. "And bloodshed revenge?"

"Totally screwed up, right?"

"Not at all," Julian said. He blew out the match, looked around for somewhere to put it. But there was nowhere. No one smoked but Brandon, weed when he could get it. Julian stuck the burnt match back in his pocket. The high-speed processor behind his eyes switched off. "Completely defensible," he said. "Your problem is the College Board doesn't include a section for student defenses."

Brandon laughed.

"And therefore?"

Brandon shrugged.

"Therefore, Brandon, you have to think like them."

"Like the College Board?"

"Not so hard. Not hard at all, in fact. Imagine the kind of people who formulate these questions. Are they brilliant?"

"I don't know."

"Or are they smart?"

"Smart."

"Smart, not brilliant. Do they listen to the Beatles? Or do they listen to Unka Death?"

Brandon was stunned. Unka Death was practically brand-new. And Julian looked too old to know about rap, although not as old as Mom and Dad—there wasn't a line on his face, his hair was thick, his stomach flat. The light changed, or Julian's head shifted, because suddenly his eyes were like mirrors for a second, opaque and glittering. Brandon realized he'd been staring at Julian, maybe rudely, and looked away.

"You must know someone at school," Julian said, "maybe not the most entertaining of your friends, but he usually gets the right answer."

Sam. Not at his school; at Andover. But Sam.

"Tip number two," Julian said. "Think like him."

Fuck that.

Then Julian added: "Just for the duration of the test. No one will ever know."

Brandon laughed, one of those single-beat laughs, mostly through the nose. Julian was kind of funny, in a sneaky way.

Julian checked his watch. "Your ordeal is over." He rose, gathered his materials. "For today."

Brandon got up too, rubbed his eyes, tried to recall if he was grounded or whether the SAT prep was the whole punishment for New York. An important question, since there was a keg party by the pond tonight. Through the window, he saw Ruby getting into Mom's car, bow in hand, quiver on her belt. Julian was watching her too.

"Your sister's an archer?" he said.

"I wouldn't say that."

Ruby had trouble fitting in the bow, rode off with it sticking out the top of the window. It looked like Mom yelled something at her. It looked like Ruby yelled back.

"What got her interested in archery?" Julian said.

"Don't ask me," said Brandon. "She's a bit of a pain, if you want to know."

Julian turned to him. "How so?"

Brandon shrugged. "Did you have a little sister when you were growing up?"

The opaque look returned to Julian's eyes. "No," he said.

Dad came in, wearing his knee brace and tennis shorts, pulling on his polo shirt. "All done?"

"All done," Julian said, lowering his gaze for a moment to Dad's bare midsection. *Hey, Dad was putting on weight.*

"How'd he do?"

Julian turned to Brandon. "Did we make some progress?"

Brandon shrugged.

Dad came forward with a check, handed it to Julian. "And here's a little extra for filling in." He added a five-dollar bill, said, "Nice job, Bran," and left the room.

Julian gazed at the bill for a moment, like he was reading it carefully or something. Then he folded it in half, folded it again, put it in the pocket with the burned match.

He held out his hand. "Good luck on the SAT."

They shook hands. Julian's felt warm, almost hot.

"Tip number three," he said. "The College Board likes to make nice."

"So pick the Beatles answer?"

"We have made progress," Julian said.

Brandon walked Julian to the front door, watched as he got on his bike. Julian pedaled down the driveway, stopped at the street, looked back. "The Beatles of 'All You Need Is Love,'" he said. "Not 'Helter Skelter.'" Then he rode off down Robin Road. It wasn't much of a bike compared to Brandon's, never used anymore, but Julian went very fast and was soon out of sight.

7

Saturday had always meant sports: soccer, baseball, softball, volleyball, basketball, figure skating, even (for five minutes) hockey. By now, thank Christ, she was down to two:

Tennis, the family sport, for some unlucky reason. A game of running back and forth on a pattern of squares and rectangles, huffing and puffing, calling out the score in a crazy language, getting jolts up and down your arm, arguing, losing over and over to Kyla the lob-lob-lobber. Not to mention Erich, with his blond-tipped back hair curling over the collar of his polo shirt, his year-round tan the color of Dad's distressed-leather briefcase from Orvis, and those eyes, practically sharing a socket.

And archery, which was her own. No huffing and puffing in archery, no lobbing, no disputes. And the word itself, one of her very favorites. *Tennis* sounded like a disease, but *archery* the word, first encountered in a coloring book of myths and legends she'd had as a little girl, on the page with Diana the huntress—blue tunic, yellow hair—had got her interested in archery the sport. A very cool word, just the sound, and then that double arch, the arch in the bow and the arch in the flight of the arrow. Plus all the other cool words: *nock, fletching, cock feather, quiver*. Instead of boring ones like *in* and *out*, and nasty ones like *fault, double-fault*. Dumbest of all, *love* meant nothing.

Ruby stepped up to the shooting line, took one deep breath, let it out slow, the way Jeanette said. She loved the whole routine: nocking the arrow, not too snug, the cock feather—hers was yellow, the other two feathers blue—making an L with the bow; then the draw—hand, wrist, forearm, all straight, lined up with the arrow, point resting on her knuckle, string barely touching the tip of her nose, grazing her lips, anchored. The anchor position: she could make a list of the things she liked about just that one part of archery.

1. The strength of the bow before she even fired, like a living thing in her hands.
2. How her fingertips on the nock united the bow and the arrow, made it all possible.
3. Everything so still, the distant sight of the target over the top of the arrow stillest of all.
4. The center circle of the target, gold like the pot at the end of the rainbow.
5. Best of all, that little kiss good-bye of the string against her lips at the moment of release.

Ruby released. *Just let go, let the string slip away.* That slipping away part was pretty good too.

Her arrow flew, the blue and yellow of its tail blending together, blue for the sky, yellow for the sun, which was why they were her colors—not favorite colors, but colors like a knight's. Also good, the flight of the arrow, when she'd done all she could and now whatever happened happened. One New Year's Eve before she was born, when Brandon was four, Adam had tossed him a tennis ball on the very last second of the old year and Brandon had caught it on the very first second of the new. The flight of the arrow was something like that.

Thwack. Not *thwack* because Ruby couldn't possibly hear the arrow striking the target, forty yards away; but there her arrow was, in the gold. Gold, yes! In the outer, close to the red, but not touching, definitely gold. She gazed at her final six of the day, not what you could call grouped, but still: one black, one blue, two red, two gold, one of them an inner.

"You go, Ruby," said Jeanette. Jeanette ran the kids' program for the archery club. Once Ruby had actually seen her split an apple from the men's seventy-meter line.

The kids walked down the range, pulled their arrows out of the straw targets. Jeanette rolled up behind them in her pickup, hoisted the targets into the back two at a time, said, "Hop up." The kids hopped up. She drove them over to the line of parent cars, waiting by the old practice field at West Mill High, a mom or dad motionless behind every wheel, engines running, heaters on.

Ruby got in the Jeep. "You must be freezing," Mom said.

Jeanette heard that through the open window of the pickup. "Never too cold for shooting, right, Rubester?"

"Right," said Ruby.

"Keep 'em sharp," Jeanette said.

"You bet," said Ruby, holding her belt quiver between her knees. Jeanette—one more good thing about archery—reached out and closed the door for her with a thump.

Mom glanced out at Jeanette, shivered. They drove off as a huge flock of dark birds swooped low over the empty field, then up, like a rising black wave. Ruby knew she could never shoot at a bird or any other living thing, but that didn't stop her wondering if she'd be able to hit one in flight. She practiced doing it in her mind—leading, leading, release, *thwack;* and feathers drifting down.

"My aim is true."

"What's that, Ruby?"

"Nothing." Good grief, she'd said that aloud. She checked on Mom with a tricky sidelong look. Mom was thinking about something else, no follow-up coming. And the birds were almost out of sight, a tiny cloud now, darker than the rest and moving the other way. Those feathers drifting down weren't funny: she could never shoot a living thing.

"**S**erve 'em up, gentlemen," said Erich in that funny accent of his.

Saturday afternoon doubles, the only tennis Scott played now, except for batting it around with Brandon once a month or so. Not Ruby, who had walked off the court the last time he'd hit with her. *If you're going to make the ball bounce that high you can forget it.* The kids could be damned disrespectful, both of them. Brandon probably needed his tail whacked, but no one did that anymore, and Scott doubted he could have in any era. As for Ruby . . . He was still trying to find the completion to that thought when Tom laid the balls on his racket.

"Start us off," he said.

Saturday afternoon doubles: Scott and Tom played Erich and whomever Erich brought along. They hit hard for an hour and a half, cracked jokes, maybe worked up a sweat, sat in the steam room, sometimes went out for a beer, losers paying. Today was a little different because first, Scott was planning to nudge Tom a little on the Symptomatica deal. Second, the player Erich had brought along today was Mickey Gudukas.

Why? Erich had never invited Gudukas before and although Scott hadn't actually played him, he'd seen him on the court a few times, enough to know that Gudukas wasn't on their level. Not that they were great—Scott and Tom had both played in college, and Erich had kicked around the satellite circuit and claimed membership on the Swiss Davis Cup team at one time, although Sam had checked their rosters going back twenty-five years on the Internet and failed to find him. That made them pretty good, a long way from great, even back when they'd been at the top of their game, but too much for Mickey Gudukas, probably a 4.5 player at best.

That was one problem. The other was: *Bald lefty who foot-faults all the time? A real sleazeball?* Tom was a stickler for court etiquette. Scott, at the baseline, held up the balls and said, "Play well, gentlemen," hoping Gudukas caught the gentlemen part.

"And have fun," added Erich, in the ad court on the opposite side. *Half fun,* it sounded like. Did a funny thought hide in there somewhere?

Gudukas, waiting at the baseline on the deuce side, said nothing. He looked a little too intense for Saturday afternoon doubles, crouched low, too low, in too-tight shorts, the lights glaring on his bald head and sweat beads already gleaming on his mustache; and inching toward his backhand, the way players with weak backhands tried to make that big forehand space enticing.

Good luck. The old man had put them straight on that one before they'd even had a formal lesson: if there's a weakness, why hit anywhere else? Scott bent a slice wide to Gudukas's backhand. A real nice one, with bite: he was going to have a good day.

"Nope," said Gudukas, not even twitching.

Caught the line. Not just caught it, but landed smack in the middle, as Scott could confirm just from the set of Tom's back at the net, although Tom hadn't moved a muscle. Bad calls were even worse than foot faults. No expression on Erich's face, of course; he took whatever he could get, a habit formed in the boonies of the satellite circuit, if not ingrained.

Scott went with his kicker on the second serve, down the middle where Gudukas wanted it. Scott never used the kicker anymore because of his shoulder, and he felt this one right away, that old twinge, deep inside, but even though this match didn't mean anything he couldn't help being a little pissed.

Gudukas swung and missed completely. Fifteen-love.

"Gott im Himmel," said Erich. "Second-serve ace. Perhaps it is better we go right to the showers."

Tom came over, bounced him a ball. Their eyes met.

"What's *Gott im Himmel?*" Scott said.

"No idea," said Tom. "That showers thing's what scares me."

Scott laughed. Tom laughed too. This was fun, not half, but total. Tennis was still in their blood. What had Ruby said? Just like math? Was she going to be one of those people who didn't know how to have fun? Kind of like Linda, maybe, the way Linda was now. Scott pushed all that out of his mind and served to Erich, forehand side.

Erich was all over it, pouncing in his bandy-legged way, angling his return right at Scott's feet as he came in. Scott dug down for the ball, popped it up, practically on Gudukas's strings. An easy put-away, but Gudukas overhit it, might have been trying to put a hole in Scott, actually; and somehow popped it right back up off the top of his frame. Tom stepped across and smacked it past Gudukas's outstretched backhand in that decisive way he had, quick and sure.

Thirty-love. Gudukas had trouble patty-patting up the ball with his racquet. Erich, standing behind him, made a face, like this was going to be a long afternoon. Scott, thinking of Symptomatica, decided to go easier on Gudukas the next serve. Another slice, but not as hard as the first, and to the forehand this time, where he wanted it. Gudukas took a big backswing—a messed-up muscle-bound stroke, beyond fixing—and hammered at the ball. From the way he was set up it should have gone crosscourt, but instead it came right at Tom, a screamer. Tom was fooled completely. The ball hit him in the middle of the forehead.

"For pit's sake," said Erich.

Gudukas held up his hand to show it wasn't intentional.

Scott took a few steps toward his brother. "You all right?"

Tom turned, reached in the pocket of his shorts, bounced him a ball. "Thirty-fifteen," he said, and that was all. There was a colorless, bloodless circle on his forehead. He didn't even look at Gudukas, just moved to the deuce court, took his place at the net.

"We are all right to play?" Erich said.

Neither of them, Scott or Tom, replied. Everything, life even, was simple for a moment or two. They were brothers, on the same side, together, and would now wipe the court with Mickey Gudukas. Tom signaled behind his back: closed fist, meaning Erich's forehand again, but this time Tom would poach. Scott tossed the ball in the air, rocked back.

A cell phone went off, a loud one. Scott broke off his motion, an awkward halt that hurt his shoulder even more than serving the kicker. Gudukas yelled, "Time," and struggled with a cell phone stuck in the pocket of his too-tight shorts.

There were signs in the lobby, the locker rooms, on the double doors to the courts: No Cell Phones in the Building. Add to that Gudukas's foot faults, bad calls, clumsy game: like he'd done research on how to piss Tom off and his real purpose was to kill the Symptomatica deal good and dead.

Gudukas talked on the phone. Scott, Tom and Erich gathered at the net, Erich doing little tricks with his racquet, rolling it up and down his arms; Scott doing little tricks with the ball, bouncing it in that back-and-forth walk-the-dog style perfected by Boris Becker; Tom standing still, holding his racquet across his chest.

Gudukas was one of those people who talked loudly on the cell, like farmers on crank-up phones in old movies. "Are you fuckin' kidding me?" he said. And: "I don't fuckin' believe this." He glanced over at them. They all looked away, except for Tom, who hadn't been watching anyway.

"How is Sam?" Erich said.

"Good," said Tom.

"Still likes Andover?"

"Loves it."

"And the team is good?"

Tom nodded. "They've got one senior took early decision at Stanford and another's getting a full ride at Duke."

"Stanford is good tennis," Erich said. "I know Billy Mixer."

"Who's he?" said Tom.

"The coach."

"Yeah?" said Tom.

"We made the doubles finals in Estoril in eighty-nine," Erich said. "The kid going to Stanford—he plays number one at Andover?"

"Yeah."

"And Sam?"

"Looks like he'll be number two this spring."

"I could call Billy, perhaps," said Erich. "Put in a word."

Scott stopped doing the Boris Becker thing.

"You think Sam could play for Stanford?" Tom said. He sounded surprised, and pleasantly.

Erich considered. While he was considering, Gudukas yelled, "What a stupid asshole."

Erich blinked. "Sam's mentality is good," he said. "I'll call Billy."

"Thanks," Tom said.

Was that how big things got done? Scott thought. *So easy?*

"Hey, guys," Gudukas called, coming over. "Some shit's come up, can't wait. Just when it was shaping up to be a good match—we'll have to do it again. Thanks for the invite, Erich. See you, Scott. Nice meeting you, Tommy."

Tommy. No one called him that, or ever had.

When he'd gone, Scott said, "We could play a little Canadian."

Erich waved the idea away. "You boys play. I've got a million racquets to string."

Scott and Tom looked at each other.

"I don't know," Tom said.

"Yeah," said Scott, "let's just bag it."

Tom started toward the bench where they'd left their sweats, racquet covers, water. Scott lowered his voice a little.

"What about Brandon?" he said. Big things, so easy.

"Brandon?" said Erich, not lowering his.

"And tennis," Scott said.

Erich considered. "He must work on his consistency, of

course. But I look for him to maybe move up this year, help us out from time to time."

"I didn't mean at West Mill. I meant in the future, at college."

"College?" said Erich. Like a lot of good tennis players, his eyes were a little too close together; now the gap seemed to narrow some more. "Like Stanford or Duke?"

There was something humiliating about the way he said those two words, Stanford and Duke. "D three then," said Scott, his voice sounding sharp, but that might have been the acoustics indoors. "Middlebury, say, or Tufts."

"Middlebury," said Erich. "Tufts." He licked his lips. "What is happening now, Scott, is even D three level is getting tough."

Scott glanced over at Tom. He was taking off his elbow brace, didn't appear to be listening.

"But who knows?" said Erich, giving Scott an encouraging pat on the back. "Why don't you boys hit? Court time's on the house."

Tom turned. "Yeah?" he said. His eyes met Scott's again. It had to happen sometime. "Hell," Scott said. "Why not?"

"A quick set?" said Tom.

Scott shrugged. What did that mean? Quick for who? Unity, wiping the court with Mickey Gudukas: slipping away fast, and gone.

"Serve 'em up," Tom said. The bloodless circle on his forehead was turning red.

"Half fun," said Erich.

They hadn't played each other in years. Scott was the better player: higher-ranked with the New England USTA in the days they were both ranked; had had a better college career, dominating several players who had dominated Tom; was bigger, stronger, faster, with a much harder serve. But he'd never beaten Tom; not as little boys, not as teenagers, not as young men. Scott had been twenty-one the last time, summer of his senior year at UConn, and Tom twenty-three, working for the old man. They'd played on the slow red clay courts, now gone, below the seventeenth tee at the Old Mill C.C., all by themselves in the middle of a day too hot for anyone else. Tom: 7–6, 6–7, 7–6 (13–11). The closest Scott had ever come; closer than that was almost impossible. He'd blown nine match points, and there'd been some yelling after it was over, even shoving, almost a fight, even at that age.

Scott stuck two balls in his pocket, held up the third. Tom waited on the other side, a foot or two inside the baseline, which was annoying; not all crouched and intense like Gudukas, but relaxed. *Quick for who?*

Scott thought of saying something light like, "Half fun," but the idea was quickly shoved aside by the memory of that ninth blown match point—a memory unvisited for a decade or more. Scott could see it clear: a sure down-the-line winner that had caught the very top of the net and instead of dropping over—like Tom's previous two shots, *two!*—fell back. Pure bad luck, Scott thought as he tossed the ball in the air. Bad luck, fate, Stanford, Duke: it was going to be now, the cracking through. Big things, so easy. He went with the kicker, right off.

Tom, 6-0.

A quick set. After it was over, they shook hands at the net, eyes averted. Tom said something nice, something about flukes, good days, bad days. Scott couldn't speak. His face, body, hands, were on fire. He left his racquet where it was, smashed on the court.

Tom went into the locker room. Scott found himself

back in the weight room, lifting crazily, trying to work it all out of him. He was no fucking match for Tom; Brandon was no fucking match for Sam. Seventy-fifth percentile versus ninety-ninth. That said what there was to say. Ninety-ninth was where all the cream was waiting, the cream of American possibility, the sweet life floating above all this shit. The ninety-niners probably didn't even know it was a competition. Would it go on forever, this coming up short? He thought of Adam. Adam, who could have competed with anybody at anything.

The thought of Adam calmed Scott. Not how Adam would have competed, what a star he would have been: just Adam. He got off the bench, stripped the weights, hung them on the steel pegs. Scott loved all his kids equally, of course, the way you were supposed to. Oh, but Adam.

In the locker room, he changed into his bathing suit, walked past the steam room, not yet ready to face Tom, and outside to the deck. The club had installed a whirlpool out there, shrouded now in vapor. Scott lowered himself into the hot, bubbling water, parting the clouds with his own motion; and there was Tom, sitting on the far side.

"You scared me," Tom said.

"Yeah?"

They sat in the vapor cloud, up to their necks. The deck looked out on the town forest, the same woods that backed so close to Robin Road, but from the other side. The woods were just a dark mass through the vapor, but directly above was a clear patch, like the eye of a hurricane. A flock of birds flew over, headed for the trees.

Scott tried to think of something to say, something to make up for the racquet smashing, the curses, all that. Would Tom tell Deborah about it, or even Sam? Scott didn't know. Tom was hard to read sometimes.

"Thought you didn't like whirlpools," Scott said. There'd been one up at Tom's ski place years before, but he'd ripped it out and extended the kids' dorm.

Tom got a strange look on his face, almost as though

he'd felt a sharp pain. "I don't," he said. "The steam room was packed."

Tom closed his eyes. Silence, except for the bubbling. Scott gazed at his brother's face, wondering what he was thinking. He had no intention of bringing up Symptomatica, not now. Neither did he want to spend any more time in the whirlpool with Tom. He should just say good-bye, shower, get out of there, do some chores, chopping wood behind the house—maybe with Brandon—or cleaning out the garage.

"What about the Symptomatica deal?" he said. Just like that.

Tom opened his eyes. Their expression made Scott think: *I should have stayed in Boston, gone back for an MBA, set up my own shop, anything.*

"After the performance Gudukas put on?" Tom said. "You really want to get involved with someone like that? Get the business involved? Mom?"

Scott didn't answer. *Just don't say we're doing pretty good here, both of us. The wives, the kids, everybody.*

Tom didn't.

Brandon lay on the couch in the entertainment center. The entertainment center was cool, especially when he had it to himself. The picture, the sound—all great. The diamond in Unka Death's front tooth showed every whatever the word was, not *face* but something like that, and he heard for the first time another rapper in the background, going "Where the sun don't shine" in a deep voice every time Unka Death said "Fuck you."

Then suddenly Dad was in the room, standing between him and the TV.

"Does it have to be so loud?" Dad said.

"I can't see."

Dad moved aside.

"Let's go out and split some wood," Dad said.

"Huh?"

"At the woodpile. There's work to do."

"I'm relaxing." *Where the sun don't shine, where the sun don't shine.* How had he missed that? It was so obvious. Unka Death got behind the wheel of his Rolls-Royce. The girl in the gold shorts and the old lady wig put her head in his lap.

Dad snapped off the TV.

"What the fuck?" Brandon said.

"That's your problem," Dad said. "Too much goddamn relaxing. What've you got to be so relaxed about?"

Dad looked really pissed. "I did the SAT thing, for Christ's sake," Brandon said. "Leave me alone."

"Leave you alone?" said Dad. "You've got a long way to go, Bran. What does *lachrymose* mean? *Perfidious? Miscreant?*"

Brandon got up. "You're such an asshole." He started for the stairs but his father blocked the way.

"Don't you call me that, ever again."

They were face-to-face at the bottom of the stairs. Brandon got ready to call his father an asshole again. At that moment, they heard Mom from upstairs: "What's all the yelling?"

She came down, a calculator in her hand, a pen behind her ear. Dad backed away from him.

"What's going on?" she said, looking at one of them, then the other.

Dad's cheeks had red patches all over them. He said nothing. Brandon said: "He's gone nuts," and went up the stairs.

"**Y**ou've heard that?" Brandon said. " 'Where the sun don't shine?' " He lay across his bed, feet up against the window, watching low dark clouds going in one direction, high light ones in the other, the phone to his ear.

"How could you miss it?" Dewey said. "That's Problem."

"The guy with the cleaver in the trunk of the Rolls?"

"Not a Rolls," said Dewey. "It's a Bentley. You coming tonight?"

"Don't know," Brandon said. "I might be grounded."

"For what?"

For what? "Your mom forgot the New York thing already?"

"Blew over," Dewey said. "Your folks coughing up half did the trick. Money's like Prozac for her."

Brandon laughed. That was pretty cool.

"So I'll see you if I see you," Dewey said. "Might have some crack."

"Crack?" said Brandon.

There was a knock at his door.

"Brandon?" Mom.

"Later," Brandon said into the phone, and clicked off.

"Can I come in?"

"I guess."

Mom came in. "How's steak for dinner?"

"Sure." This was new, not steak for dinner, although that kind of sit-down thing didn't happen a lot, but getting consulted.

Mom smiled. "Good." She glanced around, kicked some shoes in the closet, closed it, noticed the open disc tray on the CD, closed that too. *Oh, fuck.* Next would come straightening the desk, the desk where nicely centered on the only unmessy part lay the *Macbeth* makeup test, with the big red F circled at the top. Might as well have been framed and hung on the wall.

Brandon got up, went over to the desk as naturally as he could, stretching a little on the way, and sat on the test, arms crossed, casual. Mom gave him a funny look.

"What's on your mind, Bran?"

"Nothin'."

"Are you upset about what happened with Dad?"

"No."

"He just wants the best for you. So do I."

"I want the best for you too, Mom." That just popped out. What a weird fuckin' thing to say. Brandon felt his face getting hot.

"Brandon!" She hugged him, kissed him on the cheek. Hotter and hotter. "That's so nice," she said, then let him go, stepped back. "You're getting so big." Her eyes were damp.

"Mom?"

"Yes?"

"Am I still grounded?"

She gave him another funny look. Maybe there should have been more lead-up to the grounding question, was that it?

"I don't know, Brandon," she said. "How did the *Macbeth* makeup test go?"

"Haven't got it back yet."

"What about the SAT lesson?"

"Not bad."

"What did you cover?"

What did they cover? Brandon couldn't think of a thing. Then he surprised himself: there were the tips, three of them, all clear in his mind. Tip one—eliminate all kind ofs. Tip two—think like Sam, but just for the test. Tip three—make nice. "Analogies," he said. "Like mustard is to hot dogs as something is to something."

"Tell you what, Brandon. Fill in those blanks and you can go out tonight."

What was he, a performing seal? There was no way he could come up with something like that just out of the—

"Like icing is to cake," he said.

She actually clapped her hands. "That's wonderful, Brandon. What process did you use?"

She sat on the bed, like she was settling in for one of those intellectual discussions when guests came over. Process? He didn't have a clue. "Julian gave me a few tips."

"Did he? Like what?"

"They're top secret, Mom."

She laughed again. He shifted a little and the *Macbeth* test crinkled under his butt.

"What did you think of Julian?" Mom said.

Brandon shrugged. "He was okay."

Mom nodded. He could feel her thinking, had felt her thinking all his life. She was the brains of the family, no doubt about that. "How was he as a teacher?" she said.

"I don't know."

"Compared to your teachers at school."

Brandon thought of Mr. Monson and his Cliffs Notes. "No one could be that bad."

Mom nodded again, like things were making sense. "Maybe we should just forget about the Sally woman and have Julian do it."

"Do what?"

"The lessons."

"I have to do more?"

"Don't start that. We have an agreement. Besides, look at the improvement from just this first time."

"Okay, okay."

"Okay what?"

"I'll take the lessons."

"But do you want me to call the agency and switch to Julian?"

Brandon shrugged.

"It's your choice, Brandon."

"I don't care."

"Sally is supposed to be good with boys too. She plays lacrosse at Trinity and has five brothers."

"Call the agency," Brandon said.

Mom laughed. "I think that's a good decision, Brandon. Unless you think that maybe—"

Ruby came in with a phone. "For you," she said, handing it to Mom. "That asshole from Skyway."

"Ruby!"

"Mute's on," she said, and turned to Brandon. "Who's the poor girl with five brothers?"

"None of your fuckin' business," Brandon said.

Mom made a frantic silencing motion with her hand and went into the hall.

Sherlock Holmes's method was founded on the observance of trifles. Late that night, reading in her bed with only the desk lamp on, making a little circle of light on the book but leaving the room in shadow, Ruby tried to observe what Holmes observed, tried to solve the mystery of "The Speckled

Band" before he did. Without peeking, of course—Ruby never peeked at the end of any book.

Observe, not just see. Holmes was always going on about that. Watson saw everything Holmes did but could never make it add up. Dr. Roylott was obviously the bad guy—a dangerous man, as he said himself during the poker-twisting scene. So the question was how. How had he killed the sister of the terrified Miss Stoner? How was he planning to kill her?

What did Holmes observe? The dummy bell rope and the strange ventilator—must be vent—in Miss Stoner's room; the little saucer of milk and the dog lash in Dr. Roy-lott's room. Ruby read the part about the lash three times. *Lash* must be "leash." It was tied to make a loop. So? Did the baboon somehow crawl through the ventilator, or the cheetah? Ruby leafed back a few pages. Miss Stoner's sister had died without a mark on her, frightened to death, Miss Stoner believed, by the speckled band. Was a cheetah speckled? Maybe you could say that; and cheetahs were cats and cats liked milk. But cheetahs were big and this was a little saucer, as Holmes pointed out. Ruby was stumped.

She turned the page. *A ventilator is made, a cord is hung, and a lady who sleeps in the bed dies.* Watson saw no connection. Neither, maddeningly, did Ruby. Holmes and Watson took up their late-night vigil in the complete darkness of Miss Stoner's bedroom. Ruby's bedroom was completely dark too. Her light wasn't a light, just part of the book in some way, and she felt suspended in midair, wrapped in absolute silence.

Then: a soft sound like steam escaping, and Holmes was on his feet, lashing at the bell rope with his cane. Watson saw nothing. Holmes was deadly pale. Through the ventilator came a horrible cry. Ruby felt icy all up and down her spine, and her heart beat fast. Holmes and Watson entered Dr. Roy-lott's room. The words went by so fast Ruby hardly caught them: Turkish slippers, the looped-up lash, Dr. Roylott's dreadful rigid stare. What was this? A peculiar yellow band with brownish speckles around his head. Another bit of Turkish clothing? And then the speckled headband moved, and there reared up in the dead man's hair *the squat diamond-shaped head and puffed neck of a loathsome serpent.*

Ruby cried out, jerked her head up from the book, glanced wildly around her room, saw nothing but woolly darkness, full of movement. She slammed the book shut, sat up, breathing fast, close to panting. A snake! She hated snakes, couldn't bear the sight of them, not even the thought.

Ruby picked up the book, holding it at arm's length, as though the snake might be trapped inside, took it out into the hall, laid it on the floor. The house was quiet and dark, except for her reading light. She closed her door, went back to bed, leaving the light on. After a minute or two—or more, or less, she'd lost all track of time—she got back up, opened her closet, looked inside, checked under the bed, and climbed back in, pulling the duvet—blue with yellow sun faces—up high.

Ruby had made up a peaceful dream she sometimes used to get to sleep. In it she was a cavewoman, sitting in the mouth of a nice dry cave. Outside, only a few feet away, blew a wild storm, sometimes rain, sometimes snow. She sat there, safe and warm. The snow variation worked best. Ruby tried it now, a raging screaming whiteness, and her just out of reach.

Dewey did have a vial—he showed it around—but Brandon didn't want to try it, so he stayed on a log overlooking the pond with a few other kids, including Trish. It was cold and dark in the woods, but they were warm inside, at least Brandon was. They drank out of two bottles, one Coke, the other a forty-ouncer of Captain Morgan's Spiced Rum. They mixed them in their bodies. Never a problem getting booze when Frankie J was around, and there was plenty more tonight. Frankie J was the captain of the football team and the coach's son. None of the liquor stores in West Mill ever carded him. He sold to the kids in the woods for a five-dollar premium per bottle, plus drinking fee.

"You went to New York?" Trish said.

"Where'd you hear that?" said Brandon. Trish wasn't one of the cool girls. She sat beside him on the log, her knees tucked up under her chin.

"It was all around the school."

"Fuck," said Brandon, but he wasn't displeased.

"What was it like?"

"Decent."

"What'd you do?"

"Not much. Went to a bar in Soho, me and Dewey."

"That sounds pretty cool."

"Yeah," Brandon said. The bottles came around. Trish took a big hit off the Captain Morgan, didn't touch the Coke. Some kid on the other side of her lit a match, lighting up Trish's face. It struck Brandon that she was as good-looking as most of the cool girls, maybe all of them. When had that happened? She'd always been more or less a loser, lived in the apartments behind the Rite-Aid, worked at the cash register sometimes, like her mom, or stepmom or whatever it was.

The bottles came to him. He took a big chug of the Captain Morgan, just so he could talk to Trish a little better, even if she wasn't one of the cool girls, felt a nice *boing* inside his head, made him sit up straight. He dropped the Coke. The bottle rolled down the bank and into the pond; not into, exactly, but on.

"Hey," said a kid down the log, "it's fuckin' frozen."

"Go for a walk," said Frankie J.

"No way," said the kid.

"It's safe," said Frankie J. "I was skating this morning." The kid shook his head.

"Five bucks if you do," said Frankie J.

"No way."

"Twenty."

"Twenty?"

Frankie J took out a twenty, rolled it up in a ball, flipped it onto the ice maybe five feet from shore, just out of reach.

Night, but the clouds caught all the lights of civilization and the pond gleamed under them. The balled-up twenty sat there, real clear. The kid got up, a freshman Brandon didn't even know. *Don't do it, you asshole,* Brandon thought. But he didn't say it, and the kid took one cautious step onto the ice, then another, got both feet on the ice, bent down for the money and—

Splash. Right through of course, losing his balance, a clumsy kid, and falling all the way in, even soaking his head somehow.

Laughter. The kid came up shivering, then shaking. More laughter. "Where's the twenty?" said Frankie J. "You call that a walk? You owe me twenty."

Brandon happened to see that Trish wasn't laughing. He stopped.

A little later, standing by the big rock with Dewey, he said, "What do you think of Trish?"

"Trish Almeida? She's a pig." Dewey had the crack pipe in his hand. "Know who you should go after?" he said. "Whitney."

"Whitney?" Brandon could see her, sitting around a little fire with a few other girls, just off the path. "I thought she went out with Frankie J."

"They broke up."

Whitney's blond hair glowed in the night.

"Go talk to her."

Brandon shook his head.

"What's to lose?" said Dewey. "The girls think you're good-looking."

That was news to Brandon.

Dewey lit the pipe. "Try this."

"No."

Dewey took a deep drag, passed him the pipe. Brandon shook his head again, but the pipe got in his hand anyway, Dewey letting go. "One little hit and the magic word will come to you."

Brandon took one little hit. "Wow," he said, maybe not right away, but fairly soon. And, not long after: "Is that the magic word?"

Dewey was still laughing when Brandon wandered away toward Whitney's fire. Whitney and some other girls, all cool, some of them seniors, sat in a circle; they had cups to drink from. Brandon thought of sitting too, but it was a long way down. The girls all looked up at him. No smiles, more like, *Yeah?*

"Hey, Whitney," he said.

Her eyes narrowed.

"I know the magic word."

At least her eyes didn't narrow any more. The problem was saying *wow* at that moment might not seem as funny to Whitney and these cool girls as it had to Dewey. Another problem was he couldn't think of anything else. Then, coming up fast was a third problem that swept away everything, a sick dizziness that was going to end in puking, real soon. Brandon turned and ran, or stumbled, away.

Laughter, this time at him.

The next thing he knew, he was lying by the log near the pond, wedged under its curve. He sat up, bottles, beer cans, cigarette butts all around, but no people. He was alone.

Brandon rose, real fuckin' dizzy, and puked again. He went down to the pond to rinse his mouth out, reached in, not in, because his hand bumped up against the ice. Frozen, he'd forgotten that. Had someone actually fallen in? Oh, yeah. All refrozen now. Brandon crouched by the side of the pond, trying to feel right, unable to even rinse his goddamn mouth.

He heard a crack. A cracking sound, out on the pond. Not the ice cracking, but something striking it. He looked out and saw a big stick still sliding across the ice, not far away.

The cops? They sometimes raided the woods, but not this late, and throwing sticks wasn't their style; they came barreling right in. Some kid then, because it had to be someone, too far out to have fallen from a tree. He peered through the darkness of the woods around the pond, saw no one. Brandon thought of saying something out loud, maybe *fuck you*, decided he would if another stick got thrown.

That didn't happen. He rose, found the path no problem—he'd been in these woods all his life—started for home. The air turned funny, and he realized it was snowing. Then, goddamn it, he figured out a cool thing he could have said to Whitney: *Go with the Beatles answer.* Too late. Why couldn't—

That was when the second stick got thrown. Brandon heard it crack on the pond, now far behind him. Probably some kid, totally wrecked, more wrecked than him. He walked a little faster anyway, not quite so dizzy. Snow drifted down through the bare trees, black flakes that clung to his skin. Brandon realized his jacket, red with black sleeves and *West Mill Tennis* on the back, was gone. No shirt, either. Pants, yes, shoes, yes. Tomorrow was Sunday, sleep for fuckin' ever. He just wanted to be in his bed.

A man's hand was on Linda's breast, a beautiful hand. She awoke, nipples taut, aroused. No one was touching her. She could sense Scott over on his side, fast asleep.

Maybe now. Now when they were working together so well at the beginning of this new stage of life, getting Brandon into a good college. Linda remembered a piece of advice she'd come upon while leafing through a self-help book at Barnes and Noble, waiting for Ruby to finish her Christmas shopping: *The heat generated in the master bedroom warms the whole house.* A line that stabbed her at the time, stabbed her now. She reached for Scott. *Just don't wake up.* Another little stab—why couldn't she control her mind better, rid it of thoughts like that?—but her nipples stayed taut.

He was hard already, hard in his sleep. In a moment or two her nightie was hiked up and she was straddling him, got him inside. He made a little moan, not a moan, more musical than that, striking a note of surprise and pleasure. She felt him waking up. *Just don't speak.*

"Hey," said Scott. Only one word, but too much.

In the cave: snow, peace, nothing. And then something real bad happened. A fat, fat snake with a squat diamond-shaped head and puffed neck was creeping slowly up the inside of her leg. It looked up, looked her right in the eye with eyes of its own, knowing eyes. Then Ruby was bolting down the hall, crying *Snake, snake,* in her mind.

She stopped outside her parents' door. Sounds came from the other side, sounds that stopped her, stopped her long enough for the nightmare to break up and fall away. More sounds. She still wanted to go in, would have, maybe even a few months ago. But she was almost eleven. Ruby turned back.

But not to her own room, her own bed. No way. She went into Brandon's room instead, thinking of climbing in with him, which hadn't happened in years, or maybe settling for the floor in the sleeping bag his friends sometimes used.

Brandon's CD display was flashing. In the off-and-on green light, she saw that his bed was empty. Green, like snakes. She got out of there, went farther down the hall, up the little stairs, opened the door to the last bedroom.

Ruby could hear her breathing very clearly in the last bedroom. Emptiness made good sound. She switched on the light. Everything had been cleaned out long ago but the bed was made. Ruby understood perfectly: a bare mattress would have been too horrible. Leaving the light on, she climbed into Adam's bed and closed her eyes. The snake did not return.

Margie called Julian Sunday morning. "You were a hit," she said.

Julian was silent. The starlings were back. He tracked their flight patterns, panicky and orderly at the same time, back and forth between the two groves of trees.

"With the Gardner family, in West Mill. They want you back."

Down below and across the lane, Julian's landlady came out of the big house, looked immediately at his window—he stepped back—and got into her car.

"What about Sally?" he said.

"How thoughtful of you to ask," said Margie. "But it's no problem. This happens sometimes."

The starlings banked against a white sky, relentless in their going back and forth.

"So you'll do it?" Margie said. "Same time Saturdays and Wednesdays at seven."

Julian took a deep drag from his cigarette, first of the day. Oh, the smoke, and that tiny fire in his hand. He recollected every huge emotion he'd ever felt, but in tranquility. "I'll do it," he said.

9

Ruby and Kyla got in the back of her dad's car, Kyla clutching a pair of hot-pink wristbands, the prize for winning the round robin this time. Ruby hadn't even made it to the finals. "Got to concentrate, Ruby," Erich said. But the lines on the court were becoming a big distraction, like she was trapped in some experiment. And in school Amanda had got elected editor of next year's fifth- and sixth-grade newspaper, *The Westie*, a job Ruby had really wanted. Not a good day.

"Thanks for driving me, Mr. Gudukas," she said.

"Hey, no problem," he said. His smell filled the car, pine

or something, like a whole forest packed in there. "Your mom tied up again?"

"Yup."

More snow. The windshield wipers went back and forth. The town was beautiful, everyone's lawn all white and puffy, although that morning she'd noticed that theirs had little yellow holes, like Zippy was drilling for something. The roofs of the houses were puffy too, all the edges rounded in snow. The sight calmed her down.

"Want one of my wristbands?" Kyla said in a low voice, the two of them in the backseat.

That was really nice. Hot pink wasn't Ruby's color, but it worked for wristbands. She slipped it on, held out her wrist daintily like a model.

"Cool," said Kyla.

"Yeah," said Ruby. "Thanks."

"Want the other one?"

"You keep it," Ruby said.

Windshield wipers, back and forth. All of a sudden Ruby was very tired, could have fallen asleep right there. She stretched her legs, sticking her feet under the front seat, felt empty cans, stared at nothing.

She and Amanda, the only two candidates, had had to make speeches in front of all the fifth-grade classes. Ruby had promised big changes—a horoscope, advice to the lovelorn, and lots of contests, like the ugliest-sibling photo contest, the stupidest-thing-you-ever-heard contest, the best-limerick contest. Amanda had promised well-written articles with proper grammar and spelling that would make everyone proud of the school, better coverage of the PTA, and bake sales to raise money for student papers in less fortunate countries. Everyone had dropped their ballots in a box, which the principal took to her office and counted. The announcement came over the intercom, exact numbers not mentioned, just that it was close and both candidates were deserving.

"You know the lines on the court?" Ruby said. "They should make them all circles."

Kyla laughed. "And the ball should be square."

Ruby laughed too.

"What about your dad?" Mr. Gudukas said, half turning his head.

"Huh?" said Ruby.

"Your dad tied up too?"

"He's out of town," Ruby said. "I really appreciate the ride, Mr. Gudukas."

"Anytime, kiddo," he said. "Conference or something?"

"I don't know."

"Played tennis with him on Saturday. Him and your uncle against me and Erich."

Ruby didn't say anything. Was this the first time she'd heard *kiddo* in conversation?

"He mention that?"

"No."

"Lots of fun. We're pretty evenly matched."

They went past a streetlight. Kyla was biting her lip and her forehead was all wrinkled.

"The conference," said Mr. Gudukas, "Miami, somewhere warm like that?"

"Dad," said Kyla.

"Yeah?"

"Nothing."

"What is it?"

Kyla didn't answer. There was no more talking after that. Ruby didn't feel so sleepy anymore.

The house was dark. Ruby went in by the mudroom door. "Hi, I'm home."

No answer. She switched on the light. Brandon's jacket wasn't on its peg.

"Zippy?" she said, dropping everything—hat, gloves, jacket, backpack, racquet—near where they were supposed to go.

No response from Zippy. He was either on the couch in the entertainment center or on the love seat in the living room. Ruby went into the kitchen, turned on more lights. She had homework—math and social studies—plus Hot Jazz was tomorrow and she hadn't practiced in a week. How about social studies first, then sax, then the math? Good enough. She closed a deal with herself.

But broke it right away to make hot dogs. This time there were buns too. She sat at her place, snow coming down on three sides of her, inches away; hot dogs, mustard, relish, Sprite, *The Complete Sherlock Holmes*.

She took a bite, then a swallow of Sprite, and started to open the book. Oops. "The Speckled Band" was in there, unavoidable. Ruby got scissors from a drawer, carefully cut "The Speckled Band" out of *The Complete Sherlock Holmes*, sacrificing only the first page of the next story, "The Adventure of the Engineer's Thumb," which she quickly scanned so it would make sense later. Summer of '89, Dr. Watson gets a new patient, bloodstained handkerchief around his hand—got it.

Ruby could simply have tossed "The Speckled Band" in the trash under the sink, but would that have been as good as burning it? Not nearly. She took "The Speckled Band" into the living room instead. Zippy, on the love seat, didn't open his eyes. Ruby hadn't actually made a fire before, but she'd seen Dad do it, the odd time they had fires. It didn't look hard.

First, you pull away the screen, like so. Then you crumple up a bit of newspaper—there was some in the wood box—and shove it under the grate. On top of the grate went sticks of kindling—she arranged them in a neat square—and then two or three nice split logs, in this case three, because a triangle on top of the square seemed right. Ruby chose birch for the logs because of the way the white bark curled up when it started burning. Matches: on the mantel. She pulled up the ottoman, stood on it, reached the matches, barely.

Ruby hadn't actually lit a match before. These were from Bricco, her favorite restaurant. She always ordered the double-chocolate pie for dessert, could never finish it and had the rest the next day at home, when it was even better. Bricco had a kind of wine Dad liked, started with *Z*, and Mom always had a glass of champagne, just one. Ruby had Sprite like at home—at home when no one was around to make her drink milk. At Bricco they put a plastic swizzle stick in it, with a monkey on top.

Ruby slid open the matchbox. The matches inside were wooden, with bright red ends. She felt the rough strip on the side of the box, took out a match. On the box she read: Close Before Striking. She closed the box and holding the match at the very tip, drew it along the strip. Nothing happened. She tried it again, harder. The match broke in two. She threw it in the fireplace, took out another one, closed the box, pressed the bright red tip to the rough strip and gave it a quick scrape.

Presto! Fire, a little sparkly fire right there between her fingers. The flame steadied into a pointy-tipped oval, blue, orange, and yellow at the top. Ruby knelt and held it close to one of the crumpled-up newspaper balls. The paper browned a little but didn't catch fire. Meanwhile the flame was burning down the matchstick, closer and closer to her fingers, losing its pointy-oval shape, spreading out. Starting a fire wasn't so easy. She felt the heat of the flame and dropped the match. Maybe she'd have to rethink the cavewoman thing. She might not have been as good a cavewoman as—

Hey! Kazaam! With a tiny popping sound, fire sprang to life down among the crumpled newspapers under the grate. More popping sounds and the flames reached up, wrapped their ends around the kindling. *Crackle, crackle.* How great was this? Ruby decided on the spot to make a fire every night. She could even roast her hot dogs over it!

Zippy barked. His head was up, eyes open. She had his attention now. "Not bad, huh, Zippy? I rule." He barked again.

The kindling was burning beautifully. Big flames swelled all over the place and the white skin of the birches curled up, popping and crackling. The flames grew and grew, fat orange dancers all brought to life by that tiny pointy-tipped oval. And there was a nice smoky smell, too, reminding her of cookouts on the Fourth of July. That Fourth of July smell must have been in the caves all the time. She would have been a great cavewoman after all, would have called herself Rubyfire so the rest of the cave guys would know where she was coming from.

But had it been this smoky in the cave?

Zippy barked, barked again.

"Shut up, Zippy."

It was maybe a little too smoky. The fire itself was burning fine, all the logs burning now, the crumpled-up paper just ashes and even some of the kindling practically gone. But smoke was kind of flowing out, starting to sting her eyes. She could see it; in fact the whole room was a bit hazy, like a scene in a movie. Ruby made a scientific breakthrough: the fire wasn't drawing properly. She remembered Dad using that phrase once, and the next thing he'd done was open the window a few inches.

"Shut up, Zippy."

Ruby opened the nearest window, the one behind the Tin Man sculpture. They just called it the Tin Man; the real title was *Untitled—19*, a cool welded sculpture by a New York artist Mom had kind of discovered. Ruby felt cold air flowing in, turned to the fire, saw flames shooting up. But it wasn't drawing any better, maybe worse. Smoke was sort of boiling in now, making her cough. The screen: maybe time to put it in front of the fire.

She reached for the screen. Then came a horrible noise, so loud and piercing it jolted her body like an electric shock. Ruby didn't even know what was happening at first, just put her hands over her ears to shut out the shrieking. Zippy started howling. It hit her: the smoke alarms.

Ruby ran to the kitchen, filled a pot with water, ran

back. But Zippy was on the move. She tripped over him, or he bowled her over, and the pot went flying. Ruby landed hard against the ottoman, knocking it into the fireplace. A burning log came tumbling out, landed on the rug, a beautiful Persian rug that had been in Mom's family for—

Suddenly a big form appeared in the haze, a man—had to be Dad, even though he was in Boston. He stepped over her like the Colossus of Rhodes, not Dad, but some stranger. He stuck his hand in the fireplace at the top right-hand side, yanked something that made a clanging sound. Ruby got a good look at the side of his face: not a stranger but Julian, Brandon's tutor. Great balls of smoke got sucked up the chimney. Was there something called the damper?

Julian picked up the burning log with tongs from the fireplace tool rack, dropped it on the fire, jerked the ottoman out. He moved so fast: sliding shut the windowed pocket doors to the rest of the house, throwing open all the windows, plus the French doors to the deck. Zippy trotted around after him, wagging his tail. The smoke started clearing right away. The shrieking stopped. Then it was very quiet and everything was all right, just like that. The fire blazed merrily away, burning clean.

Ruby got to her feet, kind of stunned, almost the same feeling as when the roller-coaster ride was over. Julian was examining the ottoman. "A bit scorched." He looked at her. She'd never seen eyes quite like Julian's; they seemed to be carrying on a conversation of their own. "You're not hurt?"

"No."

His gaze went to the Tin Man. "Where's Brandon?"

"I don't know." Her voice sounded loud. Here she was, back in normality; she tried to make her voice normal too. "Was there a lesson tonight?"

"At seven."

"Sorry."

"Hardly your fault. You're by yourself?"

"And Zippy."

His eyes went through two or three changes. "Do you like playing with matches?"

Ruby shook her head, was suddenly close to tears. She was in trouble, the biggest trouble of her life, by far. She could have burned the house down, would have if Julian hadn't turned up. He knew it too: probably why he looked so—not mad, but serious, maybe, or thoughtful.

Julian picked up the ottoman, picked it up easily although it was very heavy. "Where does this go?"

"Over by the leather chair."

"That green one?" he said.

"Yeah."

He carried the ottoman over to the leather chair, put it down. "A bit scorched," he said again, looking up at her, "so the placement will be crucial." He turned the ottoman a little so that the scorched part was up against the front of the chair, invisible.

A crucial placement, the scorched part invisible: Ruby got it. "You're not going to tell?"

"Do you want me to?" said Julian.

"No." Ruby felt her stupid lip trembling.

He nodded. "Then we'll need the vacuum cleaner, paper towels, soapy water."

Ten minutes later, or even less, the living room was back to normal too, no evidence but a little damp patch on the rug where she'd spilled the water. Maybe not even Sherlock Holmes could have figured out what had gone on. Julian glanced around, Zippy at his side like a prize dog waiting for the next command. The living room looked perfect to Ruby, the way it did after Maria left, but Julian spotted something on the far side of the wood box, scattered pages—"The Speckled Band."

He picked them up, leafed through. A little smile appeared on his face. "Ah," he said, "the bell rope." He peered over the top of the pages. "I deduce that you've been reading Sherlock Holmes."

"How do you know it was me?" Ruby said.

"Good question." He didn't answer it. "The puzzle is—why has it been cut from its binding?"

"I don't like snakes." That popped out on its own, a little surprise.

Then came a bigger one. "Well, then," he said, and tossed the story into the fire. Poof: it was gone.

They closed all the doors and windows, went into the kitchen. Ruby's dinner waited on the table.

"Want a hot dog?" she said.

"I'm not hungry," he said. "Thanks."

"Sprite?"

He shook his head, looked down at his watch.

"Brandon should be here any minute," Ruby said, feeling that not just Brandon but somehow the whole family was being rude. She'd offered food and drink. What else did you do to entertain guests, not including playing the sax for them? That was out. Then she remembered that visitors liked to see the renovations for some reason. "How about a tour of the house while you're waiting?"

"That might be nice," Julian said.

"Great," said Ruby. "Over here's the mudroom, and—"

She stopped. Hanging on Brandon's peg was his jacket, the red-and-black varsity jacket with West Mill Tennis on the back.

"Hey," she called, going to the foot of the stairs. "Brandon?"

No answer.

"Brandon? Are you home?" Silence. She went back to the mudroom. His backpack wasn't there, or his boots. "That's weird," she said.

Julian wasn't paying attention. He was giving Zippy a nice scratch between the ears. Zippy was in heaven.

Maybe the mudroom wasn't that impressive. "Want to see the entertainment center?"

"Anything you say."

She led him downstairs.

10

" . . . **O**ff the satellite," Ruby said. She switched it on to show him how good the picture was. "A hundred and something channels, and that's not including cable." She hit the up-channel button on the remote, kept it pressed down to watch the hundred-and-something channels rip by. "Emeril, Springer, German tiger guys, Sipowicz, WWF, Yosemite Sam, Hitler, shopping, trial, Hitler again, that old nun, the other shopping, police chases." That was the way to watch TV, all right, like one big channel, really fast. "What's your favorite show, Mr. . . ."

"Sawyer," Julian said. He was staring at the screen: political arguing, bootie shaking, golf tips, kitchen remodeling, more political arguing—the one with the nasty little guy in the three-piece suit—more Hitler, the one when he's in Paris. That reminded her of "Springtime for Hitler"—she'd been rolling on the floor.

"You can call me Julian," Julian said. "I like the nature shows."

"Me too," said Ruby; except when they did snakes. "What animals do you like?"

"Birds."

Not really animals in Ruby's mind, but she let that go. First of all, he was turning out to be really nice. Second, she kind of owed him.

"We've got a cardinal that comes to the feeder."

He was looking through the doorway to the unlit furnace room, maybe didn't hear her. The furnace was on.

Through the shadows Ruby could see the little blue flames down at the bottom.

"Gas?" said Julian.

"Huh?"

"Is your house heated with natural gas?"

Ruby had no idea, but she liked that expression, natural gas.

Was Julian psyched for seeing more? Maybe not, but Ruby showed him around anyway. She was having fun, opening doors, giving a quick little shpeel or spiel or whatever it was, moving on.

"That's about it," she said at the end, having saved the best—her room—for last: her stuffed animals, the framed original cell from *One Froggy Evening*, the prism in the window. Julian watched her from the hall. She realized he had manners, was too polite to come in her room.

"Very nice," he said. "What's up there?"

"Up where?"

"At the end of the hall. Up those little stairs."

Ruby went into the hall. There had to be a proper name for that room up the little stairs. The spare bedroom? The guest bedroom? Those names fit, but no one ever used them. Whenever that bedroom at the end of the hall came up in conversation it was always Adam's room. "That's Adam's room," Ruby said. "My brother who died."

Julian, who'd been gazing down the hall, now turned and looked down at her. My God! He had one of those soul patches. How could she just be noticing something so obvious? The gap between her and Sherlock Holmes had to be wider than the goddamn Grand—

"I'm sorry," Julian said.

"About what?"

"Your brother dying."

"Oh," said Ruby. "Thanks."

Was that what you said at times like this, *thanks*? *Thanks* meant the next step was for the other guy to say *you're welcome*, and that seemed to be taking the whole thing further off the rails—*anytime, not at all, think nothing of it, so kind*.

"It was a long time ago," Ruby said. "Before I was born."

"Nevertheless," he said.

Nevertheless what? He didn't go on, turned his gaze on the little staircase again.

"Do you want to see it?" Ruby said.

"Just a quick peek," Julian said. "Now that you've shown me the rest of your very charming house."

Charming. Yes. It really was. Like in a fairy tale, with the red chimney, the feeder, the woodpile, the forest: 37 Robin Road, Paradise. *What's the zip for Paradise?* Ruby thought as she skipped up the stairs, opened the door to Adam's room. Empty, of course, except for the bedding, all rumpled from her sleeping in it, a detail that had slipped her mind. Would he think it hadn't been made in eleven years? Should she say something?

"Like an artist's garret," Julian said.

"Is that good or bad?"

"Oh, good," Julian said. "The most charming room in the whole charming house. Next to yours, of course."

Ruby giggled, a silly little giggle just like Kyla's.

"How did he die?" Julian said.

Ruby stopped giggling.

The story of Adam's death was kind of confusing, and at the same time her earliest memory. She and Brandon had been down in the basement, back before the entertainment center. She remembered a green rug, an empty tennis ball can she kept things in, like her magic ring with the huge ruby—what had happened to that?—and a pillow fort. She must have climbed to the top of the pillow fort and tried to stand, because she could remember Brandon looking up— he was wearing pajamas with a baseball print—and saying, "Gonna break your leg and die, just like Adam." So she'd found out about Adam and his dying all at once, only not accurately. Adam had in fact broken his leg but he'd died of something else, the word for it terrifying her for years, a word her eyes still shied away from whenever she came across it.

"First he broke his leg," Ruby said. "Then he died of leukemia."

Julian nodded, kind of like he'd expected that.

Leukemia: it could have been the name of the mother-ant creature in those *Alien* movies, movies she zipped by at warp speed whenever she came across them in her channel-zipping excursions.

Mom came in through the garage door, snowflakes in her dark hair and on her dark fur collar. Ruby and Julian were at the table, Ruby polishing off her second hot dog, Julian turning the pages of *The Complete Sherlock Holmes*. He rose. Had Ruby ever actually seen a man rise when a woman came into the room? Not in real life. Men rising when a woman came into the room: maybe the best idea she'd ever heard of. What had happened to it?

"Hi," Mom said. "Brandon taking another evaluation test?"

"Um," said Ruby, her mouth full. "Not home yet."

Mom's fingers froze on the top button of her coat. "Not home yet? But it's . . ." She checked her watch. "For God's sake. Did he call?"

"I don't know," Ruby said.

"What do you mean, you don't know?" Ruby knew right away Mom had had one of those tough days. "Did you speak to him? Is there a message on the machine?"

Might have missed a call while I was burning the house down. Ruby didn't say anything. Meanwhile Mom was at the phone on the counter, stabbing through the messages. No Brandon. Then, as though Ruby's skull was transparent and Mom could look in whenever she wanted, she sniffed the air and said, "Do I smell smoke?"

Silence, like between the lightning and the thunder.

"I lit a fire," Julian said. "I hope that's all right."

No thunder: Mom's voice lost that tough-day edge. "Of course, Julian. I love fires." She unbuttoned her coat. Then came the sound of the mudroom door opening, and in walked Brandon, also with snow in his hair, and on the shoulders of his new black Unka Death T-shirt. His eyes went to Mom, Julian, Mom. Then they closed, just for a microsecond. That was dismay, Ruby realized. He'd simply forgotten about the lesson. Observation and deduction: she was back in action.

Mom fired a series of questions that seemed to pin Brandon right there in the doorway: *Where have you been? Do you expect me to believe detention lasts until seven-thirty? Is this a nice way to treat Julian? Why didn't you call?*

Brandon had no good answers. Ruby spread a little extra relish on her hot dog, took another bite. Guilty as sin.

"And why aren't you wearing your jacket?" Mom said. "It's winter."

"Left it at school," Brandon said.

Huh? Ruby paused in midchew. Was he drunk or something? The jacket hung on the hook, practically at his elbow. He hadn't even worn it to school and—maybe hadn't been to school at all! Off with his head.

"What's with you, Brandon?" Mom said. "It's right there."

Brandon turned, saw the jacket. His eyebrows went up. That would be surprise. Then his eyebrows scrunched together: confusion. Then he actually touched the jacket, like it wasn't his or something. But of course it was his. It said Brandon, right on the sleeve. Drunk out of his mind, that was it. All the little sisters knew what went on.

Brandon turned to Mom. "I guess I . . ."

Julian picked up his green folder. "Why don't we get started, Brandon?" he said.

"**D**istance," said Julian, sitting at the head of the dining-room table, "rate and time. Not your strong suit, according to the diagnostic."

Mom, passing by on her way to the living room, closed the double doors. That fucking jacket. What a weird day, full of surprises, except for screwing up on distance, rate and time.

"Two northbound trains leave the same station one hour apart from each other on parallel tracks," Julian read from the test booklet.

Had to be Ruby, out with Zippy in the woods. Found the jacket and just hung it up there with no warning, like a booby trap. What was wrong with her? Other kids had normal sisters.

". . . ten miles an hour slower than the second train."

A weird day, starting with the wastebasket fire in the boys' can by the guidance office. They had wastebasket fires two or three times a year, always leading to a complete evacuation of the building. The same little group of assholes did it every time but never got caught. This time, waiting out in the parking lot for the bell to summon them back in, Brandon had found himself next to Trish Almeida, chewing a stick of her gum.

"I'm going to get out of this town if it's the last thing I do," she'd said.

"What's wrong with it?" Brandon hadn't gotten that at all. Get out of West Mill? It was a great place to grow up, everyone said so. Then he remembered about her living in those apartments behind the Rite-Aid.

But maybe that wasn't what bothered her, because she'd said: "I don't want to be a one or a zero."

"Huh?"

"Like in a computer program, everything's a one or a zero. That's this town."

That was kind of interesting. "You want to be a two?"

"Or any other number. But they don't let you do that in West Mill."

"Where do they?"

"New York, of course," Trish said. "Tell me about that bar in Soho."

"Been to Soho?"

"I've never been anywhere."

Julian came around the table. "Can I see what you've done so far?"

Brandon turned his worksheet so Julian could see what he'd done on the train problem. From a tiny shift in Julian's eyes, Brandon realized Julian had smelled the booze on his breath.

"I'm going to give you a shield," Julian said.

"A shield?"

"For protection," he said. A tiny pause, like an extra space between words in a sentence, and he added, "From distance, rate and time." He took the pen from Brandon's hand, gently, and in the middle of the page drew a shield, a beautiful one, actually, suggesting the curve of it and everything. The booze on his breath? Somehow Brandon knew it was cool with Julian. How old was Julian anyway? Still young enough to remember what it was like, right?

On the shield, where the coat of arms or whatever it was called would be, Julian wrote in big Gothic letters:

$$\frac{D}{RT}$$

"Take your orders from the shield," Julian said. "If they want distance, put your finger on D."

Brandon put his finger on D. They'd ended up going over to Trish's cruddy apartment behind the Rite-Aid. Trish had a bottle of Jack Daniel's, kind of a surprise.

"What does it say?"

"RT."

"Meaning?"

"Rate and time."

"*And* means 'plus.'"

"Rate *times* time?"

Julian nodded. His eyes got a little distant, like he was

watching everything fall into place. "What if they want rate?" he asked.

Brandon put his finger on R. "D divided by T."

"The DRT shield," Julian said. "Try the trains again."

Brandon reread the problem. Two trains on parallel tracks. A cruddy apartment, but Trish's tiny bedroom was amazing. She'd painted a mural on the walls, all about West Mill High, a very cool mural with lots of recognizable people in it, including himself. Some of them were doing disgusting things, like Mr. Kranepool, the parking lot monitor, down on his knees licking the hairy leg of Ms. Belsey, the principal.

"What is the core of the question?"

The core. Brandon read it again, took a flyer. "How many hours?"

"And therefore?"

"Let the number of hours the second train travels equal T?"

"Now just put it all in a sentence."

"A sentence?"

"A number and letter sentence, with *equals* in the middle. They're all pretty much the same."

All the same: Brandon was getting it, felt it coming, like a shifting of blocks inside his head. This was a kind of translation, from English into math. He'd never gotten it before, never answered a distance-rate-time question right in his life, except by accident.

He made a sentence with *equals* in the middle: $85T=75(T+1)$. An amazing room, and somehow they'd ended up on Trish's bed, surrounded by the whole cast of West Mill High—Ms. Belsey, Mr. Kranepool, Mr. Monson, reading his Cliffs Notes *Macbeth* while he jerked off on the toilet, Frankie J and Whitney dressed as homecoming king and queen, but holding burning crosses in the air for some reason, and he himself standing on the auditorium stage juggling tennis balls. Surrounded by all that and much more on Trish's bed, where she'd given him a blowjob, not ready for real sex yet, she'd said, and he'd reached up under her skirt and felt around inside her, even considering going down on her, maybe not real sex either, but he wasn't ready for that yet anyway. If ever.

"T equals seven point five."

"And the unit?"

"Hours. Seven point five hours."

Julian reached over, made a check mark on the page, beside his beautiful DRT shield. Even his check mark was nicely formed. Brandon wondered what Julian would think of Trish's mural.

"Is that an agency thing?" Brandon said. "The DRT shield?"

"Agency?"

"Like it's part of the materials they give you."

"I made it up," Julian said.

"Just now?"

Julian nodded the way he did, with that distant look. *Wow.*

Brandon tried ten more algebra problems, forming number sentences with *equals* in the middle, sometimes a whole paragraph of them. Paragraphs in math: his own idea. Julian slid over the answer sheet, let him grade them himself.

"Get them all?" Julian said.

Brandon checked. "Yeah." He heard the surprise in his own voice. "How did that happen?"

Julian didn't reply. He was gazing at the photo of Adam over the sideboard, the one where he was playing his saxophone—Ruby's now—and one of Wynton Marsalis's brothers, Brandon couldn't remember the name, was standing beside him with a smile on his face.

"That's Adam," Brandon said.

"Ruby was telling me."

What was the story of the photo? Something about a school jazz program and Adam making a big impression. "Ruby," Brandon said; *with her big fucking mouth.* "She wasn't even born."

"So I gather," said Julian, bending closer to the photo, his face no more than a foot away. "And how old were you?"

"Five," Brandon said. Adam would have been in college, maybe even graduated by now. What college would that have been?

"Do you have any memories of him?" Julian's voice was soft; not a whisper, but soft.

"Sure."

"What was he like?"

"Good at everything," Brandon said. Other than that, he actually didn't remember much—just a big presence, on the move with Mom and Dad fluttering around him. Harvard, Stanford, Princeton: that was the future Adam had missed, where the top guys went. "Where did you go?" Brandon said.

"Go?" said Julian, turning from the photo.

"To college."

"I didn't," Julian said. He started to laugh. Brandon hadn't heard him laugh before, and it was a bit weird because while Julian had a beautiful speaking voice, almost like music, his laugh was raucous, more like a crow. Raucous and contagious: Brandon started laughing too. They were still laughing when Mom looked in, pleasant surprise on her face.

11

After midnight, with three glowing things, his cigarette, last of the day, and two candles. Julian liked candles, liked those tiny flames loosely fixed to their single roots, chained prisoners, danger with the legs cut off. He'd found an old classroom desk under the carriage house, heavy oak with metal feet that had once been bolted to a floor, had cleaned it off, carried it up, placed it by the window overlooking the yard. He liked to sit there after midnight and gaze out into the darkness, darkness that came in three tones: lighter darkness of the field and lane between the carriage house and the big house, medium darkness of the big house, especially when no lights showed, as now, and the dark darkness of the woods.

It was snowing. Julian couldn't see the falling flakes, but he could hear them on the carriage house roof, very light. His hearing was excellent, eyesight better than 20/20, blood pressure 115/70, pulse 55, cholesterol 140. Easy measurements to take, but even the intangibles about him were of the same standard, as though he'd been designed for a special purpose. Of the six billion people on the planet, how many could be written off as more or less the same? Five billion, nine hundred ninety-nine million, nine hundred thousand. That left one hundred thousand who counted, who might be of interest to someone objective, some visiting connoisseur of humanity.

Julian looked down at the paper on his desk, where the poem lay waiting.

> *negligent is to forsake as*
> *mendacious is to deceive*

He held his Mont Blanc pen, double-shadowed by the candles, left and right, over the blank spot where line three would begin. A poem was locked in there, he could feel it, and if he could feel it, then he was a poet. All that remained was to break in and seize it. Grab the words, shake them up, spill them out on paper.

But no words came, not even the first one. Who was to blame? At first, he couldn't think of anyone, but then it came to him: the Gardners of Robin Road. They were a distraction of the very worst kind. How could a mind like his do its best work, the work it was designed for, when he had to deal with the Gardners of Robin Road? They were and would always be mired somewhere in the mass of those 5,999,900,000. The maddening thing about them, one of the maddening things, was that they didn't know it. Did any of them even suspect their insignificance, their mediocrity? Or the obverse: were any of them less smug, less sure, less confident? An interesting question.

A light went on in a top-floor window of the big house, startling him. A tiny light at this distance, but it destroyed the three-light source triangle, attenuating the geometry to a shape that made no sense. Julian took a deep drag of his cigarette to calm himself, to restore order, inhaled a long slow stream of hot scented smoke. Smoking tobacco was a way to connect with Mother Earth, although that fact never entered the endless discussions. Tobacco was as much a part of nature as redwood trees and baby seals; that made him an environmental activist.

Nature and those nature shows on television: that noisome child, Ruby. He let his mind wander. Was this wandering somehow connected to the hidden poem?

negligent is to forsake as
mendacious is to deceive

Julian lowered the tip of his pen to the empty space where the next word would fit. It was coming, something about nature, nature shows, some specific creature perhaps, and the child. He could feel the word coming, gathering momentum, and when it came the dam would burst, and nothing would ever be the same. He felt his penis growing hard.

The phone rang.

Phone? At this hour? He almost didn't pick it up. But: better to know.

"Yes?" he said.

"Julian?"

Someone he knew, but who? Someone, someone—the

landlady. Whatever remained of his poetic reverie broke up
and vanished.

"This is Gail."

He watched the light at the top floor of the big house,
saw a shadow moving in it, grew calmer.

"Gail Bender," she said.

"Yes?"

"I hope I'm not disturbing you. I'd never have called so
late if I hadn't seen you had lights on."

The shadow in the big house expanded. Julian considered blowing out the candles.

"I'm really embarrassed to say this but there's a bat in
my house—trapped in my bathroom, actually—and I'm terrified of bats."

Julian recalled Gail out in the yard in her red-and-black
checked jacket and heavy boots: did she look like the kind
of woman who was afraid of bats? She looked more like a
riding instructor he'd known long ago.

"I wonder if you'd mind doing me a big favor and coming over."

He took another big drag.

Perhaps she mistook it for a sigh. "I'm so sorry to trouble you."

Bats. Part of nature, of course, and nature seemed to
have something to do with the poem. "No trouble," Julian
said. "I'll be right over."

He blew out the candles, put on his coat. Downstairs
lights flashed on in the big house.

"You're a gentleman," Gail said, opening the door for
him. She wore a mauve robe; also makeup, which meant she
hadn't been to bed. But the house had been dark. Therefore
she had been to bed, and had reapplied the makeup. "You
must think me very childish," she said. "They're the only
thing I'm afraid of."

"Really?"

"Oh, yes," said Gail. "I grew up rough-and-tumble,

quite the tomboy as a girl. This was a working farm back then. We had two hundred acres, all the way down Trunk Road to where Blockbuster is now."

"But you never got used to bats."

She shook her head. "Even though I like birds."

"Bats are mammals."

"I know. Maybe that's the creepy part. They're like some Frankenstein experiment."

Julian smiled. He liked that line of talk. She smiled back; then her gaze went to the microbeard under his lower lip, the leftover tuft whose name he still hadn't learned, and the expression in her eyes changed slightly. Her eyes: without distinction of any kind.

"Take me to your bat," Julian said.

Gail laughed. He smelled liquor on her breath, possibly one of those coffee liqueurs, and pictured her in her mauve robe, sipping right out of the bottle, Tia Maria or Kahlúa; or perhaps in no robe at all, sprawled on her bed, eyeing the candlelight in the carriage house. He knew the layout of her bedroom already, sight unseen.

She led him upstairs. Her body moved under the robe. A big woman, yes, but a lot of her weight was muscle. He could feel her feeling his eyes on her.

They went down a wood-paneled corridor—the whole house seemed wood-paneled, with lots of ornate molding, combustibles *partout*—and into her bedroom. An old farmhouse bedroom, or possibly two or three bedrooms with the partitions removed, remodeled to look like something from a faux-rustic catalog. Nice furniture, nice rug, nice art, a nice bed, king-size; all as he'd imagined, if a little bigger. The only thing he hadn't foreseen were the company reports and prospectuses scattered on the bed.

"Investment club meeting coming up," Gail said. "The J. P. Morganettes. We were up nineteen percent last year."

"Congratulations."

She handed him a tennis racquet. "It's in the bathroom. My second husband always used this when it came to bats."

A crudely balanced racquet. "Was he a tennis player?"

"I don't know what he was," Gail said.

Julian moved toward the bathroom.

"Not that I don't appreciate a little mystery in a man," Gail continued, speaking to his back, "but I do like getting a clue from time to time."

Julian opened the bathroom door.

"About what's going on in their mind, if anything," Gail said.

He stepped inside, closed the door quickly behind him.

"Do you see it?" Gail called, right outside the door. She talked too much, like the child. Women who talked too much bothered him, almost more than anything else. He could picture them in their billions, tongues, lips, teeth working, mouthing mundanities in myriad languages.

Julian spotted the bat at once, of course. The creature hung on the towel rack over the toilet, as far as it could get from the lights over the sink counter, dark eyes on him.

"Don't like things too bright, do you?" he said.

"What's that?" called Gail.

"Still looking."

Julian looked. He looked at the mascara tube, top off, lying in front of the makeup mirror, a tiny brush beside it, a few fallen flakes on the marble makeup table. He opened the medicine cabinet, saw bottles of Prozac, painkillers, estrogen. He bent down to check the reading material in the straw basket by the toilet: women's magazines, a paperback romance—*Dark Is the Color of Dreams*—and at the bottom a worn hardcover, *The Mature Woman's Guide to Better Sex,* with illustrations.

"What's happening? Are you all right?"

Julian rose, looked at the bat hanging on the towel rack, an arm's length away. The bat looked at him. A rodentlike body trapped in membranous wings, its stick-limbs forever constrained. Perhaps it really was a Frankenstein's monster, some careless experiment of nature, gone wrong. Was that what the poor thing was trying to tell him with those dark eyes? Without taking his own eyes off the bat, Julian put down the tennis racquet, leaning its handle up against the toilet bowl. Then he reached out with his right hand and grabbed the bat.

Reaching out really didn't do justice to the action. It was much quicker than that; Julian was quick when he wanted to be, almost supernaturally so. The thing tried to struggle, tried to flap this or that little scrap of wing, tried to bite.

"No, no, little vampire," said Julian; soft, to calm it. Then he took the rodent head in his left hand and twisted it off, like a recalcitrant lid.

A jam jar lid: strawberry jam.

"Are you having trouble?"

"None," said Julian. He slid a window up with his elbow and tossed out the red-and-black remains, a sort of opposite to a bouquet, and he a sort of opposite to a bride. Oh, his mind was on fire. He felt terrific, in the true sense of the word.

"Then what's taking so long?"

Julian washed his hands in the sink, dried them on a fluffy red towel, closed the window, screwed the top back on the mascara tube, opened the door.

Gail was right there, arms crossed over her breasts. "What happened?" she said. "I thought you were locked in a death struggle there for a minute or two."

"Oh, no," said Julian. "Nothing like that. In fact, I let it go."

"Let it go?"

"I encouraged it to fly out the window," Julian said. "Assuming your goal was to get it out of the house, rather than end its life, however humble."

Gail's eyes opened a little wider, her lips parted; an opening response, in general. "That's very nice of you, Julian."

He shrugged. Shrugged, but the blood was surging through his body.

"I'm so grateful for your help, coming over in the middle of the night like this."

"Think nothing of it." Or he could have said *not at all*, or *don't mention it. Think nothing of it* was better somehow, elegant yet commanding.

"I wouldn't have slept a wink with that thing flying around the house," Gail said. "In fact, with the excitement, I'm not even sleepy all of a sudden." Her gaze slipped for a second to the little tuft of hair under his lower lip. "How about a nightcap?"

Julian thought about that, his eyes on hers, but seeing right inside to the strawberry jam.

"It's the least I can do," Gail said.

"That's very nice of you," Julian said. Or *you're too kind*—would that have been better? Probably not, laying it on too thick.

"I've actually got a little drinks tray right here in my room," Gail said. "In case of emergency." She moved toward it, a silver tray on the lowest shelf of an old bookcase, possibly valuable. "Kahlúa, B and B, cognac," she said. "What'll it be?"

Julian had cognac, Gail Kahlúa. He sat on a little chair, gilded and velvet, that she pulled up beside the bed for him. She sat on the only other place for sitting, the bed itself, clearing a space amid the J. P. Morganette material, leaning against the pillows, legs stretched out under her robe, only her feet showing, the toenails red-painted. Julian could tell she was proud of her feet, and well she should have been, beautifully shaped feet, nothing physically middle-aged about them but somehow deeply experienced all the same, full of promise: her best feature by far.

Gail raised her glass. "To bats."

Julian sipped his cognac. Perhaps she had used the word loosely.

"Tell me about yourself, Julian."

"There's not much to tell."

"I don't mean to pry."

"No problem," Julian said. "I'm sure your life is more interesting, that's all."

"Don't I wish," said Gail. "In a lot of ways I don't think I ever got started. I was forever getting waylaid by husbands, boyfriends, children, all of them not quite right. Not the children, of course. I've got two lovely children, a son and a daughter, long gone from the nest."

"Do they live nearby?"

"One's in Houston, the other in California." She drained her glass. "But the point I'm making is that I'm still all about potential, which is crazy at my age, thanks for not asking. To be pent up, if you see what I mean."

Julian nodded.

"You're a good listener, aren't you?" Gail said. "I don't have much experience with that ilk."

He hadn't been listening at all; she'd misinterpreted his steady gaze on her red-tipped toes.

"Mind doing me a favor, Julian? Freshening my drink an itty-bitty bit?"

She gave him her empty glass. Their hands touched. They must have been good hands once, almost as good as her feet, but now they showed their age. Julian went to the tray, poured more Kahlúa.

"You're very kind, I can tell," she said, taking the glass. For a moment, sitting by the bed in his dainty chair, he thought another toast was in the offing, but she drank in silence, blessed silence. Her face grew pinker. She looked at him, drank some more, shifted her legs a little so one foot came to the edge of the bed. "Can I say something, at the risk of being personal?" she said.

"Go on."

"I love that little beard thing under your lip."

Julian smiled.

Her foot slipped off the edge of the bed in a way that could have been accidental, settled in his lap in a way that could not. He kept the smile on his face, altering it slightly as though it were meant for her. She moved her foot around a little, the red-tipped toes turning out to be prehensile.

"Why don't you come up here," she said, "and let me demonstrate my gratitude."

"For what?"

"The bat."

No gratitude necessary. He'd already been repaid in full. *Snap:* the sound. And he could think of lots of reasons to stay where he was, or simply leave. But he'd been so hard when he'd felt the poem coming, the stillbirth of which she'd caused with her phone call, so in fact she did owe him. Plus she was convenient. And then there were those feet.

First he drank the rest of the so-called cognac, drank it in one long swallow, but without hurry. Then he got up and took off his clothes, let her have a good look.

"My God," she said, her face beyond pink now, on the way to strawberry red.

He got on top of her, spread her robe, her legs spreading on their own, and plunged inside without preliminaries.

"Oh, my God," she said, a cry between pleasure and pain that was about right.

Snap-bone and strawberry jam: he was hard, igneous.

Plunge and plunge. The difference in their strengths was like the difference between species. She grunted and squealed like a pig. "Oh, my God," she said, "this is going to be great. What am I saying? It is great already. Great, great, and that thing under your chin, oh, God, oh, just like that, just the way you're—"

"Shut up."

But too late. All the talking, all the inanity, all the mature woman's guidance to better sex, had obliterated the image of the red-tipped feet.

"Huh?" She stopped moving, if that helpless flabby flopping around could be called moving. "I'm sorry, Julian, did I do something wrong?"

Soft, but totally. He slid out of her gaping thing like a wet worm.

"Julian? Did I hurt you?"

He barked his contempt for that idea. She took the worm in her hand, began ministrations, shifted clumsily around and tried her mouth. At least that gagged off the hideous babble, but it was too late. He looked down at her bobbing head, considered all the strawberry jam inside, and got up.

Gail shrank back up to the headboard, lipstick all smeared, gathered her robe around her. "What did I do?".

Julian dressed and left without a word.

He sat at his desk in the darkness. All the lights in the big house were out, except for one that lingered in the upstairs window. Finally it went out too. Julian lit the two candles and another cigarette, first of a new day. He sucked down that first smoke ball of calming heat, felt it spread through his body and his mind. He breathed it out with a deep sigh, almost a sob. No one knew him, knew his immensity. That was to say, no one who counted knew, none of the hundred thousand. He was trapped in secret grandeur, like Nietzsche. And what had Nietzsche done? He'd written.

> *negligent is to forsake as*
> *mendacious is to deceive*

The next word, so close before, was not even a whisper now. Torment. Those dark eyes had understood what he was capable of, had felt it coming. Snap-bone. Snap-bone and strawberry jam.

Strawberry jam: his mind poised itself on the edge of something. Strawberry jam was an image, a symbol. Poems required images and symbols. Perhaps this whole problem could be approached from another direction. What else did a poem need? A subject, of course. From that promising first word, *negligent,* he would work his way toward some vast subject. And what was his subject? He knew its sounds already: grunts and squeals. *On Two Species:* an epic poem.

The hundred thousand and the rest. That was his subject, the smothering shallow ignobility of the 5,999,900,000.

An epic subject for an epic poem. But how to write about such a huge number? What had Homer done? He'd focused on a small number of characters, put them in conflict, launched them toward their fate. Julian needed some manageable cast to represent that number.

Gail? He almost shuddered at the thought of her name. But no need to dwell on her, not now. She didn't fit in his poem. He needed characters who swam in present-day society, and she seemed somewhat disconnected.

Then: *snap*. A eureka moment. The Gardners of Robin Road. They were perfectly present-day, symmetrically representative right down to their 2.2 children, if you counted the specter of the firstborn.

Julian lowered his pen over the empty space. The next word still did not come. He had a strange physical feeling, as though he were falling down a shaft.

Julian took an enormous drag from his cigarette, sucking up almost half in one inhalation. In the resulting moment of calm, his fall broken, he realized that an epic poem couldn't be dashed off just like that. It required preparation.

How to begin? With the characters? If so, what would be their situations, what their fate? Julian had no ideas.

No ideas, but his mind kept churning anyway, throwing out another question. Why not begin scientifically? Why not collect data? Perhaps the data would suggest the movement of the story, nature and art twisted together. He wriggled in his chair with excitement: was he actually in the process of inventing a new form, the living poem, nature and art blending in real time? Perhaps a living novel? Calm, calm. But he couldn't stay calm, and his cigarette was all consumed. He lit another, second of the day, and still not dawn. Perhaps it was time to violate a rule or two.

Data. To begin he would compile character sketches of the main players. Once more Julian lowered the tip of the pen, and at last he wrote. He wrote headings at the top of

four virginal sheets of paper: *Scott, Linda, Brandon, Ruby.*
What about Zippy? The thought amused him. He smiled to
himself in the night.

Julian stopped smiling, realized he'd almost made a
serious mistake, right here at the beginning. He reached
for a fifth sheet of paper and wrote one more heading:
Adam.

12

"**W**hy do you make me do this? Get out of bed."

Brandon clung to his pillow, clung to the darkness behind his closed eyelids and the remnants of a dream. A nice
dream: that weird bedroom of Trish's, but Whitney was the
girl in the bed.

"When are you going to start acting your age?" Dad asked.

Brandon heard the *drip drip* falling from Dad's razor
onto his floor. Was he supposed to answer that question, or
was it one of the other kind that were just for effect, the
name not coming at the moment? Didn't matter. He was too
tired to speak. He'd never been this tired in his life, and he
felt like shit on top of it. His throat was sore, he had a
headache, his ears—

"Get up, get up, get up."

Each repetition of the command louder than the last,
like Dad was going to lose it again. *Go ahead and lose it*—
Brandon couldn't move a muscle. He could smell his own
breath—stinking, foul. And his boxers felt a bit sticky in the
front. What the hell? Details of the dream with Whitney in
Trish's bedroom flickered just out of sight.

Then came Mom's voice from down the hall. "Isn't he up yet?"

"I'm getting him up," Dad yelled.

Silence. Maybe Dad had gone away, maybe he'd just decided, *oh what the hell, let the poor kid sleep*. Brandon felt his body starting to relax, deep sleep not far away.

"Hey," Dad said, still in the room, alarmingly close. "What's this?"

Brandon opened an eye, just one and not very wide, and peered out through a veil of gummy lashes. Dad was at the desk, sheets of paper in his hand. *Oh, fuck*. The *Macbeth* makeup test with the big red F on the front. Had he really left it out there in the open, really not thrown it away? He lowered his eyelid back to the fully shut position, unable to think of a better response.

"What's that, Scott?"

Mom. Mom was in the room.

"It looks like that makeup test," Dad told her.

Pause. Then Mom said, "Oh, my God." Like someone had been seriously hurt. "What is the meaning of this, Brandon?"

He could feel her standing right over him. Brandon opened his eyes. She brandished the test at him, like a cop with the evidence. They were so fucking relentless, especially her.

"Get a life," he said.

"Get a life? Is that what you said?"

"Get a goddamned life."

"Did you hear him, Scott?"

"You can't talk like that," Dad said.

"F," said Mom. "Where's your pride? You won't get into any college at all with grades like that, never mind an acceptable one."

"So? What if I don't even want to go to college?" There was an idea.

"Not go to college?" said Scott. "What would you do instead?"

"For God's sake," said Mom. "He doesn't even mean it. Stop humoring him."

No college. He'd be out of school forever in a year and a half, and the rest of high school would be easy, with no more CP courses, no more standardized tests, no more *Macbeth*, or *The Scarlet Letter*, coming next year, which everyone said was even worse.

"I do mean it," Brandon said. "Think I'll give college a pass." He watched his parents through those gummy veils. Just look at them: Dad with a towel around his waist, Mom with one around her body, another wrapped around her head, their mouths open in shock. Then he had another good idea. "Think of all the money you'll save." *Fuck you good as new all we do then it's through.*

"Goddamn it," Dad said. "Who said anything about money?"

Where the sun don't shine, where the sun don't shine. Problem, in the background. He had a deep, rough voice, just as good as Unka Death's.

"Why do you always get caught up in his games?" Mom said.

"But we never said a word about money."

"It's irrelevant," Mom said. "The point is he's going to college and he knows it."

"You can't make me," Brandon said, realizing the truth of his words as he spoke them. They couldn't make him. Did Problem have a record deal of his own? He'd have to ask Dewey.

"What kind of job do you think you'd get without a college degree?" Dad said.

"Bicycle messenger."

"Bicycle messenger?"

"In New York. They make three hundred bucks a day."

"That's not a real job," Dad said.

"Three hundred bucks a day isn't a real job?" Brandon said. "Do you make that much, Mom?"

Two pale circles, the size of quarters, appeared on Mom's cheeks. "There's a lot of life after high school," she said. "Do you really want to be a loser, Brandon?"

"If you don't go to college, you're a loser?" Brandon said.

"In this economy," Dad said.

"You think Julian's a loser?"

"What has Julian got to do with this?"

"He didn't go to college."

"That's ridiculous," Mom said.

"Put some money on it."

Those pale quarters turned pink. "You don't know much about people," Mom said. "All you have to do is listen to him talk for two seconds."

"I'm telling you what he told me," Brandon said.

"You must have misinterpreted," Mom said.

"Ask him."

In her cubicle—more of a corner office, really, bigger than what people normally considered a cubicle, only a cubicle in the sense that the walls didn't extend to the ceiling—Linda divided her salary by the number of working days in the year, came up with a number far short of three hundred. *You guys went to UConn, you're successful.* She liked her job, was good at it, but in New York she'd be making three or four times as much, maybe more. And instead of accounts like the Central Connecticut Realtors Association, Nutmeg Brewing Co., Skyway, she'd be handling Saks Fifth Avenue, Tiffany, some big museum.

She'd settled: settled for the small city instead of the big one, accepted other second choices as well. Did the very first one you took lead inevitably to the others, like one of the those trees they used to show the apes going one way and man the other? What was her very first second choice?

Her phone rang. Skyway. Skyway owned the Mall at West Mill, was also developing the site of the original mill, provided they got permission to cut an access road through the town forest. Her job was to provide visuals of the future development that the Skyway lawyers could use at their presentations to all the boards and commissions involved. There were problems: first, the Skyway architects had no drawings yet. Second, she didn't like the name they'd chosen, Olde Mill Estates. *Estates* was only going to annoy the planning and conservation people—there were wetlands issues as well as the right of way—and the development was in West Mill, not Old Mill. Plus there was that ridiculous *e*. She'd sent them a list of possible names, which they'd rejected, and then tried another one.

"They still like Olde Mill Estates the best," said the Skyway marketing woman.

"Better than Willowbend?"

"They didn't get that one at all."

"But there's that grove of willow trees," Linda said. She'd driven over one Sunday to check it out. "By the bend of the river, where the actual mill used to be."

"Those trees won't even be there after stage three."

"What's stage three?"

"The marina."

"The mill's gone too, for that matter," Linda said.

"I don't get you."

She didn't explain. "What about the *e*?"

"E?"

"On *Old*. I hope you're dropping it."

"Why?"

Linda didn't explain that either, just asked for time to come up with new ideas.

"The printer's waiting."

Linda started a new list: Riverbend, the Meadows at West Mill . . . She sat in her office, tapping her pen, thought: Willow Stump Mansions. Would she be doing this in New York? Or even Boston, the city she'd finally persuaded Scott to try first, a halfhearted attempt on his part that had ended up costing him his equal share of the family business—an inequality of inheritance that would be passed on and on.

Linda dialed the A-Plus Tutorial number, got Margie on the phone. "Is it true Julian didn't go to college?"

"Would that be a problem for you?" Margie said.

"Apparently it's what he told my son."

"A lot of our people don't have degrees," Margie said, "since so many of them are college students themselves."

"Julian's a little older."

"If someone older with a degree is what you want, I've got a retired English teacher from Loomis on the staff."

"No," Linda said. "We're not unhappy with Julian."

"That's what I understood."

"It's just a bit of a surprise, if true."

"Did someone in this office lead you to believe he had a degree?"

"No," Linda said. "He seems highly educated, that's all."

"Julian is highly educated. He gave a lecture at a university several years ago—he showed me a reference from the master of Balliol. Unlike some of my competitors, who shall remain nameless, I get references from all my applicants."

Linda couldn't quite place Balliol. Was it in Wisconsin? "Beloit?" she said.

"Balliol," said Margie. "One of the colleges at Oxford."

"Julian gave a lecture at Oxford University?"

"I believe it led to several seminars as well."

"On what subject?"

"Nothing to do with the SAT, if that's what you're thinking."

"I'm just curious."

"Hang on."

Linda heard a drawer open, heard paper shuffling. The Meadows at West Mill—what was wrong with that? Margie came back on the line.

" 'Vipers in My Backpack: Zoological Fieldwork in Up-Country Gabon' was the topic," Margie said. " 'How pleasant to learn that the tradition of the bold amateur naturalist lives on,' it says here."

"My goodness."

"But I wouldn't bring this up with him," Margie said.

"Why not?"

"He didn't want me to spread it around."

"Oh?"

"He's afraid it might sound pretentious. Kind of refreshing, don't you think?"

Three hundred bucks a day. Was it possible bicycle messengers in New York made that much? Scott could almost feel the freedom of it.

"You still there?" said a shaky old phone voice in his ear.

"Just looking that up for you. . . ." He left the client's name unsaid because he couldn't remember whether this was Mr. Insley or Mrs. Insley and they sounded the same. "It's under your umbrella."

"So we're covered?"

"Yes."

"We don't have to pay?"

"No."

The Insleys squabbled for a moment in the background. "What about our premiums?"

"This won't affect them."

"Oh, that's wonderful, Scott. Please mention us to your mother next time you're talking to her."

"Yup."

The freedom of it. Scott could remember racing down stairs three or four at a time without a thought. When had he stopped doing that? If he hadn't stopped, if he'd kept doing it every day, would he still be able to? He tensed one of his biceps and was squeezing it in an exploratory way when the door to his office opened and Sam burst in.

The truth was Sam just came in quietly; it was the energy suddenly in the room that made Scott have that bursting thought.

"Hey, Uncle Scott," Sam said, a smile spreading across his face. He came forward, hand extended. Scott rose. Sam had grown again, was as tall as Scott, maybe the tiniest bit taller.

They shook hands. Sam had a strong grip, a direct look, his eyes smiling too. He wore a blazer and a loosely knotted tie with a tennis racquet pattern.

"How're you doing?" Scott said, found that he was smiling too, couldn't help it.

"Great," said Sam.

"No school today?"

"I'm kind of playing hooky."

"You are?"

"It's a class trip, really. I got permission to meet the bus down here. Dad's going to take me to lunch first. Want to come?"

"Sounds good. Where's the trip to?"

"New York."

"What's on the schedule?"

"They're taking us to a play."

"Yeah? What one?"

"*Macbeth*," said Sam. "Only instead of medieval Scotland they do it as gangsters in the thirties. Could be kind of funny, someone like Joe Pesci going on about tomorrow and tomorrow and tomorrow."

An angry red F, with a big red circle around it. "So you're studying *Macbeth*?" Scott said.

"Finished a few weeks ago," Sam said. "We're on *Twelfth Night* now. Hard to believe the same guy wrote both of them."

Scott remembered studying *Macbeth*, knew nothing of *Twelfth Night*. "Because *Twelfth Night*'s not as good, you mean?"

"More like because they're so different," Sam said. "But I'm no judge—it takes me hours just to get through each act."

Tom came in, gave Scott a quick nod, turned to his son. "All set?"

"Uncle Scott's coming too," said Sam.

"Fine," said Tom. "Primo's all right, Scott? The Andover bus is meeting Sam at the mall."

"I just remembered something," Scott said, and made up a sketchy little excuse. "Have fun in the big city, Sam."

"Thanks," said Sam. "How's Brandon?"

"Great."

"Say hi to him for me."

"Sure thing."

They went out the door, Sam a good two inches taller than his father and broader-shouldered, but the walk was the same. A confident walk. The energy level in Scott's office went way down.

His phone buzzed. "Mrs. Insley again on line three."

"I'll call her back."

Scott got up, put on his coat, left the office. It wasn't airless, exactly, more like all the molecules were paralyzed. He got in the Triumph—he loved the car, a '76 TR6, the last year they were made, kept in perfect shape by Tony at European Motors—and drove to Briny's, the opposite direction from Primo's and the mall. The engine made a comforting sound, like something coming from deep in the throat of a formidable dog. He didn't have a formidable dog, of course, didn't have a lot of things.

Scott ate at the bar. He had chowder, a dozen Waquoits and a pint of ale, a good ale from a microbrewery they'd had a chance to invest in, an investment Tom had done some research into and ended up not liking. Goddamn good beer anyway. Scott ordered another. This wasn't a bad way to eat sometimes, by himself, no questions, no problems. He glanced up at the nearest monitor, caught a no-look pass and a two-handed dunk.

Then someone slapped him on the back. "Scotty, my man. Drinking alone?"

Scott turned. Mickey Gudukas. He had a flower in his

buttonhole and a bottle of champagne—Veuve Clicquot, Scott recognized that orange label—in his hand.

"How're you hittin' them?" Gudukas said.

"Hitting them?"

"A glass here for my friend," Gudukas said, "champagne glass."

"Not for me," Scott said.

"Tennis," said Gudukas. "How're you hittin' 'em?"

Scott shrugged.

"We'll have to finish that match one day soon," Gudukas said. "That brother of yours is some quick."

Gudukas was drunk, of course, but wired too. The bartender laid a glass on the bar. Gudukas filled it to overflowing.

"Maybe I could keep the bottle for you, Mr. Gudukas," said the bartender.

Gudukas laid a bill on the bar, put his finger over his lips, said, "Shh." A hundred-dollar bill. He handed the brimful glass to Scott.

"A toast," he said. "To Symptomatica."

"Why Symptomatica?"

Gudukas looked surprised. "You haven't heard, Scotty?"

"Heard what?" He hated that nickname.

"The enzyme thing failed. They killed two hundred and sixty fuckin' chimps, Scotty! The stock's at—" Gudukas whipped out his Palm, punched a few keys. "Seventy-three cents. And the SEC's stepping in. That's my Boxster, right out the window. I'm rich."

13

The observer who has thoroughly understood one link in a series of incidents should be able to accurately state all the other ones, both before and after. Ruby awoke on Saturday morning with that remark in her mind, a remark she'd read late the night before in "The Five Orange Pips," just before falling asleep. She looked it up again, page seventy-five of *The Complete Sherlock Holmes,* read it over three or four times. Was it true? If it was, how amazing! You'd appear just like a magician to other people, which was the way Holmes did appear, of course, although "The Five Orange Pips" wasn't her favorite: it seemed kind of strange having Sherlock Holmes and the Ku Klux Klan in the same story.

One link in a series of incidents. It would be nice if she had an example to go on, something simple. Ruby tried to think of some simple series of incidents. There was the F Brandon got on that stupid makeup test. An earlier link was blowing off studying for that New York trip with Dewey. A later link was Mom and Dad going ballistic. She understood how those three fit together pretty well, even thought she might have been able to leap from one to another. But what was going to happen next, what was the next link in the chain? Ruby didn't know.

Then, despite the fact that she needed to pee pretty bad, she thought of another example, this one not understood at all. And more like something out of Sherlock Holmes: The Mystery of the Varsity Jacket. She tried to reconstruct the whole thing in her mind. It was the day she lost the *Westie* editor election to Amanda. Kyla had given her a pink wrist-band on the way home from tennis. She'd gone in the house, turned on the lights, seen that Brandon's jacket wasn't on the peg. Call that link one.

Then came inspiration from God-knows-where to burn "The Speckled Band." That had led to the smoke extrava-ganza and Julian arriving to save the day. After that came the tour of the house, but just before they got started, she'd spot-ted Brandon's jacket, now hanging on the peg. She'd called his name up the stairs, got no answer, noticed that his back-pack and boots weren't in the mudroom. Link two.

After that, there was the tour, which was fun, and the stuff about Adam, which wasn't. Then Mom arrived, got mad that Brandon wasn't home, smelled smoke. The next thing was Brandon walking in wearing his Unka Death T-shirt—the one with Unka Death looking so mean, and that scary Problem guy standing behind him, wearing his gold AK-47 medallion—and telling Mom he'd left the jacket at school. Mom didn't know what the hell he was talking about, the jacket hanging right there beside him, and when he saw it he'd looked kind of like Adam Sandler when some-thing the least bit complicated was happening. He'd even touched the jacket, like a village idiot. Anything else? Not that she could think of. Call that part link three.

And the answer was? She had no idea. Was she a Wat-son, not a Holmes? Maybe the jacket had been hanging on the hook the whole time and she'd not seen it somehow. But even if that was true, how did it explain Brandon's confu-sion? He was confused because he hadn't expected it to be there. Did he leave it at school, as he'd said? Hey! Were there two jackets? Her excitement over that idea cooled fast. If there were two jackets, why would Bran be surprised? He'd be running into his jackets all the time. So she was no fur-ther ahead. Holmes would probably have figured the whole thing out already. A Watson, not a Holmes. Was she going to spend her life saying *jolly good* and *well done, old chap* to some preening asshole?

Ruby started to get out of bed and only then remembered what day it was. Had she turned stupid overnight? That crayoned cake with the burning candles had been right in front of her face all month. And what was the last thing Mom had said to her the night before, for God's sake? She ran into the bathroom and had her very first pee as an eleven-year-old, a real long one, mature. What was that word for "very first"? *Inaugural.* She'd had her inaugural pee.

Aruba Nicole Marx Gardner: practically a teenager. Aruba, for God's sake—named after the island where she'd been conceived. She hadn't known what *conceived* meant when she was little, and had fallen like a sap for her parents' smooth explanation about celebrating the place where they first thought of having her. Later, after checking the various definitions of *conceived* in the dictionary, she'd decided to change her name officially to Ruby the second she was old enough. Her name was for her, right? She could name her own self Bora Bora the first time she had sex there, which was going to be never. There or anyplace else.

Ruby went downstairs. Dad and Mom were up, Dad making coffee, Mom at the toaster. And on the butcher block lay a huge present wrapped in yellow and tied with blue ribbon. They both gave her a big hug at the same time.

"Birthday girl!"

"The big one one," Ruby said. Maybe it was time to start drinking coffee.

This was going to be a great day. After archery, Mom was taking her and Kyla and a few other friends to see a movie at the mall—either *Practically Dead* or *That Thang Thing*, they'd take a vote—and then have pizza at Signor Capone's, best pizza in town. Later came cake at home, just with the family, which was the way they always did it because that was how they'd done it in Mom's family going back to the Middle goddamn Ages. *Whoa there, girl.*

But there were surprises, like Julian, for example. Not that he appeared for Brandon's lesson; that was expected.

Also not that Brandon was asleep. But while Mom was up-stairs waking Brandon and Dad was changing into his tennis things, Julian took a package out of his coat pocket and handed it to her.

"Happy birthday," he said.

A small package with shiny black paper and thick red ribbon, very classy, like in one of those movies that took place in Italian villas.

"Thanks, Julian. How did you know?"

"A little bird told me," he said.

Ruby laughed, remembering at the same time the tour of the house and Julian looking in her room from the doorway. He might have seen the calendar from there, with the birth-day cake in that all-important square, if his eyesight was very sharp. Hey! Maybe this was one of those links-in-a-chain things. On the other hand, maybe Mom or Dad just told him. But why? It would be like begging for a present and they were too cool for that. Not cool, just too cool for that.

"Aren't you going to open it?" Julian said.

Ruby opened it. First the card, that was only polite. On the front stood a big brown bear with a present behind his back. He was saying, *I can bearly contain myself.* Inside it said, *Happy Birthday,* and Julian had added, *And many more—Julian.*

Then the present: She removed the wrapping carefully the way you were supposed to, either because it could be used again or because you didn't want to look greedy, the reason forgotten. Inside was a thin box, about the size of a twin CD set. She opened the box, felt through tissue paper, pulled out a magnifying glass, a really nice one with a wooden handle.

Ruby held it over her thumbnail. It magnified that half-moon thing like crazy.

"What a great present," she said.

"Don't mention it, my dear Holmes," said Julian.

She laughed some more and, caught up in the fun of it

all, held the magnifying glass to Julian's face. His eyes went
a little funny and she realized it wasn't polite. He was on her
side, no doubt about that, the way he'd covered for her, but
there were limits.

Eleven years old. Hard to believe. Time sped up as you
got older, just as everyone said. Scott tossed his racquets
into the trunk of the Triumph, got in, hit the garage door remote on the visor. He remembered the night she was born
with the clarity of something that had just happened. An
East European nurse said, "Vunce more, honey," and then
out came Ruby's head, eyes open from the get-go. He'd
started crying, an uncontrollable flood, and had to leave the
birthing room. Everyone—not Linda, but everyone else—
had probably thought he was just another New Age dad
getting in touch with the miracle of birth. They were accus-
tomed to tears of joy, and maybe his tears, of grief and rage,
looked the same. Adam had been dead for less than a year,
and here was a new one. It was so brutal. He'd composed
himself quickly and gone back inside, where Linda, dry-
eyed, had the baby on her breast, and the nurse was saying,
"Nice verk."

Scott stuck the key in the ignition, turned it, nothing. He
tried a few more times, same result. He got out, opened the
hood, saw nothing wrong with the battery connections, tried
once more. Zip: battery completely dead. He checked the
gauges—nothing left on overnight. Completely dead, no
reason.

"Goddamn it." He shouted that, out loud, not like him.
And just like that, he stopped loving the old TR6. It wasn't
just the dead battery, he wasn't completely stupid about himself. Probably wasn't the battery at all: it was that fucking
Boxster, a blue one, parked outside the window at Briny's.

Scott took his racquets out of the trunk, went into the
kitchen. Linda was on the phone. "There were meadows at one
time," she was saying. "I've been doing some research, and—"

She listened to someone on the other end. Scott raised a

finger for her attention. She shook her head, waved him away.

He checked his watch. Ten minutes to court time, fifteen minutes away. He went to the dining room, looked in. Brandon, hair all rumpled, was bent over a test booklet. Julian stood at the window, gazing at the woods out back. Scott hesitated, but only for a moment. Who was paying the goddamn shot?

"Julian," he said.

Julian turned.

"Got a valid driver's license?" An insurance man's question.

"It's temporary," Julian said.

"Good enough."

Scott drove Linda's Jeep, Julian beside him.

"How's Brandon doing?" Scott said.

"We're making progress."

"What's his biggest weakness?"

"Confidence."

Scott glanced across at Julian. That pissed him off. First of all, Julian was wrong, wasn't he? Brandon had as much confidence as the next teenager. Second, it was none of Julian's business. Julian stared straight ahead.

"I meant in terms of the SAT," Scott said.

"So did I," Julian said.

"Oh."

A cop blew by, lights flashing.

"Know much about options?" Scott said.

"In what sense?"

"The stock market."

"A leveraging instrument?"

"Yeah," Scott said. "You can leverage a Boxster out of spare change if you know what you're doing."

"Boxster?"

He didn't know the Boxster? "A Porsche," Scott said. "Runs about fifty grand."

"Is that what you want, a Boxster?"

"Why not?"

"You don't like the Triumph anymore?"

He glanced at Julian: a pretty amazing guess, as if Julian had been following his train of thought. Julian was watching the cop car, now flying up the hill toward the Old Mill line.

"Can't really compare them," Scott said. "Like apples and oranges." But he did want that Boxster, not just the Boxster but the whole big life that went with it. The clock was ticking.

"You're active in the stock market?" Julian said.

"Not as active as I'd like."

"No?"

Scott hadn't told the Symptomatica story to anyone, hadn't planned to, but Julian seemed like a good listener, and he was on the verge of getting into it when they turned into the tennis club parking lot.

"Mind coming inside?" Scott said. "I'll wave through the window if I've got a ride home."

They went in, Scott hurrying through the lobby and onto the court, Julian moving to the viewing window. Tom, Erich, and that dentist with the wicked topspin lob were already warming up on the near court.

"Get a ride home from you, Tom?"

"Sure."

Scott waved at Julian. "All set, guys," he said, skipping his own warm-up, which you did if you were late.

Erich served. Scott hit a monster backhand down the line for a clean winner, knew he was going to play great even if he didn't feel great inside. He and Tom won the first set 6-2. On the changeover, Scott glanced at the window, saw Julian still there, watching. Was he going to get billed for this?

Scott served to start the second set, winning at love, and when he looked again, Julian was gone. His game slipped a bit after that and they ended up losing the second set just as the bell rang.

"Had it going there for a while," Tom said as they were walking off.

Scott didn't like that *for a while*, not with the memory of their singles match so fresh. "Heard about Symptomatica?" he said. It all came spilling out, and with a weird kind of relish he couldn't have explained—Gudukas, the Boxster, the money they could have made. Tom didn't say anything. His face hardened, like Dad's used to, but he couldn't look Scott in the eye, which wasn't like Dad at all.

Skyway had suddenly soured on Olde Mill Estates, not just that *e* but the whole name, and Linda's boss wasn't happy about it.

"Why couldn't you have left well enough alone?"

Ruby came into the kitchen with her bow, pointed to the clock. "What's the problem?" Linda said. "We'll just have to come up with a better name, that's all."

"The problem is they're losing confidence, Linda. I think they're already looking."

"Looking?"

"For someone else. I happen to know Larry made a quick trip to New York Friday morning."

"Mom," said Ruby.

"New York?" Linda said.

"That's all I know. The best thing you could do right now is—"

"Mom?" said Ruby.

Linda waved her away. "Sorry, I missed that."

Her boss made one of those tsking sounds, so annoying. "The best thing you could do is come up with a name they're crazy about, like today."

"Today?"

"If it's not too late already. Don't you get it? The Skyway account's in jeopardy."

Linda hung up. Was her job in jeopardy too?

"I'm going to be late," Ruby said.

"For God's sake, Ruby." Linda smacked her hand on the

table, immediately thought, *Christ, don't do that on her birthday.*

Immediately, but too late. "Forget it," Ruby said. She dropped her bow right there on the floor and walked out of the kitchen.

"Christ," Linda said, this time aloud.

Julian came in through the mudroom, her car keys in his hand.

"Julian," she said. "Can I ask you a big favor?"

"The Skyway account's driving her crazy," Ruby said. Julian glanced over from behind the wheel of Mom's car. He didn't hunch over it like Mom, so stiff, but sat back, relaxed. Ruby felt safe right away, unlike the one time she'd been in Dewey's car, for example, when she ended up getting carsick and puking out the window, mostly.

"What's the Skyway account?" Julian said.

"They own the mall and now they're putting up some houses. Mom has to come up with a name."

"For the development?"

"Yeah. She likes the Meadows at West Mill the best."

"What are some of the others?"

Ruby had gone over the list, lying on the kitchen table, over breakfast. "Riverbend, the Willows at West Mill, Something else at West Mill, that kind of thing."

"Have you got any ideas?"

"Nope." It was boring, right? But then she thought of a great one: Pooh Corner. She was thinking of trying it out on Julian when they pulled up behind the old practice field at West Mill High.

Not many cars today, maybe because some of the parents thought there'd be no archery with snow on the ground. They didn't know Jeanette. She already had the targets up, was drawing the shooting line in the snow with her boot.

"Move it, let's go," she called to the kids getting out of their cars. "Run, Rubester."

Ruby ran.

She shot great, maybe because of how bright the target colors were against all the snow, maybe because it was her birthday, maybe because she was getting better. Her final six: three reds, three golds, right up there with William Tell.

"What's Rubester been smoking?" said Jeanette, and all the kids laughed. "Don't tell your parents I said that." They laughed again. "Here's something for next week." The kids got quiet. "Practice watching the smallest thing you can see on any object."

Ruby took that in, held her breath. Right away she knew how important it was going to be, not just for archery but her whole life. Down deep in her mind archery and Sherlock Holmes locked together, a perfect fit.

The kids pulled their arrows out of the targets. Jeanette drove up in the pickup, hoisted in the targets, shoved her skis and poles to the side, drove them all back to the waiting cars. "Hold on tight," she called out the window, and fishtailed a little in the snow to give them a thrill.

Jeanette stopped by each car for a kid to hop out. The Jeep was last. She parked beside it. Julian was standing outside, a snowball in his hand. He came over, took Ruby's bow and quiver. She jumped down, noticed Jeanette looking at Julian. Mom said that Jeanette was gay, but nobody really knew, right?

"Jeanette," she said. "This is Julian. He's going to get my brother into Harvard."

"Hi," Jeanette said.

"Hello," said Julian.

Their eyes met for a second. Ruby got the crazy idea that they didn't like each other, dislike at first sight.

"Keep 'em sharp," Jeanette said, and drove off.

"You bet," said Ruby.

Julian watched the pickup till it rounded the corner by the gym and disappeared. He looked down at her. "You shot well," he said.

Ruby glanced back at where the targets had stood. "You could tell from here?" she said.

He didn't answer, was no longer looking at her, but up at the sky, where a big bird was circling.

"Is that a hawk?" Ruby said.

"Yes." And then, so quick it was like one of those cuts in a movie and the next scene had already started, he'd dropped the snowball and drawn Ruby's bow, aiming up at the hawk with one of Ruby's blue-and-yellow feathered arrows.

"Julian!" she said.

He paused in the anchor position, his aiming eye color-less as the snow. Slowly he released the tension on the string, lowered the bow. He turned to her, eyes all back to normal. "Just practicing the aiming part," he said.

"Too bad the targets are down," Ruby said. "You could have taken a shot."

"Want me to take a shot?"

"We're only supposed to shoot at targets. That's rule two."

"What's rule one?"

"Nobody in front of you."

"Very wise," said Julian. He bent down, picked up the snowball, threw it in the air, amazingly far. Then, not even hurrying, he raised the bow, drew it, didn't seem to anchor even, just let fly.

The arrow was easy to follow against the pale sky, over-cast but not much darker than the snow on the ground. It soared over the field, higher and higher, closing on the snow-ball, and just as the snowball reached the top of its arc, hang-ing there for an instant before the long fall, the arrow struck right into the fattest part of its middle. Then came a tiny white explosion and the snowball was gone.

"Wow," Ruby said.

Julian didn't hear. He was already partway across the field, on his way to get the arrow, hadn't even stayed to watch. Ruby noticed that the hawk was gone.

Was William Tell real?" Ruby asked on the way home.

"A legend."

"So the apple part was legend too?"

He didn't answer; probably a stupid question.

"Some guys hunt with bow and arrow," she said.

"Yes."

"Have you?"

There was a pause, a long one, like maybe he hadn't heard. She was about to repeat it when he said, "No."

She was glad to hear that. It wiped out the whole hawk episode. They were back on the same page, archers of the target-shooting type. "I mean, how could you shoot a living thing?" she said.

"You don't see a living thing," Julian said. "You see a gold circle inside a red one."

She hadn't meant *how* that way, more like *how on earth*.

They turned onto Robin Road. Dewey's car was coming the other way, full of kids, smoke blowing out the windows. Brandon was one of the ones in the backseat, pushing and shoving in that supposedly playful way boys had. There wasn't much space, especially with the beer keg, clearly visible. Ruby glanced at Julian. His eyes were on the road.

They went in the kitchen. Mom was still at the table, her hands in her hair, crumpled papers all over the place, an ink smudge on her chin. She looked up, totally wired.

"How about La Rivière?" Julian said.

14

La Rivière it was, and so fast: Linda called the marketing rep at Skyway, the marketing rep called Larry, Larry called his partner, and in fifteen minutes, start to finish, Linda's boss was back on the phone, and in a very different mood.

"Bull's-eye, Linda. Exactly what we were looking for, quote unquote from Larry. And he's not one for throwing compliments around, as you know."

Yes! she thought, and said something more restrained, forgotten at once.

"How did you come up with it?" said her boss.

Linda glanced at Julian, sitting at the opposite end of the table, staring out the window, a glass of water—he'd refused everything else—in front of him. "Hard to say," she said.

"Enough with the aw shucks," said her boss. "It's not you."

"Just kicked a few things around, that's all," Linda said, lowering her voice in spite of herself. Julian reached for his glass, sipped; every movement economical and hard to take your eyes off, for some reason.

"Keep kicking, girl. See you Monday."

Linda hung up. "You're a gem," she said.

"An acceptable idea, then?" said Julian. Zippy trotted in, rubbed up against his leg.

"Acceptable? They ate it up. I can't thank you enough."

She waited for him to say something, and when he didn't she said: "Good things always happen fast, don't they?"

He looked at her with interest. "The corollary," he began, "would be—"

"Hey." Ruby came in, pulling on her jacket. "We're going to be late." She'd done something new to her hair, three braids twisted together like a pyramid on top of her head. She really had no idea how to present herself, but Linda was in a good mood and let it go.

"Have you picked a movie?"

"*That Thang Thing,* vote of four to three. I broke the tie."

"Is it appropriate?"

"Oh, yeah. It's all about these drug dealers who hide out at a yoga camp."

"Wonderful," Linda said, turning one of those rueful kids-today smiles on Julian, but he wasn't watching; his eyes were on that pyramid on Ruby's head.

They went outside. Julian got on his bike. "Thanks for everything today," Linda said. "Make sure the bill reflects all the extra—"

He held up his hand.

"No, really," Linda said. How nice he was; she felt a little guilty about taking the credit for La Rivière. But what good could the credit have done Julian? "If you're not doing anything tonight," she said at the last minute, "why not come over for birthday cake? Say around seven."

"What can I bring?"

"Just yourself."

He rode off but they soon passed him, pedaling fast, gaze straight ahead. The streets were bare but it was cold for bicycling.

"Why does he ride a bike all the time?" Ruby said.

"Maybe he can't afford a car," Linda said.

"He doesn't look poor to me."

"Maybe he likes the exercise. In Europe there'd be nothing unusual at all."

"We're not in Europe, Mom."

"He did lecture at Oxford."

"So?"

Perhaps they'd get along better as Ruby got older, Linda thought. She'd read about mother-daughter relationships like that.

Mom turned off the lights and Dad lit the candles on the cake. Then they sang "Happy Birthday," five of them around the dining room table, which was where birthdays happened: Mom at her end, Dad at his, Julian on one side, Brandon next to her, the birthday girl. She sang too, *Happy birthday to me,* because she liked singing, and handled that harmony thing at the end by herself.

"Make a wish," Mom said.

Ruby gazed at the burning candles and thought. Across the table, Julian was gazing at them too: the reflections of the flames flickered in his eyes. Of all Ruby's birthday wishes, the only one she could remember was for a dog, years ago, and that had come true; she could feel her wish-come-true sniffing around for scraps under the table. While she was thinking, one of the candles, the good-luck one in the middle, went out.

"Jesus Christ," Brandon said. Saturday night and he was itching to go; his foot was tapping, a soft impatient beat that vibrated up the legs of her chair.

Dad relit the candle. When one of the yoga guys in the movie was helping one of the drug guys find his inner kundalini or whatever it was, he'd said: "The essence of the presence is in the glow of the flow." The look on the face of the drug guy when he heard that! Ruby started laughing.

Dad was watching her, looked like he might start laughing too, even though he couldn't have a clue what it was about. He was a great dad.

"What's so funny?" Mom said.

"Make a goddamn wish," Brandon said.

How about pimples, all over your face? But then it

came to her, kazam and presto, what she wanted more than anything: X-ray vision. Ruby made her wish, said to herself, *Give me X-ray vision.* To be able to see not just the smallest detail, like Jeanette said, but right inside: that was what she wanted. Ruby took a huge breath and blew out all eleven candles plus the good-luck one in a single mighty gust.

Julian clapped softly. "What did you wish for?" he said.

"If I tell you," Ruby said, "it won't come true." She fixed him with a look, tried to turn on the X-ray vision. Not hooked up yet.

"Don't look at Julian like that," Mom said. "It's rude."

"Sorry," Ruby said.

"My fault," said Julian. "I thought you might give it away, Ruby."

"Was I born yesterday?" Ruby said. Everybody laughed at that, even Bran. Because Julian's laugh was so different— surprisingly like a crow, surprising because his speaking voice was so nice, like one of those English actors—Ruby noticed how similar the laughs of the family members sounded. Lots of quick little musical sounds, real happy. All in all, a great birthday. Mom cut the cake, chocolate inside and out, and Ruby ate two pieces.

Bran got up. "See you later," he said.

"Twelve-thirty curfew," Mom said.

"One-thirty," said Bran.

Mom and Dad looked at each other. "One," Dad said.

Mom sighed. "Where are you going?"

"Just hanging out," said Brandon.

"With Dewey?"

"He might show up."

Mom got that vertical line on her forehead, but not deep and smoothing over fast. She looked pretty happy, probably about Skyway. *And it was her daughter's birthday too, for God's sake,* Ruby thought; *couldn't that be part of it?*

Brandon left. Ruby burped, but real subtle, no one could possibly have heard. "Thanks, *todo el mundo,*" she said, and went upstairs to her presents, figuring to start with the

GameCube first. *Todo el mundo*—she'd picked that up from the drug guys.

"**H**ow about a drink?" Linda said, surprising herself a little. She hardly ever drank, and felt the urge even less often.

"Good idea," Scott said. "What'll it be?"

"Have we got vodka?"

"Sure."

"Vodka and tonic, then."

Scott rose. "Julian? I've got some nice single malts. There's also wine, beer, you name it."

"A nice single malt will be fine."

"Glenfarclas? Glenmorangie? Glenlivet?"

"Have you got any without Glen in them?"

Pretty funny, especially with that straight-faced delivery. Linda laughed, and Scott joined in after a second or two.

"Highland Park," he said.

"Perfect," said Julian.

Scott went downstairs to the wet bar by the entertainment center. Linda picked at the cake left on her plate. She'd cut herself a very small piece, eaten half, plus the icing flake she now put in her mouth.

"I can't thank you enough for your suggestion," she said.

"Suggestion?" said Julian.

"La Rivière."

"No thanks necessary."

"Not true. How did you come up with it?"

"Hard to say," Julian said.

The very words she'd said to her boss in answer to the same question. Was Julian making fun of her? No sign of it in his expression: he looked thoughtful, as he often did, she realized.

"You must be the creative type," Linda said.

Julian's face, normally quite pale, flushed a little. She understood something else about him: he was modest. Was he one of those enormously able people hobbled by shyness? There were still many such women around, but she'd never come across the male equivalent.

"What do you mean by creative?" Julian said.

"What everyone else does, I guess. Dreaming up La Rivière out of the blue."

"Isn't that begging the question?" Julian said.

Was that what begging the question meant? It didn't mean inviting the question? She'd been misusing it for years. Linda caught herself frowning, knew that damned vertical line was showing on her forehead—she'd glimpsed it unexpectedly often enough in store windows and the lenses of other people's sunglasses.

"No offense," Julian added, maybe misinterpreting her frown.

Scott came in with drinks on a tray. "No offense about what?" he said.

"We were discussing creativity," Linda said.

"Linda's a great one for intellectual discussions," Scott said, handing out the drinks. She noticed he'd used the Waterford glasses, the three that were left from their wedding service, all the rest broken over the years and replaced with something practical from Williams-Sonoma.

Julian raised his glass. "To Ruby."

"That's sweet," Linda said. "To Ruby."

"To Ruby," said Scott. He shook his head. "What a kid. You know she plays the sax?"

"I didn't," Julian said.

"Not on a level where it's going to be useful," Linda said.

"Useful?" said Julian.

"In terms of her future." Linda had been thinking of her boss's daughter, a year younger than Ruby, who'd already played the violin—a much more sensible instrument to begin with—at a specially arranged audition with a Juilliard professor. The same girl was also seeing a math tutor once a week, had started algebra. "She doesn't even know her times tables yet."

"Whoa," said Scott. "Where did that come from?"

"I believe there's a correlation between musical and mathematical abilities," Julian said.

"Exactly," Linda said, although it was news to her.

"I'm sure you know the story about Einstein and Heifetz," Julian said.

"Who's Heifetz?" said Scott.

"A famous violinist," Linda said; her father had played his recordings, especially the Beethoven concerto, and more especially the cadenza at the end of the first movement, over and over.

"Now I know," said Scott, taking a big drink.

Julian told the story, a funny story with Yiddish accents Linda didn't find the least bit offensive, ending with Heifetz's exasperated "Can't you count, Einstein? Vun two three, vun two three."

Linda laughed. Scott said: "Because he's a scientist, right?"

Right, Linda thought, and sipped her drink. She realized she'd forgotten to specify diet tonic. Julian was so lean compared to the two of them. "What do you think of the idea of math tutoring for Ruby?" she asked him.

"For what purpose?" Julian said. He glanced at his glass; Linda noticed it was empty.

"To give her a leg up," she said.

"I don't see how it could hurt," Julian said. "Do you, Scott?"

"I guess not," said Scott. "Freshen your drink?"

"Thanks."

"Stick with the Highland Park?"

"You're very generous."

"Hey," said Scott, "plenty more where that came from."

The phone rang as Scott was getting up. He answered it, raised his eyebrows at her.

Linda mouthed, *Who is it?*

"Who's speaking?" Scott said, and mouthed, *Larry*.

That was a first. Linda took the phone into the kitchen.

Scott came back to the dining room with the bottle of Highland Park. Julian was studying a photograph of Tom and him holding up a trophy. Scott heard Linda talking in the kitchen.

"Your brother?" Julian said.

Scott filled their glasses. "We used to play a few tournaments in the summer."

"A good team, from what I saw."

"You play too?" Scott said.

"At one time," Julian said.

Scott drank. Highland Park, not bad at all. The bottle had stood there unopened since last Christmas. He'd have to remember that line about anything without Glen in it. "Tell you the truth," Scott said, realizing it was the truth as he spoke, "I'm getting a little tired of it."

"Tennis?"

"With the same partner."

"Why is that?"

A good question. "We're together a lot at work, running the business and all. We own a little insurance outfit, did I mention that?"

"Someone did."

"Maybe not the most glamorous work in the world, but . . ." He searched for the right word.

"Solid."

Scott liked the sound of that. "Reliable," he said.

"The foundation."

"Yeah." The sound of that was even better. He felt a little more solid himself, all of a sudden.

"But not offering much leverage," Julian said.

That was right too: the good and the bad of the business summed up by Julian in thirty seconds. Scott studied him over the top of his glass: intelligent, educated, something more he couldn't name. Julian drank. His glass was empty again. Scott pushed the bottle across the table.

"So there's a little too much propinquity," Julian said, pouring an inch, even less, in his glass.

"Huh?"

"Being with your brother—Tom, is it?—at work and at play."

"I enjoy playing with him, don't get me wrong."

"Maybe you should play against him," Julian said. "Liven things up."

Scott paused in midsip, put down his glass. A little wavelet of Highland Park slopped over the rim. "Singles, you mean?"

"A better workout."

Scott was silent for what felt like a long time. Julian just sat there. Finally Scott said, "There are drawbacks."

"Such as?"

Scott considered not responding to that question, or making up some answer. But he said simply: "I've never beaten him." Maybe it was the Highland Park.

"No?" said Julian.

"You sound surprised."

"From the little I saw," Julian said, "I would have thought you the better player."

"That's the funny thing," Scott said, leaning forward. He stopped right there. He'd never spoken about this to anyone. How could he, without sounding like some whining loser?

"You beat all kinds of people who beat him," Julian said. "And you were always ranked higher."

"How did you know?"

Julian shrugged. "It's not that unusual. I take it he's older?"

"Two years and three months."

"I would have guessed more."

"Yeah?"

Julian drained his glass, poured some more, maybe only a half an inch this time. "Four or five years at least," he said, and smiled to himself, as though he'd had a funny thought. "Would you like to beat him?"

"It's not important anymore," Scott said. "I don't know. Sure."

"I couldn't help noticing a few things," Julian said.

"Such as?"

"Just little things. I suppose you try to move him around a lot."

"Yeah."

"And use your power to overwhelm him."

Scott nodded.

"Three suggestions," Julian said, putting down his glass, empty again, and pouring a quarter of an inch. "First, don't try to move him around."

"Hit right at him?"

"He's very good moving to the ball, not so good at getting out of his own way. Second, don't try to overwhelm him. Just keep the ball deep. Use your power only when he starts trying to overpower you."

"He never does."

"He will," Julian said, his glass empty. "More of this nice single malt?"

"Sure," said Scott. "What's the third suggestion?"

Julian poured more Highland Park, a big shot for Scott, not much more than a few drops for himself. "Let's keep that in reserve," he said. "Two should be enough."

"Tell me," said Scott. "I won't use it."

"But what if you did by mistake?" said Julian. "Funny things happen in the heat of battle. You wouldn't want to beat him too badly."

"No?"

"Think of his self-esteem."

Scott laughed. He felt disloyal to Tom, but only a little. Had Tom ever thought of his self-esteem?

Julian raised his glass. "To victory."

"To victory," Scott said. He couldn't wait.

15

"**W**hose victory?" Linda said, going back into the dining room, feeling pretty good. Larry had big plans, plans her boss didn't even know about, and he might need someone like Linda in the not-too-distant future.

Scott looked a little confused by the question; Linda glanced at the bottle of Scotch, much emptier than when she'd left the room. Julian said, "Just victory in general."

"I'll drink to that," Linda said; feeling really good, in fact. *Not-too-distant future:* Larry's exact words. She'd settled, settled for small instead of big, but maybe it wasn't too late. Linda picked up her vodka and tonic and sat down, not in her usual place at the end of the table, but in Brandon's chair—a wad of gum was stuck on the leg—making a more compact conversational group. She drank, not her usual cautious sip, but a generous mouthful. It tasted delicious, so sharp and . . . alive.

"What's that expression they have for spirits?" she said.

"Spirits?" said Scott.

"*Eau-de-vie* is the French," said Julian. "But most European languages have some variant. The Latin is *aqua vitae.*"

"Meaning?" said Scott.

"Water of life," said Julian.

Vie, vitae, life—sharp and alive: that was what she'd been after.

Scott shook his head. "How do you know all this stuff, Julian?"

Julian looked down, able but shy, as she'd thought. Yet he'd had the self-confidence to give a lecture at Oxford University. She wanted to ask him about that, but Margie had told her in confidence; Julian didn't want it spread around, didn't want to appear pretentious.

Scott picked up the bottle. Highland Park: the label showed a nice picture of a sunny but cold-looking vista. Linda had never had the slightest inclination to visit Scotland, until now.

Julian held up his hand in the stop position, but Scott poured some in his glass anyway, and then in his own. "Linda tells me you gave a talk at Oxford University in England," he said.

Julian went still.

Goddamn it, Linda thought. She'd told Scott not to mention it. He was so tactless sometimes; more than sometimes. She glanced at him with annoyance—couldn't help herself. He gave her a puzzled look in return. It was absolutely hopeless sometimes; more than sometimes.

Julian picked up his glass, shook it slightly, starting a tiny whirlpool inside. "You've been discussing me with Margie," he said.

"Not discussing, really," Linda said. "Just following up on Brandon saying you didn't go to college."

He gazed at the whirlpool. "Did the agency ever claim the contrary?"

"No," Linda said.

"And therefore your motive?"

"Motive?"

"Your reason for making the call."

"As I said," Linda began, "when Brandon—"

Scott interrupted. "It's more that she was checking up on Brandon, not you."

Did he have to put it like that? Linda was about to soften the statement in some way, when Julian said, "So it's not a disqualification, then, my lack of education."

"Oh, no," Linda said, "nothing like that. It's the exact

opposite—you seemed so educated, we just couldn't believe you'd only been to high school."

Julian looked up. The whirlpool stopped spinning in his hand. "Perhaps I'd better leave now," he said, the faintest smile turning up the corners of his lips. "I didn't go to high school either."

Scott laughed, spraying a tiny mist of Scotch. "Ever tried stand-up comedy? You've got that dry delivery down pat."

"So it's a joke?" Linda said. "You must have gone to high school."

Julian sipped his drink, then tilted the glass and took a much bigger swallow. "I was the beneficiary of what used to be called a private education."

"What's that mean?" said Scott. "Prep school?"

"No school at all," Julian said. "I was educated at home."

"Home schooling, sure," said Scott. "Like that couple—what's their name, Linda?—who moved to Maine."

"I don't know if Julian's talking about that kind of alternative thing," Linda said. "Making collages with a mom in Birkenstocks."

"My mother went barefoot much of the time," Julian said. "But I was mostly taught by people who came into the house."

"Tutors?" Scott said.

"Not professional tutors. More like people my father knew with special knowledge of this or that."

"Sounds fascinating," Linda said. She went to drink from her glass and found it empty, poured more vodka, almost unthinking. They had diet tonic in the fridge but Linda didn't want to miss anything. She added a very small amount of the regular tonic, compensating for the extra calories. "What sort of special knowledge are you talking about?"

"Yeah," said Scott. "Give us an example."

"If it's not prying," Linda said.

"Top off your drink?" Scott said.

From the expression on his face, Linda thought Julian would refuse; instead he held out his glass. She felt herself starting to relax. "You're too kind," he said.

"No problem," Scott said. "If we kill this off, there're still plenty of Glens in reserve."

The line struck them all as funny. Julian was the first to stop laughing. "Here's an example," he said. "There was a priest in the village who'd written a book on Verlaine and Rimbaud. I studied nineteenth-century French poetry with him."

"You lived in France, then?" Linda said.

"Briefly," said Julian. "But the village in question was in Cameroon."

"Cameroon?" said Scott.

"Were your parents missionaries?" Linda said.

"Broadly speaking," Julian said. "They were in the oil business."

"Yeah?" said Scott. He got that interested look on his face, a look that made it seem thinner, more like Tom's; a look she hadn't seen in some time. "With one of the big companies, like Chevron or Shell?"

"No company. He was an independent."

"A wildcatter?"

"He wasn't fond of that term."

"No?" said Scott. "I would have been."

Julian smiled.

"You were exploring for oil in Cameroon?" Linda said.

"Among other places."

"Like where?" Scott said.

"Tunisia, Kazakhstan, Fernando Po, Gabon, others."

Linda wasn't sure where all of them were.

"I don't even know where half of those are, for Christ's sake," said Scott.

"No?" said Julian.

Linda found her glass empty again, refilled it once more, just a tiny bit of vodka this time, barely any at all, and even less tonic.

"You had tutors in all those places?" she said.

Julian was swirling another whirlpool into existence, didn't seem to hear.

"What a life," Scott said. "Total enrichment."

"Exactly," said Linda. Scott could be acute sometimes.

"And no tests at the end of the day," Scott added.

"Oh, there were tests," Julian said. The whirlpool spun very fast.

The three of them watched it go round. Linda sipped her drink, added a little more vodka, just a splash or two more of the water of life. Then she and Scott began talking at the same time.

Linda said: "If you don't mind my asking——"

And Scott: "Let me get this straight——"

Julian looked up, smiled. "Ask away," he said. "My life's an open book."

"Go ahead, Scott."

"I'm just wondering," he said, "about your plans."

The same question she'd been about to ask, only not so bluntly.

"Plans?" said Julian.

"For your future," Scott said. "Someone of your background, if you see what I'm getting at, slaving away as a mere—not mere, but—"

Linda interrupted. "I think Scott is trying to find out in his way if you're sort of between things right now."

Julian's eyes went from her to Scott, seeming to grow more opaque. "That depends on what happens next, doesn't it?" he said.

Linda laughed. Scott was right: Julian had a wonderfully dry wit. For a moment she'd worried that he'd been deeply offended.

"Couldn't you always go back to the oil business?" Scott said.

"There is no more oil business."

"Your parents retired?"

"They're dead."

"Oh," said Scott.

"I'm sorry," said Linda.

"Nothing to apologize about," Julian said. "You didn't do it."

There was a silence. Then that little smile appeared at the corners of Julian's lips, and Linda realized he'd made another joke, even drier than the others. Scott laughed, but she didn't: not her kind of humor, even though she knew jokes like that were a coping mechanism, hiding the pain underneath. She was about to offer more cake as a way to change the topic when Scott said: "Has it been long since they passed on?"

"A number of years," Julian said.

"Have you got any other family?" Linda said.

"Not in the usual sense of the term," Julian said. "Would it be very rude to ask for another slice of Ruby's cake?"

"Of course not," Linda said, cutting him a piece, the knife halving the *y* in *Ruby*, and one for Scott too before he asked.

Scott ate the icing end first, in two forkfuls, washing it down with Scotch. His face was pink; Linda could feel that hers was too; Julian was pale but a tiny drop of sweat glittered in the hairs of that wispy thing under his lower lip. Linda took another drink, felt her muscles relaxing a little more. It took effort to keep her legs together.

"What's the story of this Oxford lecture?" Scott said. "The snakes and everything."

Julian swallowed the last of his drink, laid his knife and fork properly on his plate, rose. "If you don't mind," he said, "perhaps we can cover that another time."

"We don't have to cover it at all," Linda said.

"It's just that I've still got a few things to take care of."

"We haven't kept you?"

"Not at all. I assume I should return at the usual time?"

"For Brandon's lesson?" said Linda. "Why not?"

"The job is still mine?"

"Hell, yeah," said Scott.

"Although," Linda said, "you might want to emphasize to Brandon the importance of a traditional college education."

"There's a thought," Scott said.

They awaited Julian's reply. "We're all on the same page," he said.

"Love that expression," said Scott. "Why don't I give you a lift? We can throw that crummy old—your bike in the Jeep and—"

"Thanks," Julian said. "I prefer to ride."

"Have you far to go?" Linda said.

"No," Julian said. "And there's a handy shortcut."

"There is nothing more deceptive than an obvious fact," said Sherlock Holmes in "The Boscombe Valley Mystery." Ruby started reading the story in bed on her birthday night, but her eyelids got very heavy all of a sudden and closed just as Holmes was taking out his lens—must be magnifying glass—and lying down to examine the ground where the murder took place. Through her eyelids came that dull reddish glow, vibrating slightly, that meant falling asleep with the light on. Ruby was much too tired to do anything about it. She felt the weight of *The Complete Sherlock Holmes* lying open on her stomach, comforting, and went down, down, so fast there was no time to summon up the cave.

Down, down: she was in a field of flowers, leaning forward to examine one with her magnifying glass. Then something real bad happened. Because it had happened once before, although not quite like this, she knew it was going to happen again just before it got started. That was what scared her the most, the certain knowledge that this was not going to be a one-time event. She peered through the magnifying glass and the squat diamond-shaped head with the knowing eyes, blown up big, peered back at her.

Ruby opened her eyes, sat up with a start. *The Complete Sherlock Holmes* slid off the bed like something alive, fell on the floor with a thump. The light was on, thank God, her room a strange shade of yellow, brownish yellow, like paper about to go up in flames. She got out of bed, careful to put her feet nowhere near the book, and opened the door. Everything normal, the house same as always, serpent-free.

Ruby heard voices from down in the front hall. Mom, Dad, and another she didn't know at first, then recognized: Julian. She couldn't very well go down there and admit to nightmares, probably couldn't have even had it been just Mom and Dad. She was eleven, after all. So what would be a good cover story—thirsty, too hot, too cold, sore throat, couldn't get to sleep? Childish, one and all.

Ruby went the other way, to Adam's room. It had worked before. An obvious fact, and therefore deceptive, according to Holmes. She got into the bed, pulled up the covers. It was working again—no matter what Holmes said—she felt that right away; but she threw in the cave for added safety.

When was the last time she'd had three drinks in an evening? Linda couldn't remember. Not even in college, where sometimes a single drink had given her a headache. Not tonight. She felt great, expansive; partly because of the drinks, but more because of some new excitement that was in the air, probably having to do with the good news from Skyway.

Maybe now. She glanced at the bedside clock. Fifteen minutes to one: Brandon not yet overdue. Maybe now was the moment to get past Tom, Adam, the whirlpool. Her mind made a connection between her whirlpool and the one in Julian's glass. She sensed some hope for her in that connection, some promise that she would be all right, that she and Scott would be all right. Perhaps the lesson was to gaze into the whirlpool, as Julian had done, rather than avert the eyes, as she had for so long. *The heat generated in the master bedroom warms the whole house:* she wondered what Julian would think of that idea, felt herself growing hot.

"Kind of a fun evening, huh?" said Scott, lying beside her.

"Yes." He had a right to talk in bed without turning her off, a right to say anything he wanted.

"Remind me to call Tom first thing in the morning."

But did it have to be that? Why not, if looking directly in the whirlpool was the only way? "Are you going into work?" she said.

"Nope. It's about tennis."

Perhaps he wasn't in the mood. She put her hand on his thigh.

"Hey," said Scott. "You should get blitzed more often."

"Am I blitzed?"

"No, no, I was just using a bit of whatchamacallit, that word for exaggerating on purpose."

Linda couldn't think of it either. She could ask Julian on Wednesday. She took a deep breath. "Maybe I am blitzed," she said. "I know I haven't been what you want in bed."

She felt him go rigid, all but the part that should have been, which would be just goddamn perfect. Then he surprised her. "I understand," he said. "It's all since Adam."

What more did she want, even if he didn't really understand? The image that always waited in a tiny corner of her mind expanded now: a whirlpool bubbling out from between her legs, frothing with leukemia. She tried to squash the image back down, pulled Scott on top of her, wrapped her legs, legs that didn't want to stay together tonight, around his back.

"I love you," she said.

"Yeah?"

And if she ended up having to fake it, as she'd had to the last time and the infrequent times before that going back so long, she would make it a performance he wouldn't forget. She would generate fake heat that neither Scott nor anyone else could ever tell from the real thing.

"Do anything you want to me," she said.

"Really?"

The phone rang. They both jumped at the sound and Scott went soft, just inside the entrance to her, like that. He picked up the phone.

"Hello?"

She checked the bedside clock. Ten after one. *Not again, God. I couldn't bear it.*

"Okay," Scott said, and hung up.

"What? What?"

"Brandon got busted for underage drinking—some party in the woods. They've got him locked up at the station."

Linda started crying. Scott rose and got dressed.

16

"Scott Gardner," said Scott to the sergeant behind the counter. "I believe you've got my son Brandon."

"That we do, Scott," said the sergeant.

Scott would have expected *Mr. Gardner*, looked at the sergeant more closely, saw it was a guy who'd been a year or two behind him at West Mill High, had played on the same football team; something D'Amario, a guy he remembered not liking.

"Hey, how're you doing?" said Scott.

"No complaints. Got the insurance agency now?"

"Yup. What's the story?"

"Underage boozing in the town woods. On the noisy side, evidently, and we got a call from some concerned citizen."

"Name of Stromboli, by any chance?"

"We don't give out information like that. Anyways, we sent some cars down the old cart path, rounded up the ones too pissed or slow to get away. No one under eighteen was actually arrested—we don't do that if there's no other factors."

"So he's not in a cell?"

The sergeant paused for a moment. Scott realized he must have alcohol on his own breath, now detected. "They're in the lunchroom. I'll have your boy sent up." The sergeant reached for his phone, but before he could speak, an angry man in a long leather coat hurried up, bumping against the counter.

"You'll be hearing from my lawyer first thing Monday morning," he said. "My son would never touch a drop of alcohol."

Sergeant D'Amario said nothing. That made the man angrier. "Who do you think organized the DARE bottle drive?" he said, raising his voice some more.

"Why don't we go on back?" said the sergeant. "Might as well come too, Scott."

The sergeant led Scott and the angry man down a corridor past empty offices and into the lunchroom. The lunchroom had a row of vending machines lining one wall and about a dozen cheap tables with fixed benches. A cop sat at one of the tables, doing her nails. In the opposite corner of the room, as far from her as possible, sat Brandon, looking not too bad. At a table in the center sat the only other person in the room, a kid bowed over a plastic trash can, one of those big family-size ones. He made a gagging sound and puked up an enormous load of yellow liquid with orange bits in it; must have had pizza for dinner, Scott thought—he could remember back.

The sergeant turned to the angry man. "Which one's yours?"

D'Amario gave the boys a little talk in front of their fathers, no one getting too close to the kid with the barrel.

The town had a zero tolerance policy for underage drinking and that was that. Since neither of them had been in trouble before, he was letting them go with a warning.

"But next time, if you're dumb enough to have a next time, means arrest and charges, the whole"—turning to the angry man's kid—"enchilada." Scott didn't remember D'Amario being this funny; one of them must have changed.

"And I don't know if either of you's involved in sports up at the high school," the sergeant added; the other boy was wearing a vomit-streaked sweater, but Brandon was in his varsity jacket. "The AD has a strict zero tolerance policy, too. Caught drinking once and you're off the team for the season. Twice and it's forever."

The tennis thread, strengthening Brandon's potential application to some D III school, if not Amherst then Union maybe or Hamilton, for Christ's sake—was that going to unravel, too? "Is he going to find out?" Scott said.

"The AD's a her, Scott—things have changed since we were banging heads," said D'Amario. "But there's no communication of that kind between her and the department." He looked at Brandon and added, "Not yet."

"Thanks, Sergeant," Scott said. The angry man didn't say anything. His mouth was still hanging open. His son rose to his feet, white-faced and shaky. "Let's go, Brandon," Scott said. Brandon got up, not shaky, but not quite steady either. He didn't meet Scott's eye, which was disappointing, and he had a defiant hunch to his shoulders, which was a piss-off. Scott fought off the temptation to yank him by the sleeve. They walked toward the door.

"One other thing," said D'Amario. "Either of you boys know a kid named David Brickham?"

Brandon and the white-faced boy shook their heads.

"Calls himself Dewey," said the sergeant.

The boys shook their heads again. D'Amario's eyes were on Scott and caught him glaring at Brandon. Scott looked away, too late.

"Hasta la vista," said Sergeant D'Amario.

Brandon didn't say a word, not walking across the parking lot, not getting in the car. His door thumped shut. There was defiance in that thump.

"Buckle your goddamn seat belt," Scott said. He heard fumbling, then a click. Scott started the car, drove out of the lot. "How drunk are you?"

No answer.

"I asked you a question."

"I'm not fucking drunk."

"You watch that goddamn fucking mouth," Scott said. He hadn't really been all that angry inside the station. Now he was furious, although he didn't know why. "And what did you mean by saying you didn't know Dewey? Of course you know Dewey."

"So?"

"So? What kind of answer is—"

"Watch out, Dad."

He'd crossed the center line and headlights were coming the other way. Scott swerved back into his lane. They drove the rest of the way in silence.

Linda was standing in the kitchen when they came in, robe over her nightie, arms crossed. She gave Brandon a cold look; a cold look, but her eyes were red. "Well, Brandon?"

"Well what?"

"You're slurring your words."

"So are you."

"Don't talk to your mother like that," Scott said. He saw that Brandon's hands were balled into fists, then realized that his were too.

"Can't you see where this is headed, Brandon?" Linda said. "F's in school, cutting class, getting arrested?"

"The electric chair," Brandon said. He swayed back and forth a little.

Linda turned to Scott. "Couldn't you have talked some sense into him on the way home?"

Completely unexpected. "Wait a minute," Scott said.

"You guys talk sense," Brandon said. "Charlie Manson's hitting the sack."

"Come back here this instant," Linda said. Scott said nothing. Brandon didn't come back. They heard his feet, heavy on the stairs.

"What was that about talking sense to him on the way home?"

"He's floundering, Scott."

"That's not what I asked." A green light shone on the phone, indicating one of the lines was in use. Scott grabbed the receiver, heard a girl say, ". . . assholes," and Brandon grunt in response. "Get off the goddamn phone," he said, and slammed it down.

"Is that better?"

"Sorry," she said. "I'm worried, that's all. What are we going to do?"

"He's not getting his driver's license until he cleans up his act, that's for sure," Scott said, recalling his own father's ultimate weapon.

Linda nodded. "But we have to do something positive, too."

"Positive?"

"What about boarding school? It doesn't have to be Andover."

Their eyes met, and Scott knew they were sharing a thought: Andover wouldn't look at him. And though there were other boarding schools that would, how could they afford it? They hadn't even finished paying for the renovations. Scott didn't say that, though. He said: "I'm not sure how positive that is. What's the point of having kids if you send them away?"

Her eyes fell. She dabbed at them, just once and lightly. She wasn't a crier, which was why her reaction to the call from the station was a bit surprising. He wasn't a crier either: they were all cried out after Adam.

"Why not just flat out say I'm a bad mother?"

"I'm not saying that," Scott said; but pretty close. Would things be different with Brandon if she'd stayed at home? But then they wouldn't have a house as nice as this, there would have been no renovations, not as many trips, lots of other stuff. On the other hand, Linda wasn't working just for the money. Did that make her a bad mother?

Their eyes met. She'd followed his thoughts, every one.

"Can we afford Julian?" she said.

"Sure."

"Then maybe he could come more often. He's a good influence."

She was right. They'd found a compromise, a way to go forward, no one getting hurt. "And let's sign Brandon up for the SAT next time around," Scott said. "See exactly where we stand."

"Good idea." Linda made a note on a pad she kept in her pocket.

They went back to bed, lay on their respective sides. Scott waited for something to happen, but all that happened was a lot of fragmenting inside his head. Music leaked in from Brandon's room, almost too faint to hear.

negligent is to forsake as
mendacious is to deceive

Perhaps, his brain chemistry altered by the consumption of Highland Park—not bad at all, and no doubt Scott would be serving it exclusively for the rest of his life—perhaps the next line would spark to life somewhere deep in the neurons.

Nothing.

Julian lit a cigarette, fourth of the day, or first of the next one. He knew very well he'd been exceeding his allotment lately; on the other hand, he was an artist, and artists, the best artists, those who changed the world, were always excessive. The two candles burned on either side, the cigarette glowed in the middle: he was back in his triangle, could sense its pulsing force.

But nothing.

Then: an idea. Suppose the next word was *nothing*. Was

that what his brain had been trying to tell him all this time?
Julian lowered his Mont Blanc pen to the page and wrote
nothing. No following word or phrase came to mind. He
read over what he had so far:

> *negligent is to forsake as*
> *mendacious is to deceive*
> *nothing*

And saw it was good.

Julian took a deep, satisfied drag from his cigarette and
turned to the character sketches, beginning with Scott. He
wrote: *inferiority complex esp. re Tom; fundamentally lazy;
a gambler with no notion of odds; falsely believes himself to
be ambitious, but all he wants is more of the same; lack of
more of the same is all that makes him unhappy—not a good
enough reason, not nearly; IQ 110.* Scott was easy. Was
there some way to actually see the tennis match? Perhaps
not. *To do: friendly discussion of investment strategy, esp.
options trading; find out more about family insurance firm;
does Tom have children?*

*Linda: ambitious in real sense, wants to develop her
own thwarted expressive potential; developing Brandon—
the next best thing; many problems with Scott—explore; lies
well (Gabon paper episode); IQ 120.* If her career, as she no
doubt thought of it, happened to take off—he hoped she'd
get the accent right in La Rivière—would she lose some of
that tension inside her? Similarly, if disappointment lay
ahead, would the tension be ratcheted up to a new level?
These were interesting questions, questions the responsible
writer must pose. *To do: find out much more about Adam;
become good friends.*

*Adam: Superboy—the paragon under whose boot they
lie. Needed: time line—broken leg, leukemia.*

*Brandon: normal kid, might actually have grown up to
be a happy person in other circumstances; IQ 125. To do:
more of the same (get details of party denouement).*

Down to the last civilized inch of his cigarette, Julian stubbed it out, immediately felt hungry. He wished he'd said something nice about the cake before leaving, inducing the inevitable offer to take some home. Not bad at all, the cake.

Ruby:

Julian gazed down at the blank sheet with her name at the top, shadows pushed by random expansion and contraction of the candle flames shifting back and forth across the page.

Ruby:

He found he couldn't write a thing about her, not one word. He tried: *IQ.* And found he had no idea. She was just a silly little girl, much too talkative, who did ridiculous things to her hair. Yet there was that business with the fire. He had a disturbing thought: did they have something in common? Impossible. He must be tired.

Julian laid down his pen, leaving Ruby's page blank, and read over what he had done. He wasn't impressed; except for that one phrase, *the paragon under whose boot they lie*—surely that was prose of the highest possible order? The rest was rather obvious.

> *negligent is to forsake as*
> *mendacious is to deceive*
> *nothing*

After *nothing* nothing came. He considered this new form he was inventing, the living epic poem, nature and art blending in real time. Given the natures of the characters involved and the developing plot they were in, it was actually more of a novel in poetic form. Character, situation, fate: all these still more or less obscure. But he knew his subject: middle-class American life. He was perfectly poised to observe it. Observe and so much more, to participate, experiment, control, because the living novel would be a flesh-and-blood form, first of a kind, with an unprecedented tension, exciting and evolving, between the characters and their auteur. Only the auteur mattered in the end, of course, and therefore how perfectly bathetic were the Gardners, unquestioning, homely believers in their own mattering. Perhaps he should change the title from *On Two Species*, a little dry, to the simple but gravid *At Home*.

Yes! He was in the belly of the beast—hackneyed phrase that would never find its way into his own work—or, to alter the anatomical arrangement slightly, he was on the tumescent verge of fucking it up the ass. And it felt great.

Julian peered through his window to see if any light shone in the upstairs window of the big house. None did. Was there some way that bats could be introduced into Gail's bedroom as needed? Where did you go for bats? After this bout of creative activity, he was in the mood for and deserved something purely physical.

Still, imagining a prospective second bedroom scene in an honest way, Julian had to admit that there would still be the problem of her inane chatter, on and on. Would a gag of some sort be acceptable? He could see her actually liking it, getting turned on, asking for the gag the next time and the time after—he was just being honest with himself.

The lights stayed off in the upstairs window of the big house. Julian went to bed hungry.

17

Was there anything better than Sunday morning? Just to lie in bed reading, all snug and cozy, no practices, no lessons, nothing to do but turn the pages, stretch a little from time to time, listen to passing planes high above, like bowling balls in heaven. Sunday morning: why couldn't there be one or two more scattered through the week? What use was Tuesday morning, for example? Monday mornings—the very worst—wouldn't suck so bad if you could look forward to another Sunday morning the very next day. Whoever planned all this out could have done a better job. Throwing in lots of Sunday mornings would be her number one commitment to the American people if she ever ran for president.

Bowling balls in heaven: where Adam was, if you believed in heaven. And if you didn't believe, where was he? Probably better if there was a heaven, but by now, after all these centuries and centuries of dying, it would be very crowded, more packed than the planet Earth itself, with all the problems of crowding—pollution, rudeness, long lines for everything.

Ruby lay in her bed, thinking about heaven as an environmental disaster with a lot of pissed-off people, when it suddenly struck her that although she was indeed lying in her bed and had awakened in it, she had gone to sleep down the hall in Adam's room; and didn't remember coming back. That scared her a little. Was she sleepwalking? Or had Dad found her and carried her back? She got up and went downstairs.

Zippy was slurping out of the toilet in the little bathroom. "Stop it," she called. No more slurping sounds, but she could picture him very well, head raised over the toilet bowl, ear cocked, waiting to see if she'd follow up. Ruby went into the kitchen, heard the faint sound of the next greedy tongueful.

Dad was at the stove. Yes! French toast.

"Morning, sweetheart."

"Hi, Dad."

"How does French toast sound?"

"Yummy."

"Have a good sleep?"

"Uh."

"Uh? What's that?"

"Good, yeah. And you?"

"Me?"

"Did you have a good sleep, Dad?"

"Pretty good."

"Solid?"

"What do you mean by solid?"

"You know, slept like a baby, right through, no getting up and wandering around or anything."

Dad turned to her, spatula raised. He was using that walnut bread with the scallions, her absolute favorite for French toast. "What are you getting at, Ruby?"

Complete bafflement on his face, like when the bad guy blows the safe and there's nothing inside. Since Mom probably wasn't strong enough to carry her and would have sent Dad anyway, that meant she'd been sleepwalking. "Nothing, Dad. Just polite chitchat, back and forth."

He looked like he was going to say something else, but then sizzling came from the pan and he turned his attention to that. "How hungry are you?"

"Hungry."

"Two slices or three?"

"Three," Ruby said. She set the table for the two of them, put out the maple syrup and the sugar and cream for Dad's coffee. Sleepwalking could be a sign of emotional problems, she knew that from "Dear Abby." Could you have emotional problems and be happy at the same time? She was at the point of asking Dad when he suddenly said, "Shit," making her jump, and shook his thumb in the air.

"You okay, Dad?"

"Yeah, sorry."

"That's all right." She sat down at her place, poured OJ for both of them, waited while he finished cooking. When just waiting got boring, which was pretty quick, she picked up a crayon lying on the table and began writing a poem on her napkin. First the title:

Golden Lanes

Then what? How about something like this?

How's the bowling up there, Adam?
Are you knocking down those pearly pins?
Racking up those strikes and

"Hey, Dad, what's that thing in bowling where you knock them all down in two balls?"
"Spares."

spares?

Sure must be getting good by now
With God to show you all the tricks
In three persons, blessed trinity.
You can show me too someday
And how to eat like the gods,
heavenly hot dogs, sacred Sprite, etc.,
While we tote up our scores,
Fun forever
All together
But not too soon.

"What are you writing?" Dad said.

He was at the table, French toast on both their plates, stirring his coffee. Breakfast underway: somehow she'd missed the start.

"Oh, nothing," Ruby said, and placed her napkin on her lap, as all well-bred young ladies did. She poured a nice little pool of maple syrup on her French toast, watched it flow over the golden-brown cliffs in a waterfall of thick amber.

"Hey. Easy on the syrup."

"Oops."

She sliced off a corner of the top piece, dipped it, soaked it—"What's that word where something's full of a liquid?"

"Full of a liquid? I'm not sure."

"And any more, it just rains out?"

"Saturated?"

"Yeah." Saturated that walnut-scallion French toast in maple syrup, genuine grade A amber from Vermont, none of that sneaky ungenuine crap that left out the key word—*maple*—and took that first bite.

Dad was watching her. "How is it?"

"The best you've ever done."

He gave her a big smile. It really was great. Her mouth was in heaven. Heaven popping up again. Right then, she got an idea for another poem. In fact, the whole thing—maple tree, farmer, cross—appeared in her mind, all at once. All she had to do was write it down later. Or get someone else to do it while she reclined on something fabulous and munched bonbons. She knew right then that if nothing better came along, she could always be a writer.

"What do you think Brandon's going to be when he grows up, Dad?"

Dad put his coffee down. Uh-oh. He looked kind of grim all of a sudden. "Is he going to grow up? That's the question."

Major mood change. But why? Then she got it: had to be the curfew. "Brandon's home, right?"

"Oh, yeah."

"On time?" Ruby said.

"Not exactly."

"How late?"

"There was a little more to it than that," Dad said. He sighed, put his elbows on the table, made a frame with his hands, rested his chin on it.

Speed it up a little, Dad. Ruby kept that one to herself.

"This time the police were involved," Dad said when he finally took up the story.

"How?"

"A bunch of them were drinking in the woods, I guess it got noisy, and someone called the cops. Brandon was pulled in for underage drinking."

"Like behind bars?"

"No. And there are no charges or anything."

"This time," Ruby said.

He gave her a look, sat up straight. "Right."

Questions popped up all over the place in her mind, lots of them, like flowers blooming in one of those time-lapse documentaries. She dealt with them in no particular order.

"What were they drinking?"

"I don't know. Beer, probably."

"Did Dewey get busted too?"

"I don't know. They were asking Brandon about Dewey, in fact."

"Asking him what?"

"If he knew him."

"He denied it?"

"How did you know that?"

From your tone of voice. "Just a guess," Ruby said. "Who dropped the dime?"

"What dime?"

"For God's sake, Dad, don't you know the lingo that goes with this? Who called the police?"

"Oh. They don't give that out."

"But it's pretty obvious."

Dad nodded.

"Mr. Stromboli," Ruby said. She used her deepest voice, the voice of doom. *Stromboli* sounded pretty scary that way. "Maybe we should throw a stink bomb down his chimney."

"That's a joke, right?"

"Except there's a problem."

"With throwing stink bombs? Damn straight there's a problem. I don't ever—"

"The problem, Dad, is how did the Strombolis hear the noise from their place?"

"Why not?"

"What time was this?"

"I don't know, exactly. Between midnight and twelve-thirty, maybe."

"Were you asleep then?"

Dad seemed to have to think about that for some reason, and it didn't make him happy. "I was awake."

"Did you hear any noise?"

"No."

"And we're closer to the woods than the Strombolis."

"So it couldn't have been them—is that what you're saying?"

"Not necessarily," said Ruby. "Mr. Stromboli could have been out walking, maybe even walking in the woods himself."

"Why would he do that?"

"He's a weirdo, Dad. You know that."

Dad sipped his coffee. "We'll never know," he said. "Anyway, it's beside the issue."

"What's the issue?"

"Brandon screwing up." He gazed at her over his coffee cup. "You're not going to do stuff like that, drinking in the woods, are you?"

"Hell, Dad," Ruby said, "I was there last night."

"Very funny," said Dad. "Eat your breakfast."

They ate their breakfast. It was nice and quiet, no sound but those flowers popping open in Ruby's head, out of Dad's hearing.

Getting a stink bomb would not be a problem. If Dewey couldn't lay his hands on a stink bomb, who could? The problem was finding out whether Mr. Stromboli had gone walking in the woods. Normally on a Sunday morning like this, Ruby might have gone back to bed, curled up with *The Complete Sherlock Holmes*, or maybe had a bubble bath with something extra special from the Body Shop, listening to CDs on the bathtub player. Today she got dressed, put on her blue jacket with the yellow trim, her yellow mittens and her blue hat with the yellow tassel: a perfect outfit. She stuck her magnifying glass in her pocket, clipped Zippy to his leash, and went outside.

Not too cold. Could she see her breath? Yes. Could she

see Zippy's breath? No. Why was that? "Are you breathing, Zippy?" He lifted his leg and peed right there, on their own front steps. "Zippy!" She tugged him away. He kept peeing, three legs dragging, one still raised, leaving a wiggly yellow line in the snow.

It all depended on the snow, of course, she knew that already. When was the last time it snowed? She couldn't remember. She could be so dumb sometimes. *Are you awake in there, Rubester?* She could see it wasn't fresh, anyway. There were lots of footprints in their yard, including hers, the smallest, and these over here, bigger, deeper, most likely . . . She knelt, took out her magnifying glass, examined the corrugated ridges of the sole, so detailed under the glass, could even spot two words, faint and backward in the snow: *Dr. Martens*. Brandon, as she'd thought.

She crossed the street. "Down, Zippy." Very few tracks over at the Strombolis': not a surprise, the Strombolis didn't do a whole lot of playing in the snow, probably went in and out through the garage most of the time, in the car. There was just one set, in fact, huge footprints leading from halfway down the shoveled walk across the front lawn to a ring-shaped depression in the snow, and on to the driveway. She'd seen a ring-shaped depression like that before, in her own yard. And it would be? Yes, the mark left by a trash can lid on garbage day, when the trash guys zoomed off in that wild way of theirs, scattering trash cans and lids behind them. The trash guys were great. One year Dad left them a case of Bud for Christmas; they'd started popping them open on the spot, trash cans all over the street that day, except for theirs, neatly stacked. The special treatment had lasted for at least two weeks.

So last trash pickup day, Mr. Stromboli had come out the front door, cut across the lawn, picked up the lid, muttering *goddamn fucking trash guys* and stuff like that, taken it into the garage. Ruby stepped into their yard. Zippy growled. "Be good," she said, keeping her voice down and looping the leash hard around her wrist.

Ruby took out the magnifying glass, bent over, watched an unmarred print swim into view. Mr. Stromboli's feet were enormous. He was one scary dude, no doubt about it. His soles had left funny little square patterns, except at the heels, which were worn and smooth. There was even a tiny groove in the right heel that didn't appear in the left. These prints would be real easy to identify. If she found them in the woods, it would be case closed, definite proof that Mr. Stromboli was the villain, smoke bombs away and damn the torp—

The front door opened. Ruby, down on all fours for some reason—how had that happened?—felt her heart kick into a violent beat. Mrs. Stromboli peered out, wearing a quilted pink housecoat and matching pink slippers with pompoms on the toes. Zippy barked, tried to bolt right at her. Ruby yanked the leash with all her might, stretched full-length in the snow. His bark ended in a high-pitched sound like a car jamming on the brakes.

"Is there a problem?" said Mrs. Stromboli, every feature pointing down.

"Just doing some detective work," said Ruby, getting up, brushing snow off her face; some had already got down her neck. She held up the magnifying glass.

"What are you looking for?" said Mrs. Stromboli.

"The blue carbuncle," said Ruby.

Mrs. Stromboli smiled. A stunning development. "You have to look inside a goose for that, if I remember."

Ruby smiled back, her cutest smile. "I'm just pretending," she said, not quite a lisp, but close.

"You go on and pretend," said Mrs. Stromboli. "Long as you don't mind the cold."

"Oh, no," said Ruby. "I had such a good sleep last night." Not a very smooth cut to the chase, but nothing better came to mind.

"That's nice, dear."

"It was so quiet and peaceful, don't you think, Mrs. Stromboli? But especially quiet."

"I really didn't notice."

"No? So you didn't think it was maybe a bit noisy?"

"Noisy?"

"Yeah. One of those noisy kind of nights."

Mrs. Stromboli looked puzzled. "We live in a fairly quiet neighborhood, don't you think?"

"Except for us, right?"

Mrs. Stromboli laughed. "Mr. Stromboli's bark is worse than his bite."

What about when he tried to murder Zippy with the golf club? "So it was a quiet night for you and Mr. Stromboli?"

Mrs. Stromboli blinked. Then she blushed a little. "Is this part of your detective work?"

Ruby nodded. "My method is founded on the observance of trifles."

"Then yes," said Mrs. Stromboli. "We had a quiet night. Fell asleep watching the news, as usual, without seeing hide nor hair of the blue carbuncle."

"What time was the news, Mrs. Stromboli?"

"We always watch the ten o'clock on channel fifty-six. Do you need to know what was on? There was a fire in Hartford, if I remember, and—"

"That's all right, Mrs. Stromboli. You've been very helpful."

"Anytime," said Mrs. Stromboli. "Hope you find it."

"We'll do our best."

"I get it. Your dog's Dr. Watson."

A great idea, but Ruby didn't have time to dwell on the possibilities, getting Zippy one of those deerstalker hats, for example. She had to focus on the problem: if not Mr. Stromboli, who?

The real Dr. Watson, on his very dumbest day, would have had no trouble identifying the scene of the party in the woods. All around the far side of the pond lay empty bottles, beer cans, cigarette butts, pizza boxes, candy wrappers, and footprints on footprints, down to the mud under the snow. There was even a beer keg, abandoned, Ruby supposed, when the kids ran away, still dripping slowly from its hose. Zippy found a slice of thick-crust sausage and pepperoni, gobbled it up.

"How the hell," she said, watching him sniff in the snow for more, "are we going to find what we're looking for in all this?"

A huge man stepped from behind the big rock. He wore a navy blue jacket with a silver badge on the front and three stripes on the arm. "Depends what you're looking for, little lady."

Was that what a heart attack felt like, when your heart sprang up and tried to escape through your mouth? "Zippy lost his toy in here the other day," she said, backing up, her voice real squeaky, kind of like Amanda's.

"What kind of toy?" said the man.

"A red rubber bone," Ruby said, finally standing her ground; he'd actually had a toy like that at one time. "But now it's all so messy."

"Sure is," said the man. He reached down, picked up a wallet, glanced inside, dropped it in a black bag. Brandon had once lost three wallets in a week.

"Are you a policeman?" Ruby said.

"Yup."

"And the stripes mean you're a sergeant?"

Pause. "You live around here?" he said.

"Yeah," said Ruby, waving vaguely, and in the wrong direction.

"What's your name?"

"Ruby."

"Ruby what?"

"Ruby the Kid."

He started to smile; didn't actually smile, but his eyes looked like he was thinking about it. "Like Billy the Kid?" he said.

"But deadlier."

Now he smiled. "I'm Sergeant D'Amario."

"Nice to meet you, Sergeant D'Amario. Are you supposed to clean this up? If you've got another bag, I can help."

"That's real nice of you," said Sergeant D'Amario, "but I'm not cleaning up. The DPW takes care of that. This is an evidence bag."

"Was there a crime here?"

"Yup."

"Littering?"

"That too. But we rounded up a bunch of kids for underage drinking last night. Not kids like you, Ruby the Kid."

"You work hard, huh?"

"How's that?"

"Patrolling the woods on cold nights and everything."

"Not here," he said. "We don't do that."

"Then how did you know about the drinking?"

"We got a call from someone complaining. An anonymous call, which is usually the way it is."

"Anonymous?" said Ruby.

"Just a big word that means they don't leave their name."

That's not what I'm getting at, for God's sake. "But don't you have caller ID down at the station?"

"You going to be a detective one day?"

Was that better than a writer? Probably. "Maybe," said Ruby.

"We identify every incoming call, of course. This one happened to come from a pay phone."

"Oh."

"Can you figure out what must have happened?"

"No."

"Some neighbor, bothered by the noise but not wanting to be identified, drove down to the pay phone by the Shell and—"

"Dropped the dime."

"Bingo."

"People don't want trouble."

"No, sir. Are the kids in jail?"

"We don't put kids in jail for that. We just send them home with their parents."

"That's nice of you," said Ruby. "What evidence are you looking for, then?"

He gazed down at her. "Know what crack is, Ruby?"

"A very dangerous kind of cocaine that comes in these little vials and you smoke in a pipe."

"You pay attention in health class."

"Just say no."

"Then I don't have to tell you that crack's a serious matter, not at all the same as a little beer drinking in the woods, you see what I mean."

"The kids were smoking crack?" Brandon: her heart sank.

"We don't know that. But we're hearing stories that someone at the high school's been driving down to Bridgeport and bringing back crack. We'd like to find that someone, meaning find him with the goods."

Someone with a Fuck You You Fuckin Fuck bumper sticker, all of a sudden not so funny, especially if Brandon was in the passenger seat. She watched Zippy digging for pizza. He found something else instead. Ruby sidled over and stepped on it, very casual. Zippy pawed at her foot.

"What's he want?" said Sergeant D'Amario.

"Pizza," said Ruby.

"Here's some," he said, moving toward one of the logs by the edge of the pond. Ruby bent down real quick, snatched the crack pipe under her foot, jammed it in her pocket. Sergeant D'Amario came back with a pizza box, almost full. "How much can he have?"

"Just a slice, thanks," said Ruby. "He's on a diet."

Sergeant D'Amario fed Zippy a slice of pizza, the Hawaiian kind with pineapple and ham. Zippy wagged his tail. Sergeant D'Amario patted him. "Where's his tag?"

"Oops," said Ruby. "Are you going to throw me in the hoosegow?"

"Next time," said Sergeant D'Amario.

Ruby walked home, starting in the wrong direction, down the cart path, past Sergeant D'Amario's squad car, then doubling back. The crack pipe was like a pulsing, living thing in her pocket. She dropped it down a big knot in an old rotten tree trunk.

Almost out of the woods, where the trees started thinning out and the back of the house came into view, she spotted the tracks of a fat-tired bike in the snow. Must have been made by Julian, on his way home after the birthday party. There were no birds at the feeder. She ran the rest of the way. Zippy liked that: he thought they were having fun. She slapped that rabies tag on him the moment they got home. No way Sergeant D'Amario was taking Zippy down.

18

Back in the kitchen, Dad was on the phone.

"Sure I'm sure," he was saying. "It's only a game, right? So why take it too seriously?" He listened for a moment. If he wasn't taking whatever it was so seriously, why was his body so rigid? Ruby smelled some horrible perfume, which meant the Sunday magazine was nearby. Then Dad said, "Okay, Tom. See you at four."

"What's only a game?" Ruby said.

"Tennis."

A lousy, stupid game. "Now that you mention it," Ruby said, "I'm thinking of maybe easing up on tennis."

"Easing up?"

"Cutting back. Like maybe to a tennis-free situation."

"Dropping tennis? Is that what you're suggesting?"

"Makes sense, doesn't it, Dad?"

"I don't see how. You've only got two sports as it is,

and that's counting archery as a sport. When Brandon was your age he was playing something every season, soccer, tennis, baseball . . . he even had basketball in there at one point."

And now he's a jailbird. Ruby tried to use her X-ray vision to plant that connection—sports and legal trouble, which should have been obvious just from watching *Sports-Center*—in Dad's mind. She was able to create an area of intense pressure in the part of her brain just above the eyes.

"Why are you looking like that?" Dad said. "Are you okay?"

But obviously nothing got through.

"I'll stick with it a little longer."

"Good girl."

Ruby went upstairs to Brandon's room. She knocked on the door. No answer. She knocked again, harder, still heard nothing from inside. She turned the knob and quietly opened the door.

Brandon's room was dark and smelled like a men's locker room. Ruby had never been in a men's locker room and hoped to stay that way forever, but she knew this was the smell. That whole argument between the evolution people and the creation people? All you had to do was smell that smell to understand that Darwin was right: we come from the animals. At least men did. Hey! Maybe both sides were half right, men evolved, women were created; and she was a little angel.

"Brandon? You awake?"

Silence. Her eyes adjusted to the murk. She saw piles of this and that, Brandon's trophies gleaming dully on a shelf, the only orderly arrangement in the room, and a new poster over the bed, with Problem peering at her over Unka Death's shoulder. She realized that Problem had been in *That Thang Thing*, her birthday movie, playing the role of the voodoo king. Brandon was fast asleep, the covers up to his chin, looking surprisingly young, younger, she thought, than her.

"Brandon?" She gave him a little pat on the shoulder.

He said something, all thick and full of mucus. It might have been, "Five more minutes."

"You can sleep all day if you want, Brandon. It's Sunday."

His eyes opened, or one did, the less gummy eye. "Then why are you bothering me?"

"We need to have a little talk."

"Huh?"

"Are you going to be speaking to Dewey today?"

"What's it to you?"

"That's a cool poster."

"What's wrong with you? I'm sleeping."

"Problem was in *That Thang Thing*."

"Duh. Who do you think produced it, dumbass?"

"Problem?"

"You don't know anything, do you? Unka Death produced it. He's got a movie deal with Paramount."

"I know one thing," Ruby said. "It's time for Dewey to go to New York and start that bicycle messenger job."

"What the fuck?"

"Sergeant D'Amario—did you meet him last night?—knows that Dewey's selling crack."

The other eye opened. "Bullshit," Brandon said, sounding wide awake at last.

"What's bullshit?"

"Dewey's not selling crack."

"Sergeant D'Amario thinks otherwise."

"How do you know what Sergeant fucking D'Amario thinks?"

"He told me. I was walking Zippy in the woods and he was examining the scene of the crime. We got to talking."

Brandon gave her one of those mean looks. "You're weird, you know that?"

"At least I'm not a crackhead."

"What the fuck are you talking about?"

"You're not smoking crack, are you, Bran?"

"Keep your voice down," he said, glancing at the door. Ruby went and closed it. Brandon sat up, groaned, like his head hurt all of a sudden. "Do Mom and Dad know about this?"

"No," Ruby said, and just to get him to stop talking so mean to her, added, "not yet."

"Not yet? What the fuck—" She gave him a warning look. "What do you mean, not yet?"

"Some older brothers are nice to their little sisters."

"Who? Name one."

"Peter."

"Peter? We don't know anybody named Peter."

"In *The Chronicles of Narnia*," Ruby said.

He gazed at her, not mean this time, just looking. "Do you have any friends?" he said.

"You know I have friends." But all of a sudden, she wondered. She silently named all the kids who'd been to her party, added a few more, but the wondering didn't stop.

"You won't if you keep on like this," Brandon said.

"Keep on like what?"

He didn't say anything, just shook his head.

That pissed her off. A whole flood of being pissed off surged through her; she didn't remember ever feeling quite like this, angry. "I'm just trying to help you," she said, real loud, aware that he was trying to shush her but refusing to be shushed. "If you are smoking crack you're a jerk because first it's bad for you and second Sergeant D'Amario doesn't want it in West Mill and he's ten times smarter than you and Dewey put together."

He went to grab her or take a swing at her, but she jumped back. Then he did something that made up for a lot. He glanced at his hand, still raised, and tucked it down under the covers, like something to be ashamed of. "All right, all right," he said. "I'm not smoking crack. Just keep your voice down."

"And another thing," she said, lowering it a little. "I bet you lost your wallet last night."

"Huh?"

"Sergeant D'Amario found one that looks just like yours. Your temporary license is in there, isn't it?"

"Shit," said Brandon. "Do me a favor. Go down and check my jacket pocket, see if it's there."

Ruby left Brandon's room. Mom, her face and neck plastered with that green rejuvenator stuff, saw her from the top of the stairs. She smiled. "You and Bran having a little time together?" she said.

"Yup," said Ruby, the way Sergeant D'Amario did, giving away nothing.

"That's nice."

Ruby went down to the mudroom. Brandon's jacket hung on its peg. She realized she now had two mysteries to solve: The Mystery of the Varsity Jacket and The Mystery of the Anonymous Caller. Her caseload was getting out of hand.

She reached in the nearest pocket, took out Brandon's wallet. False alarm. Then she reached in the other pocket, just because. Her hand closed around a little vial. She left it there, didn't even pull it out to look.

So many characters to keep track of: Julian had never understood the responsibility that weighed on the shoulders of the auteur. He had to encompass all his people, their strengths and weaknesses, hopes and fears, habits, desires, casts of mind, all within his head. As he ate a working Sunday brunch at his desk—coffee, plain yogurt, toast with strawberry jam, an excellent deep red jam with whole berries, imported from France—he felt sincere admiration for masters like Tolstoy and Dickens, so adept at riding herd on vast swarms of characters. On the other hand, had either of them created a new form? He felt a little thrill, the auteur of *At Home*, a complex tale with a deceptively domestic setting; a work-in-progress.

Through his window upstairs in the carriage house, Julian saw cars coming up the long lane. They parked in front of the big house and women got out. Ah. The J. P. Morganettes. He watched them going inside, some actually moving with what they must have considered a certain style; but *herd* could not have been more apt.

Julian gazed at the blank page marked *Ruby*, tried to get back to work. His concentration, the sine qua non of the artist, had been broken. Not his fault: these bourgeois sightings could be so disturbing. Suddenly he couldn't sit still, felt the need for action, understood how even a lesser artist like Hemingway had swung back and forth between his work and outdoor pursuits.

But what action? He could think of only one possibility, earlier rejected as clumsy and therefore risky as well. Now, a way to give clumsiness grace suddenly presented itself, as needed, and he phoned the tennis club.

"Checking the court time for Gardner, please?" he said.

Rustle, rustle. "Four o'clock."

A good match time. Scott's hangover, if any, would have cleared by then.

Julian called the house at 37 Robin Road.

"Hello," said Brandon.

"Hi, Bran. Julian here."

"Oh, hi, Julian."

"How're you doing?"

"Not bad."

Julian laughed. "Sounds like you had a rough night."

"Sort of."

"Don't worry. I'll never tell."

Brandon laughed.

"Your dad there by any chance? I just wanted to check the schedule."

"He's gone to play tennis. And I think Mom's in the bath."

"Another time, then. And Bran?"

"Yeah?"

"Nothing beats a Bloody Mary for what you've got, but you didn't hear it from me."

Brandon laughed again. Julian heard a tiny interruption in the line. "Got another call here," Brandon said.

"**R**uby?" Brandon called. "Gram's on the phone."

Ruby took it. "Hi, Gram."

She heard Gram coughing on the other end, one of those smoking coughs. "Well, this is a special day, isn't it dear?"

"It is?" said Ruby.

"Why, your birthday!" said Gram. "What could be more special than that? Ten years old, my, my."

"Eleven," Ruby said. She didn't bother about the wrong day—it was hopeless—but she wasn't going to be treated like some baby.

"Eleven, is it?" said Gram, and started coughing again.

You said *bless you* when someone sneezed, but what about for coughing? *Had a chest X-ray lately?* Something like that?

Gram stopped coughing. There was a little silence. She could say, *How's Arizona?* and Gram would say, *Hot.* Then she could say, *How're you hittin' them?* and Gram would say, *No more tennis for me, dear. Just golf now, and only nine holes, at the end of the day when it's not quite so unbearable.*

Ruby said: "How's Arizona?" This was her grand-mother. They should talk about something.

"Hot."

"How're you hittin' them?"

Pause. "I don't play tennis anymore. On account of this horrible arthritis. I thought I mentioned that when we spoke at Christmas."

"At least there's golf," Ruby said.

"That's gone too," said Gram. "Money okay for your present? There's nothing in the stores."

"Money's great," Ruby said. "Thanks, Gram."

"Bye, dear."

Nothing in the stores? What did that mean? "What's

Arizona like?" Ruby said. Brandon had been there one summer for tennis camp.

"Hot," Brandon said. Some genetic connection. He left the room, a tall glass of tomato juice in his hand, ice cubes clinking softly.

From a table by the glass window in the upstairs bar, Julian had a good view of the match. It went as he had expected. The brothers shook hands. Scott was trying to restrain his smile, not successfully. He was babbling something, patting his brother's shoulder, shaking his head with false modesty, beaming. Tom was being good about it. Perhaps the years of domination had been a burden for him too; in which case, the older brother didn't have it either.

Julian had a sudden craving for strawberry jam. He went to the bar, ordered a Bloody Mary, took it back to his table along with a dish of honey-roasted peanuts. The honey part took the edge off his craving, but only a little. He was recalling the way Gail Bender's bat had gazed up at him with its dark eyes when the brothers walked into the bar. His thoughts went to the to-do list, Scott subsection: *friendly discussion of investment strategy, esp, options trading; find out more about family insurance firm; does Tom have children*? There weren't many people in the bar and Scott spotted him right away, surprised, then delighted, then conspiratorial, or at least showing awareness that there might be a sudden need for conspiracy: exactly the type of reaction that was going to make the creation of the living epic novel so gratifying. Julian gave him a wave, friendly-like.

"Hey, Julian," said Scott. He felt like jumping up and down with happiness and relief, so light on his feet, light all over, as if he might rise and float around for a while. "What're you doing here?"

"Just happened by."

"Julian, my brother, Tom. Tom, Julian."

They shook hands.

"You a tennis player, Julian?" Tom said. Tom had an expression on his face Scott had never seen there before, kind of stunned. He gave Tom a little pat on the back. The muscles in there were like stone.

"Thinking of getting back into it," Julian said. "I'm checking out some of the local clubs. You gentlemen care to join me?"

"Good idea," Scott said. "Something to drink, Tom?"

"Water," said Tom.

Scott went to the bar, ordered a bottle of water and a draft.

"Half pint or full?" said the bartender.

"Full."

He carried the drinks back to the table. Tom was saying, ". . . just one, a sophomore at Andover."

"Talking about Sam?" Scott said. "You should see him play, Julian," he added, swept forward on a sudden tide of magnanimity.

"I'd like to," said Julian. "My father was captain of the team."

"At Andover?" said Tom. "When was this?"

"In the wood racquet era," said Julian.

"Hey," Scott said. "How come you never mentioned that before?"

"It's not the kind of thing that comes up often," said Julian. He turned to Tom. "Does your son plan to play in college?"

Tom nodded. "The Harvard coach called yesterday, in fact."

"He did?" Scott said, glass halfway to his lips.

"Mostly to badmouth Stanford," Tom said. "It wasn't his finest moment." Tom sipped his water. "You an alum too, Julian?"

"Negative."

This was the place to say something about Julian helping out with Brandon's academics, but Scott would be damned if he did.

Tom rose. "Got to drive him back up there, in fact," he said. "Nice meeting you, Julian. Thanks for the game, Scott." And left. The water trembled a bit in his almost-full bottle, still on the table. The magnanimity tide turned, or at least stopped flowing.

"I have a confession to make," Julian said. "I didn't just happen by. I called your house about the schedule and Brandon mentioned you were playing tennis. I couldn't resist."

"Yeah?" Everything was suddenly more comfortable, just the two of them at the table. "I appreciate that."

"Honey-roasted peanuts?" Julian said, sliding the bowl across the table.

No magnanimity, but the core of his happiness was intact. Scott ate a few peanuts, took a big swallow of beer, heaved a sigh that would have been a blob of thick black tangles if sighs were visible. Julian was watching him, eyebrows raised. "Seven-five, six-two," Scott said. *I won, I won, I won.*

Julian smiled, a smile of genuine pleasure, Scott could tell. *I'm making a new friend,* he thought, and said, "I can't thank you enough."

"Sure you can," said Julian. He laughed. Scott laughed too. They high-fived.

"Another Bloody?" said Scott.

"To mark the occasion."

Scott went to the bar, brought back two more drinks. "It went just like you said, Julian. Like we were following a script or something."

"Very gratifying," said Julian. "But I'm sure you would have come upon the same strategy eventually."

That was a thought. Scott considered it. Julian was probably right. "Still," he said, "this saved me a lot of time."

Julian's eyes changed a little, like when clouds go by and the ocean changes tone. "Happy to be of service," he said.

"Thanks," said Scott. He took another drink. "Whoo. I feel great."

"Your brother seemed to take it well."

"He's got his code of behavior."

"Doesn't everyone?"

"Oh, sure," said Scott. "I meant he's more of a gentleman from the old school."

"In what way?"

"Good question." Scott put down his beer, leaned forward a little. "Here's an example. Remember I was telling you about options, securities options?"

"Vaguely," Julian said.

"I guess it's all pretty boring if you're not a business type. Your father really went to Andover?"

Julian went pale. What was this? "I don't understand your question," he said.

"I was just surprised, that's all."

"You think I would make something like that up? To impress your brother?"

"No, no," Scott said, suddenly realizing that Julian was from the old school too, had some honorable code of his own. "No offense intended. Sorry, Julian."

Julian gazed at him for a moment. "No problem," he said. "Maybe it is a little hard to believe, with me being a mere tutor."

"Hey," said Scott. "Don't talk like that. No one would call you mere."

"Very kind of you, Scott. You were telling me about options."

"This is more about short selling, actually." Scott took another swallow. Beer and tennis—winning tennis—went together so well. "Have you met Ruby's friend Kyla?"

"No."

"Her father's a broker. He's a bit sleazy maybe, but that doesn't change the fact that he gets good information sometimes. Tom can't do business with anyone he wouldn't have over for dinner. I'm not like that."

"Of course not."

"It's a whole new world."

"You said it. What's this broker's name?"

"Mickey Gudukas."

"That was probably the end for Tom right there," said Julian.

Scott laughed. "Exactly." He told Julian the Symptomatica story—Gudukas's tip, the margin requirement, Tom's refusal to involve the business, mass death of the chimps, Boxster.

"Now I understand," said Julian. "About leveraging a Boxster out of spare change. What an amusing way of putting it."

"Thanks," said Scott.

"But what I don't understand—none of my business, of course—"

"Go on."

"—is why you didn't put up some other capital."

"There isn't any. Not in the amount I needed. You can't touch retirement accounts for that kind of thing, and as for the house . . ."

"Not valuable enough?" Julian popped a honey-roasted peanut in his mouth.

"It's valuable enough," Scott said, "even with the mortgage."

Julian stopped chewing, looked puzzled. *What the hell,* Scott thought, *it's not a state secret.* "The problem is the house is jointly owned, me and Linda."

"And that precludes this type of arrangement?"

"Not in a legal sense. It's just that Linda never would have approved."

"Ah."

19

When Ruby went downstairs Monday morning, Mom and Dad were already gone. Brandon sat at the table, eating a bowl of Mango Almond Crunch. He had gel in his hair, like some cool guy in the Abercrombie catalog. Did he have a secret girlfriend?

"Hey, Bran."

"Hey."

"Any more of that left?"

"Finished it."

Ruby got a bagel from the fridge, sliced it, dropped the halves in the toaster. "I'm making hot chocolate," she said.

"So?"

"Want some?"

"Yeah." *Slurp slurp, crunch crunch.* "Thanks."

Ruby made hot chocolate in a pot, using milk instead of water, and whole milk at that. Hot chocolate meant going all the way. She brought two steaming mugs to the table, sat down across from him. They sipped their hot chocolate.

"Good, huh?" said Ruby.

"Yeah."

She spread cream cheese on the bagel halves, generously, like in a restaurant where the customer was always right. "How many jackets have you got, Bran?"

He screwed up his face. She wished he wouldn't do that. Winston, dumbest kid on the bus and eater of nose pick, did the same thing, and Brandon wasn't dumb. "What are you talking about?"

"Your West Mill jacket, Bran, for being on the varsity—how many have you got?"

"One. What's wrong with you? No one has more than one. You just sew on the crests for every sport and add a bar for every year."

"Where are you going to be on the ladder this year?"

"I don't know."

"Number one?"

"What difference does it make to you?"

She ate more bagel, sipped her hot chocolate. His bowl of Mango Almond Crunch was huge; he must have poured half the box in there.

"Got a theory on what happened to that jacket, Bran?"

"What the hell kind of a question is that?"

Oops. Was he thinking crack vial in the pocket? "Remember that night you came home late and kept Julian waiting? You told Mom you'd left your jacket at school, but it was hanging on the peg."

"So?"

"So what do you think happened?"

"What do you mean, what happened? I forgot where I left it. You never forget anything, Miss Suck-up?"

She gave him a look, an X-ray look that said, *Keep it up, buddy boy, and that crack vial is on the six o'clock news.*

"What's that stupid look supposed to mean?" She kept it on him, pinning him to his chair. "All right, you're not Miss Suck-up."

"Apology accepted," Ruby said, even though he might have muttered something about Ms. Suck-up. She took another bite of bagel, toasty crispiness plus creamy cream cheese, like the perfect married couple. "The problem is that when I got home from school that day, it wasn't there."

"What wasn't where?"

"Your jacket. On the peg. I always look to see who's home."

"You must have made a mistake."

"Nope," Ruby said. "I remember."

"So you remember. What's your point?"

"My point is that one link can give you the whole chain."

"What are you talking about?"

"When was the last time you had your jacket before then, that's what I want to know."

"Why, for fuck sake?" But he didn't say it in an angry way, and his eyes shifted to one side, like he was thinking or remembering: some mental activity, thank God.

"I just told you—one link can—"

The side door, the one that led to the garage, opened and Dewey came in. Gel in his hair, too. "Hey," he said.

"Hey," said Brandon.

"You set?" said Dewey.

"Yup," said Brandon, vacuuming up the last of the Mango Almond Crunch.

"Hi, Dewey," Ruby said.

"Hey, Ruby, how's it goin'?"

"Great. Want some bagel?"

"Thanks." He took half. The Darwin thing was so obvious. Men had hardly evolved at all, were still pretty much neck-and-neck with the apes, except that some of them—not all by any means, as a visit to the beach always proved so shockingly—had lost their fur.

Brandon grabbed his books and they headed for the door.

"Try to remember, Bran," Ruby said.

"Remember what?" said Dewey.

"Don't pay any attention to her," said Bran.

"The jacket," Ruby said, pretty loud. The door slammed in response.

Ruby ate what was left of her bagel, started braiding her hair—a prim and proper crossover called Little Scarlett. Then a big surprise. Zippy came trotting over for a pat. He never did that, wasn't the kind of affectionate dog other people seemed to have, more a different kind of dog with his own agenda.

"Zippy, you cutie pie," she said, bending down to give him a big kiss. He gave her a big one back, if a lick up and down the face with his wet and scratchy tongue was a kiss, and Ruby knew it was. "I love you, Zippy," she said. He wagged his tail. "And you love me, too." The moment her back was turned, he got his nose in the cream cheese container. Didn't mean he didn't love her, though. Everybody had to eat. That thought led her right over the edge of a cliff: everybody had to eat, the Aztecs ate people, she'd forgotten all about her social studies homework, a worksheet on Cortés.

Why did the Spanish treat the Aztecs so badly? That was the assignment. She had almost three inches to fill on the bad treatment question and Ms. Freleng was a stickler for filling those inches. Ruby started writing, big fat letters: *The Spanish, who are sometimes called the Conquistadors, which means "conquerors" in their native language of Spanish, sailed all the way across the mighty Atlantic Ocean from Spain to the New World, which was new to them but not to the Aztecs, who had been living there for some time, practicing the art of human sacrifice in peace and quiet. All that peace and quiet was gone with the wind when the Spanish, arriving in their ships, sailing ships because this was long before the days of motor boats* . . . and soon the three inches were packed nice and full. There was a bonus question: *What is plantain?* Ruby wrote: *Funny banana.* Homework done.

She glanced at the clock: and suddenly it was panic time. Two minutes. Mr. V. was never late, never early. He always said Mussolini made the trains run on time, whatever that meant. She could almost feel the school bus rolling down Robin Road, *rumble, rumble.* Ruby threw everything together, flung open the front door; and banged it shut just as fast. Coming slowly down the road was a cop car, and at the wheel of the cop car sat Sergeant D'Amario, his eyes on their house. Had he seen her? If he had, the game was up. He could probably arrest her for giving false information to an officer of the law—that waving in the wrong direction when he'd asked where she lived. She stood stock-still in the front hall, hardly breathing, waiting for that knock on the door.

No knock came. After a while, she rose on her tiptoes and took a quick peek through the fan window. The coast was clear. She breathed a sigh of relief, opened the door and looked out. The school bus was just disappearing around the corner. Her backpack slid off her shoulders, mostly by itself.

Missed the bus: a first. And now what? She could walk to school, which would take ages, West Mill Elementary miles away, a mile and a half, anyway; or possibly three-quarters of a mile, she forgot whether Dad had been talking about her school or Brandon's. But ages on foot, whatever the exact distance. Or she could ride her bike. It was cold for bike riding, and she'd never ridden in the winter, but Julian did, so it wasn't impossible.

Ruby went into the garage. Her bike—blue, with yellow streamers dangling from the handlebar grips—hung from a hook on the ceiling, where Dad stored it for the winter. Ruby dragged over the stepladder, climbed to the top step—not the tip-top, which said Danger, Not a Step right on it—from where she could reach about halfway up the frame of the bike. Ruby had no choice but to climb to the tip-top, slow and careful. Now she could reach the handlebars. One two three, lift. And off it came in her hands, but very heavy, and all of a sudden the ladder was gone and she was in midair, like she was performing some amazing bike trick in the X Sports Games. Then crash, an incredible noise, cymbals gone crazy, and she rolled a couple of times on the cold cement floor and came to a stop, completely unhurt. Ruby got up—bounced up—invincible. She put on her backpack, mounted the bike and rode off, returning after a minute or so to close the garage door and start again. Zippy barked like a madman in the house. Invincible; that was pretty cool.

She pedaled down Robin Road in the direction the school bus had gone, turned left onto Indian Ridge. It wasn't too cold at all. This was fun; fun, except she'd forgotten her helmet. Yikes. That was a big rule, like don't talk to strangers. Too late to go back now, but whatever happened she wouldn't talk to any strangers she met on the way to school, wouldn't even look at them, to make up for the helmet violation.

Indian Ridge to Poplar Drive. Poplar Drive turned out to be downhill all the way. Funny she hadn't noticed before. She zoomed, not even pushing the pedals until the road leveled out near the fire station. This was great. Why had she never ridden her bike to school? The bus was history.

But: the fire station? Had the fire station always been on the way to school? She'd gone past the fire station many times of course, but on the bus? No. Or at least not that she could recall. Had she taken a wrong turn somewhere? She hadn't turned at all, was still on Poplar Drive, right? Ruby came to the next intersection, checked the street sign: Central Avenue. And the other street was Main. What was going on? Ruby had the strong feeling that the school was over there somewhere. She turned right on Main, pedaling faster to make up for lost time. Huff and puff, huff and puff, pedal pedal pedal, then *bumpity bump. Bumpity bump*—she'd gone over the railroad tracks, hadn't even seen them coming. The railroad tracks were nowhere near West Mill Elementary, she was almost sure of that. She felt her lower lip quiver.

Hey! None of that. Eleven years old, and you're not lost or anything—you're in your hometown, for God's sake, born and bred, like a native tracker. For example, here was the Shell station, always the most expensive gas in West Mill, according to Dad. And they had a pay phone, just outside the office. Did she know Dad's work number? No. Mom's? No. They were written down on the blackboard in the kitchen with the new area codes, but she didn't know them by heart. Ruby rode into the station, got off the bike, leaned it against the glass window of the office.

Then it hit her: the pay phone! She was looking at the very pay phone where the anonymous caller had dropped the dime on Brandon and his friends, Saturday night. Case number two: The Mystery of the Anonymous Caller.

Ruby went inside, nice and warm. A guy in a Shell uniform that said Manny on the front was at the cash register, counting money. His fingers were huge and greasy, his oily fingernails surprisingly long. Ruby would have kept hers short if she was involved in garage work.

He looked up. "Something I can do for you?"

She'd meant to say, *Can you give me directions to West Mill Elementary, please?* But what came out was: "What time do you close on Saturday night?"

Manny blinked. "Say again?"

Ruby said it again.

"You taking a survey?" said Manny.

Good idea, thanks Manny. "Yeah. For school. I got the gas stations." Oops. How was she going to get to asking directions to the school from this little corner she'd backed herself into?

"Close at nine on Saturdays," said Manny. "Except on holidays. You need to know the holiday times?"

"No," said Ruby. "So let's say someone came by and used the pay phone around midnight, you wouldn't see him."

"How could I?" said Manny. "I wouldn't be here."

There was another cyclist on the road. He turned into the station and stopped by the air hose, on the far side of the pumps. From out of nowhere came a tremendous idea. "Have you got a security camera?"

Manny went all suspicious. "What's it to you?"

"We're supposed to ask. My teacher's very strict."

Manny pointed a huge blackened finger at a camera on the wall.

Remarkable, my dear fellow. Ruby had no Watson to say it for her, so she had to say it to herself. "Just so I can tie them together," Ruby said, which didn't make sense, even to her, "does the camera take pictures of the pay phone?"

"Nope," said Manny. "We don't own the pay phone."

"Ah," said Ruby.

She thanked Manny and went outside, paused by the pay phone. She began reading the instructions for making different kinds of calls, mostly because it was hard for her not to read if written words were visible. It gave emergency numbers down at the bottom. Police—911. Ruby had never dialed 911 before, but of course the anonymous caller had. He'd picked up the receiver just like this, pressed these three little numbers and—

"Nine one one, recorded line," said a man on the other end, a tough-sounding man, real fast-talking. "What is your emergency?"

Ruby whipped the phone back on the hook, like it might bite any second. Manny was watching her through the window. She gave him an innocent little wave as she got on her bike, but probably not convincing; her mind was elsewhere. Recorded line: that meant one thing and one thing only. The voice of the anonymous caller was on tape, down at the police station; like the camera solution, but a bit more complicated. All she'd have to do, Ruby thought as she rode across the gas station lot, was listen to the tape, then go around the neighborhood striking up conversations with all the neighbors until she heard the same—

"Ruby?"

Ruby turned. The other cyclist, over at the air hose, had called her. Surprise, surprise: it was Julian.

"Julian!" She was real happy to see him. For one thing, she was still lost, not lost, really, but he'd be a big help anyway. He always was.

Julian looked down at her. "No school?" he said. "Or am I missing something?"

"I'm on my way," Ruby said.

Julian checked his watch. "At ten fifteen?"

"Ten fifteen?" How did that happen?

"And I thought the school was on River Drive," Julian said. "The gas station is in the exact wrong direction from your house."

"Maybe it's a little roundabout," Ruby said. "But I'm working on something."

"Oh?"

"A case."

"That sounds interesting."

"The Mystery of the Anonymous Caller."

"I like the title."

"Thanks." She was very pleased. "But this isn't make-believe, Julian. It's a real case."

"God forbid," said Julian.

Ruby laughed. "It's all about the woods, and Brandon and Dewey and Sergeant D'Amario and—"

Julian held up his hand. "Whoa," said Julian. "There's a Starbucks a few blocks down. You can tell me the whole story over a cup of hot chocolate."

"I already had hot chocolate today."

"Another cup won't kill you," Julian said. "Then I'll get you on the right track to school."

Another cup of hot chocolate sounded great, actually, but she didn't want to take advantage of Julian. He probably didn't have much money, a grown-up riding around on a bike all the time. It was only fair to warn him. "I don't have any money on me."

"My treat," Julian said.

20

Ruby realized one thing right away: her hot chocolate was better than Starbucks. Maybe one day she'd go against them, head to head: Ruby's Hot Chocolate Heaven, coast to coast.

"Biscotti?" Julian said.

"Thanks," said Ruby, taking the chocolate-coated one. "How come everything's in Italian here?"

"To justify the price," Julian said.

Ruby laughed. Julian was very funny. She considered dipping her biscotti in the hot chocolate, but maybe it wasn't polite.

"Feel free to dip," Julian said. "I won't tell."

Very funny, and uncanny too. Ruby dipped the chocolate-coated biscotti in the hot chocolate. Bliss.

"Have you ever been to Italy, Julian?"

"Questo è l'inizio della fine."

"That sounds so beautiful," Ruby said. "What does it mean?"

" 'Where is the bargain shopping?' " said Julian. "Loosely translated."

"Which one is shopping?"

"Fine."

"How do you spell it?"

"We'll do some Italian one day," Julian said. "But right now I'm much more interested in The Mystery of the Anonymous Caller."

Julian rubbed his hands, like an eager spectator who couldn't wait for the play to start. "The thing is, Julian, this is going to have to be like the smoke incident."

"Between you and me?"

"Yeah."

He extended his hand. Ruby shook it. Julian's hand was hot, like he had fever, although he looked fine. No wonder he didn't mind riding around on his bike in winter. "Deal," he said.

"Deal," said Ruby. "Guess what happened on Saturday night?"

"Zippy ate the rest of the cake."

Ruby laughed. "He didn't. Must have had an off day. But this is about Brandon. You know the woods?"

"Nicest feature of the whole town."

"They have parties in there, drinking parties. Brandon got busted. Dad had to go bail him out."

"Yikes," said Julian. "I hope there were no charges."

"No charges. But Sergeant D'Amario is doing an investigation."

"An investigation? Of teenagers drinking in the woods?"

"There was a little more to it. But the main thing is that Sergeant D'Amario told me they got an anonymous call. Somebody dropped the dime on Brandon and his friends."

"Your dog-loving friend across the street, no doubt."

"The Strombolis. That's what I thought. But they're in the clear."

"How do you know that?"

"I did a little investigation of my own."

"Meaning Sergeant D'Amario told you?"

"He's a cop, Julian. You get nothing out of him."

Julian stirred his hot chocolate. "How is it you were talking to him in the first place?"

"I was out walking Zippy in the woods. Sergeant D'Amario was hunting for evidence."

"Evidence of what?"

Ruby shrugged. She didn't want to actually lie to Julian, but why go into the whole crack thing, especially when it had nothing to do with the mystery of the anonymous caller, which was about noise, not drugs? "The point is I found a way to solve the mystery."

"Oh?"

Ruby leaned forward. "Get this," she said. It was fun talking to Julian. He understood things right away. "Those anonymous calls all get taped down at the police station." She waited, triumphant, for his reaction.

But there wasn't one; he just stirred his hot chocolate with one of those little spoons. "I don't quite follow," he said, gazing at a chocolate whirlpool he had going, faster and faster, in the cup, a whipped-cream island in danger of getting sucked down. Ruby made a little mental adjustment: he understood *most* things right away.

"Don't you see?" she said. "The voice of the anonymous caller is on that tape. All I'd have to do is go around the neighborhood and talk to people until I find the voice that matches." No reaction. What was he missing? "I don't have to bring up the call or the party or anything like that. Like, 'Hey, your lawn's looking pretty sharp this year, Mr. Neighbor,' and then he says, 'Why, thank you, young lady,' and whammo."

"Whammo?"

"I got him. From matching the sound of the voice."

"I understand," said Julian. "But then what?"

"Then what? Mystery solved. Case closed. We could maybe drop a stink bomb down his chimney or something immature like that."

"So Brandon's in on this?"

"My investigation? I won't need him till the stink bomb stage."

"But first you have to listen to the tape."

"Right."

"Do you think Sergeant D'Amario will let you do that, given that you're Brandon's sister?"

"He doesn't know I'm Brandon's sister."

Julian had bought a mini-sized jar of strawberry jam at the counter. He opened it now, dipped a biscotti, bit off the red-tipped end. *Crunch.*

"At least I don't think so," Ruby added, remembering the whole reason why she'd missed the bus in the first place.

"He didn't ask you your name, out in the woods?" Julian said.

"Sort of," Ruby said. "But then he got distracted."

"So you haven't discussed this idea with Sergeant D'Amario?"

"No."

"Not even as a little joke?"

"What kind of joke?"

"One of those fanciful and characteristic non sequiturs."

"I don't know what that means, Julian."

He dipped his biscotti in the jam again, a little too hard maybe, because it cracked in two, one half falling on the floor. He laid the other on the table. "It means nothing," Julian said. "I'm asking if there's any reason to suspect that Sergeant D'Amario knows what you're thinking."

"No."

"Did you discuss it with anyone else?"

"Why? Do you think someone else might tell him what I'm up to?"

"You never know in a mystery," Julian said.

"We're safe, then," Ruby said. "You're the only one."

Julian smiled, leaned back in his chair. "Quite remarkable on reflection, this idea of yours," he said. He sipped his hot chocolate. "You've been very clever."

"Thanks." She was pleased.

"Another biscotti?"

"Thanks."

"So what comes next?"

"You mean how am I going to get to hear the tape?"

Julian nodded. He had a tiny blob of whipped cream caught in his soul patch. For a moment, biscotti raised, Ruby felt that strange queasiness in her stomach, the same feeling she'd had as a little girl on the car trip when she'd been eating the baloney sandwich and listening to the story about the frog. Now she was older; she mastered it, although her enthusiasm for biscotti vanished temporarily, mixed up as it was now with those facial hairs.

"You can't just walk in there and ask to hear the tapes, huh?" she said.

Julian smiled. "What would happen to anonymous calls?"

"They'd stop."

"Then where would Sergeant D'Amario be?"

"Out of a job?"

Julian nodded, suddenly became aware of the whipped cream problem. He dabbed at his chin, surprisingly annoyed, Ruby thought; she could see how he'd be as an old man, the fussy but kindly type.

"So what's your plan?" he said.

"I don't know," Ruby said. She realized something important about Julian, something she liked very much: he talked to her like an adult. "Any ideas?" she said.

Julian took a notepad from his pocket, a nice one, leather-bound, and a fountain pen, also nice. He turned the top page, which had a few interesting-looking lines on it, and on the next one wrote *Ideas*. Ruby shifted her chair closer so she could see.

One, he wrote. *Technological.*

"What's that?"

"These recordings must be digitized. That means they're on some combination of computer tapes, disks, hard drives, vulnerable to hackers. Do you know any?" Julian wrote: *Hacker?*

"Not unless you're one."

He shook his head. "Hackers are reductive."

"What does that mean?"

"They're basically small-minded, like all techno enthusiasts."

Ruby didn't know about that. She'd have to think. But she did know that Julian was a great teacher. Ms. Freleng never discussed stuff like this. Not only that, she got the feeling he was teaching all the time; Ms. Freleng was out of the parking lot like a shot at 3:01.

On the next line, he wrote: *Two.*

"What's two?"

"Your turn," he said.

That was it: a good teacher made you think. Ruby racked her brain. She liked that expression. Rack was a kind of torture, right? Didn't Mel Brooks put Jews on a rack in *History of the World, Part One*? There was also "cudgel your brains," same idea. She racked. She cudgeled. Nothing.

"I can't think of anything," she said.

"Me either," said Julian. "Maybe it's not worth the trouble."

"What?" said Ruby. "Are you saying just give up? Don't

you want to solve the mystery? Besides, whoever made that call caused a lot of trouble for Brandon."

"I don't see how. Didn't he get off with a warning?"

"It's a little more complicated," Ruby said.

"In what way?"

The cashier came over. "If that's your bike outside, sir, would you mind moving it? It's blocking the delivery entrance."

Julian rose, went outside. Ruby stared at the notepad page. *One: Technological.* So two wasn't going to be technological, at least she knew that. No ideas, technological or not, came to her. She turned back the top page for a little peek.

> *negligent is to forsake as*
> *mendacious is to deceive*
> *nothing*

Cool. Julian was making a poem out of one of those SAT problems. She had a pretty good idea what all the words meant, except *mendacious*, but it was clearly something bad. She picked up Julian's pen—it felt nice—and right away words started coming. She wrote them down.

> *negligent is to forsake as*
> *mendacious is to deceive*
> *nothing you can't depend on*
> *will ever depend on you.*

So the poem was going to be about trust. A real good subject. She could work in the part in *That Thang Thing* where Problem orders the killing of the wrong girlfriend, the one with the Santa Claus tattoo on her butt. But right now, if she could remember it, would be a good spot for that bargain shopping line of Julian's, *questo* something, and *fine* meant shopping, don't forget that. In fact, she could sprinkle the whole poem with Italian, *bella, signor, latte*—they were all great, worth the extra price. The price of trust, that was where the poem wanted to go—shall we break biscotti together, my friend?—whatever *friend* was in Italian.

Julian was coming back. Ruby flipped the poem page over, putting *Ideas* on top.

"How do you say *friend* in Italian?" she said.

"*Amico* for a male, *amica* for a female."

"They have different endings?"

"Kind of appropriate, don't you think?"

Was that some kind of double meaning? Ruby was shocked and embarrassed, even though she heard way worse things all the time, had even walked in once on an X-rated movie when Brandon and Dewey were down in the entertainment center. She felt herself reddening, then caught Julian looking at her in a funny way. Puzzled, maybe. Perhaps she'd misinterpreted.

"Lots of languages have gender," he said.

Yes, completely misinterpreted; her fault. "They do?" she said.

"French, Spanish, Portuguese, German—Latin has three."

"Three genders?"

"Including neuter."

"English is all neuter, right?"

"You could put it that way."

"All neuter is best," Ruby said.

"Why?"

It just was; she couldn't explain it.

Julian gazed at her for a moment or two, then looked down at the *Ideas* page. "How are we doing on number two?"

"Nothing."

"You were about to tell me why this isn't just about drinking in the woods."

Not exactly. More like she was considering it. "That's all it is, really," Ruby said. "This extra thing can't possibly have anything to do with it."

"Absolutely impossible?" said Julian. "Or just improbable?"

She knew what was coming: "The Sign of Four." Was anything better than when books and real life came together?

" 'When you have eliminated the impossible,' " Julian said, " 'whatever remains, however improbable, must be the truth.' "

Probably the most important thing Holmes ever said, at least from what she'd read so far. "We've still got our deal?" Ruby said.

"Always."

"Crack," said Ruby. "Dewey's selling it and Sergeant D'Amario's on to him." She felt better right away. Getting it off her chest—a true expression, like there'd been something squeezing her heart ever since she'd found the crack vial.

"Is Bran involved?"

"Oh, no," Ruby said. "Not the selling part." She couldn't prove that, just knew. Brandon didn't care about money—wasn't that what losing all those wallets meant?

Julian glanced around. No one nearby; in fact, they had Starbucks to themselves. "Crack is serious," he said. "For one thing, colleges ask about criminal records on the applications."

"Mom and Dad would freak."

"Would they not," said Julian.

"What are we going to do?"

"The right thing," Julian said.

"You mean tell on Brandon?"

"Right and wrong can be tricky," Julian said. "Telling on Brandon, as you put it, could lead, through a series of unpredictable events, to the very result we don't want—a criminal record."

"So what's the right thing?"

"Whatever inflicts the least amount of pain on the fewest people."

"Which is?"

Julian laughed. "Who knows?" He reached for his pen

and the leather-bound notepad, like he was going to start a new category. The top page flipped back over. His gaze went to it casually, then not so casually. Uh-oh. Probably not nice to write in someone else's notebook. Was he mad? She couldn't tell because his eyes were on the page, reading what she'd written. There was something strangely transparent about his eyes, even from Ruby's angle, something new. It was as though she could see right inside him for a moment, and she saw he was so smart it was almost frightening.

Julian looked up. Whatever had opened was now closed. His eyes glittered a little, opaque like the sea on a cloudy day.

"Sorry, Julian," she said.

"For what?"

"Messing with your poem," Ruby said. "I didn't mean anything—I was just doodling away."

"Doodling?"

"You know. Fooling around."

"Nothing to be sorry about," Julian said. "And it's not a poem. Whatever gave you that idea?"

"It kind of looked like the start of a poem."

"It's an SAT analogy," Julian said. He pocketed the notepad. "Nothing more. Nothing less."

"I thought you were mad there for a second."

"Why would I be mad?"

"I don't know."

"No reason," Julian said. "And I'm not the type to do things for no reason."

"I know," Ruby said. That was probably what made him so reliable. She gave him a smile. He smiled back.

"Tell you what," he said. "Why don't we check out the scene of the crime?"

"Great idea," Ruby said. "But what about school?"

Julian checked his watch. "We've got to be rational about this," he said. "Doesn't there come a time when even the most diligent student might as well bag it?"

"Eight thirty-one," Ruby said.

He laughed, that funny crow laugh but pretty soft this time. "On the other hand, we don't want you to get in trouble."

"I'll just say I all of a sudden felt sick and stayed home."

"Have you ever done that before?"

"No."

"There's a first time for everything, as folk wisdom tells us." Julian dipped his biscotti in the jam jar, took a bite that left a tiny red smear at one corner of his mouth. "Unless, of course, someone was still home when you left."

"I was alone," Ruby said.

"*Perfetto*," said Julian. "Got your magnifying glass? Can't sleuth around in the woods without that."

"It's at home."

"Got a key?"

"Sure."

"Then we'll pick up the magnifying glass on the way. All set?"

Ruby drained her cup. Gritty chocolate particles from the bottom stuck to the roof of her mouth. They got up.

"After you," Julian said.

They moved toward the door. It opened and someone came in, someone familiar.

"Hey, Jeanette."

"Ruby?" Jeanette looked down at her, then up at Julian. "No school today?"

"Well," she began, and turned to Julian. "You remember Julian?" she said.

"Yes," said Jeanette.

"It seems the bus was a little too early for Ruby today," Julian said, "and she set out on her bike. We ran into each other at the Shell station."

"The Shell station?" said Jeanette.

"Exactly," said Julian. "We're on our way back now."

"Back?" Jeanette's gaze went to the little red smear at the corner of his mouth. Julian took note at once, wiped it away with the back of his hand.

"I planned to ride back to the school with her," he said, "just to be on the safe side."

"You're on a bike too?" Jeanette said. "West Mill Elementary's five miles from here. I'll drive her."

"But—" said Ruby.

"Excellent idea," said Julian, "if it's not too much trouble."

"No trouble at all." Jeanette rumpled Ruby's hair. "I'll just throw her bike in the truck."

"Isn't it a bit late for going to school?" Ruby said.

"I'll give you a note," Jeanette said.

"That takes care of that," Julian said. "See you, Ruby."

"Got a little turned around there, Rubester?" said Jeanette as they went by the Shell station the other way.

"I guess."

"And then you ran into Julian?"

"Yeah."

"At the Shell?"

"Yeah."

"What was he doing there?"

"Filling his tires. He's a biking fanatic, or maybe he can't afford a car."

"Maybe. He's tutoring your brother?"

"Yeah. And he helped out my mom on something at work the other day. He's kind of a friend of the family. We had hot chocolate."

"Your mom lets you bike to school?"

"No. This was kind of an emergency."

"The kind that won't happen again?"

"Right. You're not going to tell, are you?"

"Not if you promise."

"I promise."

Jeanette turned into the school, parked by the front door. Recess already. Amanda had all the girls in the class playing some game with her in the middle. Jeanette found an old envelope on the floor, scribbled on it.

"Here's your note, Ruby. Take the bus home. I'll handle the bike."

"Thanks," said Ruby, getting out of the pickup. Now that she was there, it was actually good to be at school.

"Keep 'em sharp," said Jeanette.

21

"**G**ood things always happen fast," Linda had said. Julian didn't necessarily agree with that, was more interested in the corollary: bad things happening slowly. Probably not true either: take sudden death in a car crash, bad but quick. On the other hand, the bad might linger on long after the crash, possibly even grow, in the minds of the victim's loved ones. Grow and metastasize, that insight reminding him of Adam, and thus the corollary seemed to suit Linda rather well. He copied it onto the page headed *Linda*.

Julian copied his corollary as neatly as he could, but the script wasn't up to his standard, not near, because of the tremor in his hand. Artists were sensitive, vulnerable to deep upset, and he was an artist. Until that morning in the West Mill Starbucks, he'd had no idea that the auteur might have to fight his own characters for control of his own story. Plot development was his responsibility, his alone, certainly not this child's, Ruby's. Was it possible she would figure out some way to hear the 911 tape? That way lay chaos. His response must be to foresee and forestall her method. What method would he use in her position? Julian tried to put himself in her position, tried to bend his brain inside hers, found he could not. Did that make it impossible that she would succeed? No, only that he couldn't imagine how she would do it. But the problem was difficult, the chances of an eleven-year-old succeeding remote. Julian decided to keep worrying about it, but in a low-grade manner.

And what of other characters like Jeanette, not even belonging to the auteur, who nevertheless barged into the story, destabilizing its Aristotelian order? Intolerable: no auteur could work under such conditions. But what to do about it? Julian didn't know. He settled for the temporary acceptance of another low-grade worry.

Something else was bothering Julian, something much higher in grade. He reached into his pocket, was taking out the notepad, when the phone rang. Sergeant D'Amario, he thought, and an icy charge passed through him. But of course it wasn't Sergeant D'Amario.

"Hi, Julian. This is Linda."

"Hello."

"I hope I'm not disturbing you."

"Not in the least."

"Thanks again for the help with La Rivière."

Julian was silent. The help? What part of the idea was hers, exactly?

"But that's not why I'm calling."

"No?"

"I—Scott and I—have been thinking it might be a good idea if you came more often."

"For what purpose?"

"Why, to tutor Brandon."

"He seems to be doing well under the present arrangement."

"I'm glad to hear you say that. But frankly, the nonacademic side of things could be better these days."

"Oh?"

"And we thought you might be a settling influence. Maybe you could add another night or two, helping with his academic subjects if necessary, even taking him out from time to time."

"Out?"

"To a museum or something like that."

"What does Brandon think of this idea?"

"He's not in a position to argue at the moment."

"You've got him bound and gagged?"

Linda laughed. "This time of day that's up to his teachers."

Julian laughed too. "Of course, they'd be in school now, the kids. I forgot."

"It's a funny thing—these are the times I'm most productive. In the hours I'm at work before and after school"—she lowered her voice— "I get almost nothing done."

"That probably makes you a good mother," Julian said.

Pause. "What a nice thing to say."

He cringed; a very odd feeling, reminiscent to him of placing a coin on the fingerless palm of a begging leper at the Yaoundé marketplace. "In any case, if you think another session or two worthwhile, I'm happy to oblige."

"Great. And what about that idea of helping Ruby with her math?"

Julian glanced down at his notepad, was reminded of what was really troubling him.

> *negligent is to forsake as*
> *mendacious is to deceive*
> *nothing you can't depend on*
> *will ever depend on you.*

"Julian? Are you still there?"

"I'm not sure there's any urgency on that score," he said.

"Well, we can think about it."

"If you wish." But it was out of the question. The girl tested his self-control and self-control was the essence of dignity. Any further one-on-one sessions with her would be at his discretion.

"Shall I call Margie?" Linda said.

"I'll spare you the trouble."

"Thanks, Julian." Now she would resort once more to a predictable metaphor. "You're a gem."

He hung up and his eyes were immediately drawn to the poem, as if it contained some hidden force, some mental gravity. The poem: yes, matter-of-fact, the poem; the girl had begun its transformation into art. Doodling, as she'd put it. He placed his hand on the page, ready to crumple it, rip it apart or burn it, as she had burned "The Speckled Band." But he couldn't. It was good. And mostly his own work after all. He counted the words that were his: ten. And hers: nine. And felt a little better. Perhaps he could build on her contribution, quite possibly a stroke of pure luck, or maybe not even hers at all, but lines stolen from a published poet, a talented one, whose work he didn't know. Yes, that must be it. He got the feeling that the next line was about to come to him, leaned forward in anticipation.

It did not. Her big loopy letters maddened him.

He called Margie.

"Isn't that funny?" she said. "I was just going to call you."

"Yes," said Julian. "It's funny."

"I've got two more jobs for you," Margie said. "The Wexlers in West Hartford—they've got twins at Williston—and the Mandevitches in Manchester, plus there's a possibility of—"

"I'm afraid not, Margie."

"What was that?"

"Much as I've enjoyed the experience, I'm retiring from A-Plus Tutorial, at least for the moment."

"Retiring? I don't understand."

"I've taken on a rather large project."

"A tutoring project?"

"Nothing like that. This is more in the artistic line."

"You're writing a book."

"I wouldn't want to jinx anything by saying yes or no."

"I'm not surprised," said Margie. "And good luck. But what about the Gardners?"

"Naturally I'll continue those lessons," Julian said. "I'm committed to the Gardners."

"Thank you, Julian."

"And if you could just send me the letter?"

"Letter?"

"From the master of Balliol."

"I'll get it out today."

"You're very kind, Margie. It's been a pleasure."

"There's always a place for you here," Margie said.

Julian called Linda at work. She answered her own phone, rather disappointing.

"Is there really a need to inform Margie about the extra sessions?" he said. "Keeping this between ourselves would allow me to cut the rate in half."

"I wouldn't want to—"

"It happens all the time."

"That's very thoughtful of you, Julian."

Some things were easy.

And some were not. Julian turned to the empty page headed *Ruby*. The auteur must fight for control of his own story. Julian leaned over the page and fought with all his might. He fought to understand her, to see her whole—like a specimen in a jar—the way he understood all the others. Time passed, how much he didn't know. The texture of the paper seemed to come alive, patterns of off-white fibers changing shape under his gaze. Changing, even writhing: at last, Julian wrote, *"The Speckled Band."*

Julian gift-wrapped a jar of that strawberry jam from France, wonderful strawberry jam, thick and plasmal. It was important to give good presents, to wrap them nicely, to tie a proper bow with matching ribbon. Women liked that sort of thing. If it was true that women had a special talent for speech—not thought, but speech—then perhaps that included a talent for symbolic speech as well. It made them vulnerable to thoughtful gifts.

Gail's eyes were wary when she opened the door. That

was too bad. Julian wanted good landlord-tenant relations. Perhaps their last encounter hadn't been entirely smooth. On the other hand: a few drinks, a woman's bedroom, two recent acquaintances, misconnection—surely part of the American experience, like a trip to Disney World. He gave her a big smile.

"Here's a little something," he said.

Gail took it, with some hesitation. Those little details—hesitations, inward looks, lower lip softly bitten—couldn't be said to make life worthwhile on their own, but they added to the enjoyment, like *amuse-gueules* in a good restaurant. The symbolic conversation was off to a good start.

"This is nice of you," she said. "But really, there's no need to—"

"It's nothing," Julian said. The vocalized conversation was rockier, but moving in the right direction—two civilized acquaintances intent on burying a little past unpleasantness. "I've also brought the rent."

"It's not due till next week."

He handed her the money envelope, perhaps the only symbolic transaction understood equally well by women and men. "Maybe the J. P. Morganettes will capitalize on the extra days."

"Funny you should mention that," Gail said.

"Oh?"

"Do you know much about investing?"

"Not a thing," Julian said, the soul of affability.

She relaxed a little, seemed rounder and shorter almost at once. "That's how I was before the Morganettes. It's like anything else. You have to do your homework. We outperformed Warren Buffett last quarter by almost two percent. On a smaller scale, of course."

"I'm impressed," said Julian. "And it's all about homework?"

"Almost always. Very occasionally we get a tip, but then we still go to work on the fundamentals the way we would with any other stock."

"For example?"

"Are you really not into the stock market, Julian?"

"Cross my heart."

"Because you're acting like a tip seeker."

Julian laughed. "I'm just curious, that's all."

"The fact is, we did learn something interesting at the last meeting. It's not inside information or anything like that—we wouldn't act on inside information even if we had it, much too risky."

"Who wants trouble?"

"Can you imagine? The feds swooping down?" Gail glanced up at the sky. Julian followed her gaze: no feds, but a wave of starlings in a single formation, like a giant stealth bomber coming over the trees.

"The feds," said Julian. "What a thought." He almost managed a shiver.

"But there's no law against keeping your eyes open," Gail said. "Not yet, anyway."

Ah, a nice libertarian component. "Thank God."

Gail gave him a look: two acquaintances with more in common than she'd thought. "One of our members was out visiting her sister in San Francisco a couple weeks ago when her nephew—the sister's grown-up son—came over for dinner. He was driving a brand-new sports car, right out of the showroom—"

"A Boxster?"

"How did you know?"

"It's de rigueur."

Gail blinked.

"Just a lucky guess," Julian said.

"Oh," said Gail. "And he came racing in to tell his mother that something great had happened that he wasn't allowed to talk about yet. But the whole family knows he's been working on some revolutionary gizmo—he's got a computer-engineering Ph.D. from Cal Tech—for years. So we did our research and found that the company's solid, with or without this gizmo, and we're placing an order tomorrow for three hundred and twenty-five shares."

"You'll be running the country soon," Julian said. Could he have been more convivial?

"You're just teasing," Gail said.

"I wouldn't dream of it."

Her gaze dipped to the tiny beard under his lower lip; very brief, but Julian caught it. They were back on an even keel, all patched up, perhaps even steaming forward on their previous course.

A whistle, a steam whistle, went off inside the house, an appropriate confirmation of their rapprochement. "I'm just making tea," said Gail, "if you'd care to—"

"How kind," said Julian. "Another time, I hope. But work calls." He stepped back.

"Thanks for the present."

"Don't mention it," Julian said. He turned, paused. "If you don't mind my asking, how much would say, ten shares of the stock you mentioned cost?"

Gail laughed. "Hooked," she said, "just like that."

Julian shrugged helplessly.

"It closed at eight dollars and change yesterday," Gail said.

"Thanks," Julian said, and started walking away.

"Don't you want to know the name of the stock?"

Julian slapped the side of his head.

Gail laughed again. "Codexco," she said. "On the Nasdaq."

Was it difficult to go into the Old Mill Library, sit at a computer, learn the name of this happy nephew, only Cal Tech Ph.D. on the Codexco payroll? No; so quick and easy that Julian had extra time to read a little in Conan Doyle, skimming here and there, lingering over "The Speckled Band." Was it then difficult to find the bar Mickey Gudukas liked to visit on his way home from work, to dress in the manner that would impress him, to slide onto the vacant stool beside him, to lay a folder bulging with papers on the bar and exhale deeply, a hard worker laying down his burden at last? No; all very easy, and fun, too.

"Tough day?" said Mickey Gudukas.

Julian turned to him. He'd already smelled the pine forest. Now he took in the other basics, and how basic they were: big mustache, little eyes, a bald pate divided into two regions, the natural horseshoe-shaped one shiny, the shaved sides and back dull, as though some designer had treated them with two different finishes for sadistic effect. "Boy oh boy," said Julian.

Gudukas nodded. He took in the suit, the tie, the folder.

"If business is slowing down," Julian said, "why aren't I?"

Little eyes got littler. Too complex, somehow. He would have to ease off on the mental throttle.

"What can I get you?" said the bartender.

Julian glanced at Gudukas's drink, something blue in a martini glass. He wasn't going to go that far. "Single malt," said Julian. "Highland Park, if you've got it."

"Coming up," said the bartender.

"Highland Park?" said Gudukas. "Haven't heard of that one."

"It doesn't have Glen in it," said Julian. "That's what appeals."

"Huh?"

A simple grunt, placing Gudukas several notches down from Scott on the evolutionary scale. How low did it go?

The bartender brought his drink. Julian took a sip.

"Is it good?" said Gudukas.

"And one for this gentleman," Julian told the waiter, adding, "on me," taking nothing for granted now on Gudukas's part.

"Hey," said Gudukas, probably expressing thanks, and "Not bad," after he'd had a taste. "Cheers," after that. They clinked glasses. "What line of work you in, stays busy in this shitbox economy?"

"Venture capital."

"Yeah?" Greed expressed itself in the contraction of specific facial muscles, possibly hardwired, certainly so in Gudukas's case. "What outfit?"

"I'm retained by several."

"As what?"

"A technical consultant."

"What's that when it's at home?"

"The VC firms have their own people to evaluate the financial side of companies they're interested in, but sometimes they need help on technical and scientific issues. That's me."

Gudukas eyed him with care; it gave Julian that peculiar feeling when one of the zoo animals gazes back. "You don't look like a techie," Gudukas said.

"I'm not," said Julian. "I'm a mathematician."

"Yeah?" said Gudukas. "Never met one of them before."

"It's really no different from any other job," Julian said. "You search for patterns."

"Search for patterns," said Gudukas. He went still. For a moment, Julian wondered whether some medical emergency was in the offing. Then Gudukas spoke. "I like that." He actually wrote it down—*search for patterns*—on a napkin and stuffed it in his pocket. Then he downed his single malt in one gulp, taking another look at Julian over the rim of the glass. "Working on anything interesting lately?"

"Naturally I can't discuss specifics," Julian said. "I've just been checking out a company in California."

"Who shall remain nameless, right?"

Julian smiled. "Those are the rules." Although not those of grammar.

"What kind of company, you know, in general?"

"Software design."

"That's kind of broad."

Good for you, Mickey; Julian was pleasantly surprised. "Too broad, in this case," he said.

"How do you mean?"

"I could answer that," said Julian, "but you'd have to know about number theory in general and Mordell's conjecture in particular."

"I'll pass," said Gudukas. He was back on the blue drink. "But your point is you found some screwup in this company."

"Broadly speaking, yes."

"And now what? You tell the VC boys to stay clear?"

"Or unload."

"Unload? So they're going to dump their shares?"

"I really can't answer that," Julian said.

"Gotcha," said Gudukas. "So did you lay the news on these Silicon Valley guys?"

"I never mentioned Silicon Valley," Julian said. "And my job is simply to file my report."

"And pick up your check, right?"

Julian smiled. "What field are you in, if you don't mind my asking?"

"Sales," said Gudukas. "Pretty dull in comparison."

Julian made some conciliatory remark. Sales. True in a sense, but was there a stockbroker alive who would have given that answer to a prosperous-looking stranger in a bar, who wouldn't have handed out his business card? Everything was set.

Julian waited till the bartender left to hook up a new keg in the cellar, then excused himself and went to the bathroom, leaving Gudukas alone at one end of the bar, folder in reach. When he returned it was exactly where he'd left it, and Gudukas was turned the other way, gazing with what looked like great interest at a Depends commercial on TV.

Julian sat down. Gudukas finished his drink, pushed back his stool. Would he check his watch too? Yes. "Well," he said. "Nice talking to you. And thanks for the drink."

"You're welcome, Mr. . . ."

"Mike," said Mickey Gudukas. "Be seeing you." He couldn't wait to get out of there, leaving no trace.

Julian finished his Scotch, paid his bill, left about ten

minutes later, taking the folder. Inside was the rough draft of a memo outlining Codexco's bleak prospects, based on the failure of Gail's friend's nephew's project. Beneath the memo lay pages and pages of mathematical equations Julian had copied at the library. He dropped the whole thing in the first Dumpster he saw. Good things happened fast. He owed Linda one.

22

"I can't believe how big your house is," said Trish Almeida.

"Yeah?" said Brandon. They lay on Brandon's bed, music playing soft, TV on, mute button pushed. He'd been in big houses—his cousin Sam's in Old Mill, for example—and knew this wasn't big. He stretched out, relaxed but not at all sleepy in his boxers; Trish wore her bra and nothing else. Another hard-on would be along soon. They'd left school a little early, both having last-period spares with a sub in charge this week, and the sub-spare combo lowered the chances of getting a cut sent up to the office to almost zero. And if they did get cuts, so what? He was only at level two and Trish hadn't had a single infraction all year. But even at level nine hundred and ninety-nine, Brandon knew he would have done the same thing. Come on, school or this? Besides, he kind of liked Trish, admitted that to himself, even if she wasn't one of the cool kids, didn't dress right, rode the bus.

"I think the chief is stirring," she said.

That was what she called his dick, something about a resemblance to one of those fireman's helmets. They'd gone beyond oral sex—Trish had decided she was ready for real sex now—and it was good, but in a way Brandon preferred the old days of the oral kind. This way they were face-to-face, and sometimes their eyes opened simultaneously, like right now, and he had to look into hers. She had nice eyes, beautiful, actually, and looking into them wasn't bad, exactly, just too much, like whatever went on inside her was way too intense. It made him feel he should protect her, like some knight, a crazy idea she probably would have hated. Still, he was always surprised when she could talk normally right after.

"Know what I'd like?" she said.

He guessed it was going to be some kind of snack, but wasn't sure and kept his mouth shut.

"I'd like to go down to that bar in Soho."

"Yeah?"

"Now, Brandon. I'd like to jump in the car and go right now."

"What car?"

"Maybe we could get my mom's."

"What are you talking about? You're fifteen."

"You could drive."

"I've only got a permit. And my second lesson is next week." Other than a few informal lessons with Dad, not good. " 'Hey, Mrs. Almeida, can I take your car down to New York? I'll be getting my license pretty soon.' "

"You just don't want to go."

"Fuck I don't," said Brandon. "I'll talk to Dewey."

"I don't want to go with Dewey."

"Then who?"

"You."

He looked in Trish's eyes. They were normal, almost. "This isn't working out," he said.

"What isn't?"

"Me being the mature one."

Trish laughed. "You're so funny," she said. "The chief is funny too. Aren't you, chiefy?" She gave the chief a little shake.

There was a knock at the door. Trish went still.

"Bran?" Ruby called through the door. "You in there?"

"What is it?" Brandon said. Trish was tugging silently at the sheet, hopelessly tangled beneath them.

"Phone."

"Tell them to call back on my line."

"No."

"What do you mean, no?"

"It's Julian."

"Shit. What does he want?"

"To talk to you. That's what it means when someone calls you on the phone."

"Jesus Christ, I'll be right down."

"I've got the portable." The doorknob started to turn.

"I said I'll fucking be right down."

It stopped turning. Brandon thought he heard footsteps retreating.

"Your sister?" Trish whispered in his ear.

"The biggest pain," he said in a normal voice.

"What was that?" said Ruby, from not far off at all.

"Get the hell away."

"You talking to yourself now, Bran?"

"I mean it."

There was no sign of her when he left the room, wearing only his jeans. He closed the door behind him and went downstairs.

Ruby, standing in the linen closet with the door opened just a crack—really one of her best ideas—watched Brandon go by. Hair gelled again. Also a funny kind of scratch on his back. She waited till the coast was clear, stepped out of the closet and boom—Brandon's door opened. Out came a girl, a teenage girl, very pretty, slipping a rubber band on her ponytail.

"Hi," she said.

"Hi," said Ruby.

"You're Brandon's sister?"

"Among other things," said Ruby.

"Gotcha," said the girl. "I'm Trish. Nice to meet you."

"Nice to meet you, too," Ruby said. "But he should lose the gel."

"You tell him."

"**P**retty good, Julian. How're you?"

"Could be worse," said Julian. "I'm just calling about the new schedule. Did your mother mention I'd be coming more often?"

"Something about it."

"Ghastly turn of events, right?"

"I wouldn't say that."

Julian laughed. "You know that some of these visits won't be strictly academic in nature."

"Yeah."

"Your mother said something about visiting museums."

"Yeah."

"But if you could come up with any ideas of your own, I'm sure they'd be considered."

"What kind of ideas?"

"Cultural, I suppose, but in the broadest sense."

"Like trips?" Brandon said.

"Depending on their nature."

"To see culture."

"Yes."

"Like how far?"

"How far?"

"How far a trip?"

"Up to your parents, of course. But I'm sure it's nego-tiable. To a point. Indian casinos would be stretching the cul-tural definition."

Indian casinos! What a great idea! "When's the next lesson?"

"Tomorrow," Julian said. "Geometry again."

"Maybe we can talk more about it then." An idea was taking shape in his head.

"Why not?" said Julian.

Trish and Ruby entered, in the middle of some conversation. "I could whip up a batch of hot dogs," Ruby was saying.

"Sounds great," said Trish.

Then they both looked at him funny. "What?" Brandon said. "What?"

Ms. Freleng had a thing about Cortés, but Pizarro, forget it. He was even worse, what he did to the Incas. Ruby kept waiting for Ms. Freleng to say something about the adventure part of the whole story, how it must have been amazing from that point of view, but Ms. Freleng never did. Tonight's assignment was to make a diorama of Machu Picchu before the Spanish came, showing the Incas at work and play. The first thing Ruby did was crayon in a couple of sailing ships on the right-hand side, just to add a little tension to the scene. She included big red crosses on the sails and black cannons on the deck. Why not fire one of them? She was testing various oranges for the flame—Ruby had the Wizard's Giant 120 Crayola box—when she half remembered that maybe Pizarro hadn't come by ship. But the ships were too good to lose. If Ms. Freleng objected, Ruby could say the ships were a vision of the Inca shaman. Unable to choose between Atomic Tangerine and Neon Carrot, she ended up firing two cannons.

Ruby got bored when the ships were done, took a break. She practiced her Oscar acceptance speech in front of the mirror on her closet door. "Wow," she said, holding up one of Brandon's tennis trophies. She had none of her own: archery was the only sport she was good enough to win trophies in, and Jeanette didn't give them. "Wow." Ruby panted; a long run from her plush seat to the stage. "I don't believe this. Amazing. I want to thank just everybody, everybody on the whole planet Earth." She giggled. Waves of adoration swept over her. "I love you all. Thanks to the folks at Disney, you know who you are. But especially my mom and dad, my brother Brandon, and his new girlfriend—what does she see in him?" Pause for laughter. "And Adam? This is for you." Then she hurried offstage, keeping it short and sweet.

Back at her desk, Ruby began making an Inca temple out of toothpicks. The boredom was intense, maybe like building a real temple. Did the Incas get excited when they first saw the ships, thinking something was going to happen at last? She decided to have one tiny Inca spotting the ships and breaking out in a big grin. After that, her mind wandered to other stupid school projects, then to her pretend project that had fooled Manny down at the Shell station. And then: inspiration. Just like that, she thought of a way to hear the 911 tape, to solve The Mystery of the Anonymous Caller.

Why not a school project? Kind of one night in the life of the guy taking the 911 calls. She'd go into the police station, interview the 911 guy, then ask to hear some 911 calls. It had to be a specific night, of course, a specific Saturday night, because . . . because the class was doing a portrait of West Mill on that particular night, and her assignment was the 911 calls. Wow. It was perfect.

Ruby checked the time: 7:15. Not too late. Why not do it tonight? No getting lost this time. She went to MapQuest, typed *37 Robin Road* in the *from* box and *West Mill police station* in the *to* box. Up came the directions; not even far, 2.1 miles. She printed them out, went downstairs—no one around—put on her blue jacket with the yellow trim, opened the kitchen door to the garage. No cars, Mom and Dad not home yet. And no bike either. No bike? For a moment, she thought it had been stolen. Then she realized Jeanette hadn't brought it back yet.

The 911 project would have to wait. She went back into the house, hung her jacket on the peg next to Brandon's. Then she fought the temptation to check the pockets of the varsity jacket. Checking the pockets was wrong. Would she want someone checking her pockets? No. Were there rights in this country? There were. Was checking someone's pockets as bad as reading their mail? Yes. Was there anything positive to be said for checking someone's pockets? No.

Ruby checked Brandon's pockets. In one she found a crumpled geometry quiz. *17/20,* it said, *nice improvement, Brandon.* In the other pocket was nothing but a stick of Bubblicious gum. Innocent as the baby Jesus. Check out these all-American pockets, Sergeant D'Amario, and back off. Of course, they didn't have crack in the baby Jesus' day. Probably another boring time, like the Incas, until he came along, or He, depending, shaking things up a little like Pizarro and Cortés and the rest of the Conquistadors, but a much nicer guy.

The next thing she knew, the gum was in her mouth. Bubblicious was one of Ruby's favorites. Chewing gum helped you think, no doubt about that. Did Einstein and that crowd chew gum? Probably, and if not they would have done better if they had, like maybe explaining everything so people could understand.

Ruby stood in the mudroom, chewing gum. She could see Zippy lying under the kitchen table. He opened an eye, saw her too, raised his tail sideways, let it flop back down to the floor. Why so affectionate all of a sudden? Was there a mess waiting in some hidden corner of the house?

She entered a kind of bubblegum trance. Her mind left Einstein and Zippy behind, settled on her cases. There were two: The Mystery of the Varsity Jacket and The Mystery of the Anonymous Caller, in order of when they'd happened. Funny thing: at the moment, she was working on case two, the anonymous caller, work that involved checking the pockets of the very jacket that was the subject of case one. Whoa, right there. Did that mean the two cases were connected? What did *connected* mean? Did it mean that the anonymous caller himself—or herself (some girl jealous of Trish?)—was involved in the strange disappearance and reappearance of the jacket? Had to be; even elementary, my dear Ruby. *When you have eliminated the impossible, whatever remains, however improbable, must be the truth.* Perhaps that thought didn't quite apply yet to the linking of the two cases, but Ruby felt its might behind her just the same.

And linking! Here we go. *To thoroughly understand one link in the chain:* there were two chains, the varsity jacket chain and the anonymous caller chain, and the link she'd got hold of was special, the one that joined the two chains together.

"Wow."

Zippy opened his eye again, raised his tail, let it fall. A puff of dust rose off it under the table. The dust filled with light that came through the crack where the two halves of the table joined together. Ruby was gazing at this sight when the side door opened and Dad came in.

"Hi, Dad."

Dad was talking on his cell, didn't see or hear her. He kept going toward the living room.

"Lightning strikes twice," Mickey Gudukas said.

"How do you mean?" said Scott.

"I mean this is your lucky day, again. You're not going to let this one slide by too, are you, Scotty? Most people don't even get one lucky day."

Scott tried to convey his displeasure with that in his tone. "This another stock tip?"

"More like investment advice," Gudukas said. "I think of Symptomatica and opportunities of that magnitude as having a classier nature than just a tip." He said something else, lost in cell phone breakup, that ended in ". . . short."

"Didn't get all of that," Scott said.

"Christ," said Gudukas, "do you want to make a shit-load of money or don't you?"

Scott stood beside the Tin Man sculpture, *Untitled—19*. Linda and Deborah had taken an interest in the artist, back in the days when the four of them had done things together, like trips to New York. The artist's career hadn't gone any-where, but Scott liked the Tin Man, although he couldn't have begun to explain what it meant. He'd given it to Linda for Christmas, then had to fight to make her keep it. She loved the sculpture, thought it was the best thing the guy had done, but the price: two grand, more than a stretch in those days, and still significant. When wouldn't it be? How nice not to have to even think about two grand here or there, or even twenty. To spread out a little, breathe deeper, do something interesting with his life, maybe open a restaurant one day—call it Untitled 19 and stick the sculpture on the bar. The kids and all their friends would have summer jobs, guaranteed. He could picture Ruby in a chef's hat.

"Because there are people who don't want to make a shitload of money," Gudukas said. "Strange as it may seem. They're content to be comfortable, whatever the hell that means."

Scott didn't find it strange. Tom was like that. "I'm listening," he said.

"Codexco." Long pause.

"Go on."

"Codexco." Gudukas said it again, the pause shorter this time. "That one word's going to change your life."

"Never heard of it."

"Where are you going with that?" said Gudukas. "The world's full of five-hundred-million-dollar companies no one's heard of."

"It's a five-hundred-million-dollar company?"

"Been on the Nasdaq for ten years, actually started paying dividends last quarter," said Gudukas. "I'm rolling the whole Symptomatica score into this one."

"I thought you were rich already."

"Not rich enough to buy an island in the Bahamas."

"You're buying an island in the Bahamas?"

"Part of one, anyway. After Codexco. It's already got a tennis court for Kyla."

"What do they do?"

"Who cares?" said Gudukas. "Happens to be software development for heavy engineering. You know that big thing in China where they flooded out all those peasants? Codexco was in on that."

"What's so good about them?"

"What's bad is what's good," said Gudukas. "They had a hotshot Ph.D. from Cal Tech working on some algorithm shortcut that was going to cut costs by a third and wipe out the competition. Spent fifteen million on it so far, funded a new lab. The good news is it's not going to work and no one knows but us chickens."

"So this is a short sell?"

"Exactly. Lost our fear of those by now, I hope."

"How do you know the shortcut won't work?"

"You guys," said Gudukas.

"What guys?"

"Like you and your brother, don't believe anybody. You don't see a pattern here? Have I ever steered you wrong? Stentech, Symptomatica, now this. Searching for patterns— that's what investing's all about."

"Call it searching for patterns, then," said Scott. "How do you know?"

"My source is confidential, but I've seen internal documents. Had them in my hands—a one hundred percent negative evaluation, backed up by a shitpile of math, charts, graphs, equations. The fifteen mil is gone and their VC backers are pulling out. As soon as that leaks out the stock's in the toilet. Not down to zero, like Symptomatica—this one's more diversified—but they should lose half their value in a day."

"What's it trading at?"

Click, click on Gudukas's end. "Nine and a quarter. Up twenty cents from yesterday, good for us."

"So you think it might go down to five?"

"Four or five, something like that. Maybe even two or three."

"When?"

"No one knows when. But it's always sooner rather than later, plays like this."

"Full-rate commission?"

"Preferred client rate, you go through me."

Say it went down to five, to be conservative. Five from nine is four. Fifty thousand shares would be two hundred grand, a hundred thousand would be four hundred grand, a hundred and twenty five thousand would be half a million; restaurant money. And what did he have to put up? Nothing but collateral.

"Put you to sleep, Scotty?" said Gudukas.

"It's Scott."

"Shit. Why didn't you say anything before? I can't guess these things. Hell, I like that everybody calls me Mickey."

"I'll get back to you, Mickey."

"You know best, Scott," said Gudukas. "But the clock is ticking."

23

"**D**on't you think Linda should know about this?" Tom said. They sat in Tom's office, the day dark outside, lights on: Tom's green-shaded banker's lamp on the desk, the floor lamp at the end of the couch, next to Scott, and the little brass light over their father's portrait on the wall. It hid the old man's face behind a shiny glare, also shone on his gold watch, a watch Tom now wore.

That was fair: Scott had inherited the mother-of-pearl cufflink-and-stud set. But Tom's question pissed Scott off. "Does Deborah know every little thing you do?" he said. That wasn't the kind of comeback he'd have made before the last tennis match, certainly wouldn't have said it so roughly.

It reddened Tom's face, and that was fine with Scott. He shouldn't have had to beg for this, not after what happened with Symptomatica.

"There's risk involved, that's all," Tom said, "and she'd be part of it."

"What's all this worrying about Linda?" Scott said, and had the satisfaction of seeing Tom go a little redder; this new tone was satisfying too, just the sound of it. The tennis match had changed things. At the same time, he had no intention of exploiting it in a habitual way: they were brothers, after all. "She's my responsibility," he added in a softer tone. Tom's blush or whatever it was didn't disappear, intensified if anything. Maybe he was sick, like everybody else this week; the sun hadn't been out once.

"And second, there's no risk," Scott said.

"How can you say that? The risk is open-ended. Short selling's one of the riskiest things there is, everyone knows that."

"Didn't I just explain all this?" Scott said. "Gudukas has seen internal documents. That's like tomorrow's head-lines today."

"Why do you trust a guy like that?"

"It has nothing to do with him personally. It's his record. Stentech. Symptomatica. Don't you see the pattern? He gets good information. I told you that from the very beginning."

"How come he gets such good information?"

"You're a snob, you know that? Why shouldn't he get good information? Because he wears loud clothes and plays lousy tennis? Gudukas has good contacts and he works his ass off. Isn't that enough?"

"Who's his contact on this?"

What a question; a question someone on the other side of a generation gap might ask. "You expect him to reveal that?" Scott said. "It's better not to know, for our own pro-tection."

"That's the kind of talk that scares me, right there."

Tom scared too easily. "Reading between the lines, I got the impression his source is a VC guy," Scott said.

"What's that?"

Jesus. "Venture capital. That's the trigger, when they start dumping their shares."

They gazed at each other, their heads in separate pools of light. Scott felt the power of that expression, venture capital, hanging in the air.

"Is this us?" Tom said.

"What do you mean?"

"Are we guys who play in that game? Venture capital, selling short, putting money into companies like Codecto—"

"Codexco."

"—that we can't even understand what they do?"

The power of the expression was real, but their responses were different. Tom shrank from it; Scott embraced it. What had Julian said? *A little too much propinquity.* Julian was smart, not because he could throw around words like propinquity that Scott only half understood, but because he could get to the heart of things. A hundred and twenty-five thousand shares, half a million dollars, meant no more enforced propinquity, meant the freedom to make his own decisions. But it wasn't just him: the whole family would benefit. Brandon could go to boarding school next year, or as a day kid to Loomis or Choate, maybe get into Harvard after all. Julian could still come in the summer and on vacations, ramping up that SAT score. He wondered if Ruby would want a horse.

"The fact is," said Scott, "I guess we end up being different. One of us is a guy who does play in that game."

"Then you'll have to do it by yourself," Tom said.

"Meaning?"

"Meaning I can't involve the business."

"That's not entirely up to you," said Scott. "Mom owns forty percent."

"I talked to her."

"About what?"

"This kind of thing, the Symptomatica deal specifically."

"What did she say?"

"Nothing. But a week later she sent me a book." Tom opened his desk drawer, took it out: *The Stock Market for Dummies*. He opened it to a bookmarked page. "She underlined this passage." Tom held out the book, expecting Scott to get off the couch and fetch it. Scott stayed where he was. Tom walked around the desk and handed it to him.

Scott read the passage. Tom returned to his desk. His phone rang. He ignored it.

Short selling is not for the faint of heart. Big corporations and commodities traders use it to hedge their bets. If you're not playing in that game, give it a miss.

"So?" Scott said.

"So you can talk to her," Tom said, "but I think that's her answer."

"Sure you didn't send her the book first, maybe with the underlining all in place?"

"What's going on with you, Scott?"

"Nothing."

"How can you ask me a question like that?"

"I take it back," Scott said. "Didn't mean to imply I don't trust you. Of course I do."

Tom went red again, which made no sense. He picked up a pencil: their hands were identical. "How many shares were you thinking of?"

"A hundred thousand, maybe more."

"At nine?"

"It's up to nine thirty-five this morning."

"What if it keeps going up?"

"That's why I need collateral—to cover any little blips like that. But in the end it's going down."

"What if it blips up to eighteen?"

"That's not happening. There isn't time, for one thing."

"But if it did, you'd owe the broker nine hundred grand, is that right?"

Hands identical, but inside they were different, all right, maybe growing more so. Scott recalled Julian's tennis advice: hit right at him and use your power only when he tries to overpower you. And there'd even been a third suggestion, which Julian had held in reserve. Scott smiled.

"What's so funny?"

"I just realized I'm the one who's like Dad. I always thought it was you." Hitting right at him.

"Dad never bought a single share of stock in his life."

"But he built this business."

Power for power. There was a long silence. Then Tom leaned back in his chair, nodded. The battle was over; what worked on the tennis court worked in the office.

"Can I just ask you one more thing?" Tom said. "Does your share of the business plus the equity in your house and all your other investments come close to nine hundred grand?"

"Where are you getting that number? It's a fantasy, Tom, a ghost. I'm not afraid of ghosts."

Something hard, hail or sleet, clattered against the windows. The lights dimmed for a moment, went back to full power. "Tell you what," Tom said. "I'll buy out your share of the business."

Scott didn't get it. "You mean after?"

"After what?"

"The Codexco payout."

Tom shook his head. "Now. But temporarily, just so you'll have the collateral. After you cash out, you can buy back in."

"That's very nice of you, Tom. Buy back in with interest, goes without saying."

"Goes without saying."

Yes! It was going to happen, not in the way he'd expected, but did that matter?

"No reason we can't draw up an agreement right here, the two of us," Tom said. "We'll have to put some value on the business. They used two and a half times revenue last time, as I recall. That acceptable?"

"Sure." Although then they'd been after a conservative value, for tax reasons. Still, somewhere between two and three times revenue was standard.

Tom was busy on his calculator. "Revenue last year was eight hundred grand plus, we'll plug in the exact figure later. Two point five times eight hundred thousand is two million, times your share, point two five, makes five hundred grand."

"Wait a minute," Scott said, maybe a little late in the game. "Where are you going to get the five hundred grand?" This was a real five hundred grand—*real* was the wrong word, more like in the present, Scott corrected himself—as opposed to the equally real but future five hundred grand estimate of the Codexco score.

"I can raise it," Tom said.

"How?"

"There's the home equity line, for starters." That made sense: housing values in Old Mill kept rising, and Tom had owned his place for years. "I could also mortgage the ski place if necessary."

Scott realized that Tom was already where he himself wanted to be. Didn't seem to be enjoying it, didn't seem to be stretching out, but he was there.

"We'll get the agreement drawn up and cut the check by end of business tomorrow."

"Thanks, Tom."

"Hope like hell it works out," Tom said.

"Relax."

Tom was quicker than that: the agreement—Tom bought Scott's share of the business, Scott retaining the option to buy it back at the same price, with interest at prime plus one—was signed, witnessed and notarized at eleven the next day and Scott deposited the check at Gudukas's brokerage in an interest-bearing account an hour later. Five hundred seventeen thousand, two hundred and sixty-three dollars, seventy cents.

Gudukas took him into the conference room, closed the door. "How big do you want to go?"

"I was thinking a hundred thousand shares."

"You can go a lot higher with this behind you." Gudukas waved a photocopy of the check. "I'm in for three myself."

"Three hundred thousand shares?"

"No blue-light specials in the private island market," Gudukas said.

"What's it at?"

Gudukas checked a monitor on the conference table. "Eight eighty-five, down twenty cents from the opening."

Scott moved around to look at the screen, saw Codexco, the price, the volume: all real. "Where was it when you got in?" Scott said.

"Nine-oh-five," Gudukas said.

"So you could buy back right now and make—"

"Sixty grand," Gudukas said. He didn't even have to think. The screen flickered and the price fell to eight eighty.

"Jesus Christ," Scott said. "Is it happening already?"

"Could be," said Gudukas. "So what's the number?"

"Maybe a hundred and ten," Scott said.

Gudukas clucked like a chicken.

"All right, one twenty-five."

"One twenty-five's better," Gudukas said. "But one fifty multiplies a lot easier."

On the screen in front of him, Codexco dropped another nickel, down to eight seventy-five. Fifteen grand for Gudukas, twice what Scott had forgone by not getting in two minutes ago, at the one fifty level.

"One fifty it is," Scott said.

"My man," said Gudukas.

Scott sold one hundred and fifty thousand shares of Codexco he didn't own, borrowing them from Gudukas's brokerage in the standard way. The trade went through at eight seventy-five—one hundred and fifty thousand times eight seventy-five equaling one million, three hundred twelve thousand five hundred. By the time he left Gudukas's office Codexco was at eight sixty-five. He'd made fifteen grand already.

Sleet, wind, all the streetlights on: even darker than yesterday, the bellies of the clouds dragging through the treetops. But Scott was lit up inside. Fifteen grand already! He was on his way. He had to force himself to go back to work, to stay at his desk, to write insurance—life, disability, medical, homeowner, automobile, umbrella; everyone paying a premium just to try to hang onto what they already had. He was moving to another level, getting more, so much more that the hanging-on part would never be relevant again.

Codexco ended the day at eight and a half, down twenty-five cents: $37,500 to the good. It wasn't about paying premiums; it was about multiplying. What if Codexco didn't stop at four or five, but fell all the way to three, even two? Scott played with the numbers. They were beautiful. On the way home he stopped at the travel agent, gave himself the pleasure of dropping four plane tickets on the kitchen table that night.

"What's this?" Linda said.

"Atlantis."

"Hey!" Ruby said.

"What's going on?" said Linda.

"We're going to Atlantis?" said Brandon.

"When?" said Ruby.

"Tomorrow morning," said Scott. "Nine forty-five, nonstop from Bradley. Be there in time for a nice swim before lunch."

"What's Atlantis?" said Linda.

"You can't be serious," Brandon said.

"Paradise Island, Lin," Scott said. "The resort with that underwater park where you walk through a glass tunnel."

Ruby danced around the table.

"But tomorrow's Friday," Linda said.

"Back Sunday night," Scott said. "With fresh tans and salt in our hair."

"Friday's a school day."

"Mom!"

"And a work day."

"I've already called in sick," Scott said. The kids laughed, because he could take off work whenever he wanted, although he never did. "You can catch whatever I've got tonight."

The kids laughed again, but Linda's brow furrowed the way it did, that vertical line digging deep. "What are you up to, Scott? We can't afford this."

"Sure we can."

"What did you pay? Is it refundable?"

"We're locked in," Scott said. "Locked and loaded."

"Have you been drinking?" Linda said.

"Not yet." He wished he'd picked up a bottle of champagne, maybe two.

She stared at him, then opened one of the folders, leafed through the ticket pages. "First class?" she said. "Have you gone crazy?"

"First class!" said Brandon.

"I'm ordering everything," said Ruby.

"Scott, I want an explanation this minute."

He went over, pulled her close. "You know you love the sun," he said. "Brings out those beautiful Mediterranean skin tones."

"I hope I don't have them," Ruby said.

Linda backed out of his grasp.

"I had a good day today, that's all," Scott said. "It's a poor heart that never rejoices."

"Did you make that up?" Ruby said.

"What kind of good day?" said Linda.

"In the stock market."

"You're playing the market?"

"Is that your Jewish grandmother imitation?"

"Like on *Seinfeld*," Ruby said.

Linda turned on her. "Shut up," she said. "And leave the room. That's a disgusting thing to say, Scott."

"Sorry," said Scott. "I didn't mean anything bad. But playing the market? Come on. It's not foreign territory—you've got a four-oh-one K. I simply made an informed investment."

"How much did we make, Dad?" Brandon said.

Scott scaled down the figure, thirty-seven five, perhaps too high for credibility. "Seventeen grand and change," he said. "So far."

Brandon high-fived him; that felt good.

"And the trip cost less than a quarter of that, everything included," Scott went on. "So what do you say?"

Linda looked at Brandon, who was watching her in a surprisingly detached way that gave Scott an insight into how he might turn out; at Ruby, who'd made no move to leave the room and was close to jumping up and down; at him. He was pretty sure she was thinking about the poor heart remark. Linda smiled. Not much of a smile, and the vertical frown line was still deep, but she said: "Okay."

Then came a few moments of happy pandemonium. Zippy lost control completely, barking, clawing at the trash bag, knocking a carton of Mongolian beef off the table with his tail.

"What about him?" Linda said.

"We'll have to call the kennel first thing in the morning," said Scott.

"You can't do that," Ruby said. "He hates the kennel."

"And didn't they say he could never go back after the last time?" said Brandon.

They all gazed down at Zippy. He was eating Mongolian beef off the floor, growling at the same time for some reason.

"What about Julian?" Ruby said. "Couldn't he stay here while we're gone? Zippy loves him."

"Brilliant," said Scott. "What's his number?"

"Isn't it a bit of an imposition?" Linda said.

"We'll pay him, of course," Scott said.

Scott called Julian. "How're things?"

"No complaints," said Julian. "And you?"

"Pretty good, in fact." Scott heard the wind outside. Icy sheets came slapping against the windows in waves. Tomorrow at this time he'd be sitting at one of those in-pool swim-up bars, watching for the green flash. "We've got a little favor to ask you."

"Yes?"

Scott explained. "And we'll pay you, goes without saying," he added at the end.

"No payment necessary," Julian said. "A change of scene will do me good."

Ruby ran upstairs to pack.

24

"**W**hat room shall I take?" Julian said.

Ruby came down the stairs with her backpack, blessedly free of school things, now scattered around her room, and full of airplane carry-on things—CDs, player, crayons, gum, candy, *The Complete Sherlock Holmes*. Dad was looking at Mom.

"The bedroom at the end of the hall, I guess," Mom said. "The empty one."

"Or would you prefer I make up one of the couches," Julian said, "perhaps in the entertainment center?"

"No, no," said Mom. "Of course not."

Enough chitchat, Ruby thought. To get her point across without being rude, she said, "Brandon up, I hope?"

"First one, in fact," said Dad. "He's loading the car."

"My God," said Ruby. The prince of sleep in action, and still dark outside.

Ruby went into the garage. There he was, doing lots of things crisply, showered, neatly dressed, gelled to a fare-thee-well, or maybe fair-thee-well, both expressions probably on their way out of the language, and good riddance. And that one too.

"Here," he said, "give me that."

Ruby handed him her backpack. He fitted it into a perfect space beside the tennis bag.

"What about the snorkeling stuff?" she said.

"All set."

"Mine too?"

"Are you coming on the trip?"

"Yeah."

"Then yours too."

The prince of sleep wakes up as Mr. Helpful. She had a crazy impulse to throw her arms around him and give him a big kiss, maybe kicking up one of her heels at the same time like a war bride cutie pie. She fought off the whole thing in less than a second.

"Does Trish know you're going?" she said.

"What's it to you?"

And they were back on track. A quick little kiss: now she wished she'd squeezed it in while the moment was right.

Zippy came in, trotting in tight circles and making a whiny sound.

"He's crying," Ruby said.

"What a pussy," said Brandon, stowing the hard little square suitcase with Mom's toiletries.

"He doesn't mean that," Ruby told Zippy, kneeling and giving him a big hug. "Everybody loves you." He licked her face in a frantic sort of way. "Oh, the poor thing," she said. "He knows, he knows." She took him into the kitchen, filled his food and water bowls to the brim. He didn't even glance at them, not like him at all. "We'll be back in no time," she said, stroking his ears. He kept whining, gazed up at her with big eyes like a saint in one of those paintings by the guy who made everyone so long and thin.

"Don't worry," said Julian. She turned. He was watching from the door. "I'll take good care of him."

"Thanks, Julian. He's no trouble at all, really. You'll have lots of fun." She opened a cupboard under the counter. "He needs a bowl of this every night, but sometimes he gets hungry in the morning, too. And he likes the occasional can of this stuff. These are for treats, and here are some toys. If you've got a chance, he could use a little refresher on his retrieving skills—he's part retriever, did you know that?—and the rawhide bones—"

"Ruby!" Dad called from the garage. "What's the holdup?"

"Don't give him real bones," Ruby said. "They could kill him."

"Point taken."

"Even though he's a carnivore."

"Ruby!" Dad came in from the garage.

"Bye, Zippy." She kissed him and kissed him. "I love you, I love you, I love you." He kissed her back like there was no tomorrow.

"For God's sake, Ruby!"

"He doesn't want me to go."

"Any Mongolian beef left?" Dad said. "That'll ease the pain." He came over, grabbed her hand, pulled her toward the garage. "Thanks for everything, Julian," he said.

Mom poked her head in the door, frantic all of a sudden. "We'll never make it."

"If I drove you," Julian said, "you wouldn't have to worry about parking."

"Good idea," said Dad.

"Sure you don't mind?" said Mom.

"Not at all," said Julian. "And it'll give Zippy a chance to collect his thoughts."

. . .

"**C**ollect his thoughts?" said Brandon, laughing in the car. "Where's he going to find the first one?"

They drove to the airport—Dad and Mom in front, Julian, Brandon, and Ruby in the back, Ruby in the middle, where Brandon never sat, not ever, like it was against his religion—laughing all the way, until they came to a car fire on I-91. Ruby had never seen a car fire before: smoke, flames, and a woman crying beside an ambulance.

"Oh, dear," said Julian.

The car fire caused a backup. Fifteen minutes before departure, they squealed to a stop in front of the terminal—actually squealed, like a sound effect on a cop show—and everyone jumped out, Julian too, to help with the bags, and ran to the ticket counter. There was a huge line.

"Over here," said Dad.

A huge line; but in first class no line at all.

"My, my," said Julian.

"We never do this," said Linda as Dad handed over the tickets. "One of those upgrades."

Brandon and Julian heaved the bags on the scale. Ruby gazed at the economy-class line with satisfaction. Everyone in it was real tense. She herself was wonderfully relaxed, like the woman who said, "Peel me a grape." Beyond the line, the sliding glass doors to the outside opened and three people came in—a man and a woman in long matching fur coats and a girl of about her own—

"Hey, there's Kyla!"

Dad turned. "Kyla Gudukas?"

"Here you go, sir," said the agent, handing him the tickets. "Gate nineteen."

They started toward the gate, crossing paths with the Gudukases. Mrs. Gudukas had dyed her hair blond. She looked very small in her fur coat.

"Well, well," said Mr. Gudukas. "Great minds think alike. Where're you off to?"

Dad told him. "And you?"

"Paris," said Mr. Gudukas. "Weekend getaway. We're staying at the Ritz."

"Bring me back one of their shampoos," Ruby told Kyla.

The Gudukases went on, towing leather baggage with bright gold fittings.

"Julian, thanks so—" Mom began. They all looked around. Julian was gone.

"Maybe he saw a cop," Dad said.

"A cop?" said Ruby.

"They tow," Dad said.

"Wouldn't want that, would we, Bran?" said Ruby.

"Too bad you said that," said Bran. "I was going to let you have the window."

They settled into the front of the first-class section. Ruby sat in her seat, aisle, not window, but the most comfortable seat ever invented, and tried every possible position. Across the aisle, she heard Mom say, "Paris? I had no idea they were doing so well."

"Times are good," Dad said.

A champagne cork popped nearby. The flight attendant smiled down at Ruby.

"What would you like?" she said.

Would *peel me a grape* be going too far?

Julian was not in a good mood when he drove back to 37 Robin Road, hit the button on the visor of Linda's Jeep to open the garage door, parked, entered the kitchen. Plot development was his responsibility, but some of the characters, even minor ones like Mickey Gudukas, kept having their own ideas. If he hadn't heard that little chirp—*there's Kyla*—all his work would have been ruined, an unsatisfying, popgun climax, at once demeaning and absurd, like being pelted with rotten fruit. A near thing: his hurried exit, while unremarked at the time due to sheer choreographic happenstance, was bound to raise questions. He could imagine the answers to those questions—police, tickets, towing, answers probably supplied by Scott—but he couldn't be sure. He couldn't even be sure, not one hundred percent, that Gudukas hadn't seen him. Gudukas, still in the rubber-matted entrance between the sliding doors, beyond the economy-class line, hadn't been looking his way, and Julian had instantly turned his back and walked off, but he couldn't be sure. Two more low-grade worries, like trickles suddenly appearing on a dike: how was he expected to work in this atmosphere?

Julian lit a cigarette, dropped the match in the sink, tried to calm himself. Not so easy, especially when he saw they'd left dirty dishes—two mugs, one plate, one bowl, three juice glasses. Who was expected to clean them? He took deep tobacco breaths, gazed at the dishes.

Why does the boy worry so much? He'd overheard his father asking that once, on the verandah at the tennis club above Freetown, as he came up the path from those strange African courts, well supplied with ballboys but too long by almost a yard. And his mother's reply: *Because he's marked for great things.* The words had thrilled him then, thrilled him still. Great things were happening at last: a fitting memorial, perhaps. It struck him at that moment that burning human flesh smelled like any other barbecue.

Was that the next line of the poem? He took out his notepad, wrote standing by the sink.

> *negligent is to forsake as*
> *mendacious is to deceive*
> *nothing you can't depend on*
> *will ever depend on you.*
> *burning human flesh—*

He stopped right there. It was not the next line of the poem, perhaps belonged in some other poem; perhaps in no poem at all. He sucked on his cigarette, smoked it long past the point of elegance, down to an addict's nub.

Something pressed the back of his leg, startling him.

Julian whirled, heart pounding. Only the dog. It pressed up against him, wagging its tail. Julian backed away.

"None of that," he said.

Then he saw what should have been obvious from the moment he came in: a turd, right in front of the doorway leading to the dining room.

"Come here, Zippy."

Zippy came.

Julian took Zippy's collar. "New regime, Zippy," Julian said. "Meet Robespierre."

He led Zippy toward the dining room. He'd had a dog once, briefly, growing up. His father had trained the animal, name now forgotten. You trained a dog like this.

"Like this, Zippy."

But Zippy dragged his feet, and as they got closer to the mess he'd made, dropped down into a sitting position. Julian pulled him along, brisk and matter-of-fact, the way his father had done, at least at the start of training sessions. Brisk and matter-of-fact, but his father had had a rough hand: with a smile he'd give your shoulder a little encouraging squeeze, a squeeze that always hit a nerve, carrying a countermessage.

"Here we go, Zippy."

They stood over the stinking pile. His hand tight around Zippy's collar, Julian forced the dog's head down and down. The dog whined, resisted with all his strength; the difference in their relative strengths was delicious.

"Making the connection, little doggie?" Julian said. "This is what we never ever do." He pushed Zippy's face a little farther down, to be absolutely sure the message got through, that all nerves got touched. Then Zippy growled, the hairs on the back of his neck rising. Julian heard himself growling back, but louder, felt the hairs on the back of his neck rising too, and hot chills shot through his own nervous system, rebounded around. He shoved Zippy's muzzle right into the shit, held it there, mushed it around a little. *Never ever, Mommy and Daddy.*

Julian let Zippy go. The dog bolted from the room, tail down, spirit altered. Julian's mood lifted. Now he didn't mind cleaning the mess, was hardly aware of doing it. Hot chills still circulated inside him, but less intense. He felt much better, more comfortable, at home.

Julian carried his suitcase up to the empty bedroom at the end of the upstairs hall, the one raised a few steps to its own level, Adam's room. Like an artist's garret: it really was the nicest room in the house, quite suitable.

The bedding was still rumpled, as before. Julian stripped off the sheets, piled them by the doorway for laundering on his next trip downstairs. First he had to familiarize himself with his new personal space. This was basic, a fundament of the military arts. He flipped the mattress, opened the closet, all the drawers in the desk and chest of drawers, found nothing. The boy hadn't even carved his name on any of the wooden surfaces.

On the wall, Julian found two or three bits of transparent tape where posters had been hung, but no posters, not rolled up among the dust balls under the bed, not fallen behind the chest of drawers or the desk. Just as well: the sight of some now retired athlete or has-been movie star would have been mildly depressing in a predictable sort of way. But what was this? Behind the desk, wedged between the wall and the tin of the baseboard radiator: a yellowed sheet of paper. Julian withdrew it with care, restored the desk to its precise previous position.

He moved to the window. Another dark day, almost colorless. He held the paper to what light there was; funereal, he couldn't help but think.

Book Report
Adam Gardner
Ms. Freleng, Third Grade

The Wind in the Willows is my favorit book I ever read. By Kenneth Grahame. This is all about a bunch of animals that live by a river. Some of them are Mole Rat and Badger, but the funniest one is Toad. Toad is rich and lives in Toad Hall. Also he is a very bad driver. He cant stop himself from stealing a beuatifull car. He gets thrown in gaol, which is jail in there country, for twenty years but he escapes. When Toad says things like I wonder if this sort of car starts easily, get reddy for a big adventure.

The reasin for the title is there is a Wild Wood in the book with willow trees and sometimes the lone wind blows.

Good, it said at the bottom, *but not a full page. Watch spelling and punctuation.*

Julian folded the paper and put it in his pocket: excellent data for the Adam page in his notebook, to be analyzed later. *Superboy—the paragon under whose boot they lie.* Paragon or normal kid? Decidedly normal—probably not much brighter, if at all, than his brother, the project. Was there something in the very nature of these family people, these complacent exemplars of the 5,999,900,000, that marred their vision of each other? What a helpful insight that might be!

Julian explored the house. He didn't find and hadn't expected any dark secrets. Checkbooks, bank statements, report cards, common prescription medicines, none psychotropic— he added details but learned nothing new. He did come across the blueprints to 37 Robin Road in a desk in the master bedroom and borrowed them temporarily. Scott's toolbox he found in the furnace room, a Santa Claus card still taped to the handle, the tools inside shiny and in their virginal slots.

Julian made lunch, two English muffins with strawberry jam and a glass of milk, studying the blueprints while he ate. *Questo è l'inizio della fine,* but he had no *fine* in mind. Must an auteur know *Z* before he set down *A*? How limiting—

surely it was somewhere in the *LMNOP*'s that the very best *Z*'s were born. You had to give yourself something to work with, even if there were many blanks ahead, must wrestle with the *LMNOP*'s, trusting your talent to find *Z*. It was hard work, and daring. But he was marked for greatness.

Julian took a ride in Linda's Jeep, the Triumph, his preference, being too conspicuous. He was a nice suburban fellow, driving down to Bridgeport, radio tuned to NPR. He heard a lot of earnest stuff indeed.

Was it a challenge to find a low-life bar in Bridgeport, the kind where after a drink or two—bottled beer only, Julian had no faith in anything else in such a place—the right contact would lead him into an alley where a second contact would make the transaction? No, it was easy. Difficulty in buying drugs would have signified some other country. Julian could barely understand this second contact, a brother citizen no doubt, but his dialect extreme. Money and drugs went in opposite directions, Julian keeping his gloves on the whole time. The contact, runny-nosed, walleyed, a barbarian, pure and simple, made some remark that might have looked toward future commerce. Julian felt momentary empathy with those vegetarians who admitted no human superiority over any other animal.

But of animals: task one, easy; task two, to find the right pet store, was much harder. Hours went by. What's wrong with this one? they would say. Or that one?

"Not speckled enough," he would tell them.

"Not speckled enough?"

Night had fallen before he returned to 37 Robin Road.

The blueprints showed an attic, but there was no access to it from anywhere but a small painted-over hatch cover in the ceiling of the upstairs hall, totally inconvenient. Julian carried the toolbox to Adam's room. He was no expert with tools but he understood the concept of tools very well: instruments for getting what you wanted. He opened the toolbox, first reading the card *(Merry Xmas, Daddy. Mom bought this but I thought it was a good idea. Love, Ruby. P.S.: Think treehouse)*. Then, plugging in the saw, he went into the closet and cut a square out of the ceiling, about two feet by two. He rolled in the desk-chair, and standing on it, placed blueprints, tape measure, auger, and flashlight on the surface above. After that he hoisted himself through, pencil in his teeth. Like a studious pirate, he thought: he must have looked rather dashing.

Ten feet six inches, read the blueprint, from the hinge side of the closet door to the wall where the two bedrooms met, Adam's and Ruby's. Julian crouched his way along the attic floor, soft and slightly springy from the layer of pink insulation, paying out the measuring tape. Eight feet four inches to the near side of her windows, a pair of double-hungs, five feet two inches more to the far side of the windows; and the head of her bed should be here. He rolled back the insulation, checked his measurements once more, penciled a thick black *X* on the exposed plywood.

Julian bored a half-inch hole with the auger. This was more in the nature of reconnaissance; a bigger hole, although not much bigger, could come later if necessary. *Auger* was completely unrelated to *augur*, two different mother languages, but still he couldn't help making the pleasant connection. A tiny pile of wood dust accumulated on the floor; then resistance ceased abruptly and the metal bit slid through with a little lurch. He thought of Gail.

Julian bent over the hole, shone the flashlight through. It glowed in the eyes of some animal, down there in Ruby's dark room, startling him. His eyes made the adjustment: only a bear, a teddy bear, lying on her pillow. Perfect, on the first try. He turned out to be good with tools.

Julian gathered them up, crept back through the attic, lowered himself down through the square hole in the ceiling of Adam's closet, his feet feeling for the chair. Then came a different shock, far more powerful and unnerving than the teddy bear. Standing just a few feet from the open closet door, watching his descent, was a woman. He recognized her at once: Jeanette. He had no idea how she came to be there, but he understood the deeper meaning of her appearance, or reappearance, certainly reappearance, considering the Starbucks scene: this was Nemesis.

25

Julian took the pencil from between his teeth. "Jeanette, if I'm not mistaken?"

She nodded. Somehow the auger overbalanced and fell from the edge of the hole he'd made in the attic, crashing down in the closet behind him. Her eyes went to it, then back up to his. Not up, really: she was almost his height, perhaps an inch or two shorter. She offered no explanation for being in the house, putting him in the absurd position of having to justify his presence first.

"They've gone for the weekend," Julian said. "Well-deserved respite. I'm taking care of Zippy and doing the odd repair, just to make myself useful, et cetera."

"Yes," Jeanette said, "Zippy. I was returning Ruby's bike and I heard him through the garage wall. Heard him from the street, actually."

"He does like to bark," Julian said.

"He was howling, not barking," said Jeanette. She had a direct way of speaking, a direct way about her in general, that he didn't like at all. "So I looked into the kitchen."

She paused there, watching him. He'd closed the big garage door, of course, but there was another door at the back of the garage that she must have used. The door from the garage to the kitchen was never locked, and he'd adopted local custom, thoughtlessly perhaps.

"And?" Julian said.

"The dog was in a bad way."

"He was?" said Julian. He had the saw in his hand, made a rueful little gesture with it. "I didn't hear a thing."

She paused again. He noticed that she was wearing bib ski pants over a turtleneck, hazarded a guess.

"On your way up to the mountains?"

"Yes," she said, peering beyond him, into the closet.

"Skiing should be good," he said, "if it doesn't get too cold. Where do you go?"

"Killington," said Jeanette. "Don't you want to know what was wrong with your charge?"

"My charge?"

"I thought they left you in charge of the dog."

"Of course," he said, "although it's no charge at all in the sense of burden—he's such a fun little guy."

"You think he was having fun, tied up like that?"

"Tied up?"

"Hog-tied is more like it. I've got a camera in the truck, and I'm tempted to take a picture the ASPCA might be interested in."

"Hog-tied? I haven't the slightest idea what you're talking about."

"No?" she said. "I'll show you." So direct, and clearly a woman of action, too: still, Julian thought he detected a little doubt in eyes unaccustomed to showing any.

He followed her out of Adam's room, along the hall to the stairs. Julian was close behind as they went down. She was a very fit woman, with trim but well-defined muscles across her shoulders and up the sides of her neck. They were rigid.

A jump rope, now cut in three unequal lengths—perhaps cut in haste or with strong emotion, to judge from how widely scattered they were—lay on the kitchen floor. No sign of the dog at first: but then Julian saw him, back in the shadows under the table.

"There you are, Zipster," he said. "Come on out, fella."

The animal shrank under Ruby's chair, against the wall and out of sight.

"Hey, boy—what's wrong?" Julian said. He glanced at the lengths of jump rope. "What's all this?"

"I cut him free," Jeanette said.

"He was bound with the jump rope?" Julian said.

"You're pretending not to know anything about this?"

Julian raised his hands, palms up. "I swear."

"How could you not know he was tied up down here, his four paws all together and his head so far back he could hardly breathe?"

"Oh my God," Julian said. He blinked a few times, like a strong but sensitive man fighting to contain strong but sensitive emotions. Then he passed his hand over his forehead, looked her in the eye, but humbly, and said, "I've got a confession to make."

Her gaze, hard to begin with, hardened some more. She was a formidable figure, square in front of him in those bib ski pants, a Killington lift ticket dangling from one of the zippers; and her hands were big, weather-roughened, capable.

Julian took a deep breath, sighed. "Zippy ran away this afternoon. I had him outside with me while I was shoveling the walk, and all of a sudden, out of the blue, he just took off. Like a streak. Of course I ran after him, but I'm not much of a runner, Jeanette, and he got away. Clean away."

"So?" said Jeanette. "What are you saying?"

Julian made a fist, pounded it into his open hand. "Mr. Stromboli," he said. "That sadistic son of a bitch."

"Excuse me?" said Jeanette.

"And naturally we can never prove anything, damn it to hell."

"What are you talking about?"

"Mr. Stromboli, across the street. Ruby never mentioned him?"

"What's Ruby got to do with this?"

"Nothing. I just wondered whether maybe she mentioned him. You know the way she babb . . . The point is Mr. Stromboli hates Zippy. Ruby's a bit afraid of him, truth to tell. I once had to step in before he struck Zippy with a golf club."

"Is that true?"

"Ask Ruby. It was a rather unforgettable moment. He was on his lawn in robe and slippers, the club a six iron, I believe."

"So you're saying . . . ?"

"He must have," Julian said. They were starting to think along the same lines at last. "He must have caught Zippy, tied him—done what he did—and delivered him over here. I didn't hear a thing, busy as I was with the repairs."

"That's horrendous," Jeanette said.

"Poor little dog," Julian said. He knelt down. "Come on out, pup." Zippy shrank further into the shadows.

"I'm going right over there," Jeanette said.

"As I mentioned," Julian said, "nothing can be proved, and based on my brief but indelible interaction with the man, I'm quite certain he'll deny everything. My suggestion is to wait for Scott and Linda's return, offer the information to them in the least upsetting way—no point ending their vacation on a sour note—and allow them to decide a course of action."

A splendid verbal flow, coming at just the right time: Julian could feel it sweeping away her doubts. "You won't forget?" Jeanette said.

"Certainly not," said Julian. "In fact, I'll jot down a memo at once, to be sure I've got the sequence right." He took out his memo pad and the Mont Blanc pen.

Her gaze went to pad and pen, then his face. "All right,"

she said. She bent down, looked under the table. "Come on out, Zippy."

He didn't move.

Julian opened Zippy's cupboard, found one of the rawhide treats. "Here you go, boy," he said. No response. "Perhaps if we just put it here on the floor for him and leave him alone for a while, he'll pull himself together."

"You're probably right," Jeanette said, and started toward the mudroom at last.

"Thank God you came over when you did," Julian said, opening the mudroom door for her. "Have fun on the slopes."

She nodded and stepped outside. Julian closed the door behind her and went upstairs. Through the window in the master bedroom, he watched her backing the pickup out of the driveway, her skis, boots, and poles lying in the bed of the truck. She drove off down Robin Road, headed in the direction of Indian Ridge and 91, north to Vermont.

Julian returned to the attic, widened the hole in Ruby's ceiling to a diameter of about two inches. He left the flashlight by the hole, shining there to mark the spot, then crept back to his Alice-in-Wonderland entrance in Adam's closet. He lowered himself down into Adam's room, and from under Adam's bed withdrew the terrarium from its quiet resting place. The speckled band lay coiled in its miniature jungle. A cliché, certainly, to find the creature beautiful, yet there was truth in clichés: no worm, despite the similarity in shape if not size, could ever be called beautiful.

"Come, Prettyface," said Julian, looking down through the steel mesh screen over the terrarium. "Places, everybody."

He carried the terrarium into the closet, climbed onto the chair, hoisted it up on the attic floor. Then he pulled himself up and, crouching, advanced the terrarium somewhat awkwardly in gentle bumps toward the shining flashlight, a small flashlight but nicely balanced and very bright, a tribute to Linda's gift-buying skill, her thoroughness, perhaps even her thoughtfulness. No, not that: stop at thoroughness.

"Ready?" he said, sitting himself by the enlarged hole in the attic floor, more than big enough he saw, now that he had the talent on stage. He shone the light on the terrarium. What a calm performer, a trusty old pro! Julian removed the steel mesh screen, no hurry, laid it down. "Set?" he said, and reached in, quick and decisive, the way his father had taught him, grabbing Prettyface firmly but not roughly by the neck, if Prettyface's strange adaptive bulge could be called a neck.

Prettyface didn't like that, of course: who would? But this was only a one-dimensional creature, after all, that dimension now erased. How frustrating for it, as Julian could feel from the peristaltic writhings. He lowered Prettyface's head to the two-inch diameter hole, squeezing perhaps a little harder than necessary, just to show who was boss, or in this case, director, or—to convey the whole truth and nothing but the truth—the auteur. Also—why not admit this?— it felt good. He wasn't made of stone.

"Go," he said, and shoved Prettyface's squat, diamond-shaped head and puffed neck through the hole, encouraging the rest of him along with a two-handed shove, like a card player betting poker chips, a card player with an ace in the hole, as it were. Prettyface vanished with a last panicky flick of the tail.

Julian scrambled to a kneeling position over the hole, shone the light through, angled his eye close. Down below, Prettyface had already landed on the pillow. The whole episode must have been deeply unsettling: Prettyface had turned on the teddy bear, was striking, striking, at those glowing eyes. They stopped glowing.

"Cut," said Julian. He crawled back to Adam's closet as fast as he could, dragging the terrarium, dropped through, hurried down the hall to Ruby's room. He flicked on the lights. Prettyface was on the bed, slithering around in an abrupt fashion, still agitated. Ruby's quiver hung on the closet doorknob. "There, there," said Julian, withdrawing an arrow. He advanced on the bed, arrow extended. Prettyface curled up onto it, in the manner of his kind, and easy as that, Julian thrust him down into the terrarium and clapped the steel mesh cover on top.

"What the hell is going on?" said someone behind him.

Julian forced himself not to whirl around, not to succumb to a reptilian panic of his own. Not just someone, but a woman; not just a woman, but Jeanette. He turned slowly, his control complete, at the very summit of the evolutionary chain.

A vein was throbbing in Jeanette's neck. Her eyes darted around: the terrarium, the hole in the ceiling, the sawdust on the bed, back to him.

"Nothing, really," Julian said, "merely—"

Her voice rose. "No one's home at the Strombolis'. The woman next door says they left for Florida yesterday."

"I'm just baffled," Julian said. She must have circled the block. He thought furiously, seeking some explanation, innocent yet convincing, of what had happened to Zippy, and now of what she'd seen in the two bedrooms. "Have you met Ruby's little pal yet?"

"Ruby hates snakes," Jeanette said. "This is a matter for the police." She drew a cell phone from the pocket of her ski pants and walked out of the room. Julian needed time to think and she wasn't giving him any. He hurried after her.

Jeanette was halfway down the stairs, cell phone in one hand, index finger of the other poised over the keypad. "Police?" said Julian, starting down after her. "Don't you think that's a little extreme? After all—"

Over her shoulder, Julian saw her index finger hit the 9. He continued with whatever reasonable clause came next, but at the same time leaped ahead, reached around her—a kind of punch, to be accurate—and struck the cell phone from her hand. It clattered down into the front hall. Nine-one-one was out of the question—he knew its dangers now.

Jeanette whirled around, balanced there, four or five

steps from the bottom. "You're going to regret that," she said.

"I hope not," Julian told her. In fact, he was quite sure: he had the higher ground, another tenet of the military arts. "We really should talk, Jeanette. I think you're being somewhat unreasonable."

She gave him a look loaded with negative emotions—anger, suspicion, even contempt, that last closing so many doors in his mind—and turned without a word, headed down the stairs toward the phone. Julian grabbed her shoulder, not violently or even roughly.

Jeanette must have missed that consideration. She batted his hand away with a movement that was rough, was violent, a movement that ended with her elbow jabbing him right below the sternum, leaving him suddenly breathless. The next thing he knew she was down in the hall, scooping up the phone, her fingers at the keypad once more.

Julian dove from where he was, about halfway up. His shoulder caught her in the ribs. He heard a quick and gratifying rip of human tissue—his hearing was acute. They fell together onto the floor, his hands around her neck as they rolled, a roll that ended with him on top. But not quite ending: she gave a little twist, some subtle movement of Asian origin, and the roll kept going. At the same time, Zippy came racing in, barking wildly. Now Jeanette was on top, straddling him, and before he could move a knife appeared in her hand, a wood-handled folding knife, the blade not especially imposing, but pressed against his neck. An outdoorsy woman: why had he assumed she'd cut the jump rope with something from a kitchen drawer?

"Don't move," she said. Zippy circled them, barking his head off. Julian didn't move, although of course he would have to, and soon. Instead he relaxed his body, hoping hers would relax too in unconscious imitation. It did not. Without taking her eyes off him, Jeanette felt around with her free hand, found the cell phone. She brought it into his field of vision, hit the 9 once more.

At that moment, Zippy lunged forward and sank his teeth deep into Julian's right shoulder. Julian cried out in pain, genuine pain, genuinely felt. Jeanette's gaze shifted to the dog, and as it did, some clumsy movement of his hindquarters knocked the phone from her hand. For an instant, Julian no longer felt the blade against his neck. The instant to move: and he moved. An instant after that, the knife was in his hand, his left hand but good enough. Another instant—or several more, because more than one thrust was necessary—and Jeanette was no longer in the story. She had no business being in it in the first place.

And Zippy, who still hadn't let go, who had those teeth sunk into him so deep, who growled so hatefully? There: he was out of the story too.

Julian didn't like mess. Here was mess indeed, both physical and organizational. But first he must listen. He listened and heard nothing, the outside and inside worlds quiet. Then he had to attend to himself. He pried Zippy's jaws apart, an awkward and painful process that almost made him cry out again. After that, he checked the tag on Zippy's collar. His shots were up to date, as Julian had assumed they would be.

In the downstairs bathroom, he took off his shirt, washed his wound in soap and warm water, bathed it in hydrogen peroxide he found in the cabinet, applied Bacitracin he found there too, taped on a gauze bandage. In the mirror he looked rather calm, and in a way handsomer and more full of life than he'd ever seen himself, especially once he'd washed the blood—mammalian, he couldn't be more specific than that—off his face. Julian went down to the entertainment center and helped himself to a modest portion of Highland Park, pouring with a hand that was almost steady.

Back upstairs, he turned off all the lights, presenting a proper late-night facade to the neighborhood. Then he checked outside. The Strombolis' house was also dark, of course—how careless not to keep an eye on them, but understandable, why be too hard on himself?—and the two or three other houses visible from 37 Robin Road were dark too. Julian went to the driveway and brought Jeanette's skis, boots and poles into the house, laying all the gear down in the front hall with everything else. Then he locked up and drove her pickup to Killington.

The last few carloads of après-ski traffic were still on the highway, even at the late hour Julian reached Killington, but the road to Bear Mountain was deserted. He followed it up to the base lodge. Except for a few cars here and there, the vast parking lot was empty. No one sat in any of the cars, no lights shone anywhere, other than the snow cats grooming the trails, so high above they might have been flying. Julian parked near the lodge, borrowed ski gloves, hardly tight at all, and a ski mask he found on the passenger seat—the night being so cold—and left the pickup there, locking it and pocketing the keys.

Julian walked down the Bear Mountain road to the highway, turned toward town, saw a bus sign. He followed it to the Killington Peak access road, found the little open bus shelter, sat on the bench. A cold night and a colder dawn: Julian wasn't the only boarding passenger wearing a ski mask when the first southbound bus came along. Organizational mess in hand, physical to come. What a creative person he was! That was Julian's last thought before he fell asleep in the back, lulled by the motion and the warmth.

26

Practice watching the smallest thing you can see on any object. Why not? Soaking up some bonus rays on a terrace at the airport—the flight home delayed a few hours, even more if they were lucky—Ruby sipped a tall cold Coral Splash, mostly Sprite but blue in color, with a bright red maraschino cherry at the bottom, the coral, of course, and looked here and there for smallest things. She'd learned so much on this trip already. One, she could hold her breath and dive to fifteen feet and sometimes find lobsters at the bottom, their antennas poking out from under rocks, very alert. Two, Bahamians spoke a different kind of English, hard to understand at first, then all of a sudden easy, and finally you couldn't stop yourself from talking the same way. Three, she had to get very rich so she could have a house down here one day. Four, European men wore tiny bathing suits but pranced around like nothing was wrong. Five, what was the big deal about caviar?

Mom came through the automatic doors, sat in the shade of the umbrella. She looked great, those Mediterranean skin tones glowing.

"They still don't know, mon," she told Dad.

Dad laughed, sipped a cold one, wiggled his bare toes, still a little prunelike from the last ocean swim. He looked great too. So did Brandon, but he was inside the terminal somewhere, probably having a beer or maybe a Goombay smash, no problem down here, out of Mom and Dad's sight. No problem about Brandon paying for it, either. He'd won a five-hundred-dollar jackpot on the slots, and given Ruby a hundred of his own free will. And Dad was up almost fifteen hundred dollars in blackjack. The rich got richer, just like they said. Ruby reached into her Coral Splash, fished out the cherry, popped it in her mouth.

"Another cherry or two, miss?" said a passing waiter.

"Why thank you," said miss.

"Maybe I should call Julian," Mom said, "tell him not to bother picking us up."

"Sure," said Dad. "We'll take a cab."

"But it's expensive," Mom said.

Dad shrugged. Ruby had never seen him so relaxed: he was practically brain-dead. Mom took out her cell, left some message on the machine. Ruby wasn't really listening; she was eyeing the smallest thing she could see on one of those geckos. The geckos were great, but bringing one home, her initial idea, was out of the question, Zippy being the only-child type. This one was doing push-ups on the railing, a few feet away. His smallest thing was a tiny red dot over one eye, like one of those Indian caste marks, but misplaced. The smallest thing on the Rastafarian guy chopping at weeds with his machete on the other side of the railing was also red, a drop of blood, maybe from an insect bite, inside the first *O* of *One Love* on his T-shirt. And the girl of about her own age, but dressed to kill, at the next table? Her sunglasses, for sure: the tiniest, coolest sunglasses Ruby had ever seen.

The girl gave her a little smile. Oops: Ruby knew she must have been staring.

"Hi," she said.

"Hi," said the girl, only she said it a little funny. Maybe she was from LA or somewhere. That would explain the shades.

"Not a bad island, huh?" said Ruby.

"Fantastico," said the girl.

That would be the latest slang, no doubt, moving east like the weather.

"You from LA?" said Ruby.

"No," said the girl. "You are?"

"Connecticut," said Ruby.

The girl found something funny in that, giggled for a moment or two. "Me I am coming from Roma," she said.

"In Italy?"

"Sì. But you are saying Rome, am I not correct?"

"I'm saying Rome, yeah," said Ruby. She checked out those sunglasses, those clothes. She knew nothing about Rome. Ms. Freleng hadn't gotten to it yet, probably never would, bogged down as they were with Cortés and Pizarro. Was it possible Rome was even cooler than LA? Maybe just the women, since the men would be running around in those tiny bathing suits all summer. There was nothing cool about that and never could be. "Your English is pretty good," Ruby said.

"I am studying of it in school," said the girl.

"Me too," said Ruby. The girl laughed again. She had a jumble of teeth, just like Ruby. Ruby laughed too. "I know some Italian," she said.

"Yes?" said the girl.

"I know how to say, 'Where is the bargain shopping?'"

"Oh," said the girl, laughing again. "That is very, very critical."

Could she remember the whole thing? *Fine* was "shopping," *questo* was "where is," and what was the rest of it? Boom, it came, just like that: *"Questo è l'inizio della fine."*

The girl wrinkled up her forehead.

"Excuse the accent," said Ruby.

"This is not a question of the accent. But what it is you are saying is not of the subject of bargain shopping."

"No?"

"For where is the bargain shopping, we say *'Dove si può trovare i prezzi buoni?'"*

"That sounds a lot different," said Ruby.

"Sì."

"So what did I say?" said Ruby.

"Questo è l'inizio della fine?" said the girl.

It sounded so much better when she said it. Italian had to be the most beautiful language on God's green earth. She would start learning it as soon as she got home. "Yeah," said Ruby. "Does it mean anything?"

The girl nodded, pursing her lips a little. "It is meaning this is the initiation—*scusi*—perhaps you would be saying beginning, no?"

"Yes."

"Thus, beginning," said the girl. "This is the beginning of the end."

"That's what it means?"

"Sì."

"This is the beginning of the end?"

"*Sì.*"

"It isn't like some kind of code for shopping, maybe in Venice or somewhere?"

"Venice?" said the girl. "Code?"

"Veneshia," said Ruby, remembering they had their own word for Venice. "Coda."

The girl blinked. "Would it be a phrase, this beginning of the end, you perhaps heard at the cinema?" she said.

"Sure sounds like it," said Ruby.

"I am loving the cinema," said the girl. "I have been meeting Brad Pitt."

"You have?"

"Oh, certainly," said the girl. "My father is doing many face liftings for the stars."

Ruby glanced over at the girl's parents. They looked like movie stars themselves. Wrapped in silk and holding those tall skinny champagne glasses, they stared out at the palm trees, waving in the tropical breeze.

I don't have to go to school, tomorrow, do I?" said Brandon.

"It is tomorrow," said Ruby.

The taxi—one of those town cars, lots of room in the back—rolled through West Mill, the whole town fast asleep. Ruby's skin had lost that tingly feeling from the ocean. It looked cold out there, plus something else she couldn't put her finger on, something about Sunday night and no one in all those dark houses eager for Monday morning. What did they call it? The rat race. All the rats were resting up to race each other again, starting at seven, eight, or nine. And the races were all organized, even for kids: Brandon had the SAT, she had the Mad Minute and the other little contests with Ms. Freleng's funny names, air quotes around *funny*. As they turned onto Poplar Drive, the headlights of the town car swept past a lost-dog notice, taped to a telephone pole. Ruby's souvenir coconut rolled against her bare ankle, the milk sloshing around in there, very faint.

"Next house on the right," Dad said.

They parked in the driveway. Lights glowed in all the windows. The mudroom door opened as they got out of the car and Julian came to help with the bags.

"How was the trip?" he said.

"Great," said Dad, paying the driver. "How's everything here?"

"Good," said Julian. They took everything into the house, Ruby suddenly too tired to carry anything but the coconut. Was it her imagination or did it feel warm in her hands? "Except for one thing," Julian added as they plunked everything down on the mudroom floor.

Ruby went into the kitchen, glanced around. "Zippy," she called.

"It's all my fault," said Julian.

"What is?" said Mom.

They all turned to him, Mom, Dad, and Brandon still in the mudroom, Ruby in the kitchen. Julian bit his lip.

"Did something happen to Zippy?" Ruby said.

Julian squatted down to her level, faced her. "He ran away, Ruby. I'm so sorry. We were out shoveling the walk and a car went by with a dog poking its head out the side window, the dog barked at him—" Julian's voice cracked "—and Zippy just took off." Julian rose, looked at the others. "I ran after him, of course, calling and calling, but he just kept going and finally I lost sight of him on Indian Ridge. I just know he's going to come back, but he hasn't yet. I've been to the pound every day, I've put up signs, I've canvassed the neighbors." He raised his hands helplessly.

"What if he got run over?" Brandon said.

Julian looked pained. "The pound keeps track," he said. "No reports of anything like that."

"Could someone have taken him?" Mom said.

"Would Zippy let that happen?" Julian said. "I for one don't believe it." He swallowed.

Ruby started crying, hot tears, a flood. She ran outside:

"Zippy! Zippy! Zippy!" Dad pulled her gently back in the house.

Julian was showing Mom and Brandon the flyers he'd made. *Lost Dog,* it said at the top. *Generous Reward.* In the middle was a picture of Zippy, the Halloween one where he was sitting by the pumpkin. At the bottom it said *Have you seen Zippy? Please, please call,* and then the number.

"Maybe the kids could hand these out at school tomorrow," Julian said.

"Good idea," said Dad.

"But what if—" Ruby felt the tears coming again, somehow got a grip. "What if he comes back and there's no one home?"

"He'd wait out on the lawn, wouldn't he?" said Dad.

Ruby lost hold of that grip, heard her voice rising to a note that shamed her, kind of hysterical. "But what if he doesn't?"

Mom and Dad looked at each other. Julian said, "Why don't I return in the morning? I can watch for him during the day."

"That's very nice of you, Julian," Mom said.

"It's the least I can do," said Julian. "I feel so bad."

"In that case," said Dad, "you might as well stay the night."

"If that's all right," said Mom.

"Oh, certainly," said Julian. "It's my duty, under the circumstances."

Ruby took a deep breath. "Don't feel bad, Julian," she said. Through her teary eyes she could see his dampening too, a double blurriness. "It's not your fault."

"We'll just have to keep looking and looking," Julian said.

"Call the school the moment he shows up," Ruby said.

"Count on it."

They all went to bed. Ruby's teddy bear's name was Beamish, a word she'd loved the moment she first heard it, listening to Mom reading *Through the Looking-Glass*. She could remember the beamish part, word for word:

> *"And hast thou slain the Jabberwock?*
> *Come to my arms, my beamish boy!*
> *O frabjous day! Callooh! Callay!"*
> *He chortled in his joy.*

What could be happier than that? Ruby took Beamish under the covers with her, something she hadn't done lately, maybe not for a year or two. She'd been neglecting him, hadn't even noticed that his plastic eyes were cracked.

The house was quiet; last night she'd heard the ocean. Ruby turned off her bedside light, gazed up at the ceiling, all fuzzy and dark but with a very faint reddish tinge from the glowing digits of her clock. She had pretty much decided that there was no God. The fact that people had been squabbling about it for so long was proof enough. If she was God, she'd make damn sure that every single earthling knew about it in no uncertain terms from the get-go. Or there'd be hell to pay, she thought, and almost smiled for a second in the darkness. So, almost certainly no God: but that didn't stop her from speaking out loud just before falling asleep, to no one in particular: "Please bring Zippy back."

Scott was at his desk, connected to the Raging Bull live-time quote site, when the market opened. Codexco: $8.40, down another dime. Another dime meant another fifteen grand.

Tom poked his head in. "How was the trip?"

"Great."

"What'd you do?"

"Hit a little. Snorkeled. Ate like pigs. Brandon went on a scuba trip. I played a little blackjack."

"How did you do?"

"Up about a grand or so."

"And the stock?"

Scott glanced at the screen: down another nickel, made $7,500, just sitting there talking. "Doing what it's supposed to," he said.

"You're on a roll, bro," Tom said.

Bro was new.

At school, Ruby got the office ladies to make lots of copies of the Zippy flyer. She gave one to Ms. Freleng and to each kid in the class, including Amanda, who surprised her by saying how cute Zippy looked and promising to keep an eye out for him, and Winston, who asked why she didn't just get another dog. Amanda surprised her again: "Don't have a clue, do you, Winston?"

Winston didn't say another word, sat quietly on the bus going home, not even picking his nose. Ruby watched for Zippy the whole way, saw no dogs at all. Her house came in view. No Zippy out front, no pawprints on the fresh sprinkling of snow on the lawn or the driveway, and Julian hadn't called the school. That left a little window of hope, the possibility Julian had gone somewhere to get him while she was on the bus. But she knew Julian: he'd be waiting with the front door wide open, Zippy beside him, probably on his leash.

Ruby handed a flyer to Mr. V. as she got off. "Don't you worry," said Mr. V. "He'll turn up."

"You think so, Mr. V.?" said Ruby, pausing on the bottom step.

"They almost always do," said Mr. V. Then, while a few cars, a FedEx van and a Poland Spring truck waited behind the bus, its red lights flashing, he taped the Zippy flyer to his side window, facing out, at the same time telling a long story about a dog Mrs. V. had owned before they got married, a half-Schnauzer half-beagle who'd gone missing and ended up walking home all the way from Meriden. "Look what the cat brought in." That was what Mrs. V. said when the poor mangy thing came staggering up the driveway. "So don't you fret, beautiful," said Mr. V.

Ruby got off the bus. There were things about Mr. V.'s story that didn't add up, but she felt a little better anyway.

She went in the house, heard Julian on the phone. "... wearing a blue collar," he was saying. "Answers to the name of Zippy." He hung up as she entered the kitchen. "No news, I'm afraid," he said. He sat at the table, surrounded by lists, notes, phone books, balled-up pieces of paper. "I've been putting ads in the community newspapers."

"Good idea," Ruby said.

"I also bought this staple gun," he said. "I was going to tack up more flyers, maybe even a few in the woods."

"I'll do it," Ruby said.

"Want me to come with you?"

"You've done a lot already."

Ruby took her binders out of the backpack, stuck the staple gun in there with the remaining flyers.

"Heavy homework night?" Julian said.

Ruby nodded. Spelling, worksheets on the Mayans, the Toltecs and one other bunch she couldn't remember the name of, plus extra math: she'd had her worst Mad Minute ever, not even beating Winston.

"Can I help?" said Julian.

"I'll be okay."

Julian smiled. "No doubt in my mind," he said.

Ruby went into the garage. Her bike wasn't hanging from the hook. Right: Jeanette had it. For a moment, Ruby was a little annoyed that she hadn't brought it back yet; not annoyed, how could she be annoyed at Jeanette? But she needed the bike. And then she spotted it, leaning against the wall beside the lawn mower. A Post-it note was stuck to the seat: *Here's your ride, Rubester—use with care. J. P.S. That means a helmet.* Ruby found her helmet, dusted it off, hit the door button and rode out of the garage.

Lots of flyers were already up in the neighborhood, on Poplar Drive, Indian Ridge, Larchmont. Ruby went farther, across Larchmont as far as West Mill Wine and Spirits, back all the way to the health food store in the other direction. The health food store had a big bulletin board outside. Ruby was stapling the Zippy flyer right in the center when a woman coming out with a bag of groceries stopped beside her.

"Oh, yes," she said.

Ruby whipped around, looked up at her. "You've seen Zippy?"

"Unfortunately not," said the woman. "But I know about him. A very nice man was going up and down our street yesterday. He was so concerned. I'm sure your dog will show up—that's what I told him. I had a dog once who . . ." And she told a long story, a lot like Mr. V.'s except her dog walked all the way back from Waterbury instead of Meriden, and was missing an ear.

Ruby stopped at the pound on the way home. The pound was next to the Little League fields, and Ruby had often wandered over there during Brandon's games. She saw Zippy flyers on the boarded-up Little League concession stand and on a telephone pole by the pound office. The dogs heard her coming and started to bark.

Ruby walked around the office to the kennels at the back. The dogs were in their individual fenced-in cages, each with an opening at the back for going inside. They stopped barking when she came in sight—two big skinny ones and a little fat one. They watched her closely, tongues hanging out.

A door opened and a man in a green uniform came out. "Help you?" he said.

"My dog's lost," said Ruby, handing him a flyer.

"Right," said the man, "Zippy. Nothing so far. I'll call soon as I got news, like I said." The man smelled strongly of dog, wore a patch on his arm that said Animal Control Officer.

Ruby gazed up at him. "You're an expert, right?"

"Expert?"

"On this kind of thing."

"You might say that."

"So where is he?"

The animal control officer rubbed his chin; she could hear the rasp of his stubble. "Lots of possibilities," he said. "Specially if you're a dog."

Ruby waited for the rambling story of some dog's strange journey home—really wanted to hear it this time—but it didn't come.

Beyond the outfield fence lay the town woods, with a path that led to the pond and just past it the crossing path to her own backyard. Ruby walked her bike through the woods, the snow packed hard and slippery by the feet of others. She stopped from time to time to staple Zippy flyers to the trees, and once called out, "Zippy! Zippy!" A sheet of snow slid off a branch above, thumped down nearby.

Ruby came to the pond, saw that all signs of the high school party—bottles, cans, butts, boxes, keg—were gone. A thin coat of black ice covered the pond, except out in the middle where she could see tiny ripples. She stapled a flyer to a big tree by the water, where anyone circling the pond would see it. All of a sudden, there in the quiet woods where Zippy loved to play, even if he wouldn't fetch sticks thrown in the pond like he was supposed to, Ruby had a strong feeling that this flyer would be the one. She took a felt pen from her backpack and wrote at the top: *I miss him.* She hadn't meant to write that, had meant to write *Please help*, or underline the reward part, or do something else a little more useful.

Ruby rounded the big rock, came to the spot where Zippy had found the slice of sausage and pepperoni pizza. No pizza now, the snow smooth, even Sergeant D'Amario's deep footprints all gone, and of course gone too the tiny depression where Zippy had dug out the crack pipe. Ground zero in The Mystery of the Anonymous Caller. And that case was connected to The Mystery of the Varsity Jacket. Now here she was again, working on a third case, although it felt so different she didn't like to call it that. The Mystery of Zippy's Disappearance was so much realer. Not realer—they were all real—but bigger, maybe. That didn't mean she didn't care about Brandon, just that he wasn't missing and Zippy was.

None of that realer or bigger part had anything to do with the point she'd been trying to get at, though. She shoved it from her mind. The point had to be this: here she was again at ground zero for case two, which was tied to case one, only she was working on case three. At that moment, she thought of "The Musgrave Ritual," one of her favorites, where Holmes discovers the secret chamber under the stone floor of the old manor. But before that discovery, he says something very, very important. Ruby tore off her backpack, took out *The Complete Sherlock Holmes*, leafed through, found it: *"I was already firmly convinced, Watson, that there were not three separate mysteries here, but only one."*

27

Everyone was at dinner when Ruby got home, and they all seemed to be in a good mood, laughing and talking in the dining room. Did that mean Zippy was back? She hurried in and it got quieter right away. That was her answer, but she asked anyway.

"Is he here?"

"No," said Mom. "And where have you been?"

"Did anyone call?"

"Not about Zippy," Dad said.

"And I asked you a question," Mom said.

"At the pound." She froze Mom with a look, or tried to. Didn't Mom care about Zippy? Didn't any of them?

"Well, come and eat," said Mom.

"I'm not hungry."

"Gotta eat," said Dad.

Julian pushed the platter of steaks in front of her empty plate. He cared more than any of them and Zippy wasn't even his dog. Yet it had been on his watch, as he himself had said: not a nice thought, holding him to that, but Ruby thought it. She left the room.

The phone rang in the hall. She snatched it up.

"Hello?"

"Brandon there?"

"Dewey?"

"Yeah?"

"This is Ruby."

"Hey. How're you doin'?"

"Have you seen Zippy?"

"Zippy the dog, you mean?"

What other Zippys do you know, you fucking crackhead? "Yes," Ruby said.

"Nope," said Dewey. "Is he missing or something?"

"I'll get Brandon," Ruby said. She took the phone into the dining room—Dad was saying something about Codexco and Julian was listening with interest—and held it out to Brandon, not quite in his reach.

"Did you pass out the flyers?" she said.

"Flyers?" said Brandon. "Sure."

"Or did you dump them in your locker? Maybe you didn't take them in the first place."

"Huh? Give me the phone."

"Hey, kids," said Dad.

"You didn't bother, did you?"

"Back off."

"Because you didn't even tell Dewey. You don't care at all."

"For Christ's sake," Brandon said. "It's only a dog."

Ruby tossed him the phone—threw it at him, actually—and ran from the room.

"**H**eard the news?" said Dewey.

"What news?"

"Problem shot Unka Death. He's in critical condition."

"That's a joke, right?"

"Turn on your TV."

Brandon was already on his feet.

"Brandon?" said Mom. "Is it something about Zippy?"

Brandon hurried down to the entertainment center. The story was on a dozen channels: some dispute in a Manhattan strip club that afternoon, gunfire, vigil outside the hospital, clips from the video, over and over.

Fuck you, good as new, all we do, then it's through.

And Problem with that deep background voice: *Where the sun don't shine, where the sun don't shine.*

The video, over and over: the girl in the gold shorts and the white old-lady wig got in the Bentley and put her head in Unka Death's lap; Unka Death's diamond tooth sparkled as he turned the key; the trunk opened and Problem got out with the cleaver, the gold AK-47 medallion around his neck. Brandon didn't know what to think.

"What's going on?" he said.

"Life sucks," said Dewey.

Ruby was in a fury, all brake lines cut. No one really cared about Zippy. They just wanted her to get back to her normal self, weren't even trying. Take the flyers, for example, probably still in Brandon's backpack. She would take them into the high school herself, first thing in the morning.

Ruby went up to Brandon's room, hunted through the mess on his desk, on his bed, on the floor, found no flyers. She opened his backpack without compunction: no flyers. Where else? She went down to the mudroom. His varsity jacket hung on the peg. She searched the pockets. No flyers balled up in there, nothing else either.

But what was this? Through the pocket, inside between the quilted lining and the leather or leatherette outside material, she felt something hard. Ruby explored the object with her fingertips: a vial, no doubt about it. And another, and another: sewn in between the two layers.

Ruby went into the kitchen. Taking scissors from Mom's sewing drawer, she heard Julian in the dining room.

"Perhaps a college visit?"

"Perfect," said Mom. "Let's make a list."

Sing Sing, San Quentin, Devil's Island. Back in the mudroom, Ruby cut through a one-inch length of stitching at the bottom of the lining. No brakes. She could see where Brandon had done the same thing, and restitched with thread that didn't quite match, the gray slightly too dark. When had he learned to sew? And then she thought: Trish. She liked Trish. Was it completely impossible to know people on the inside?

Ruby squeezed the vials out through the hole. One, two, three—a dozen in all, like he was some kind of dealer. Ruby gathered them in her hat, put on her boots and jacket, went outside.

One of those dark nights with no moon or stars. Ruby understood how people who'd lost an arm or a leg still had those phantom feelings. Being out on this kind of night without Zippy was like that. She could feel his phantom occupying the empty space beside her, but quiet now, and unfrisky. Ruby walked into the woods, all the way to the pond. She threw the first vial, remembering while it was still in the air that the pond was frozen except in the middle. But it must have warmed up, because she heard a splash. She threw in the others, twelve splashes in all, and started for home.

Stepping out of the woods and into the backyard, just by the woodpile, Ruby noticed a tiny red glow. First she thought it came from inside the house, then realized it was outside, by the silhouette of the bird feeder. She got a little closer and saw a second silhouette.

"Julian! You smoke?"

"Oh my God," he said. "You scared me." The red glow spiraled away, vanished with a faint sizzle.

"Sorry," Ruby said.

"I didn't see you, that's all." He came closer. "Out for a walk at this hour?"

"Looking for Zippy."

"Ah." She smelled tobacco smoke when he said that. "I can't tell you how sorry I am."

She didn't want to hear that anymore. "I'm not giving up."

"Of course not," Julian said. "Me either."

"Thanks," Ruby said. At least he was helping, which was more than she could say for the members of her own family. But he smoked. That was stunning.

Tuesday was a half day, another teacher conference about the statewide tests. Brandon liked half days. The classes whipped by twice as fast, and sometimes the teachers showed a movie, or let them talk about whatever they wanted. In the afternoon came parties in adult-free houses. But not this afternoon: Julian was taking him on a college tour.

Trish passed him a note in English: *unka death's in a coma.*

He wrote *duh* and passed it back. Mr. Monson started handing back last week's grammar and vocabulary test. Trish passed him another note: *this aft—yr place or mine?* He wrote *can't*, started handing it back.

"Hope I'm not interrupting anything, Brandon," said Mr. Monson.

"No," said Brandon.

"Would that missive be of general interest, by any chance?" said Mr. Monson.

"No."

"Sure about that?" said Mr. Monson. "Sure you know what I'm talking about? The meaning of *missive*, for starters?"

"Note," said Brandon. "Message."

Mr. Monson's eyebrows rose. "You're surprising me

lately, Brandon." He dropped Brandon's test on his desk. At the top it said: *100*. The first perfect score he'd had in high school. "Been eating your Wheaties?" said Mr. Monson.

Someone groaned.

"What?" said Mr. Monson. "They don't say that anymore?"

"Can we talk about Unka Death?" said someone else.

"Unka Death?" said Mr. Monson. "Who dat?"

Brandon didn't even have to look to know that the three black kids in the class didn't like that at all; he could feel it. Mr. Monson was an asshole.

"A better poet than half the old farts we study in this class, Mr. Monson," said Trish.

Mr. Monson reddened, right up to his comb-over, whether because of the statement itself or just the word *fart*, Brandon didn't know. There was a knock at the door just as Mr. Monson had his reply ready. He closed his mouth, opened it again, said: "Come in."

Ms. Belsey, the principal, entered. "Pardon the interruption, Mr. Monson. Do you have Brandon Gardner here?"

"Yup."

"May I borrow him for a few minutes?"

"Borrow them all," said Mr. Monson.

Ms. Belsey smiled a tight little smile that showed no teeth and hardly moved her lips. "Brandon?" she said. He rose. She crooked her finger. He followed her out into the hall, thinking of Trish's mural with Mr. Kranepool, the parking lot security guy, licking Ms. Belsey's hairy legs. Glancing down, he saw that Ms. Belsey's legs, clothed in sheer stockings, were smooth and hairless, actually kind of nice, like she worked out after school. But funnily enough, there was Mr. Kranepool out in the hall. Plus Mr. Brack, the gym teacher.

"What's up?" said Brandon.

"Mind showing us your locker?" said Ms. Belsey.

"My locker?" said Brandon. "How come?"

"We'll get to that," said Ms. Belsey. Mr. Kranepool, and Mr. Brack stepped up on either side of him.

Brandon shrugged. "Whatever," he said.

His locker was 817, down the stairs and around the corner by the guidance office. Frankie J was coming the other way.

"Dude," he said. "Whassup?"

"If you don't hear from me by sundown, call the cops," said Brandon. Maybe the coolest thing he'd ever said, and to just the right person for spreading it around. But why not? There was nothing bad in his locker.

Frankie J laughed and kept going.

The cops were already there, two of them, standing in front of locker number 817. One held a German shepherd on a leash; the other wore sergeant stripes on his sleeve.

"Open your locker please, Brandon," said Ms. Belsey.

"Why?"

"Because the courts have ruled that under certain circumstances we have the right to open it, and therefore it would look better if you did the opening yourself."

That sounded like bullshit to Brandon. "What circumstances?" he said. Being in the clear was a nice feeling.

"If we have reason to believe, which we do, that there are illegal substances inside," said Ms. Belsey. "Especially if confirmed by the K-9 unit, a confirmation that I believe has been made, Sergeant D'Amario?"

"Yes, ma'am," said the sergeant. He looked at Brandon. "Hello, Brandon. Didn't know we'd be getting together again so soon. How's your dad?"

Sergeant D'Amario: who knew Dewey was selling crack, who was ten times smarter than him and Dewey put together. Confirmed by the K-9 unit—how could that be? Brandon had a crazy thought: he wished that his sister was there beside him.

"He's good," Brandon said.

"Your dad was a big man on campus at West Mill High,"

said Sergeant D'Amario. "Captain of the tennis team, if I remember right. I'm sure he'd want you to do the right thing."

"What's that?"

"Open the locker."

At that moment, Brandon thought of Unka Death, in a coma at some hospital in New York. *Fuck you, good as new, all we do, then it's through.* He started to say Nope, changed it to a plain "No." And felt his spine stiffen.

"Mr. Kranepool?" said Ms. Belsey.

Mr. Kranepool flipped some pages on his clipboard, mouthing, "Eight one seven," like the retard he was, checked the corresponding numbers—each locker had its own permanent combination—and dialed it on the four brass counters. He opened the locker.

"Show us where it is," said Ms. Belsey. "You can still make things easier for yourself."

Brandon said nothing.

They all stared into the locker. On the top shelf lay a comb, hair gel, and some scratched CDs; on the hooks hung his backpack and his varsity jacket; on the floor was all kinds of shit—old tennis shoes, a single hiking boot, books, papers, someone's belt.

"Do we have your consent for this legal search?" said Sergeant D'Amario.

"No," said Brandon. He was shaking a little now, but his voice sounded steady. There was nothing in there, whatever the dog thought.

Sergeant D'Amario nodded to the other cop. The other cop pulled on surgical gloves and emptied the locker while Sergeant D'Amario held the leash. The cop dumped out the backpack, searched every compartment, shook out the tennis shoes and the boot, took the hair gel apart. He went through all the papers and the books.

That left the jacket. The cop removed it, dug his hands in the pockets, patted the lining inside. Then he gave it a shake and patted the lining again. After that he turned it inside out and tried once more. The adults exchanged blank looks. Sergeant D'Amario handed the other cop a little fold-ing knife.

"What the hell?" said Brandon. He should have said *What the fuck?* but he wasn't brave enough.

"Language, please," said Ms. Belsey.

The cop cut through the stitches at the bottom of the lin-ing, extending a little hole already there, and thrust his hand up inside. He turned to Sergeant D'Amario and shook his head.

Sergeant D'Amario knelt, went through the books and papers again. "What's this?" he said.

"We've lost our dog," said Brandon. "Like it says."

D'Amario rose in a hurry. "What was that?"

Brandon said nothing.

"Pat him down," D'Amario said.

"Face the wall," said the other cop.

Brandon faced the wall. Something savage woke inside him. He made himself be still.

"Hands up, legs apart."

Brandon raised his hands, spread his legs. The cop pat-ted him down.

"Nothin'," he said.

Brandon turned. He could have looked them in the eye forever.

"I guess there's been some mistake," said Ms. Belsey, picking the jacket off the floor. "We'll have this resewn for you by dismissal time, Brandon."

"You think I'd wear it now?" said Brandon, and his god-damn voice betrayed him, cracking a little. "It's shit." He walked away before anyone could do anything, leaving the whole mess for them to deal with, kept walking down the hall and right out of West Mill High.

Brandon started toward the student parking lot because that was what he always did. When was dismissal? Half an hour or so. He headed for Dewey's car. For the first ten or twenty yards, he was almost crying, maybe even did a little.

Then he got control; good thing, because a car rolled up alongside and someone said: "Out already, Brandon?"

Mom's Jeep, with Julian at the wheel. The college visit: he wasn't in the mood.

"Your mom told me noon," Julian said.

"Then you're early," said Brandon.

"To ensure a good start," said Julian. He glanced up at the school doors. "No one else seems to be coming out yet."

Brandon shrugged, got in the car, moving the Fiske, Princeton Review, and Insider's college guides out of the way.

Julian was watching him. "You're not in trouble, are you?" he said.

Brandon took a deep breath, almost a shuddering one. "For what?"

Julian licked his lips. "Leaving school too soon."

"No."

"Because you look a little distraught, if you don't mind my saying so."

"Let's just go," Brandon said.

Julian put the car in drive and stepped on the gas, maybe a little roughly, from the gear-grinding sound. "If there is some difficulty at school," he said, "you know you can rely on my discretion."

"Thanks, Julian. I got out a little early, that's all."

"Very well," said Julian.

They drove in silence for a while, came to 91. "Where are we going?" Brandon said.

"I thought we'd look at Amherst first. A reach at this stage, but why not see what a reach looks like? We can check out Trinity on the way back."

"I thought Trinity was a reach too."

"Not with the way you're improving."

"Yeah?" For the first time, Brandon thought that maybe college might not be such a bad thing after all. At least he'd be out of West Mill High. Then he had an idea. "What if we went the other way."

"South?"

"To New York. What's in New York?"

"Columbia. NYU."

"Reaches?"

"Columbia, certainly."

"But no more than Amherst, right?"

"Probably not."

"Then let's go to New York."

Julian pulled over to the side of the road, switched off the motor. He turned to Brandon. Brandon felt Julian's intelligence, like his mind was being scanned. "Not impossible, Brandon," Julian said, "but first I'd have to be sure there will be no ramifications from your early dismissal."

"Jesus Christ," said Brandon. "You're just like all the others."

Julian's eyes changed a little, a brief glint, then darkness. "Is that really your opinion?"

"I guess not," said Brandon. "They opened up my locker, Julian, the cops and everything, looking for drugs."

"My God," said Julian. "Did they have a warrant?"

"They don't need one. It's happened to other kids before."

"Outrageous," said Julian. He shook his head. "But I hope that at least the search itself wasn't too invasive."

"They didn't strip me or anything like that. But if cutting the lining out of my jacket makes it invasive, then it was."

"They did that?"

Brandon nodded. There was a silence. Brandon felt himself starting to shake again. He wanted to punch somebody—D'Amario, the cop who'd patted him down, Ms. Belsey, Mr. Kranepool, Mr. Brack, all of them. Even compared with him and all his fuckups, they were worse, dirty even. Compared to someone like Trish, they were scum. And the K-9 dog, a complete bluff. Ruby was right: D'Amario would do anything to keep crack out of West Mill.

"That must have come as a shock," said Julian, "when they cut the lining."

"It was like they expected to find something there."

"It goes without saying that their search was unsuccessful?"

That question mark at the end made Brandon mad. "You think I'm a drug dealer?"

"Of course not, Brandon. I'm on your side, as I thought you knew." He turned the key. "Let's hit the big city."

They drove to New York, saw NYU first, then Columbia. Lots of the kids looked weird, but some were okay.

"There's one more thing I'd like to see," said Brandon.

"What's that?"

"Beth Israel."

"But it's a hospital."

"Unka Death's inside."

"Ah."

Julian drove across town to Beth Israel, double-parked on a side street while Brandon got out. The vigil was taking place in a little park across the street from the hospital. Brandon joined the—*what would you call them, vigilantes?* he thought, suddenly understanding both words at once. There were hundreds of them, some in NYU or Columbia T-shirts. They gazed up at the hospital, passing around joints and beer cans, sometimes chanting: "Fuck you, good as new, all we do, then it's through."

The rap echoed off the stone walls of the hospital. "I think he's in that corner room up there," said a girl beside Brandon.

"Where that nurse waved a while ago?" he said.

The girl gave him a look. A college girl, no doubt about it. "Yes," she said.

Brandon said the first thing that came into his head: "I hope she's wearing the gold shorts."

The girl laughed, one of those bursts, the surprised kind. There was life after West Mill High. He was going to have to work his butt off, but it wasn't out of the question. Already he could handle *ramifications* in ordinary conversation.

Brandon got back in the car. They drove across the bridge, up into Connecticut, taillights glowing endlessly ahead. Julian looked tired: fun things tired adults out just as much as work. He was gripping the steering wheel too hard, just like Mom.

"Thanks, Julian," Brandon said. "You've been a big help."

"My pleasure," said Julian. His grip got a little tighter.

28

Standardized tests were great. Maybe not the tests themselves, which went on and on, especially the math—halfway through Ruby had been down to answers only, leaving the questions unread—but who could be upset about all the arguing they caused, and the half-day conferences that resulted?

The bus rolled to a stop. The flashing lights went on and Mr. V. glanced in the mirror. Ruby saw momentary disappointment on his face, probably at the sight of the lone truck behind them. Mr. V. lived for long backups.

"Chin up," he said.

Ruby tilted up her chin, got off the bus. Normally on a half day she'd take out a recipe book and bake fudge, just to establish the right mood. Then maybe she'd practice the saxophone for a while. When was the last time she'd touched it? And the next Hot Jazz performance, at an old-folks home, was less than two weeks away. Those old folks loved "It Don't Mean a Thing"—they tapped their old feet and beat time on their walkers—and Ruby sometimes had trouble with the slur after the eighth rest in the seventh measure; she didn't want to let the old folks down. After that she might put on a CD, real loud, and dance around the house like a banshee, or dervish, whichever it was. The dancing always got Zippy going like crazy—once he'd tried to take a bite out of the toaster.

But none of that today. Today was for finding him.

First, she checked the messages. Lots for Brandon—from Trish, Dewey, Frankie J, other kids whose names she didn't recognize—but nothing about Zippy. Then she was hungry. She opened the fridge, took out peanut butter, Marshmallow Fluff—and how about a little jam, just to add that healthy fruit element? Three kinds—blueberry, apricot and, over by itself on the top shelf, strawberry, the French one Julian liked. Strawberry wasn't her favorite and she couldn't reach it anyway. She chose blueberry, whipped up a glass of chocolate milk for that all-important calcium element, sat down to lunch.

Mom called just as she was washing up. That was nice.

"What are you doing this afternoon?" Mom said. That was nice too.

"Looking for Zippy," Ruby said. "Did you know Julian smokes?"

"What makes you think that?"

"I saw him out smoking last night."

"Cigarettes?" Mom was quick.

"Yeah."

Mom lost interest right away. How did that fit in with the quick part? "Lots of people smoke," she said.

"I know," said Ruby. "But Julian?"

Phones rang in the background at Mom's end. "See you tonight," said Mom. "And Ruby?"

"Yeah?"

"There may come a time when you'll have to start coming to terms with . . ." Mom left the rest unsaid; maybe she could sense through the wires the reaction that was already building in Ruby.

Beep.

"I've got another call," Ruby said.

"Bye."

"Bye."

"Hi."

"Hey." Kyla. "Wanna hit sometime this afternoon? My dad could pick you up."

Tennis on a free afternoon, completely voluntary? Madness. "Can't," said Ruby. "Some other time." *Like a year starting with three.*

"I'll have to hit with my dad," said Kyla.

Ruby knew how bad that could be, but didn't relent. "He's got a half day too?"

"He takes them whenever he wants now."

"You're rich, huh?"

"I think so."

"How was Paris?"

"We went to the Eiffel Tower," Kyla said. "There were some college boys. Big Green—is that Dartmouth? They peed off the top deck."

Dartmouth—was it on Mom and Dad's wish list for Bran? "What are you eating?" Ruby said.

"Gummy bears."

Ruby hated gummy bears. Why didn't they just include dental floss in the packages? She listened to Kyla chew.

"Hear about Problem?" Kyla said.

"The guy from *That Thang Thing*?"

"Yeah. He shot Unka Death."

"Killed him, you mean?"

"He's in a coma," Kyla said. "And Problem's in jail."

"What happened?"

"They were in a strip club." Ruby waited for more explanation, but none came. "It's on TV right now," Kyla said.

"Later."

"Later."

Ruby went down to the entertainment center, switched on the TV. She ripped through the channels—woman with the red-framed glasses, Molto Mario, shopping, nun, ab cruncher, skateboarding, Hitler—found Problem. He was rapping onstage in one of those orange prison jumpsuits, the gold AK-47 medallion bouncing on his thick chest. Were they letting him perform in jail, or was this from before, the jumpsuit part of his image, a part that came true?

The announcer was talking but Ruby couldn't concentrate. Something was bothering her, something that had flashed by as she'd torn through the channels, somewhere around the nun. Ruby hit the channel down button, went back more slowly.

WWII, WWF, ab cruncher, nun and—there it was. A picture of someone she knew: Jeanette. They had her name up there, and under that *Old Mill, CT*. Ruby turned up the volume.

". . . did not appear for work on Monday and is now considered missing. Police are asking anyone with information to please call—" Then came a number, and they moved onto the next story. Ruby raced through the channels, found nothing more about Jeanette.

She called Mom, got her voice mail. She called Dad; not yet back from lunch. She went upstairs, found Mom's address book, called Jeanette's number.

"In case I didn't reach everybody," said Jeanette, "there'll be no archery the twenty-third and twenty-fourth." The Atlantis weekend. "Classes as normal next Saturday. If you need to leave a message, wait for the tone."

The tone came. Then silence. Ruby spoke into it. "Jeanette? This is Ruby. I hope you're all right." Then more silence. After a few seconds, Ruby said, "Bye," and hung up.

She called the rec center, where you signed up for the archery classes.

"Rec center."

"Hi. I'm in archery with Jeanette. Is it true she's missing?"

"We have no information."

"But is it true? Missing where?"

"I'm sorry." Click.

Missing where? What kind of missing? And Zippy was missing too. Ruby sat down at the kitchen table, sat down hard, as though her legs had suddenly forgotten the timing, or lost their strength. She put her head in her hands, tried to think. Was this another case, tied to all the others? That was her first thought, an obvious one, at least in her mind. But didn't Holmes warn against obvious things? *There is nothing more deceptive than the obvious* something or other, he told Watson; maybe in "The Boscombe Valley Mystery." Also it was childish: Jeanette was a person, meaning this was on another level. On the other hand, the levels had been going up and up the whole time: Varsity Jacket, Anonymous Caller, Zippy, Jeanette. Was there something that tied it all together? She had a crazy feeling she knew all she needed to know already, that if she just smacked herself in the head everything would fall into place, neatly unscrambled. Ruby smacked herself in the head, open-handed but pretty hard. Nothing happened.

She called the pound. "Have you found Zippy yet?"

"You're the little girl?"

"I'm the girl."

"Still got your flyer. I said we'd call."

"You could have lost it."

"Is this the number?" He said their number.

"Yeah."

"What's your name?"

"Ruby."

"We'll give you a holler, Ruby, moment we know anything."

"But where is he?"

"Lots of possibilities."

He'd said that the last time. "Like what?"

"Specially if you're a dog. Say you smell something kinda inviting in a backyard shed, you mosey in and then the wind comes up and blows the door shut. Boom, locked in, easy as that. There's a possibility right there. Had one like that just the other—"

"Thanks," said Ruby, hanging up. Moseying in: Zippy to a T. She would have to think like a dog, specifically one very special dog she knew better than anybody.

Ruby put on outdoor things—blue jacket with yellow trim, yellow hat with blue stars, mittens, boots—shoved her magnifying glass in a pocket, went outside. First stop, the driveway: he'd been out shoveling with Julian. Shoveling usually got Zippy pretty hyper; lots of bounding at shovelfuls of flying snow, lots of that crazy starting-and-stopping thing he did, lots of barking. So he'd have been practically out of his mind already when the car went by and the dog in it barked at him. Or maybe Zippy barked first, that would be it, began the whole thing. Then he took off. In what direction? She thought back, remembered Julian's voice cracking: *I ran after him, of course, calling and calling*—Ruby could practically see it—*but he just kept going and I finally lost sight of him on Indian Ridge.* She could practically see it, but not quite: had Julian been smoking at the time, or not? A little detail that couldn't possibly matter, but it blurred things just the same.

Ruby walked down Robin Road, turned onto Indian Ridge. She kept going, around the curve where Julian must have lost sight of Zippy, and over the hill where the woods came back in view. There were some nice houses on this part of Indian Ridge, like this one with new shingles and green shutters. Wouldn't Zippy have been getting a little pooped by now? Besides, the car would have been long gone. So what would Zippy do? He'd stop.

Ruby stopped. And then what? He'd just stand there in the middle of the road, tongue hanging out and panting, waiting for some thought to come into his head. Ruby moved out to the middle of the road. She closed her eyes, made her mind a blank—did that by picturing a squeegee sliding across a window—and waited for a thought, the first random thought, whatever it was. She skipped the tongue-hanging-out and panting part—that would have been ridiculous.

The first thought came, and it was pizza. She opened her eyes—good thing, because the mail truck was just coming over the hill—and stepped to the side of the road. Pizza! Singularity, Holmes said, was almost invariably a clue, and Zippy was singularly interested in pizza. And what specific pizza had recently entered his life, would be the first thing he thought of, now that he was out and free? Thick-crust sausage and pepperoni. But there was more—after that slice, Sergeant D'Amario had brought him a whole box of the Hawaiian kind with pineapple and ham. A pizza bonanza, in Zippy's mind: he'd be able to hold that thought for days and days, the knowledge of a pizza motherlode, out there in the woods. What would he do? Get to the woods by the shortest route possible, maybe not running, wiped as he was from the car chase, but possibly in that purposeful trot he had, even when there was no purpose whatever. Ruby walked toward the nice house with the new shingles and green shutters.

Two newspapers in plastic bags lay halfway up the driveway. Ruby stepped over them, kept going around the side. The house backed onto the woods just like hers, had a feeder just like hers, with a cardinal watching from the perch—she hadn't seen her own cardinal in ages—but unlike hers also had a shed. A cute shed, with new shingles and a little green door, closed, that matched the shutters of the house.

"Zippy?" Ruby's heart started pounding and she was on the run. There was one of those metal pieces for a lock on the door—rasp, clasp, hasp, something—but no lock. She could see how the whole thing happened, just like the animal control officer said. Ruby turned the knob, pushed the door open.

"Zippy?" But no Zippy, no sign of Zippy, no life of any kind. It was still inside the shed, and smelled like a library.

Cardboard boxes were stacked neatly in rows along the back, floor to ceiling. They all said *Income Tax* on the side, and then a year, the earliest one, down at the bottom left, being 1949. That gave Ruby a creepy feeling. She got out and shut the door.

No Zippy. That didn't mean the shed idea was wrong. It didn't mean the pizza idea was wrong either. Pizza was right. She knew Zippy. Pizza was one of those links in the chain—so many links now, so many chains, she felt like Jacob Marley dragging them around—a link that thoroughly understood would reveal all the befores and afters. Pizza had drawn Zippy into the woods.

Ruby went in after him. No actual trail led from the shed into the woods—if the people in the house were paying taxes in 1949, they'd probably been in wheelchairs for years—so Ruby just wandered through the trees, bearing sort of left, which she thought was the direction of the pond. She saw tracks in the snow, small shallow ones like brush strokes, probably made by squirrels, bigger sloppy dog ones—but she had no idea what Zippy's looked like specifically—and once those neat precise triangular kind that meant deer. She'd seen deer several times out here, but not for a long time; nice to know they were still around, now that the woods had been turned into a crack house.

Ruby came to a path, followed it to another path that seemed familiar, took that, went up and around a bend and presto: the pond. A born tracker. Cortés and Pizarro must have had trackers, but Ms. Freleng had left that out. Either they'd been local trackers, in which case the native people had helped cause their own downfall, or they'd been Spanish, in which case the Conquistadors had at least been good at something. She walked around the shore of the pond, completely unfrozen today, pale under a cloudy sky, toward the big rock where Zippy had found that first slice of sausage and pepperoni.

No pizza now, all cleaned up, but Zippy couldn't have anticipated that. He'd be puzzled. There'd be some clawing

around, although she didn't see any signs of it, but snow
came and went, changing everything, and he'd be making
that whiny noise he made when he'd reached his wit's end,
which wasn't a long distance, and then—

Ruby saw something a few yards ahead, a shiny little
blue thing, wedged into the bark of a tree root that crossed
the path, sticking out of the snow. She knelt, took off her
mitten, picked it up: a dog tag in the shape of a heart. On one
side, under the year, it said: *West Mill Vet, Rabies Vacc.* On
the other side, it said: *Zippy.*

Ruby looked around. The tag felt cold in her hand.
Zippy had been here, no doubt about it, here at ground zero.
But then what? She gazed at the pond. Zippy didn't like the
pond, would hardly ever fetch anything, except on the hottest
days of summer, or that one time she'd tried tossing in
Cheez-Its. He'd gone in dozens of times for the Cheez-Its—
they floated on the surface, making it easy—finishing the
whole pack. A tiny memory, just a trifle, but that was her
method, the observation of trifles leading to a conclusion.
The conclusion: Zippy would go in the pond for food any
old time.

Suppose the pond had been frozen, which made sense
since it was partly frozen yesterday and ice-free today, and
the DPW guys had maybe missed a pizza slice, or a whole
box, that the wind had blown out onto the ice. The wind: a
factor, as the animal control officer had predicted. What
would Zippy do? Pretty obvious. Easy to visualize the scene:
Zippy out on the ice, falling through somewhere out in the
middle where the ice was thin, paws scrabbling frantically,
panic; the effort came in trying not to see it. But she had to
know. Ruby walked home, Zippy's tag warming in her fist.

Ruby returned to the pond dragging her SnoTube, the
round fat one big enough for two, inflated as full as she
could get it with the bike pump. On the SnoTube lay her
mask and snorkel, faded a little from the Bahamian sun. She
had no intention of going in, nothing crazy—the water was

much too cold—but going on was different. She knew where to draw the line.

Ruby took off her jacket, laid it by the rock. She took off her mittens, rolled up the sleeves of her lone Abercrombie sweater—she was still too small for Abercrombie, but she'd had to have it—and pushed the SnoTube down to the edge of the water. Then she spat in her mask—a nice man called Moxie at the Junkanoo Beach Hut had shown her the whole routine—swished it around in the water, yes, very cold, and put it on top of her head, snorkel hanging down the side. After that, she lay prone on the SnoTube, shoved off with her legs, and whoosh—she was skimming across the pond.

Ruby paddled a little, but not too much because the water was so cold, steering toward the middle of the pond. When she got there, she lowered the mask, stuck the snorkel in her mouth, wriggled forward to the front of the SnoTube and lowered her face into the water.

Wow. That woke her up. But the mask stayed on tight, just her cheeks and chin going numb. She breathed through the snorkel, peered down into the depths of the pond, saw nothing except stuff that looked like dust motes. No sign of the bottom. How deep was the pond, anyway? Funny how she'd never brought her snorkeling stuff in the summer, only thinking of it when they went to the ocean.

Ruby paddled a little bit one way, a little bit another, didn't see the bottom or anything else, except for the dust mote things. All of a sudden something moved, way down there. The SnoTube passed over before she could get a good look. Ruby wriggled a little farther forward, got her face in a little deeper, better for looking back, and there it was: a fish, on its way up. A brown fish—in the winter!—with delicate fins, sort of blue, not the electric blue she'd seen in the Bahamian—

Then she was in the water. So fast: like a giant wave roared up and tipped her over. Down she went, jolted through and through with cold so shocking she couldn't move a muscle, do anything but gasp. Gasping meant swallowing water. She swallowed water, coughed, swallowed more, sank, boots filling up, clothes so heavy. On the way down, Ruby caught a glimpse of the bottom, a jumble of beer cans, bottles, tires, weeds, tree trunks, a ski pole. Then another jolt went through her, this a desperate one from inside. Ruby's arms and legs started moving, thrashing around; sounds of struggle bubbled past her ears. She came to the surface, coughing and gasping, glanced wildly around for the SnoTube, spotted it on the far side of the pond, bobbing by the shore. The wind again: she was no smarter than Zippy, maybe dumber.

Ruby thrashed. Mask and snorkel gone, boots gone, socks gone, Abercrombie sweater gone, she thrashed herself to shore, pulled her practically naked body up in the snow. She reached for her jacket, shivering, teeth clacking together like those Spanish dancer things, dropped it, picked it up with both numb hands, tried to put it on. Wouldn't go on. She wrapped it around her and got herself home, running, stumbling, crying a little, barefoot in the snow.

No one home. She had a long hot bath, climbed into bed, turned on her TV. Snowy parking lot; yellow tape; Jeanette's pickup.

Reporter: ". . . an excellent skier. Police are working on the theory that sometime over the weekend, she skied into a gladed area, possibly out of bounds, and came to grief. Searchers are now combing every inch of Killington's six mountains, as well as neighboring Pico and unmarked terrain, but as another cold night descends on ski country, the hope for a successful outcome to this winter drama dims." Shots of searchers in the woods, on skis, on snowmobiles, with dogs. Sound of the dogs barking.

"Ruby?"

Ruby opened her eyes. It was dark in her room. Mom was there, her face lit by the blue-white glow of the TV.

"Are you okay?" Mom said.

"Must have fallen asleep." Her head was all fuzzy. "Have you heard about Jeanette?"

"It's terrible," said Mom. "But there's every reason to hope—she's such a strong woman."

"How long does it take to freeze to death?"

"It depends."

"What if she hit her head on a tree?"

"I don't know."

"Do they keep searching at night?"

"I'm not sure."

Ruby sat up. "What's going on, Mom?"

"What do you mean?"

"Zippy," Ruby said. "And now Jeanette."

Mom came closer, put her hand on Ruby's forehead, a cool hand, cold, in fact. "You feel a little warm," Mom said. "Why don't you come downstairs? It's a Blue Dragon night, but I can heat some chicken soup."

"Not hungry."

"I'll bring something up."

"Don't want anything."

Mom bent over, kissed her forehead, left the room. Ruby gazed at the TV. They were showing the pickup again but it was the exact same report as before, shot in the daytime. Now it was night. It got cold in the mountains at night, way below zero. She'd been up at Uncle Tom and Aunt Deborah's ski place once, had stepped out at night just to see how way-below-zero felt. Ruby pressed the off button on her remote.

Dad came in. "Got it pretty dark in here, sweetheart." He switched on the lights. "I hear you're not feeling tip-top." He sat on the bed, put a tray on her bedside table: chicken soup, orange juice, white rice with plum sauce.

"What's going on, Dad?"

"How do you mean?"

"Zippy. Jeanette."

Dad shrugged. "Unfortunate things happen sometimes.

But lost dogs get found all the time. And Jeanette's a tough cookie."

"Zippy's not coming back."

"We don't know that," Dad said.

Ruby did know it, almost 100 percent, but going into the whole pond episode would mean big trouble. "And what if they don't find Jeanette in time?"

Dad sighed, rubbed the back of his neck. "Let's not worry about that unless we have to. Worrying never helps, Ruby." He felt her forehead; his hand felt cold too, but not as cold as Mom's. "Feel okay?"

"Yeah."

"Try to eat something. Then get a good night's sleep. You'll be good as new in the morning."

"Thanks, Dad." He was a great dad and she would have felt a little better just from his gentle tone if he hadn't said *good as new*, which led right to Unka Death. *Fuck you, good as new, all we do, then it's through*. It was one of the best records she'd ever heard, maybe because the meaning scared her so much.

Dad gave her a little kiss on the forehead, as Mom had, and started toward the door.

"Dad? How's the stock?"

Dad turned. "Doing just what we want, sweetheart. Try not to worry so much." He left the room.

Ruby sat up. Not easy: she was so heavy, all of a sudden. She tried the soup, had to make a big effort to get a single spoonful down. She took a sip of orange juice. Rice was out of the question, despite her love of plum sauce. One of the worst things about getting sick was the way your mind played tricks on you. The plum sauce, for example: it glistened on the rice in a creepy way, like it had some sort of bad plan for the rice, a smothering one. At that point, she forced herself to get out of bed, before things got worse.

Ruby went into the hall, now feeling very light, like a reed, and very tall, so that every step was dangerous. Julian's voice drifted up from downstairs.

"Columbia?" he was saying. "A bit of a reach at this stage, certainly, although not impossible. But if you want my opinion . . ."

"Of course," said Dad.

"I think he preferred NYU."

"Do you?" said Mom, in that tone she had when she was getting real interested in something.

"And it wouldn't be a bad choice, in my view," Julian said. His voice faded as Ruby went down the hall, trailed by half-audible snippets: NYU, Columbia, SAT, GPA, community service. She opened Brandon's door.

He was at his desk, a textbook in front of him, yellow highlighter in hand. Had she ever actually caught him doing homework before? The animal smell wasn't as strong as usual, but that might have been because her nose was clogging up. She went in and closed the door. He turned at the sound.

"Ever heard of knocking?"

She couldn't think of anything sharp or biting to say back, didn't have the strength. "We have to talk."

"About what?"

"Weird things have been happening."

"Like?" He was tapping his foot.

"Let's start with your jacket."

He glanced at the door. "What do you know about my jacket?"

"A lot."

"Did Dewey say something to you? Trish?"

"About what?"

He put down the highlighter. "What do you know about my jacket?"

"It's central to the case."

"What case?"

"Or cases, I meant. Remember that time you came home without your jacket and were surprised to see it on the peg?"

"We're going through that again?"

Ruby got a little dizzy, sat on the bed. "How come we argue all the time?"

Brandon shrugged.

"I'm going to tell you something. You can get as mad as you want."

"What?"

"I took your crack. I threw it away."

He checked the door again. "What are you talking about?"

"There's no point in lying, Brandon. I had it in my hands last night."

"Last night?"

"I was so mad that maybe you hadn't given out the flyers. I looked for them here and then in your jacket. That's when I found the crack."

"There was crack in my jacket?"

"For God's sake, Brandon."

He got up, came closer. Ruby was afraid. But all he did was sit beside her on the bed. "How much crack?" he said.

He really didn't know? She looked into his eyes, eyes a lot like Mom's, and couldn't tell. "You really don't know?"

"Know what? I don't carry crack around. I'm not a crackhead, Ruby. I tried it once or twice, that's all."

"Promise you'll never do it again."

"Jesus Christ."

"Promise."

"I promise."

"There were twelve of those vials."

"Sewn in the lining?"

"How did you know that if you didn't—"

"Because they searched my locker today—that D'Amario guy and the principal—and they cut it open."

"They cut your varsity jacket?"

He nodded.

They sat in silence for a while. From Brandon's headphones, lying on the desk, came tinny sounds of rap.

"Someone tried to get me in trouble," Brandon said.

This was a moment for saying *duh*, to pay him back for all the *duhs* he'd sent her way. "Like who?" Ruby said instead.

"No idea," said Brandon. "Whoever it was must have planted the stuff and called the school."

"Anonymously?"

"I don't know."

"Do they tape the calls?"

"That's coming next year," Brandon said.

"School's a gas," said Ruby.

Brandon laughed, actually put his hand on hers. "Hey," he said. "You're burning up."

"I'm okay," said Ruby.

He looked at her, kind of funny, like he was meeting someone new. "You saved my butt," he said.

"True," said Ruby. "What are we going to do now?"

"I'm going to find whoever did it and beat the shit out of him."

"How are you going to do that?"

"I've got friends at school. We'll think of something."

"What if it was one of them?"

Brandon thought about that. "What's your suggestion?"

"The place to start is that day you were surprised to see your jacket on the peg," said Ruby. "Like I said."

"All right, all right," said Brandon. "I got hammered at a party in the woods, an earlier one, and must have left it there. I kind of thought you brought it back."

"Me?"

"Out with Zippy."

Didn't he know her better than that? "I would have said."

"Oh," said Brandon. He was silent for a moment. Then he said, "Are you telling me whoever brought the jacket back planted the crack, that it was there all that time?"

"I don't know."

Brandon rose. "Maybe Mom or Dad was here when the

jacket came back, maybe the guy just handed it to them." He headed for the door.

"I don't think so."

"Why not? I'll go down and ask."

It didn't fit, but she couldn't explain why, not before he went out. She listened to the tinny rap: Unka Death, but like a ghost. Brandon came back a minute or two later, shook his head. "They all looked blank," he said. He handed her a glass of water and a pill.

"What's this?"

"Advil. You look a little sick."

"Thanks," Ruby said.

He watched her swallow the pill, drink the water. "So what are we going to do?" he said.

Ruby thought. At first it seemed impossible. What did they know? Only one thing: some person had done this. What did they know about this person? Nothing. Then she realized, by simply putting herself in the unknown person's place, that they did know something, one little fact: that person would be pretty puzzled right now, wondering what had gone wrong with the plan. "Whoever it is may come to you," Ruby said.

"To try and find out what happened?" said Brandon.

Ruby nodded. This was getting easier, talking to Brandon; maybe they weren't as different as she'd thought. "But it'll be in a sneaky way," she said.

"You're right," said Brandon. "I'll keep my eyes open."

Ruby shivered.

"Are you all right?"

"Yeah."

"You should go to bed."

"Okay."

"I'll pass out those flyers in the morning."

She shivered again.

Ruby went to bed. She fell asleep, woke up, fell asleep, woke up. The Mystery of the Varsity Jacket was partially solved, but now there seemed to be a second anonymous caller mystery. The cases went round and round, and she got hotter and hotter. Ruby hated getting sick, hated how it messed with your mind, the real world getting less real, acting imaginary; the unreal one, the imaginary one, coming true. Her mind had to be normal right now: all she needed to know was already in there.

She had to sleep, had to get well. She tried the cave dream. Ruby the cavewoman sat in the mouth of her nice dry cave, safe from the blizzard outside. But snow led directly to Jeanette. Ruby knew without looking that Jeanette was deep inside the cave, also knew that loathsome serpents were writhing all over her. They were inside her too. After that, the real world started its routine, crossing over into the imaginary one, sending down soft little sounds from the ceiling above her, like the house was coming to life.

29

Ruby opened her eyes. Morning. She felt better, maybe a little light-headed, but not hot. The strange warping of the world that sickness caused was gone too. She was seeing clearly, very clearly, in fact: she noticed for the first time in all these years that a little patch of the white ceiling just above her head didn't quite match the rest of the whiteness. That would have to be fixed before it drove her crazy.

A fat snowflake drifted past her window, gliding mostly sideways. Then another, and a few more. Every snowflake was different; true of people too, of course, excepting twins, but the differences in snowflakes were hard to spot, whereas you could never confuse one person with another. And the better you knew people, the more different from each other they got. Did everyone believe that? Certainly not advertising guys—they had to believe that huge bunches of people were pretty much the same. Take Gap, for example, all set up to appeal to millions of girls. She, Aruba Nicole Marx Gardner, despite that one-of-a-kind name, was just one of millions, maybe billions. Ruby didn't want to push this any farther, didn't want to back herself into a corner where she'd have to take some sort of stand against Gap. Gap was one of the foundations of her life. *So shoot me.*

She glanced at the clock. Nine thirty-five. Nine thirty-five? What was this? Nine thirty-five on a Wed., said so right there. She'd overslept, missed the bus. Missed the bus, also missed math, where come to think of it there was a test she hadn't studied for, and health, where there was also a test she hadn't studied for, although you never had to in health as long as you stuck to the position that smoking, drinking, and drugging were bad.

Ruby got up. A little bit weak or something, and real real hungry. She went to the bathroom, then downstairs and into the kitchen. There was Julian, having breakfast at the table, gazing at the countertop TV. He'd slipped her mind.

"Good morning, Ruby," he said, turning to her; on the screen those stock market numbers were streaming by. "Feeling any better?"

"Yeah." And she was; seeing clearly—his soul patch, getting just a little scraggly, maybe time for a trim. Smelling clearly too: she caught a cigarette whiff, although he wasn't smoking and there were no butts around.

"Your mom and dad decided not to wake you," he said. "I'm holding the fort."

"So I don't have to go to school?"

"Free as a little bird," Julian said. "Can I get you some breakfast?"

"Thanks," said Ruby, glancing at what he was having—

coffee and toast with strawberry jam, spread thick. "I'll get it."

Ruby checked the cupboard: a brand-new unopened box of Mango Almond Crunch. Mom: on top of things, this week. She poured a big bowl—no need to add sliced-up bananas or berries, this cereal had everything—brought it to the table, sat down at her place by the window, across from Julian.

"That looks good," he said.

"Want some?"

"Thank you, no."

Ruby had a big spoonful, then a few more real quick she was so hungry, milk dribbling down her chin. She wiped it off on her sleeve. Julian didn't notice; his eyes were on the screen.

"Was there health class when you were a kid?" Ruby said.

"Health class? I suppose."

"Was it the same stuff? Smoking is bad, that kind of thing?"

He turned to her. "I didn't actually take health class. My education was a little different, as I mentioned to your parents."

"Oh, yeah," said Ruby. She took another spoonful, this the most mangoey one yet. A good taste, but nothing like those huge ripe mango fests at Atlantis. "You had tutors, right?"

"Correct."

"Is that how come you went into tutoring?"

"No."

She waited for more explanation. Maybe he was thinking about it while he spread more jam on his toast. After a while, she said, "But you like doing it—tutoring."

"Certainly."

"Working with kids, et cetera? Some of my teachers don't like kids at all, which is kind of weird."

"Very," said Julian, raising a piece of toast toward his lips.

"I bet I can guess something about you," Ruby said.

"Oh?" he said, putting the toast back on the plate. She noticed it was one of those special Wedgwood plates from Gram, plates that were kept in the dining room cabinet and only came out at Christmas.

"You're doing this while you work on being a writer."

"What makes you say that?"

The beginning of that poem on his notepad, of course, the one about *negligent is to forsake*. But she'd had no business reading it, let alone adding to it, so instead of doing anything to remind him of that episode, she said: "You know all the words."

"You think that makes a writer?"

"At least you've got something to choose from."

He gave her a funny look, one of those looks where you could see inside to how smart he was. It made her a bit nervous, and out popped the next thing that came to mind: "And in Italian too, if you want."

Julian picked up the toast, took a bite, savoring that strawberry jam; she could tell from the slow way his lips moved. *Sensual,* was that the word? Or was it *sensuous*? She didn't want to ask him that kind of thing, could look it up later in the big dictionary on the—

Italian. Wait a minute. This and that collided in her mind. Kaboom. And out came a question mark: hadn't he gotten *Where is the bargain shopping* all wrong? Wasn't it possible that Julian's Italian was actually a bit shaky?

"Where did you learn your Italian anyway?" Ruby said.

Julian took a sip of coffee, a delicate sip; sometimes he reminded her of a European aristocrat, the kind in movies since she'd never seen a real one. "Mostly in Cameroon," Julian said.

"They speak Italian in Cameroon?" Ruby wasn't clear on where Cameroon was, but knew that European languages were spoken in Africa, Nelson Mandela and the French Foreign Legion being two good examples. And the Italian spoken in Cameroon probably wouldn't be the same as the original Roman kind spoken by the girl at the airport, so that could explain the bargain shopping problem.

"At the Italian embassy they do," Julian said. "I had lessons with the ambassador's children."

Oh. "Were they from Rome?"

"Milan, I believe."

"How's the Italian in Milan?"

"I beg your pardon?"

"Is it the authentic kind, like in Rome?"

Julian gazed up at the ceiling, maybe giving it careful thought. Then he looked at her. "Do you ever think before you speak?" he said. He took another sip of coffee.

At first, Ruby didn't believe she'd heard right. Julian was always so nice and kind. But it had been a very simple question made up of very simple words, and her hearing today, like all her senses, was extra sharp. She'd heard right. Her face was telling her that by going red, and her dumb lower lip too, by quivering.

Julian's eyebrows rose. "Oh, my God," he said. "Did I say that?" He put down his cup, put it down hard, coffee slopping into the saucer. "How awful. I'm so sorry, Ruby." He put his hand to his forehead. "I'm not feeling too well myself today. Of course, I didn't mean it at all. I think the world of you, really I do. My mind was back at that dreadful embassy, that dreadful town, Yaoundé. White man's graveyard, as they say, where they—we—all end up snapping. Please forgive me." He reached across the table, patted her on the arm.

"No big deal," said Ruby. Adults did snap. Just about every adult she knew snapped at one time or another, some of them lots, like Ms. Freleng; and Mom, of course. The color of her face returned to normal; her lower lip shaped up.

"Thank you, Ruby. Erring human and forgiveness divine, as I'm sure you've heard."

"I haven't."

" 'To err is human, to forgive divine.'"

Beautiful. So beautiful it took her breath away. "Did you make that up, Julian?"

"Pope," said Julian. " 'Essay on Criticism.'"

Any particular pope? Ruby wondered. She'd forgiven him now—didn't anyone who could come up with stuff like that deserve it?—but she didn't want to risk a dumb question. Ruby went with a smarter one: "How would you say it in Italian?"

Julian smiled. "Now that's a good one," he said. "How about *'sbagliare è umano, il divino è perdonare'?*"

"Sounds good," said Ruby.

"Interestingly enough, the Italians don't say it. What they do say is *'sbagliare è umano, pefervorare è diabolico.'*"

"Meaning?"

"To err is human, to persist is devilish."

Ruby thought that over. Julian knew so much. How many years would it take her to even get close? As for his Italian, it was obviously *perfetto.* So why did she even bother asking the next question? "What was 'Where is the bargain shopping' again?" To be devilish?

"Dove si può trovare i prezzi buoni?" Julian said.

Exactly what the Italian girl had said, word for word. Just as Julian finished saying it, his eyes shifted slightly, like maybe he'd had a thought. Ruby had the feeling she'd just observed one of those trifles. That other phrase—*questo è l'inizio della fine*—had nothing to do with shopping, not in Venetian slang or anything else. So why, since he'd known the right way of saying it, had he led her astray? Was it some kind of joke? If so, she didn't get it.

"Something on your mind, Ruby?"

"Italian," she said, at the same time thinking, if not a joke, what? What was funny about 'This is the beginning of the end'? Was it possible that this, the Italian Mix-Up, was in fact another case? "It sounds so beautiful."

"So people say."

And if it was a case, she needed to know more, a lot

more. Holmes always enumerated the essential facts of a case to Watson early in the story, but you had to have them first. "What other languages do you speak, Julian?"

"French, Spanish, Portuguese, some Arabic, some Russian, a little German."

"Mom said your family was in the oil business."

"Correct."

"That's why you lived all over the place."

"Not all over," said Julian. "But various places."

"What was your favorite?"

"London."

"There's oil in London?"

Pause. "We were based there."

"I'm not surprised," Ruby said.

"Why is that?"

"You talk a bit like you're English, except you don't have an accent."

"Have you known many English people?"

"No."

"But you've seen them in the movies."

Ruby nodded.

"You're considered rather creative, aren't you?" Julian sounded thoughtful as he spoke, like he was observing a trifle or two himself. He held up both hands. "Innocent question," he said, and smiled when he said it.

Ruby had never thought much about how she was considered. "I don't know."

He gazed at her for a moment, smile slowly vanishing, although his lips stayed pretty much in the same position. "My mother was English, in fact."

"And your dad?"

"American."

"From whereabouts?"

"He was a New Englander, just like you."

"Mom says your parents are dead." Oops. You were supposed to say *passed on* or something like that.

"Correct."

"Were you still a kid when they died?"

"I was of age."

Still, Julian looked pretty young to have dead parents. She made another guess. "Did they die in an accident or something?"

"A fiery explosion," Julian said.

"Oh my God," said Ruby. "I'm sorry. Like a big blowup in the oil fields?"

"A big blowup," Julian said.

"That's so terrible. I can't imagine living without Mom and Dad."

"No?" Julian said.

For a second or two, she actually tried to imagine it; and caught a glimpse of a gray emptiness, like an endless cloudbank. There'd be Brandon, of course, making it a little better. "Do you have brothers and sisters?" she said.

"I was an only child."

"What were they like, your parents?"

Julian reached into his pocket, took out a cigarette that must have been lying loose in there. "Now that you know my big secret," he said, "do you mind if I smoke?"

Ruby didn't know what to say. No one had ever smoked in the house before.

"Tell you what," he said, "I'll open a window and keep all the carcinogens at bay." He raised the nearest window about a foot—a crow was at the feeder—lit his cigarette with a match, gazing for a moment at the blue-tipped flame, then tossed the match out the window, resting his arm on the sill so the cigarette burned outside. Ruby felt the cold air right away.

"That speech you made at Oxford—" Ruby began.

"Your mom and dad mentioned that?"

"Mom did."

"Ah."

"Something about hiking in Africa."

"And animal collecting—did she mention that too?"

"No."

He smiled. "Go on."

"Were your parents there?"

"Where?"

"At the speech."

"Why do you ask?"

"Just that if they were, they must have been proud."

"They were, in fact."

"What did they say after?"

"I don't recall."

"Something nice, I bet."

Julian took a big drag, let the smoke out through his nose and mouth; Ruby thought of dragons. She was about to ask who Julian looked like, his mom or his dad, when Jeanette's face appeared on the TV. Ruby jumped up, grabbed the remote off the counter, hit volume.

". . . less and less likely after another subzero night here in the mountains. Ski patrollers from other resorts, both in Vermont and New--"

Julian shook his head. "Awful," he said.

Ruby didn't like the way he said that, no hope at all in his voice. "How long can someone survive up there, say they broke their leg and fell into a crevasse?" she said.

"There are no crevasses in the Green Mountains," Julian said. He took another drag from his cigarette. "But in my brief encounters with her, Jeanette struck me as a very capable woman. There's every reason to hope."

Ruby felt a little better. Julian flicked ash out into the falling snow; more flakes now, the ash disappearing in their midst. Snow seemed to bring Jeanette nearer.

"How about if you and me go up there right now," Ruby said, "and join in the search?"

"What a cliché that would be," said Julian.

Cliché? Wasn't *cliché* some unimaginative way of saying something, like stubborn as a mule? "How do you mean?" Ruby said.

"Simply the idea of amateur rescuers bumbling around

in the snow," Julian said, "possibly getting in difficulty themselves."

"Oh." All at once, Ruby didn't feel so good; maybe it was the cigarette smoke. She sat back down at the table.

"Are you all right?" said Julian.

"Yeah."

"Perhaps a glass of water," he said, going to the cooler, pouring a glass, setting it in front of her, holding his burning cigarette in the same hand. How finely shaped his hand was, although the top third of the nail on his middle finger had been torn off, and there was a little purple bruise.

Ruby drank half the glass.

"How's that?" said Julian.

"Good," said Ruby. "Thanks."

He took one last drag, tossed the cigarette out the window, closed it. "You've been full of questions this morning," he said.

"I have?"

He laughed. "There's another. Is turnabout fair play, Rubester?"

"Turnabout?"

"I've got a question or two myself."

"About what?"

"Brandon," Julian said. "The fact is, I'm a little worried about him."

"How come?" said Ruby.

"On the way to New York yesterday he told me a rather disturbing story."

"Oh?" said Ruby.

"I wonder if he told you as well."

"Depends on the story," said Ruby.

He looked at her, then reached in his pocket. Another cigarette already? She'd had no idea. But he came out empty-handed. "This story concerns a search of his school locker."

"Oh, yeah," said Ruby. "He said something about it."

"What, precisely?" said Julian.

Ruby gazed at him, not a gaze in the sense that it lasted a long time—it was hard to look into Julian's eyes for a long time, because he was so smart, no fault of his—just in the sense that hers was a deep look, that *precisely* sounding so strange. At that moment, just before she turned away, Ruby remembered what she'd said to Brandon last night when she'd been sick; maybe she was still sick, but not like last night. Last night, she must have been in some kind of altered state because what she'd said then now sounded so grown-up in her mind; still her, still Ruby, but an older version, if that made sense. She'd told Brandon, *Whoever it is may come to you. But it'll be in a sneaky way.*

"Are you cold?" Julian said.

"I'm fine."

"Feverish?"

"No."

"You shivered."

"I'm okay." The cases all started twisting around in her head. She had to think.

"It's just that I'm concerned about Brandon," Julian said. "Naturally anything you say will fall under the terms of the fireplace precedent."

Fireplace precedent? She got it. "Meaning you won't tell."

"Correct."

He'd been so good about that, when she'd almost burned down the house. Ruby did feel hot all of a sudden, was probably messing things up in her mind, like a bad drug trip. But what about the Italian problem? Was it possible she was confused about that? Maybe; but then what about his smoking? She couldn't get past that; totally crazy, on her part. "There really isn't anything to tell, Julian. Brandon said locker searches happen all the time."

"Searches that involve cutting linings out of jackets?"

"That was mean," Ruby said.

"So he told you?"

"Yeah."

"Did he give you any idea what they were after?"

"Had to be drugs."

"What drugs?"

Ruby shrugged.

"You do recall our conversation in Starbucks?"

"Yeah."

"When you brought up this crack issue yourself."

"Right."

"Of your own volition."

"Yeah."

Silence, except for the TV: the stock market numbers were flowing by; two guys were talking about cement.

"What puzzles me," said Julian, "is why they had such a specific target. Do you think there ever was any crack sewn into that lining?"

Julian did look puzzled, an expression she'd never seen on his face. On any other face, she would have called it anger. *Puzzled:* the word stuck in her mind, she'd used it herself so recently. *That person would be pretty puzzled right now, wondering what had gone wrong with the plan.*

Ruby took another sip of water; not feeling well, for sure. And certainly all mixed up about Julian, who always treated her well—except for that remark about not thinking before she spoke—who made her laugh, who appreciated Sherlock Holmes, who talked to her like an adult. *Yes, there was crack in the lining,* she wanted to say. *I found it and took it out. Help us figure out who put it there. What's going on, Julian?*

Ruby came real close to saying all that. But she couldn't. Why not? In the end, it wasn't the Italian—she was no language expert, was familiar with only two, after all, English and Bahamian. It wasn't even the smoking—what did that have to do with her? It was something else, one tiny detail, a detail that might not even have mattered to Sherlock Holmes: *Do you ever think before you speak?* He'd hurt her feelings. For the first time, she grasped the idea of forgiving but not forgetting.

30

"Nope," Ruby said.

"Nope?" said Julian, like it was from a foreign language. He rubbed his shoulder as though he'd felt a twinge.

"No crack," Ruby said. "No crack in the lining at any time."

She looked Julian in the eye, or tried to. He wasn't buying it. "Maybe at Starbucks I exaggerated the crack thing a bit," she said, shooting a bunch of words into his gaze, like fighter planes in a war movie. "Turns out Brandon's not into crack at all. Or any other drugs. It was a once or twice kind of thing. Peer pressure."

"Is that what he told you?" Julian said.

"I believe him."

"He's your brother."

"That's only part of it," Ruby said. "Look how well he's starting to do in school. Is that what you'd expect from a crackhead?"

"A crackhead with my assistance," said Julian.

That one stunned her too; so many things wrong with it. "You think Brandon's a crackhead?"

"Of course not," Julian said. "Do you have a monopoly on exaggeration?"

"No," said Ruby; maybe she'd misinterpreted. She rose, cleared her place and her mind at the same time. "So since we've both been exaggerating, let's stop worrying about Brandon." She loaded her dishes in the dishwasher, catching sight of Zippy's water bowl in the corner, half full. His DNA was in there; maybe one day they'd be able to clone him just from that. What a big effort that would be, and all for nothing: she would always want the real Zippy.

"Done," said Julian, behind her. She heard the clink of cup and saucer. "So what are your plans?" he said.

"Plans?"

"For the day."

"Go back to bed, I guess," said Ruby.

"Good idea."

She turned to him. "I'm okay by myself, if you've got things to do."

"Don't worry about me," Julian said.

Ruby went upstairs, closed her door, lay down. Her mind was up to something. She tried to picture it, tried to get some idea how it worked. The brain was easy to picture: there were pictures of the brain all over the place. The mind wasn't so easy. It had to have shifting parts, for one thing; Ruby could feel them now, unstable and threatening to move, like those geological layers or whatever they were that caused earthquakes and volcanoes.

All those cases: The Varsity Jacket, part one—the disappearance and reappearance, part two—the planting of the vials; The Anonymous Caller, also with parts one and two; the Italian Mix-Up; Zippy; Jeanette. One link could give you the whole chain. She felt big blocks shifting in her mind, but way down deep, out of sight, and no earthquakes came.

How about going back to the original case, The Mystery of the Varsity Jacket, especially since she now knew what had happened to it in the first place? Brandon had left it in the woods after a party. Lost it, in his mind. Then Ruby got home from school, and it wasn't on the peg. Next came the fireplace adventure, Julian's timely arrival, 37 Robin Road saved. After that, she'd taken Julian on a tour of the house, including the mudroom, where she'd spotted the jacket, now on the hook, and called Brandon's name up the stairs. Then Mom arrived, snowflakes in her hair, smelled smoke. Julian covered up for her, saying he'd lit a fire. Finally Brandon walked in, wearing nothing on top but his Unka Death T-shirt. Mom had asked why he wasn't wearing his jacket. Brandon had lied, saying he'd left it at school. Mom had pointed it out, hanging on the peg.

That was it, the whole story, not even especially complicated. This one didn't require Sherlock Holmes. Anyone with half a brain should be able to figure it out. "Don't I even have half a brain?" she said to Beamish. He gazed back with his broken eyes, no substitute for Zippy. Zippy was her Dr. Watson, as Mrs. Stromboli had said. She missed him so bad.

Lost jacket.

Empty peg.

Fire.

Timely arrival.

Mom.

Jacket on the peg.

Brandon.

Correction: timely arrival, jacket on the peg, then Mom and Brandon. Julian's timely arrival.

Ruby sat up. Julian's timely arrival, and the timing, when it came to the jacket, was right. She got up, looking out the window toward the woods, but not really seeing. Julian? Julian used the woods as a shortcut, she'd seen the tread of his fat tires in the snow, coming back from her encounter with Sergeant D'Amario. Ruby could feel the earthquake coming now: Julian had brought the jacket back from the woods. Who else could have done it? Maybe one of Brandon's friends, but none of them would have known the right peg, most likely would have left it on the steps outside or tossed it in the garage. Julian fit, maybe not beyond a cockamamie doubt, but surely beyond a reasonable one. She had solved The Mystery of the Varsity Jacket!

But Julian? He was so nice, except for that one little thing, when he'd hurt her feelings. Maybe she was making a big deal about nothing. After all, bringing back the jacket was a nice thing. Then why wasn't she having nice feelings about it? That was simple: because he hadn't told Brandon, had left him in the dark. The next thing Ruby remembered was Brandon, last night: *Are you telling me whoever brought the jacket back planted the crack?* Were all her cases connected, like a super Musgrave Ritual?

Big blocks were rumbling around in Ruby's mind now: she understood one link in the chain, although maybe not thoroughly enough. Sherlock Holmes said she should now know what had gone before and what came next, and she didn't.

What did Holmes do when he didn't understand a case thoroughly enough? He hunted for more evidence. In "The Speckled Band," for instance, he had searched Dr. Roylott's chamber, where he'd found the saucer of milk and the dog lash. Dr. Roylott was an obvious villain. You knew that from the way he'd tried to scare Holmes off with the poker-bending bit, never mind that quibble about how he could do that while holding his riding crop at the same time. Julian wasn't an obvious villain; in fact he was nice, except for that one little slip. He wasn't a villain at all, more of a big help in fact, saving the house, raising Brandon's grades, giving Mom the La Rivière idea. So why was she taking care to open her door very quietly?

Ruby stuck her head out into the hall. She heard music, saxophone music, drifting up from downstairs: "It Don't Mean a Thing." For a moment or two, she thought it must be a CD, but there were no other instruments, and besides, she knew the sound of her own alto. So it had to be Julian. He was so good, playing really fast and softly, almost like he was just running through it in his mind. The only thing she didn't like was the way every time he came to that E, where "swing" was, he played a whole ugly crash of notes instead. She closed the door behind her, turning the knob so there wouldn't even be a click. Then she went down the hall to Adam's room, bare feet silent on the carpet.

The door stood open. Ruby walked in, the sound of "It Don't Mean a Thing" fainter now, but still audible. This wasn't going to take long. She wanted to check out that leather-bound notepad, with the poem inside. First Ruby tried the desk. On top lay the green SAT folder, several college guides and a letter from A-Plus Tutorial addressed to Julian at 840 Trunk Road, Old Mill. In the desk drawers, nothing. She tried the bureau, found two neatly folded shirts, two pairs of briefs, two pairs of socks. She opened the closet. A blazer hung from the rod and a pair of sneakers lay on the floor. She checked the pockets of the blazer. No notepad, just a book of matches from a restaurant called Suharto's in London.

Ruby went back to the desk, picked up the letter. He'd already opened it. All she had to do, not that it was right, although Holmes never hesitated about this kind of thing, was stick the tips of her thumb and index finger inside like this and pluck out the letter.

> *Dear Julian:*
>   *Enclosed please find your last check, excluding a final accounting with the Gardners. Good luck with your novel. I'm sure you'll be famous one day, but if you ever want to get into tutoring again, the door is always open.*
>   *Warm regards,*
>   *Margie*

He was working on a novel, no surprise there. Ruby refolded the letter, slid it back in the envelope. The notepad might be in his pocket; the pages of a novel were harder to carry around. She really wanted to see that novel. Maybe he kept it under the bed, under the bed being an obvious place to try anyway, probably at the top of Holmes's checklist. Ruby took a step in that direction before realizing that something was wrong. A moment or two passed before she figured out what it was: he'd stopped playing. The house was quiet.

Ruby glanced out into the hall. Empty, but did she hear a footstep on the stair? Probably her imagination, but on the other hand her senses were acute today, and—

The next thing she knew she was running down the hall, on tiptoes, silent. Yes, footsteps, quiet footsteps, coming up the stairs, and quickly. Was there time to reach her room? No. She ducked into the bathroom, leaving the door open, and turned on the tap.

"Ruby?"

Ruby glanced up from the sink, where she was busy splashing cold water on her face. Julian stood in the doorway.

"Yeah?" she said.

He glanced around the bathroom. "Everything all right up here?"

"Huh?"

"You're feeling okay?"

"Pretty good," said Ruby, and did some more face splashing, the picture of a plucky kid home sick. After a second or two, she didn't feel his presence anymore, like there was more breathing space. Ruby turned off the tap, dried her face, went into the hall. The door to Adam's room was closed now. She heard a drawer open, the desk or maybe the bureau. Ruby went into her own room and shut the door.

She sat on her bed, listening. After a while, Adam's door opened and closed. Footsteps in the hall, approaching, pausing outside her door, moving on and down the stairs. Ruby jumped up, logged on, went to MapQuest. Under *from*, she punched in *37 Robin Road,* under *to, 840 Trunk Road.* She wanted to see that novel. *A crackhead with my assistance:* make that two bad things he'd said.

Ruby printed it out: 6.3 miles, which seemed like a lot, but not too complicated, all the directions fitting on one page. She folded it, stuck it in her pocket and went downstairs. No sign of Julian. She put on her blue jacket with the yellow trim, her yellow hat with the blue stars, wrote a note—*Gone looking for Zippy, back soon*—left it on the table and went into the garage. Ruby was disentangling her bike from the lawn mower when she spotted Jeanette's Post-it note on the floor. She read it again: *Here's your ride, Rubester—use with care. J. P.S. That means a helmet.*

The first time she'd read that, Jeanette hadn't been missing. Not quite true: no one knew she was missing. So she hadn't given it much thought, just good old Jeanette, bringing back the bike. But when had she done it? Not before they left for Atlantis on Friday, so it had to be between them leaving for the Bahamas and Jeanette leaving for Killington. When had that been? Friday afternoon? Saturday morning? Probably no later than that, because she'd canceled archery for Saturday and Sunday, no point in canceling if she was going to be around anyway. But Ruby would have bet on Friday afternoon. Jeanette would want to squeeze every second out of a ski weekend. It was even possible she'd dropped off the bike on the way. And therefore? Ruby wasn't sure. She hit the button and the garage door slid up.

Julian was standing in the driveway, facing her. He had her note in his hand. Ruby stuck Jeanette's Post-it in her jacket pocket, felt Zippy's tag in there too.

"I thought you were sick," Julian said.

"I'm feeling better all of a sudden," Ruby said. "Ten times better."

"Your parents wouldn't think this was a good idea."

"I'll be right back," said Ruby. "I'm only going around the block, maybe try Indian Ridge again."

"To what end?"

"I'm not going to stop looking, Julian. He's my dog."

He stepped aside. "Half an hour," he said. "It wouldn't be responsible of me to let you out any longer."

"Thanks," said Ruby, pedaling past him. When she got to the street she paused, looked back. He was watching her, snowflakes landing gently in his hair. Maybe it was the snowflakes that reminded her, snowflakes being some distant cousin to salt, at least visually. She remembered getting on the bus the day she started "The Speckled Band"—must have been the same day Brandon got his SAT results, come to think of it, hard to forget the scene that night with Dewey's mom—and how she'd glanced back like Lot's wife. Had Mrs. Lot—Ms., no doubt, since she obviously had an independent streak—seen someone like Julian? Probably not. People back then must have been pretty gross-looking, what with the lack of grooming products, and Julian was very handsome.

Ruby felt another one of those shifts in her mind. Friday. They'd been running late. He'd driven them to the airport. Then what? It raised a question, like one little volcano popping off.

"Hey, Julian," she said.

"Yes?"

"Did you happen to see Jeanette on Friday or Saturday?"

Too far away to see some tiny reaction on his face, and if there was a big one, she missed it. "Jeanette?" he said after a moment or two. "I don't understand."

"That's when she must have brought my bike back," Ruby said.

"I didn't see her," Julian said. "But I wasn't around much."

"No?"

"I was out looking for Zippy." He sounded a little offended.

"Oh, yeah."

Ruby pedaled off, following the MapQuest directions. Once she took off her mitten, felt in her pocket for Jeanette's Post-it and Zippy's tag: her two biggest cases, in there together.

Julian watched till Ruby had turned up Indian Ridge, vanishing around the corner. He went back in the house. The bike. He'd forgotten all about it, worse, hadn't even seen it as a point of vulnerability. No doubt the police were trying to trace Jeanette's movements, discover who had seen her last, plodding through their checklist. Would they be interested in this visit? Oh, yes. But the police didn't know. Only the girl knew. Was she smart enough to understand the importance of the bike, to act upon that understanding? Julian didn't know. Until recently, he'd have said no. She was just a little girl, often annoying, independent, perhaps, but not especially clever. But now, just this morning, he wasn't sure.

Julian went upstairs, looked in her room, saw nothing unusual, checked the bathroom, then his own room. She'd said she was going back to bed and now she was out looking for the dog. She had indeed gone upstairs, but he'd found her at the sink in the bathroom, not in her bedroom. Also, he'd had the feeling she'd been in his room, was almost certain he'd heard her running in the hall as he came up. But not totally certain, despite the excellence of his hearing, of all his senses. He'd checked the room of course: looking up in the closet where the square he'd cut out of the ceiling was in place, its sawed-through outline, angle-cut to stay in place, invisible in the shadows; and under the bed, where nothing had changed. The desk, the chest of drawers—nothing out of place, no sign of prying eyes. He picked up Margie's envelope, took out her letter and reread it, put it back.

How infuriating this bike development was! Another example of characters developing their own plots, the worst one yet because now they were acting in concert, forming alliances against him. Perhaps not the worst: someone had found the crack vials, not inexpensive, in the lining of the varsity jacket and cut them out. Who? Not Brandon; Julian had established that to his satisfaction on the way to New York. The boy was an innocent, not smart enough—never would be—to fool him for a moment. Then who?

Julian returned to the bathroom, splashed water on his own face. It seemed untroubled in the mirror; a credit to his self-possession. He went into her room, sat at her computer, hit a key. AOL came up. She had two screen names, RobinR@aol.com and Zippy37@aol.com. He tried RobinR, was asked for the password. Julian thought, but not long, five or ten seconds, then typed in *Rubester*. And was in.

Julian went to *History*. The last site she'd visited was MapQuest. He went to MapQuest, hit the button for *Last*

Search. Up came the directions to his own place, the carriage house at Gail Bender's farm.

Julian ran down the stairs, swung around the post toward the kitchen, on the way to his own bike in the garage. How far ahead could she be? The door, that busy door from the kitchen to the garage, opened just as he put his hand to it, and Linda came in.

31

"**O**h," said Linda, "you scared me."

She didn't look scared. "My apologies," Julian said, backing into the room. "Completely unintentional."

"I know that," Linda said. She gave him a big smile. Why was her face so unusually pink? Why were her eyes so lively? What was she doing home at this hour?

Linda set a bag of groceries on the counter. "I've brought some treats. How's she doing?"

The concerned working mom checking on the sick child: that hadn't occurred to him. "Much better," he said. "The fact is, she's out looking for Zippy." He had a sudden thought, somewhat alarming. "You might have seen her."

"No," Linda said. She glanced out the window; a few light flakes were falling.

"I was just going out to get her," Julian said. But how would that work now that Linda was home? Characters again acting on their own, leading to plot complications without end. "Perhaps I could borrow your car for a few moments. She can't have gone far." But then what? A muscle twitched under his shirt.

"Let her keep looking a little longer," Linda said. "It'll probably do her good."

"How would that be?"

"Psychologically," Linda said. "In terms of coming to some sort of closure—if we don't get Zippy back, that is." She looked him in the eye, a look of some intimacy, as though they were close. "What do you think, Julian—will we get him back?"

"I'm hopeful," he said.

"I love your optimism. Did you know it's one of the basic characteristics of a leader?"

"I wasn't aware."

"According to a seminar I went to last fall."

He could see she was in the mood for one of those discussions that passed for intellectual in her circle. Julian wanted no intellectual discussion with her, now or ever. What he wanted was her car. A possible course of action had come to him, one that didn't involve meeting Ruby at all. The essential point was not preventing her from entering the carriage house, but making sure that nothing she shouldn't see was there. How long would it take her? An hour, probably more: a DRT problem. Slightly disguised, it might make a good exercise for Brandon: R leaves on a bicycle etc., how long after must J leave in a Jeep, given that etc., etc. Brandon would need his DRT shield; he himself required the Jeep.

"We don't want to risk Ruby's cold getting worse, do we?" Julian said. "I could just kick myself, letting her out at all. Why don't I—"

"Stop worrying, Julian. She'll be fine—Ruby's pretty independent, as I'm sure you've noticed. But I appreciate your concern. The truth is, I appreciate how much you've helped in every way, today more than ever. I had some very good news this morning."

"Oh?"

"Larry offered me a job—head of marketing at Skyway!

All of Skyway, Julian. I'm a VP. I never dreamed. I'll even be going to New York once a week."

"Congratulations."

"It never would have happened without you. La Rivière started it all. I feel very grateful." Linda reached into the grocery bag. "Here's some of that jam you like. Far from adequate, I know, but all I could think of."

Julian took it. Their hands grazed: did the grazing go on a little longer than necessary at her end? "How kind," Julian said. A huge round thick-glass jar of jam, heavy on his palm, like a weapon. He needed the Jeep. Where were her maternal instincts? How to trigger them?

"Ruby's independence is a credit to you, no doubt," he said, "but recklessness is another matter. Think for a moment of Toad."

"Toad?"

"Of Toad Hall, who said, as I recall, at the beginning of one of his misadventures, 'I wonder if this sort of car *starts* easily.' "

"You're referring to *The Wind in the Willows*?" Linda said.

"It was my very favorite book as a boy," Julian said. Perhaps he could have done without the *very*. Laying it on a little too thick; on the other hand, subtlety was so often wasted.

Linda sat down, slowly, as though her legs were dying beneath her.

"Is something wrong?" Julian said, putting down the jar.

"No, not wrong exactly. I should have been prepared for this."

"For what?"

She took a deep breath. "Ever since you arrived I've had the thought, couldn't help it, that you're the kind of man Adam would have grown up to be. And now, with you in his room, it's almost as though . . ." She started to cry, composed herself. "He was such a helpful little boy, so kind. I love my other kids, of course, they're wonderful, but they don't have that gift."

Julian handed her a tissue from the box on the butcher block.

"*The Wind in the Willows*," she began, and burst into tears. She gazed up at him through the bleary mess, and some inner pain suddenly distorted her face, some thought or memory that must have been torture, reminding him in turn of an illustrated book of medieval torture he'd had as a boy, and before he could react, she fell forward and buried her face in his chest. "It was Adam's favorite, too." The words came out of her not as normal speech, but as torn things, literal sound bites. Julian felt them through his skin.

"I'm sure that's true of many children," he said. He noticed that she dyed her hair: some of the roots were gray.

Linda shook her head, her face still against him. Perhaps this was a moment for patting her on the back. And perhaps not. Then another surprise: he felt himself getting hard.

"No," she said, looking up at him now, breaking contact, making a huge effort to control herself, "it's like fate or God has sent you, a little consolation at last. I don't even deserve it."

He could read her watch upside down. Still time enough, and he'd never feel right about abandoning such a promising interview. "Why don't you deserve consolation?" he said, realizing at that moment what a good priest he would have been; and now gave her that pat, nice and soft on the shoulder, stroking, consoling. There was no answer.

"Everyone deserves consolation," he said. The priesthood: what fun, confession most of all. "Except for the truly monstrous, I suppose, and you're certainly not that."

"But I am."

"What nonsense. You're a fine person." More fun, saying things like that. The tutor and the priest: hadn't the same man performed both roles at one time?

"You're so wrong," Linda said. She was crying again, but silent, just the tears flowing steadily, as though some inner dam had failed.

"What could you have possibly done to merit this self-laceration?" he said.

"I can't explain."

"Can't or won't?"

"It's the same."

"Then how will you ever understand your own life?" Julian wasn't satisfied with that question, a formulation more suited to the talk-show hostess than the man of the cloth.

But it worked, got down deeper, because racking sobs came now and the racked look was back. "I understand my life all too well."

"In what way?"

"I was responsible," she said.

"For what?"

"Adam."

"I thought Adam died of leukemia."

"But first he broke his leg."

"Which didn't heal properly, is that right? Leading to the discovery of the leukemia."

"Yes."

"A terrible tragedy," Julian said, "and my heart aches for you, but how could it be your responsibility?"

"It is, it is." He stroked her more softly, in inverse proportion to the noise.

"How can that be?" he said. And how gentle his voice, like a lullaby. "Didn't he break his leg skiing? You didn't beat him or anything?"

"Yes," she said. "Yes, I did."

"I don't believe it," Julian said.

"Oh, Julian, you overestimate me, you really do. I did a terrible, terrible thing." He got a little harder.

"I can't imagine you beating him."

"Not in a physical sense. But he died in a physical sense, didn't he? Where do you think I was when he broke his leg?"

"On the same trail? You collided?"

"I wish that was true. I wish I could make that happen,

be out there on the hill, falling down with him." Tears still flowed, but her eyes had an inward look now, building some scene, perhaps, of an alternate and better history.

"But?" said Julian.

"I wasn't even skiing."

"Where were you?"

"Where I shouldn't have been," she said.

"In the bar?" Julian said. "Completely understandable on a ski vacation. Why are you being so hard on yourself?"

Her voice rose, partly in anger, partly at him. "I wasn't in the bar."

"Then where?"

The tortured look returned. Linda bit her lip, so hard a droplet of blood appeared. "You poor thing," Julian said. *Child* would have been better, but he wasn't a priest, after all. Good enough, however: new sounds came up from deep inside her, ragged and uncontrolled. He lowered his voice, made it almost inaudible, like a thought of her own. "Nothing could be that bad," he said.

Linda sagged, as though she had no strength left but for crying. Somewhere in the crying came a little phrase, almost lost. "I was back at the cabin."

He began to see. "It doesn't matter where you were, Linda," he said in that same low voice. "You didn't do anything bad."

"But I did. Only once in my life, but it happened when Adam fell."

He stroked her shoulder. "Don't, Linda," he crooned. "Don't."

She shook herself free. "Stop being so nice to me. Don't you understand? I was in Tom's Jacuzzi."

She gazed up at him, blurred eyes waiting for his reaction. How biblical this was, and primitive, swift and disproportionate punishment for her transgression. "You know there is no causal relationship," he said. "Forgive yourself. Scott must have forgiven you long ago."

"He doesn't know."

Ah.

"No one does."

"Then let us speak no more about it," Julian said. "You forgive and I'll forget." That was truly beautiful. He leaned forward, kissed the top of her head—you put your lips together and then parted them with a smacking sound. Surely she was aware of his erection by now. Was she more interesting than he'd thought? He backed away, shirt-dampened. Perhaps things hadn't gone so well with Gail on the carnal side, but he knew that no performance with this woman could ever go wrong. All he would have to do was think of that Jacuzzi scene and snap of the bone to stay hard as adamantine, adamantine being the fitting trope; he was very good.

But all that could come at his leisure. He had lots of time—what interesting nocturnal wanderings lay ahead!— but everything depended on one specific timing challenge: reaching the carriage house before Ruby. He took the box of tissues off the butcher block and slid it across the table to her.

"I'm worried about Ruby and I'd like to go get her," he said, simple and plain.

Linda dabbed at her eyes. She looked exhausted and used up, like a woman after a long, hard childbirth.

"The keys are in the ignition," she said.

He started toward the door.

"It was *The Wind in the Willows*," Linda said, maybe to herself.

The power of the written word: Julian understood. He also understood for the first time that intelligence alone had not raised him above the billions. He also had deep insight into the human heart. The Jeep fishtailed just a bit as he took the corner at Poplar Drive.

Scott checked Codexco: $7.95, below eight for the first time. One hundred and fifty thousand times eighty cents made $120,000. He went out to lunch.

And on the way, took a little detour, about twenty miles, to the nearest Porsche dealership. They had a single Boxster on the lot, a blue one. He took it for a test drive. Zoom. While he was zooming, "Born to Be Wild" came on the radio, as though Porsche and the radio station were part of some conspiracy. Scott laughed out loud. "Head out on the highway," he sang, dead center in the most awesome sound system ever, "lookin' for adventure."

"Better than sex?" said the salesman, back on the lot. Probably what he said every time, except to female customers, but Scott wasn't in a judgmental mood. He was in a great mood, as though gravity had lost some of its power. Fresh air was reaching the bottom of his lungs for the first time in years.

"I'd like it in silver," Scott said; even his voice was deeper.

"Best color," said the salesman. "No question."

They went inside, sat down at the salesman's desk. The salesman got on the phone, calling other dealerships in search of a silver Boxster. Scott leafed through the brochure. Snowflakes drifted past the big windows. On the wall of his office hung a very nice snowflake that Ruby had made. He smiled to himself. His cell phone rang.

"Scott?"

"Hi, Mickey," said Scott, "guess where I am?"

"That's easy," said Gudukas. "In the toilet, like me."

"What's that supposed to mean?" Scott said. Across the table the Boxster salesman, phone to his ear, gave him a thumbs-up.

"You don't bother checking the stock?" said Gudukas.

"Sure I do. It was under eight less than an hour ago."

"It's at twelve and a quarter this very second," said Gudukas.

Twelve and a quarter. The words made no sense. He couldn't have heard right. "What did you say?"

"Twelve forty now."

"What the hell are you talking about?"

"It's going up like a rocket on the fucking Fourth of July, that's what I'm talking about."

"But it's at seven ninety-five," Scott said. "I'm up a hundred and twenty grand."

"You're down, down five hundred and forty grand, more or less. Not as bad as the shit-kicking I'm taking, but—"

"What was that? What number did you say?"

"—you're going to have to come up with two hundred grand minimum."

"Why? How?"

"Got to cover. Standard procedure. You've got ten minutes. Or you can close out right now. That's what I'd recommend. I'm doing it as we speak."

"Close out?"

"Buy back the shares at market. Come on, Scotty, think."

"And lose everything?" Scott said.

"This ain't everything," Gudukas said.

"What the hell are you talking about?"

"Infinite exposure. Say it goes all the way to twenty, thirty, ninety. Shit like that happens. They'll still want the shares. That's losing everything."

"But it's going down." Even as he spoke, Scott remembered Tom: *What if it blips up to eighteen*? "You said it was going down."

"Not today—Codexco issued a press release fifteen minutes ago. That algorithm bullshit worked after all. They're signing a billion-dollar contract with the government of Japan."

"But what about the venture capitalists?"

"What about them?"

"Aren't they going to dump their shares?"

"Who the fuck knows?"

"You do. You're the one who talked to them and you said it was going down." Scott was on his feet now; the salesman, still on the phone, was watching him, his pencil hand still.

"Ten minutes," Gudukas said. "And my boss says make it three hundred grand if you're hanging tough."

Scott stood there, the cell phone in his hand, showroom cars gleaming all around. Had he imagined the whole thing? Was it some brain chemistry weirdness? Maybe he was having a stroke. That was it. He felt paralyzed already: the slightest breeze would knock him down.

"We can have it on the lot Monday morning, Mr. Gardner," said the salesman. "I'll need a deposit, say five grand."

Scott walked out of the showroom, got in the Triumph. It was cold in the Triumph and some snow blew in with him. He went to punch in numbers on the cell, realized he still had the Boxster brochure in one hand. Mortgaging the house was the only answer. It was going down. This was a blip. How was he going to explain? He had no idea. The words would come pouring and Linda would sort them out. He called her at work. Not there. Her cell. No answer. Home, and got the machine. But Ruby and Julian were there. "Pick up, pick up," he yelled. No one did.

What next? Tom? Impossible. His mother? Horrible thought, but he had no better. Even if she agreed, it would take time. He needed time.

Scott called Gudukas. He expected to hear bedlam in the background at the brokerage, but it was quiet.

"Mickey," he said, "I need—"

"Too late," Gudukas said. "Stock's at fourteen. We closed you out."

"Closed me out?"

"Had to cover," Gudukas said.

"My five hundred grand?"

"Standard procedure."

"Gone?"

"Plus what you owe the brokerage. It all happened so fast we couldn't get you out till it hit thirteen seventy-five. Comes to two hundred grand."

"You're telling me I lost my five hundred grand and you

want two hundred more?" Scott was speaking slowly, slurring his words a bit; maybe a stroke after all.

"Plus or minus."

"You're slime."

"Want me to say I'm sorry? Think that'll bring your money back? I lost a shitload more than you, buddy boy."

"So what?" Scott said.

"Suck it up," said Mickey Gudukas.

32

It was like the three bears only she was the porridge—first too hot, then too cold, finally just right. Fat snowflakes went by, some of them catching in her eyelashes; but the road was bare. After what seemed like ages, Ruby came to the 840 mailbox and took a left down a long tree-lined lane, dodging huge piles of poo every so often. Eight forty Trunk Road turned out to be a farm with acres and acres, still inside the boundaries of Old Mill. She'd had no idea.

Ruby pedaled up a little rise. From the top she saw a small wooden house on one side of the lane and a much bigger one on the other; beyond stood some sheds, a barn, more fields, and in the distance two dense groves of trees. She was coasting down the hill, wondering where exactly in all this Julian lived, when a woman in a red-and-black checked jacket came out of the big house. Ruby ducked behind a tree, one hand on the trunk, poised on her bike.

The woman crossed the lane, walked toward the little house. She had something in her hand, an envelope maybe.

Her boots crunched on the packed snow of the path to the door. She knocked on it.

"Julian," she called. "Are you home?" She knocked again, harder. "Julian?" The woman knelt, stuck what Ruby could now see clearly was an envelope under the door, and walked back to the big house. Ruby shifted around to keep the tree between them, but the woman never looked in her direction. The door of the big house closed behind her.

Ruby got off her bike. She couldn't ride the rest of the way down the lane—what if the woman glanced out her window? Best to circle around behind the little house, but the snow was too deep for riding. Ruby leaned the bike against the tree. What if the woman went out into town, drove past? She'd see it. Ruby laid the bike down, covered it with snow. This kind of thing was so tricky. She set off in a wide circle through the fields, ending at the back of the little house.

Ruby tried the door, locked, peered through a cracked and dirty window, saw a wheelbarrow, bags of garden supplies, a shadowy hall leading to the front of the house. She stepped back, noticed a bulkhead door. Wasn't that for getting in the cellar? She raised it, went down stone steps to another door, quite small, her size. She tried this one and it opened. Ruby climbed back up the stone steps, pulled the bulkhead door shut, went down in darkness and entered the house, closing the little door, too.

All cobwebby in the cellar. Ruby waved her hands in front of her, cutting through as she moved toward a dusty shaft of light that came from a high window on the far wall. Halfway there she came to a staircase, all rickety, and went up.

She found herself at the front of the house, a bare hallway with warped and darkened floorboards. The envelope, addressed to Julian from A-Plus Tutorial, lay by the front door. Ruby opened it.

Inside was a letter with an A-Plus Tutorial business card attached. On the business card it said: *Forgot to include this last time—Margie.*

Ruby read the letter, dated November 19, 1998, and written on stationery that said *Master of Balliol, Oxford* at the top.

*Re: Vipers in My Backpack—Zoological Fieldwork
in Up-Country Gabon
Dear Mr. Sawyer:
We all of us, dons, fellows and students, so enjoyed
your talk Wednesday last. How pleasant to learn that
the tradition of the bold amateur naturalist lives on.
Do come back and regale us with an account of your
next adventure.
Yours truly,
R. M. Simkins, K.B.E*

Ruby reread the letter. Then she read it again, holding it near a window for better light. Must have been typed on a real typewriter because every letter made tiny dents in the back of the page. Something bothered her, something not quite right. She took out her magnifying glass, peered at the year, 1998. Something not quite right about that second 9. Just at the left of the tail part, the paper looked a little thin, felt a little rough, as though something had been rubbed away.

Ruby examined the back of the page under the magnifying glass, saw that while the numbers on the front read 1998, the impression on the back read 1988. Someone had erased that little bulge on the bottom left of the 8, turning it into a 9. Ruby pocketed the letter, went upstairs, creak creak, another worn staircase, but not rickety.

At the top she came to a small room: fireplace strewn with cigarette butts and burned matches, a bed on one side, a desk at the other, by the window; not much else. On the ceiling over the bed was written,

*negligent is to forsake as
mendacious is to deceive*

· · ·

Julian's room.

Ruby sat at the desk. A flock of dark birds skimmed by, followed by a whirlpool of spinning snowflakes. Nothing on the desk but a phone and a few papers, kept in place with a jar of strawberry jam. Ruby opened all the drawers, found nothing, no novel or anything else. She shifted the jam and examined the papers.

At Home, read the first page, the handwriting beautiful: *A Living Novel by Julian Sawyer.*

Ruby turned to page one: *Notes for a Living Novel: Toward a New Form. By Julian Sawyer.*

And under that:

> *negligent is to forsake as*
> *mendacious is to deceive*
> *nothing you can't depend on*
> *will ever depend on you.*

The last two lines, her lines, the test for who can be relied on, were scratched out.

Page two: *Scott: inferiority complex, esp. re Tom; fundamentally lazy; a gambler with no notion of odds; falsely believes himself to be ambitious, but all he wants is more of the same; lack of more of the same is all that makes him unhappy—not a good enough reason, not nearly; IQ 110. To do: friendly discussion of investment strategy, esp. options trading; find out more about family insurance firm: does Tom have children?*

Page three: *Linda: ambitious in real sense, wants to develop her own thwarted expressive potential; developing Brandon—the next best thing; many problems with Scott— explore; lies well (Gabon paper episode); IQ 120. To do: find out much more about Adam; become good friends. Bad things happen slowly.*

Page four: *Adam: Superboy—the paragon under whose boot they lie; time line—broken leg, leukemia.*

Page five: *Brandon: normal kid, might actually have grown up to be a happy person in other circumstances; IQ 125. To do: more of the same; (get details of party denouement).*

Page six: *Ruby: IQ—*

"The Speckled Band"

Ruby still had her jacket on, and her hat with the stars, but she felt very cold.

What else? Phone messages. Ruby found only one, not new, since the light wasn't blinking.

"Julian? This is Gail. Did you ever buy Codexco? It's going up anytime now."

Codexco? Wasn't that Dad's stock, the one that paid for the Atlantis trip? And wasn't it supposed to go down? The dark birds swooped by again, going the other way this time. And down the lane from that direction, the direction of Trunk Road, came Mom's Jeep Grand Cherokee. But not Mom. Julian was at the wheel.

For a moment, Ruby couldn't move, not a muscle. He was going to park, come through the door, up the stairs and find her at the desk, the living novel all spread out on top, and there wasn't a thing she could do. *Bad things happen slowly.* Help me. Oh, God, help. But her body was frozen.

Body frozen, but her mind kept going, on its own. Julian had the car. Mom must have lent it to him. Mom was at home.

Her body came to life. Ruby grabbed the phone, called home. "Answer, answer." She mouthed the words.

Mom answered. "Hello?"

"Mom. Call Julian right now. Tell him—"

"Ruby? He's out looking for you. Where—"

"Call the car. Tell him I'm home."

"Home?"

"Back, Mom. I'm back already."

"But why, Ruby? Is something wrong?"

"Just do it. And warn Dad about the stock."

"The stock?"

"Codexco."

"Codexco? What's—"

The car started turning off the lane, into the driveway.
"Now."

"But you're not home." Mom's voice got higher. "Why
should I lie to Julian?"

"Make him turn around, Mom. Make him turn around."

"Turn around? I don't—"

"Trust me."

The car rolled up the driveway to the little house. Mom
started to say something else, something else beginning with
but. Ruby hung up, backed a few feet from the window,
where she could still see out but knew he couldn't see in, except at night when lights were on. The car came to a stop.
The engine died. The door opened. Julian put one foot on the
ground, paused. The car phone rang; Ruby heard it.

Julian put it to his ear. His lips moved. Then they didn't.
His foot left the ground, disappeared back inside. The door
closed. His lips moved again. He put the phone down. The
engine fired. The car backed out, all the way to the lane.
Ruby breathed. The wheels turned. Next the car would
swing around, straighten out on the lane, head back to Trunk
Road, through Old Mill to West Mill, home.

But that didn't happen. Mom's Jeep stayed where it was,
halfway into the turn, didn't move at all for what seemed like
a long time. Then it did: but forward, erasing the turn and
coming back up the driveway to the little house. Ruby
backed into the middle of the room. She heard the engine die
again, the door open and close.

Ruby glanced around wildly, tried the only door there
was: on the other side a tiny bathroom, transparent curtain
hung over the stall shower, useless. She turned back to
the room, saw the pages of the living novel scattered on the
desk, ran over, piled them neatly, placed the jar on top. The
front door opened; and closed, shaking the house a little.
Ruby whirled. Under the desk? No. Under the bed? No.
Where? Where?

Up the chimney? Ruby darted into the fireplace, crouching, peering up. What was that thing, the thing that had caused the smoke episode? Damper, he'd taught her himself. This one seemed quite high up. Maybe if she rose, got her hands on it—

Footsteps on the worn stairs, *creak creak*.

Ruby stood—head, shoulders, the top half of her body in the chimney. She reached up, felt a metal plate, not sharp, got both hands on it, pulled her feet up, up, out of sight. A little blob of something fell from the chimney wall, landed with a plop. Footsteps entered the room. Step, step, pause. A long pause. She could hear him breathing. Then came a sound, a soft thump: setting down the jam jar?

Step, step, step, pause. A door opened, the bathroom door. Then a quiet silvery shriek—the shower curtain, transparent or not—yanked aside. She heard him talking: "If A, then B," he said.

Ruby's arms ached. Her hands got damp, started to lose their grip. If she could only draw her feet a little farther up, press them against the wall. Now: had to be now, while he was in the bathroom. Slipping, slipping, hands so sweaty— now. There, like that, wedged in, her legs bearing some of the weight. But how loud was that scraping sound her boot made? Another blob fell plop.

Step, step. Whoosh: bedcovers swept off. *Grunt:* Julian looking under the bed. *Step, step, step.* Then *tap, tap*: at the desk, the tap of his fingernails. The broken-off one with the purple bruise underneath—how had that happened?

Ruby could feel him thinking, like one of those weather fronts on TV, pushing, pushing, pushing that front right into her own head. A faint plastic click, and then Ruby heard the dial tone. But no dialing. A plastic impact, and the phone was back on its stand. Had he just figured out the call to Mom? The Codexco message? Both?

Step, step, coming closer. *Step, step.* Ruby glanced down. She could see through a tiny opening between her left leg and the chimney wall, down to a thin strip of the fireplace floor where two shoe tops now rested among the ashes and cigarette butts. Then came a little snick, a pause, and a match spun down. She smelled cigarette smoke. "If A, then B," he said again, but practically in her ear this time. Maybe he hadn't figured out the call or the message; if he had he'd be at C right now, or D, or even farther. *Oh, let that be true.*

Julian stayed right there, smoking his cigarette. Ruby hung on, soaked with sweat under her jacket and heavy clothes. The pressure of his mind pushed and pushed. Then the cigarette, half smoked, landed down there with the other butts, still smoking. Smoke rose. It was going to make her cough.

The shoe tops shifted, turned with a grinding sound, moved out of sight. Ruby held her breath, keeping that cough inside. *Step, step.* Then down the stairs, little quick ones. More stepping on the level below, movement of objects, then fainter sounds on the level below that. After that no sound at all. Smoke rose. The cough was coming and there was nothing she could do.

The car door slammed.

She coughed. Her feet slipped.

The engine started. Ruby lost her grip, crashed down in the pile of cigarette butts. The car drove off.

Linda watched through the living-room window. A DPW truck went by, spewing sand; the oil man; a visiting nurse; and then the Triumph. She hurried into the kitchen.

Scott came through the garage door. Her first thought was that he'd caught it too, whatever Ruby had. His face was bloodless, even the lips, and there was a tiny tremor in his hands.

"Are you all right?" she said.

He didn't answer, gazed around the room as though it were a strange place instead of his own kitchen.

"I'm worried," she said.

He nodded.

"I got the strangest call from Ruby."

"Ruby? Isn't she here?"

"She's out looking for Zippy."

His voice rose suddenly, scaring her. "She's got to stop that."

"I know. Julian's gone to find her. But she sounded so frightened."

"Frightened?"

"Of Julian. She said to warn you about the stock."

He turned to her, the muscles in his face all slack. "Warn me about the stock?"

"Scott. Are you all right?"

"Warn me what?"

"I don't know. Is there some connection between Julian and Codexco?"

Scott put his hand to his forehead, rubbed it till it reddened, a red patch on his colorless skin.

"What's wrong, Scott? Has something happened with Codexco?"

Scott took a deep breath. Red spread from the forehead patch all over his face. "I lost it."

"Lost what?"

"Everything."

"Every—" The door opened and Julian came in; she hadn't even heard the car.

His eyes went to Linda, Scott, back to Linda. "Well, well," he said. "What good parents, home to check on the invalid. Back safe and sound, thank goodness."

"No," Linda said.

"No?" said Julian. "What can you mean by that?"

"She's not here."

"But you said she was."

"She's afraid of you," Linda said.

"Afraid of me? What makes you say that?"

"She called, half scared to death."

"She called?" Julian backed toward the door, the car keys in his hand. "The poor little thing," he said. "Feverish, of course. I'll go get her. We can straighten this out after I bring her home safe."

"You know where she is?" Linda said.

"Search for her, more accurately speaking," Julian said.

"Wait a minute," Scott said. "What do you know about Codexco?"

"The stock you bought, or sold, or whatever you did? How is that relevant?"

"Linda says you know something about it."

Julian glanced at her. "I'll go get Ruby now."

"No," Linda said. "I want you to explain."

"Explain what?"

"Why Ruby's afraid of you. What you know about the stock."

Julian turned to Scott. "I know you're both under stress, Ruby sick, dog missing, other possible concerns depending on the relative acuity of your perceptions, but I appeal to you, Scott. Please make Linda see reason. I should be out looking for Ruby. She's not well."

"Linda has good judgment. Give me the keys."

Linda loved Scott then, at the very moment she knew for all time that her judgment was bad.

Scott held out his hand for the keys. Julian's hand closed around them. "Good judgment? Did she show good judgment the day Adam broke his leg?"

"Adam?" said Scott. "What do you mean?"

Julian turned to Linda. "Why have you allowed it to come to this? You might as well tell him. Probably best, in an air-clearing sense."

Linda couldn't speak.

"Tell me what?" said Scott.

"About Tom," said Julian.

"Tom? What about him?"

"A minor indiscretion, on the scale of things," said Julian, "but it's really not my story."

Scott took a step toward him, grabbed the front of his shirt. "Tell me."

"But it's so tawdry," Julian said, his face close to Scott's, appearing in no way alarmed by Scott's hold. "Footsie in the whirlpool, two tipsy people, one thing leading to another. Why don't you fill in the blanks while I get Ruby?"

Scott let go. He swayed back a little, as though he might faint. The big, thick-glass jar of strawberry jam lay on the butcher block. Linda picked it up and brought it down on the back of Julian's head with all her strength.

Ruby went to the desk, got the notes for the living novel. She opened the damper on the fireplace the way he'd shown her, lit one of his matches, burned the papers. They were no one's business.

She left the little house by the bulkhead doors, same way she'd entered, made the same wide circle back to her bike. She raised it out of the snow, brushed it off, started riding, down the lane, right on Trunk Road. On her way home, but not directly: she was going to pull a little surprise on Julian.

Snow still fell, that same light snowfall, like the beginning or the end of a storm except it just stayed that way. Ruby rode through Old Mill, into West Mill, turned right on Depot. The police station was on Depot; she'd passed it many times. But not this time. She rode and rode, shivering now, over the tracks, very tired and very slow. Main? Depot turned into Main? And there was the Shell station. She went inside.

"Hi, Manny," she said. He was counting money at the cash register again, or still.

"Hey," said Manny, looking up. "How's that school project going?"

"Not good," Ruby said. "Where's the police station?"

"Ruby the Kid," said Sergeant D'Amario, coming into the room where they'd asked her to wait.

"Ruby Gardner," said Ruby, finishing her Sprite. She'd never needed one so bad. "Brandon's sister."

"I know," said D'Amario.

"He's not a druggie and you're on the wrong track. I can tell you who's bringing crack into West Mill."

"Who?"

"But first I have to hear that tape."

"What tape?"

"The anonymous caller tape," Ruby said. "From the night you made the bust in the woods."

"Why?"

"Because it's all connected. Like the Musgrave Ritual."

The cop leaning against the wall said, "Is it a cult thing? Like David Koresh?"

"What's the Musgrave Ritual?" said D'Amario.

Ruby couldn't believe that: a professional law enforcer, and he hadn't heard of the Musgrave Ritual? Nothing had changed since Inspector Lestrade's day. "It doesn't matter." She reached into her pocket, took out the evidence: Zippy's tag, Jeanette's Post-it, the letter from the master of Balliol.

"What's all this?" said D'Amario.

"Look it over."

D'Amario glanced at the tag, read the Post-it. "What does *J* stand for?"

"Jeanette."

The cops in the room exchanged looks. D'Amario read the letter.

"What's this got to do with anything?" he said. "Is this Sawyer guy the dealer?"

Ruby handed him the magnifying glass. "Check that date," she said.

He checked the date. "It's been changed."

"What time is it in England?" Ruby said.

"Six or seven hours difference, maybe," said D'Amario.

"Earlier or later?" said the cop by the wall.

D'Amario ignored him. "What are you getting at?" he said to Ruby.

"Just trying to figure if this is a good time to call R. M. Simkins, K.B.E."

"Why would I do that?"

"Because it's all connected," Ruby said. And if so— boom. A watery memory came in view. The last big block shifted in her mind. Everything locked in place. All she'd needed was inside her head, as she'd suspected: it just needed arranging right.

"I don't get any of this," said the cop by the wall.

"What if I told you there's a ski pole at the bottom of the pond?" Ruby said.

He got that one. They all got that one. Ruby got it too, really got it. She buried her face in her hands so no one could see her.

Things started happening. D'Amario placed a call to the master of Balliol, left a message. Then they took Ruby into a room packed with electronic equipment. The guy at the controls popped a little disk, smaller than a CD, into some kind of player. After two or three seconds, a voice spoke.

"I'm calling to inform you of a very loud party in the town forest. I believe there was a gunshot, although I wouldn't swear." *Click.*

"That's him," Ruby said.

Ruby went home, riding up front in the lead cruiser, her bike in the trunk. They flashed their blue lights but kept the sirens off. The garage door was open at 37 Robin Road, the Triumph inside; Dewey's car sat in the driveway, Fuck You You Fuckin Fuck visible for all to see.

"That David Brickham's car?" D'Amario said.

"Dewey," said Ruby. "No one calls him David."

"Maybe they should," D'Amario said.

D'Amario was smart; maybe not ten times as smart as Brandon and Dewey put together, but smart.

"And the Triumph?" D'Amario said.

"My dad's."

"What's your mom drive?"

"Jeep Grand Cherokee."

"Color?"

"Blue. Dark but not navy, with some purple in it." Ruby opened the door.

"Stay in the car," D'Amario said.

"But I want to see my mom and dad."

"In a minute."

A policewoman came to sit with her. She had a box of Dunkin' Donuts, chocolate ones with sprinkles, normally irresistible.

"No, thanks," Ruby said.

The cops took out their guns and entered the house, using Ruby's key. D'Amario came out almost at once and waved her in.

They were in the kitchen: Brandon, Trish, and Dewey, with the remains of half a dozen Subway subs, and a few cops, guns back in their holsters. Dewey's eyes were darting around, as though he was planning an escape.

"When did you kids get here?" D'Amario said.

"Going to slice up more of my clothes?" said Brandon.

"Don't fool around," said D'Amario. "Not the time."

"Bran," said Ruby.

"Four-fifteen," said Trish.

"And it was just like this? No one home?"

"Yeah," Bran said.

A cop poked his head in. "Mrs. Gardner left her office at eleven-thirty, Mr. Gardner left his a little after that, they're not sure the exact time. Neither one went back."

"The Jeep," said D'Amario.

"Already on it," said the cop.

"What's going on?" Brandon said.

"Your sister'll fill you in," said D'Amario. "You other two can take off."

Dewey flew out like a cartoon character. Trish gave Brandon a little kiss on the cheek and followed.

"Cars we can find pretty easy," D'Amario said.

"Don't forget eight forty Trunk Road," Ruby said.

D'Amario gave her a look, then made a little motion with his index finger. A cop hurried out. Another hurried in with some blueprints.

"All set?" he said.

D'Amario went with him. Ruby ducked into the mud-room, saw that Mom's gray coat with the fur collar and Dad's leather jacket weren't there, tagged after D'Amario.

They walked through the house, the blueprint guy, D'Amario, Ruby. There were cops all over the place but the three of them went into every room anyway, tried every closet, checked under every bed. The house was normal, nothing out of place, nothing broken, nothing missing but the parents.

"Don't forget the chimney," Ruby said. They looked at her funny but did what she wanted.

"There an attic?" said D'Amario in the upstairs hall.

"Shows one," said the blueprint guy. "Only access is right here." He pointed to a hatch cover in the ceiling at the top of the stairs, painted over and almost invisible.

"Anybody ever go up there, Ruby the Kid?" said D'Amario.

Ruby hadn't even known there was an attic. "No."

The blueprint guy pulled in a chair from Brandon's room, stood on it, pushed against the hatch cover. "In solid," he said. "Hasn't been moved since the painters left."

D'Amario nodded.

Another cop called up the stairs: "Ready down at the pond."

"I'm coming," said Ruby before anyone had other ideas. Jeanette was loyal to her and she was loyal back.

33

Ruby regretted that decision a few hours later.

They had a generator down at the pond and lots of bright lights. The snow, falling thicker and faster now, blackened as it passed through their beams. It was colder too, but the pond didn't freeze, probably because of the divers going up and down. The divers wore dry suits and huge packs on their backs, bulky like spacemen. They brought up a ski boot, a pole, a pair of skis; then a couple of those weights, the kind that Brandon had in his room, with holes in the middle; finally something in bib ski pants, hair like seaweed. Ruby turned away, not fast enough, lost control of the shape of her face, and started crying. Brandon stepped between her and the pond.

D'Amario came over with another cop. "Take the kids home," he said.

Ruby tried to pull herself together. "What about Zippy?"

D'Amario shook his head.

"He must be down there."

"They didn't see him," D'Amario said. "We'll try again in the morning." The lights went out, one by one.

There was a cruiser in the driveway, another on the street, two cops in the backyard, one in the kitchen, one in the front hall. They went up to Brandon's room, checked his weights. He couldn't remember exactly what weights he'd had and how many. A couple looked less scuffed than the rest, like they were new, but Brandon wasn't sure about that either.

The cop in the hall called up: "England coming through."

"That phone have a speaker?" D'Amario called back.

"Yeah."

They went down. Ruby sat on the stairs. The cop hit the speaker button. D'Amario took the phone.

"Sergeant D'Amario?" An English voice, the upper-class kind that made everyone who had it sound brilliant; for some reason, this guy put the accent in *D'Amario* on the *i*, like Sergeant D'Amario pronounced his own name wrong. "This is Sir Ronald Simkins."

"Yes," said D'Amario. "Mr., uh, sir—what should I call you?"

"Ron is fine."

D'Amario nodded, but he didn't call him Ron, or anything. "I've got a letter it seems you wrote to someone named Julian Sawyer, on either November nineteenth, nineteen eighty-eight, or the same date in nineteen ninety-eight. We could use your help in sorting it out."

"In what context?" said Simkins.

"A murder investigation."

"Can you read me the letter?"

D'Amario read him the letter.

"Nineteen eighty-eight," said Simkins.

"How sure are you?"

"Absolutely," said Simkins. "Julian Sawyer wasn't even alive in 1998."

D'Amario glanced at Ruby. "We've got a Julian Sawyer here, and he had the letter," he said.

"I'm speaking of Julian Sawyer the elder," said Simkins. "Or senior, as he called himself, in your style."

"There's a junior?" said D'Amario.

"Correct. A son of some notoriety a number of years back, but these incidents recur with such frequency nowadays most of them are forgotten."

"What incidents?"

"Inexplicably violent ones. In this case, young Sawyer burned down the family cottage in Sussex, a kind of retreat they had for use between petroleum ventures. His parents died in the fire. I would have thought him still in prison, but perhaps not. Mitigating circumstances were brought out at the trial, if I recall."

"What mitigating circumstances?"

"Psychological testimony. Justifiable resentments, perhaps? Something of a hothouse environment, parents never satisfied? Analysis of that nature, plus his relative youth at the time."

"How old was he?"

"Early twenties, I believe," said Simkins.

"Did you ever meet him?" D'Amario said.

"I did. He was a student here for several months—I believe that was one of the reasons his father gave that little speech, to smooth the admission process. Marked for greatness, his father said."

"Several months?" said D'Amario.

"He was dismissed."

"Why?"

"Mistreatment of laboratory animals, if I'm not mistaken," said Simkins. "You say you've got him?"

"We're looking for him."

"Good luck."

Sergeant D'Amario sat them down in the kitchen.

"Where do you want to go for the night?" he said.

"Nowhere," said Brandon.

"What if Mom and Dad come home?" said Ruby.

"Then who would you like to come over?" D'Amario took a list from his pocket. "Whole lot of people been calling—your uncle and aunt, a woman named—"

"Does anybody have to come?" Brandon said. Ruby understood—she didn't want someone else staying there, didn't want it stranger than it already was.

"Aren't you guys going to be here?" she said.

"Of course," said D'Amario. "Cruiser out front and foot patrol out back, plus someone inside to monitor the phone."

"We'll be fine like that," Brandon said.

Ruby nodded.

"Just for tonight, then." D'Amario rose.

"Why would it go on longer than that?" Brandon said. "You said finding cars was easy."

"So where are they?" said Ruby.

"That's what we're working on," said Sergeant D'Amario.

"What can't you find easy?" said Ruby.

Brandon tore the last Subway sub in half. "Hungry?" he said, and handed it to Ruby. They sat at the kitchen table, Ruby in her pajamas, hair still wet from the shower, Brandon in sweats. Her filthy, blackened clothes—blue jacket with yellow trim, hat with the stars, all of it—lay in a heap in the upstairs bathroom, and the water spiraling down the shower drain had run black for a long time. Yet she hadn't realized how dirty she'd been and no one, not Brandon, Sergeant D'Amario or the other cops, had said anything or even given her an odd look. She took that for a bad sign and put down the sub after a single bite.

"Not eating that?" said Brandon. He started on her half. How could he be so hungry at a time like this?

"Aren't you scared?" Ruby said.

He put down the sub. They sat together, not talking, but she could feel their thoughts, similar ones, mingling in the air.

A cop came in, handed her the portable. "For you," he said.

"You all right?" Kyla said.

"Yeah. The cops are here."

"It was on TV," Kyla said. "They had a picture, from his driver's license application or something. My dad recognized him."

"How come?"

"He thought he was the VC guy."

"What's that?"

"A money guy—about that stock."

"Codexco?"

"Yeah," said Kyla. "We're not rich anymore. Neither are you, my dad says."

"I don't feel any different," Ruby said.

Kyla laughed that funny laugh of hers, a quick little giggle, really amused. "Me either," she said. Then there was a silence. "I'm going to say a prayer for you before I go to bed," Kyla said.

"You pray?"

"Course not," said Kyla. "Tonight's the only time."

Ruby knew all about that already, from Zippy. It didn't work.

At Home. An epic masterpiece required an epic feat by the hero. Julian, calm, although not as calm as he might have been with a cigarette glowing between his fingers, considered epic feats by epic heroes. Disappointing in the main, the ending so often coupling spiritual triumph with physical demise, Samson being a good example, if thicker-witted than most.

Was the second part, physical demise, really necessary? Or did it merely signify imaginative failure on the part of the artist, an inability to go far enough? The best artists—he recalled his own thought, warmed to it—those artists who changed the world, were always excessive. This, then, this predicament, what lesser men would call a predicament, was in fact an opportunity, a test of his special greatness. How he would relish this moment in future years! The moment in the living novel, the final chapter, in which the artist suddenly reveals himself, takes the stage, a flesh-and-blood giant striding over the paper puppets of his own creation. Even inside the greatest artist burns the need for recognition. He was only human.

Oh, the thrill of it: his finest hour. But not his last. Without life there could be no sequels, each one slightly more disappointing than the last. A funny thought at such a time, so insouciant: he came close to laughing aloud, despite everything. Insouciant, calm—a remarkable man, as anyone would have to acknowledge. As for a plan? The work of seconds. Demeaning to escape under cover of darkness: the epic hero, the epic hero with a brain, exits under cover of light.

They went to bed, Ruby in her bedroom, Brandon in his. A huge, heavy force overwhelmed her the moment she lay down, sleep coming like one of those tides with the Japanese name; it would come to her in a minute. She curled up in a ball. Her eyes closed.

Ruby awoke in the night. She heard the crackle of belt walkie-talkies through her window: the cops down below, in the yard. Everything came back to her, right away. She got up and went downstairs.

The cop in the hall was sitting on that tiny French chair from one of Mom's antiquing trips, eyes closed.

"Excuse me," Ruby said.

His eyes opened.

"Sergeant D'Amario around?"

"Be back later."

"Can you get him a message?"

"Yeah."

"Tell him to check the parking lot at Killington."

"Yeah?" His eyelids were puffy, might have weighed a pound each.

Ruby went back upstairs, lay down, pulled up the covers. The parking lot at Killington. That didn't make sense, but something like it did. She tried to think what, but couldn't, and closed her eyes, had to make them close this time. They popped back open. She got up, went down the hall to Brandon's room.

"Bran? You awake?"

Brandon's voice came out of the darkness. "Yeah."

"I can't sleep," Ruby said.

Silence. Then Bran said, "There's this murderer who says to Macbeth, 'We are men, my liege,' and Macbeth says, 'Ay, in the catalogue ye go for men.'"

More silence.

"When's it going to be light?" Ruby said.

"In a while."

"We already had enough death in this family."

"Adam?"

"Yeah."

"So this time it's going to be okay?" Brandon said.

"Yeah."

"You're pretty smart, Ruby."

"Thanks."

" 'Night."

" 'Night."

Ruby went back to her room. Murderer. She opened the closet, took her bow and quiver off the hook, lay down with them beside her; closed her eyes.

In *The Complete Adventures of Sherlock Holmes*, there was never that big a deal about why the villain did what he did. Always pretty much the same: he didn't get what he wanted, got frustrated and did what he had to to get it. There wasn't much talk about resentments or unsatisfied parents. The villain had bad in him and was smarter than everyone else, knew how to get the better of everyone else, all except for Sherlock Holmes. Holmes outwitted the villains and had fun doing it. Ruby realized that was what she liked best about the stories— the fun he had. That fun part was also the difference between a story and what was happening right now. Where were they?

Snow was falling harder; Ruby could hear its soft thudding on the window, like a tiny drumbeat. Snow led her into the cave dream, snow falling inside and out, and her all safe and warm. The storm rose and rose, howling over the drumbeat now, so loud it made noises on the roof of the cave, but it couldn't touch her. She was a cavewoman, safe and warm, so the storm could howl all it wanted, howl and howl; in fact, the more it howled, the safer and warmer she felt. Now it was shaking the roof of the cave, trying to punch a hole through, but that was impossible, of course, and she was safe: snow, peace, nothing. Heavy, heavy nothing.

And then something real bad happened. A fat, fat snake with a squat diamond-shaped head and puffed neck stirred somewhere in the cave. Ruby opened her eyes. But they were already open. She was dreaming with her eyes open. She must have been, because in her dream a long thick ropelike thing was suspended in midair, or maybe dangling above her. In a dreamlike way it did something no rope could ever do, curling back up on itself in a kind of fishhook shape. Then came a hissing sound, so real.

It fell. The long thick thing fell and landed on her pillow, coiling through her hair. She felt its cold, hard heavy body; a light tongue flickered against her cheek, so fast, something she wouldn't have known how to dream. Ruby screamed, screamed the scream of her life, but kept it inside: she wanted to live.

Ruby lay still, like she was already dead. It hissed again, started moving, little imperfections in its skin catching the edge of her ear, its muscles flexing under her chin, over her throat, across her shoulder, all at the same time, muscles more supple than human muscles and much stronger, and then it mostly slid off to the side, toward the wall. Now? Now.

Ruby rolled away, or jerked, panicking completely, trying to spring out of bed and throw the covers over it in one motion. Everything got all mixed up. It—not it, but the speckled band—reared out of the blankets, head high above her and hissing. She swatted with her quiver. Arrows flew everywhere, most of them backward.

The speckled band got mad, came at her in two quick spasms of its lower half, opened its mouth gaping wide, tongue motionless between the fangs. Ruby stuck out her bow just as it struck, struck so hard that the impact of its fangs vibrated up the bow and into her arm. Then she was running as fast as she could, out of her bedroom, into the hall. Another strike, a hard crack, but on the door just as she slammed it behind her.

Julian, crouched in the doorway of Adam's room, looked up. He was mostly a silhouette, lit by little flames be-

hind him, a silhouette with a gas can in his hand, the one
Dad used for the lawn mower and weed whacker. He rose, in
no particular hurry, and walked toward her. Brandon came
out of his room. Julian swung the gas can at his head, not
even looking at him, connected with a sickening sound.
Brandon fell back inside.

Julian kept coming. Ruby backed up, stepped on something. An arrow, one of the arrows flung from the quiver. She
snatched it up, raised her bow. Raised her bow and nocked
the arrow, not too snug, and drew as Jeanette had taught her,
string barely touching the tip of her nose, anchored.

"What are you doing up at this hour?" Julian said, still
moving forward, but slower, like the floor was slippery. He
didn't have a shirt on and she could see an ugly bruise on his
shoulder, surrounding a crescent-shaped pattern of little
scabs. Zippy was a hero.

"You're feverish, poor kid," he said. Was the gas can
held a little higher now, like he was getting ready to throw
it? Flames rose behind him. They had voices all of a sudden,
like a crowd getting louder and louder, a big, hot crowd.

"Stop," Ruby said. Confused sounds rose from below.

"Would you really kill a human being, Ruby, a living
thing?" Julian said. "You'll have nightmares the rest of your
life." He had a sympathetic smile on his face, like they were
friends.

"I see a gold circle inside a red one," Ruby said, feeling
the bowstring against her lips.

The smile vanished. More noise now, on the stairs; and
a split second later a big boom from Adam's room that shook
the house. Julian threw the gas can, gas suddenly igniting in
midair like liquid fire, and sprang at her, so quick. Ruby saw
a gold circle inside a red one, really did. And then came the
string's little kiss good-bye.

Her aim was true. Julian stopped, stopped like she
wanted, stopped like she told him.

"Nightmares," he said.

Then life left his eyes; all kinds of expressions, like flicking through a deck of scary cards, the last one puzzled.

Gas was everywhere, flames in Adam's room, Brandon's, the hall. Ruby stepped over Julian into Brandon's room. The downstairs cop came charging up, gun drawn.

"In the attic," Ruby said. She had to shout over the voice of the fire. "They're in the attic."

More cops. Brandon sat up, head all bloody. "You all right?" she said.

"Yeah."

But he needed her help to get up. They went into the hall. Big flames now, spreading from Adam's room. Lots of yelling, lots of sirens. A cop with enormous arms stood on a chair, banging at the painted-in hatch cover with all his strength. Something cracked. The hatch opened. He pulled himself through. Then came grunting sounds from above, and a mummy appeared, feet first, wrapped all in duct tape except for the nose. Other cops took the mummy, carried it downstairs. And then a second mummy, a little bigger. The mummies made sounds.

Something roared in Adam's room. A giant flame burst through his wall. D'Amario pushed past a bunch of cops. "Get the kids out of here. Everybody out." He lifted Ruby in his arms, carried her toward the stairs.

"Any quick thing you want to grab?" he said as they went by her room.

"Don't open the door."

Out on Robin Road, Dad, Mom, Brandon, and Ruby watched the firemen save some of the house—the garage, kitchen, mudroom, a little more. Mom and Dad were bawling their eyes out.

"We're sorry," Mom said.

"So sorry," said Dad.

"For what?" said Brandon.

"It's insured, right, Dad?" said Ruby. He was in the business, after all. Mom and Dad mixed in some laughing with the crying. They all kind of hugged. Ruby did her crying later, when the nightmares came.

Dad had written an excellent policy for 37 Robin Road, covering complete rebuilding costs including the renovation, plus a little padding he'd snuck in. Gram lent him money to pay off the Codexco debt. He got a job with John Hancock in Hartford.

Mom went to work for Larry at Skyway, made more money. There were changes between Mom and Dad, hard to understand. First came finding Dad sleeping on the couch if Ruby happened to get up early; then lots of talking by Mom and Dad in low voices; after that a kiss once in a while around the house.

Brandon took the SAT again and got in the fifty-ninth percentile. He took it once more, not hung over, and made the ninety-first.

They didn't find Mom's Jeep until the Strombolis came home from Florida and opened their garage. Mom's gray coat with the fur collar and Dad's leather jacket were inside.

No reptilian body ever turned up, a big concern to the neighbors. A real estate agent used it to explain away a disappointing offer over on Poplar Drive.

Unka Death remained in a coma.

D'Amario sent divers back to the pond twice but they didn't find Zippy. When the weather warmed up, Ruby went in herself, did no better. *When you have eliminated the impossible, whatever remains, however improbable, must be the truth.* Ruby kept an eye out for Zippy.

After some months of that, Brandon came home with a dog from the pound. Ruby had nothing to do with it. This dog didn't look at all like Zippy, was very ugly and kind of fat. One day when they were alone, he came up to her room with an unopened can of Sprite in his mouth, tail wagging. He wasn't ugly, really, more homely. She named him Watson.

THEIR WILDEST DREAMS

Mackie dreaded the mail. That was new, one of many new things in her life, none good. Lying in bed on a Saturday morning, clinging to sleep although she wasn't tired—this greediness for sleep also new—she heard the mail truck turning into Buena Vida Circle. The sound of its motor—part truck, part toy—grew louder, every little throb and rattle distinct in the desert air. Then came a squeak of brakes, followed by a pause in which she thought she heard mail thumping into the boxes at the foot of the circle; too far away to hear that, of course, had to be her imagination, if not playing tricks on her then anticipating that tricks were going to be played.

Two drivers shared the mail route—a man and a woman, both with sun-worn faces and long gray ponytails. The man always tapped the horn as he drove off. Like that: toot toot. People were friendly out West, as everyone said, and that toot-toot had sounded so optimistic in the beginning, back in the ground-breaking days. Now it made her heart race, like the opposite of a defibrillator. A wireless fibrillator: there was an idea. Niche-marketed to sadists and torturers it might bail them out, they being Lianne and her. Kevin would have to do his own bailing. Mackie got up, put on sweats, went outside.

A tangerine tree grew in her front yard. Each house in Buena Vida Estates—nine in all, arrayed like jewels around the circle as the architect had put it, crammed, as Mackie had said the first time she'd seen the plans, drawing one of those looks from Kevin—had a tangerine tree. Cost: $850 apiece. "Maybe this is a place we could cut back," Mackie had said. But Kevin wouldn't hear of it. Tangerines went with estates and the Santa Fe–style beams poking through the adobe walls and the heavy Spanish dark oak front doors, the whole concept they were selling, even if there was barely enough room to plant them. Mackie picked two bright orange beauties as she went by—pretty close to stealing from the bank.

She opened her mailbox, number four. Number four Buena Vida Circle—in her name alone now—was the original model home. And the nicest: she'd even loved it for a while, despite all the shortcuts and compromises she knew were part of it, from the foundation up. At the same time, she'd known it wasn't a permanent home, just the last and biggest sale, leading to a move even higher up. Now, no longer loving it, even closer to hate at times, Mackie wanted to hold on to this house forever.

Surprise: just one little envelope in the box, not the dammed-up cascade of overdue bills, lawyers' letters, and collection agency threats so often waiting to spring. Mackie plucked it out, one of those letters that still came addressed to her as Mrs. Kevin Larkin, even though the divorce was six months old and she'd gone back to her maiden name. A little distracted by that, she didn't notice at first that it came from the IRS.

The IRS. They never had any correspondence with the IRS; everything went through the accountant, Mr. Fertig, a careful old guy with lots of starch in his short-sleeve white shirts and neat little knots in his striped ties. Then she remembered Kevin saying something about a refund this year. Wouldn't that be something, a check he didn't get his hands on first? Mackie opened the envelope: no check. Kevin didn't slip up on things like that. She scanned the page inside, thick with type, waiting for the meaning to jump out at her. It did not. She had to read it three times, her eyes all of a sudden wild to speed ahead, faster than her mind could follow, before she understood that she owed the IRS $101,961.

Impossible. Mackie knew there were lots of people who didn't fear the IRS, but she wasn't one of them. She always made sure that Mr. Fertig had the two returns, their joint personal and the Buena Vida Development Company corporate, ready a month before filing date. It had to be a mistake. Her mind knew that, but the signal didn't get passed along to her hands, too unsteady to fold the letter and stick it back in the envelope.

She walked back toward her front door, the nine houses

of Buena Vida Estates fanning out around her, the canyon rising into the foothills beyond them, the mountains standing in the middle distance, cloudless sky above. Mountains on all sides, the first thing she'd noticed when they'd moved here, back when Kevin was still teaching tennis and Buena Vida Estates wasn't even a dream, at least not in her mind; mountains the first thing and still the best, the air a close second. She'd hiked in those mountains now, even in the heat of the summer, learned a bit about them. They weren't as green as they appeared from down here in the foothills, for example. Green came from the accumulated effect of the saguaros, like pixels, individually invisible at this distance, living up high at their own slow pace, blind to the million-dollar views of the city down below. Hiking up there, it was impossible, at least for Mackie, not to feel them doing something like thinking. Only recently was she starting to understand what was on whatever they had for minds: nothing human can make a lasting impression in this landscape.

Mackie went inside. Lianne was in the kitchen, hanging up the phone. That meant they still had service and the last check had cleared; this immediate reaction another one of those new things, not good.

"Morning, hon," Mackie said.

"Hi, Mom," said Lianne.

Who was on the phone? Mackie kept that remark, a mother's natural remark, inside. Teenagers needed space. But she couldn't help being curious because Lianne didn't have many friends. No fault of her own: she was a great kid. Going over all the good things about Lianne in her mind was one of Mackie's secret pleasures. But there'd been so many changes. First the move from back East, Lianne in the middle of sixth grade at the time. Then a few years later, when the development got going and the bank loans came through, they'd put her in private school, which was what everybody did, the kind of everybody they'd been getting to know. Now she went to Kolb High.

"Straight off the tree," said Mackie, handing Lianne a tangerine.

"Thanks." Lianne loved them.

They ate the tangerines—sweet, juicy, perfect. True luxury: $850 divided by two.

"That was Dad," Lianne said.

"Oh?"

"He's on his way over."

Saturday was Kevin's day with Lianne. That was the agreement. But he hadn't shown up the past three Saturdays, hadn't even bothered to call.

"What's the plan?" Mackie said.

Lianne shrugged. She was tearing the tangerine rind into tiny bits.

You don't have to go, Mackie thought. But unfair to say. A girl needs a father. She said: "Better get ready."

Lianne rose, pushed herself up from the table, really, like a nine-to-fiver off to work. Maybe divorce was like that for kids, an adult job suddenly handed to them, a hard one, sometimes a backbreaker.

Lianne was still in the shower when Kevin knocked on the front door. Mackie knew that knock—three taps, very quick, almost urgent. She knew every little thing about him. The big things were where she'd slipped up.

Mackie opened the door. "Oh, hi," he said, as though this were some nice surprise. "Lianne all set?"

"Not quite," Mackie said, moving aside. He came in, glancing at the mops and brooms by the door, went into the kitchen. Mackie checked his car out in the street before closing the door, in case he somehow had a new one, which would mean another big slipup on her part. But it was the same car he'd been driving since a week or two after the bank shut them down, yes, a BMW and, yes, a convertible, but this one twenty years old; and no graduate of the Yale School of Architecture waiting in the passenger seat, tapping her suntanned foot.

Kevin was leaning against the counter. Mackie sometimes still forgot how good-looking he was. From certain angles, like this one, he even appeared strong and resolute.

"Coffee brewing, by any chance?" he said.

"No."

Mackie handed him the letter.

"What's this?" he said.

"You tell me."

Kevin read the letter. She watched his eyes, beautiful deep brown eyes, like Lianne's although not so intelligent, one of Mackie's postdivorce realizations about him, and like all of them far too late. Did a little tremor cross their dark surface as he read, last faint wavelet from some deep disturbance? If so, it was gone in a flash.

"Must be some mistake," he said, handing the letter back. "I wouldn't worry about it."

"You're sure?"

"As I can be, under the circumstances."

"What does that mean?"

"It is addressed to you, after all," he said.

"What are you saying?"

"Just that I'm no longer privy to your finances."

Privy. Something about that word made her want to hit him in the mouth.

"What?" he said. "What?"

Privy. It meant free to root around. He'd rooted around in her finances, all right, to the tune of sixty thousand dollars, her inheritance and the foundation of the whole Buena Vida plan, the sixty grand turning into the down payment for the land less than a month after she got it, the land becoming the collateral for architectural, planning, and construction cost of the houses; a logical plan with millions in profits the inevitable result, golden, visible, almost tangible. Leverage was the magic word. They'd leveraged her father's heart attack.

But Mackie hadn't said no, had been caught up in the dream herself. Even now she wasn't sure how crazy it was. Who could have foretold all the bad things, the economy going one way, mortgage rates the other, and those last five houses sitting empty, month after month, no one even coming to look at them? "Unreal," as Jenna had said more than once, shaking her curls.

Jenna was the architect. Paid in full, Kevin had been scrupulous about that. She'd done a beautiful job, wedging those houses—clones, but all slightly unique, as though they'd been to different plastic surgeons or tailors—around

Buena Vida Circle. Kevin had learned a lot from her, as he'd pointed out when Mackie questioned the size of Jenna's bills. And in the master bedroom of the model house, he'd taught Mackie some of those lessons. At first, she'd assumed he'd suddenly taken to reading Maxim or one of those magazines: how to drive women wild. What other source could there be of this newfound expertise? All of a sudden he had the touch, after years of not having it, of being just slightly off. Now he was dead-on, and with new themes and variations every time, rooting around inside her and yes, driving her wild.

Mackie had figured it out eventually.

"Just tell me one thing," she said. Didn't privy also mean outhouse? Something right about that, although Mackie couldn't have said why.

"What's that?" Kevin said. He was leaning back slightly against the counter, wary, as though sensing an impending punch in the mouth, although of course there'd never been any of that.

"Tell me there are no more time bombs," Mackie said.

"Time bombs?"

"Financial time bombs you've left behind."

"How could there be?"

"That's not an answer."

"Then no. No time bombs."

"Not even one or two that could never possibly go off in a million years?"

He laughed, the kind of laugh that said, What a character. "Think."

"Your tone could be a little more civil."

She didn't change it. "Think."

He thought. "Not a one," he said. "We're in a bomb-free zone." But she saw that fucking tremor in his eyes again.

"What's funny?" said Lianne, coming into the room with her overnight bag.

They turned to her. "Hey," said Kevin, crossing the room, giving her a big hug. "Who's getting bettter looking every day?"

The top part of Lianne's face, from the eyes up, poked

over his shoulder. Her gaze was on Mackie. "What were you laughing about?" she said.

"Mom—your mom and I were just shooting the breeze," said Kevin.

"About what?" Lianne said.

"Nothing important," said Kevin.

Lianne stepped out of Kevin's embrace, came over to give Mackie a quick kiss. "See you tomorrow, Mom."

"Have fun," Mackie said.

"Do our best," said Kevin, although she hadn't been talking to him.

Then they were out the door. Mackie watched them get into the car. Kevin said something that made himself laugh. Lianne put on sunglasses. They drove off, a little too fast, which was how Kevin drove, leaving an oily cloud hanging in the air. The desert wind swept it away.

Mackie tried Mr. Fertig's office, picturing him hard at work on a Saturday, tax time only a couple months away. But no. She left a message on his voice mail, brisk and untroubled, "Helen MacIsaac here, Mr. Fertig. Got a quick question, if you could get back to me."

Mackie went into the bathroom. It had his-and-her sinks, a vanity mirror surrounded with light bulbs, and a round whirlpool bath where she and Kevin had played once or twice. A tiny spider ran down the drain.

Mackie brushed her teeth, pulled back her hair, and wound it into a tight bun, then stuck in her turquoise and silver comb, a gift to herself the day she arrived in Tucson, all about a new future and her belonging in it. Now she was a lot smarter and it was just a comb, but a nice one. Mackie gathered up her stuff—mops, broom, vacuum, cleansers, dustpan, toilet brush—and left for work.

"Where are we going?" Lianne said. Her dad had an apartment over a video store on Stone Avenue, down in the Mexican part, but they weren't headed that way, which was fine with her as it was such a pit.

"A little surprise," said Kevin, raising his voice over the

wind. It streamed through his hair like in a commercial for perfect male hair. She was the envy of all the other kids when it came to how young her dad looked, which wasn't worth thinking about for more than twenty seconds, and no one did.

"Like what?" Lianne said.

"Hardly be a surprise if I told you," said Kevin, "now would it?"

Mom and Dad were just full of surprises. For example, this hint of a Western cadence that was creeping into his speech, like he came from deep cowboy roots: why did that have to happen? Nothing stayed the same. Safe behind her bronzed Revos, slipped down her shirt at a Sunglass Hut, Lianne closed her eyes.

The ride got bumpy and she woke up. They were on a dirt road out in the desert, crossing one of those washes. A faded sign read COLDWATER WASH, but like almost all the washes, arroyos, and even the goddamn rivers out here, it was dry. Trees grew along the banks, sharing in the joke. Lianne wished she'd brought one of those tangerines. Ever since they'd moved west, she'd been thirsty all the time; not hungry, just thirsty.

"Where are we?" she said.

"Almost there," said Kevin.

Lianne pictured an endless tail of dust rising behind them. She looked back and saw it was there.

They mounted a rise, rounded a bend with steep hills on either side, crossed a gray-green valley full of cactuses, mesquite, palo verde, none of which she was sure about when it came to matching the name to the thing. Some buildings dwarfed by rocky outcrops sat at the other end.

"Feast your eyes," said Kevin.

"On what?"

"Our new home," Kevin said. "Leastwise mine, and yours too, every Saturday and alternating holidays."

Leastwise? Was he trying to be funny? She glanced over, saw no clue. Then came a sign arching over the road, the letters branded in: OCOTILLO RANCH.

"You're living on a ranch?" Lianne said.

"Living and working," said Kevin, as pavement began

and took them past stables, corrals, and outbuildings to a big lodge, much bigger than it had appeared from the valley entrance, with a long shaded porch and a stone fountain out front. Kevin switched off the engine. It was quiet, just the fountain splashing softly and a horse neighing somewhere out of sight.

"What kind of work?" Lianne said.

He turned to her. "Where'd you learn to ask all these questions?" he said, and added a big smile.

Was that some sort of jab at Mom? Lianne didn't think of her mother as much of a questioner, at least not until recently. She said nothing.

"Hop out," said Kevin, "and I'll show you."

Lianne didn't move. "Is Jenna here?"

Kevin stopped smiling. He licked his lips. "This thing," he said, "was never about her. I thought I'd got that across."

"Thing?" said Lianne.

"Divorce. People grow apart. That's the unfortunate truth. But I'm still your dad and always will be. Do you understand?"

What was to understand? Dads and their offspring, it happened all the time: pop pop pop.

He patted her knee. "Everything's going to be fine," he said. "And she's not here. Not here and won't be."

"You mean you've grown apart from her, too?" Lianne said.

"If you want to put it that way, yes."

That was fast, Lianne thought. Did it mean that maybe there was a chance Mom and Dad might grow back together? "What were you and Mom laughing about back in the kitchen?" she said.

He thought back. Whenever he was thinking hard like that, he didn't look quite so young. "I guess that was just me laughing by myself, baby," he said.

Lianne got out of the car. She felt the wind, blowing out of the north; not that she was good at directions, just assumed it was north from the chill it gave her. They climbed the steps to the front door, dark, massive, and scarred, although the brass studs were polished bright.

"See this?" said Kevin, pointing out something in the wood.

She saw an arrowhead stuck in at an angle.

"Apaches," he said.

"They didn't like the food?" Lianne said.

"For Christ's sake, Lianne, this was in the eighteen somethings." He opened the door. "Very funny," he added as they went in.

"What's funny?" said a man coming the other way, a young man in tight jeans, cowboy boots, spurs.

"Jimmy," said Kevin. "How're you doin'? This is my daughter, Lianne. Say hi to Jimmy Marz. He's the head wrangler."

"Hi," said Lianne.

"Assistant," said Jimmy. There was just a tiny still moment while he looked at her. She looked back, undetectable behind her Revos. "Nice to meet you," said Jimmy. "What was funny?"

"Just a little joke Lianne made about the food," said Kevin.

"The food at Ocotillo?" said Jimmy. "What's the joke? It's the best in southern Arizona."

Lianne laughed, not knowing why. It was funny somehow—arrowhead, gourmet cooking, assistant wranglers. Jimmy laughed, too. Small teeth, but white and even, in a suntanned face; pink tongue. "Here for the weekend?" he said.

"Overnight," said Lianne.

"At college somewhere?"

"Still in high school," said Lianne.

"Cool," said Jimmy. "See you at suppertime." He went out with a jingle-jangle of spurs that should have sounded silly, but didn't.

Lianne and her dad crossed the room, a big room with a high ceiling, stone fireplaces at either end, terra-cotta floor with scattered Indian rugs, little groups of heavy leather furniture, and flowers everywhere. On the far side stood a hotel-style front desk, suitcases lined up beside it. Behind the desk, an old man sat staring at a computer screen.

"Frozen again," he said.

"Let me have a look," said Kevin, going behind the

desk. "My daughter, Lianne. Mr. Croft, owner of the Ocotillo Ranch and all you can see for miles and miles."

"Me and Western Savings," said Mr. Croft, raising his eyes from the screen. Tired old eyes, half-shut from the heavy lids, but they brightened a little when they saw Lianne. "My, my," he said.

"There you go, Mr. Croft," said Kevin, tapping at the keyboard. "All set." A hand of solitaire popped up on the screen. "And I should have those estimates for you tomorrow."

"Mr. Efficiency," said the old man. "Your father's a breath of fresh air around here, I can tell you. Had lunch yet, young lady?"

"No," said Lianne.

"Well then, take her on over to the buffet, Kevin, and get her fed," said Mr. Croft.

"I'm not really hungry," said Lianne.

"On my tab," said Mr. Croft. "Number one."

The dining room had a view of the swimming pool, bluer than any she'd ever seen, for some reason, and three horse trails leading up into the hills, each trailhead marked with a giant saguaro. They helped themselves to lunch— eighteen-ounce T-bone and fries for Kevin, fruit salad and coffee for Lianne—and took a table by the picture window.

"Quite a guy, Mr. Croft," said Kevin.

Lianne ate a cherry. "What estimates?" she said.

"Estimates?" said Kevin, dipping a forkful of fries in ketchup.

"That you're going to have by tomorrow."

"Right," said Kevin. He raised his hand and a waiter came over. "How about one of those prickly pear margaritas, Ramon?"

"Certainly," said Ramon. "And another for the lady?"

Lianne glanced at her dad.

"Specialty of the house," said Ramon.

"Okay," said Kevin. "As long as it's mostly virgin, Ramon."

"Mostly virgin," said Ramon, moving toward the bar.

Lianne tried a cantaloupe ball, biting it in half, leaving the rest uneaten.

"These estimates," Kevin said, "are what my new job's about."

"Which is?"

"Hard to put into words. The leisure business in general, I guess you could say."

"You're working for Mr. Croft?"

"Officially, no. Not yet. We're still in the exploratory phase." He leaned forward. "But just between you and me, this is the beginning of something good."

"Like what?"

"Bringing Ocotillo Ranch into the twenty-first century. No more, no less."

Her dad's face was glowing. Lianne could feel his enthusiasm, like a warm front pressing against her. "What does that mean?" she said.

"Look around," Kevin said. "What do you see?"

Lianne looked around. "It's one of those dude ranches, right?"

"We don't say dude ranches anymore. Dude's kind of changed a bit, the meaning. They're guest ranches now. But basically, you're right. It's a place where city people can come for the Old West experience. And this is one of the best, in terms of the existing infrastructure and real estate. The problem is the riding, the horses, the desert, all that's not enough anymore. Mr. Croft knows that. He just needs someone to help him get started."

"Doing what?"

Ramon arrived with two big glasses of peach-colored liquid, thick and frothy.

"Here's to Ocotillo Ranch," her dad said.

Lianne took a sip, a sip that turned into more of a drink. Prickly pear and lots, lots more, not virginal at all: the Old West experience. She took off her Revos.

"Good, huh?" said Kevin.

She nodded.

"And good for you, too, that prickly pear juice. Grown and pressed right here on the property."

Lianne had some more. "Doing what, Dad? What are you going to be doing?"

He smiled at her, a loving smile. She realized she'd called him Dad. "I'm in charge," he said, "or soon will be, of the first phase in the redevelopment of the ranch."

"Which is?"

"I'll put it in three words," he said, chewing on a bite of steak; a juicy one because a little leaked out of the corner of his lip. "Golf. Tennis. Spa." He cut another piece. "Leaving out the later phases, condos and such, for now, since our discussions haven't reached that stage. Phase one is tennis. The estimates are for eight lighted DecoTurf courts that'll go right about there."

"Where the eucalyptuses are?"

"They'll have to come down."

She took another drink. "So you'll be teaching tennis again?"

A rider came over the ridge on the middle trail, easy and relaxed in the saddle, followed by about a dozen more, not as easy and relaxed, but looking richer somehow, even though everyone was dressed the same in jeans and denim shirts. Maybe it was their cowboy hats, all crisp and clean, except for the lead rider, his hat dusty and stained.

"I'm going to tell you something important," Kevin said. Uh-oh. Mood change.

"What?"

"Regarding that remark you made, teaching tennis again."

"A question," said Lianne, "not a remark."

"It doesn't matter. Listen up."

She felt the temptation, even at her age, to cover her ears.

He held up his knife. "When life knocks you down, you have to get right back up. If you do it quick enough no one even notices."

But what if you knock yourself down, Dad?

"What's funny?"

"Nothing," Lianne said.

"Your mother has exactly the same—" He stopped himself. "The point I'm making is that you have to develop people skills in this life. Real estate companies, vacation companies, they all come and go, but people will always be around. Do you understand what I'm saying?"

"People will always be around."

"And therefore?"

The riders came down the hill, smiling and talking, probably wondering what was for lunch. Another rider galloped into view from off to the right, rode up to meet them, a FedEx package under his arm. A hatless rider, this one, and she recognized him: Jimmy Marz. Some expression she'd heard about being one with the horse? Lianne understood it now.

"And therefore?" her father repeated.

"And therefore you have to make them like you."

Kevin sat back. "Well, I wouldn't put it quite so bluntly. But yes."

Suddenly Lianne began to understand the divorce much better. Her father sold himself. Her mother didn't.

A woman on a white horse took the FedEx package from Jimmy Marz and said something that made him laugh. Lianne finished her drink. Nothing virginal about it. She caught Ramon's eye.